READERS ARE HOT FOR
COLD VENGEANCE!

"I've just finished reading the book, and as usual, it was not possible to put it down for longer than two minutes without getting itchy fingers. Another fabulous read which leaves more questions than answers, but what a ride to the end. Keep up the good work!"

—**Paul Bevan, Basildon, UK**

"Well, gentlemen, I just finished COLD VENGEANCE. I would like to say that the book is marvelous and perfect. While I abhor the cliffhanger, I love it at the same time. I congratulate you on your latest work, and cannot wait until your next book!"

—**Adam D. Ferguson, Indianapolis, IN**

"I read COLD VENGEANCE in twelve hours. I was up till 3:30 a.m. reading, had to be at work at 6:30 a.m. I am so tired today but your book was worth the time. So many words could describe how good your book is, all I can say is 'mind-blowing.' I loved it! Thank you for the excellent read and I look forward to the next."

—**Joshua Hudson, Pensacola, FL**

"What a page-turner! I couldn't put it down, even called in and canceled several appointments because I just had to keep reading. Seriously, I want to thank you both for the outstanding writing that you do. *Really* looking forward to see what unfolds in the follow-up to COLD VENGEANCE."

—**Andreia Morrison, City Island, NY**

"Just finished COLD VENGEANCE and per usual it delivered twists, turns, and thrills! And also left this reader eager for the next Agent Pendergast novel. Your writing so captivates me that I get absolutely nothing else done until I finish a book! Thanks and appreciation, gentlemen, for such wonderful and inventive entertainment!"

—**Dawn McKeone, Nashua, NH**

"I want to thank you for the years of enjoyment your novels have given me. While I have a favorite list of protagonists: Joe Pike, Jack Reacher, John Rain, and Burke, none equal Pendergast. I love this character. I can't wait for the next novel."

—**Murphy Nolan, Toronto, ON**

"Once again, you have left me speechless and craving more at the end of COLD VENGEANCE. Cruel and inhumane to leave us hanging like this, but understandable. I love all the plot twists. Can't wait to see what comes next."

—**Steve Mueckenhoff, Woodstock, IL**

Acclaim for the Novels of Preston and Child

COLD VENGEANCE

"Before you even open the cover of a Preston and Child book, you know you're in for a good, if chilling, even thrilling time."

—Asbury Park Press

"[Preston and Child are] still going strong . . . Such is the talent of our authors that we happily follow their characters . . . all over the globe, from the moors of Scotland to the loony bins of New York City; the recipe is mixed well with a dash of assassins here and a soup-con of Nazis there, a couple of traitors and some really fascinating secondary characters . . . COLD VENGEANCE is a hot hell of a fun read."

—Examiner.com

"4½ stars! Top Pick! Preston and Child continue their dominance of the thriller genre with stellar writing and twists that come at a furious pace. Others may try to write like them, but no one can come close. The best in the business deliver another winner."

—RT Book Reviews

"Douglas Preston and Lincoln Child have outdone themselves once again, and with COLD VENGEANCE at the #1 spot on the *New York Times* bestseller list, it's proof this is without a doubt the best in the entire series. The third book can't come soon enough."

—GoodReads.com

"5 stars! This fast-paced series continues to provide the reader with many twists. What you thought you knew from prior Pendergast novels may not necessarily be true."

—TheMysteryReader.com

FEVER DREAM

"This is no dream; it's the authors' best book in years."
—*Library Journal* (starred review)

"A thrill a minute."

—*San Jose Mercury News*

"[One of the] summer's best beach books."

—*Newark Star-Ledger*

"Preston and Child up the emotional ante considerably in this thriller featuring brilliant and eccentric Pendergast . . . Once again, the bestselling authors show they have few peers at creating taut scenes of suspense."

—*Publishers Weekly* (starred review)

"Together [Preston and Child] reach an entirely different level, achieving a stylistic grace and thematic resonance neither has so far matched alone. This may be the best of the Pendergast novels . . . a definite must-read."

—*Booklist* (starred review)

"Pendergast has never been more brilliant, eccentric, and intriguing."

—TucsonCitizen.com

COLD VENGEANCE

By Douglas Preston and Lincoln Child

Gideon's Corpse	*Still Life with Crows*
Gideon's Sword	*The Cabinet of Curiosities*
Fever Dream	*The Ice Limit*
Cemetery Dance	*Thunderhead*
The Wheel of Darkness	*Riptide*
The Book of the Dead	*Reliquary*
Dance of Death	*Mount Dragon*
Brimstone	*Relic*

In answer to a frequently asked reader question: The above titles are listed in descending order of publication, though almost all of them are stand-alone novels that need not be read in order. However, the pairs *Relic/Reliquary*, *Dance of Death/The Book of the Dead*, and *Fever Dream/Cold Vengeance* are ideally read in sequence.

By Douglas Preston

Impact
The Monster of Florence
  (with Mario Spezi)
Blasphemy
Tyrannosaur Canyon
The Codex
Ribbons of Time
The Royal Road
Talking to the Ground
Jennie
Cities of Gold
Dinosaurs in the Attic

By Lincoln Child

Terminal Freeze
Deep Storm
Death Match
Utopia
Tales of the Dark 1–3
Dark Banquet
Dark Company

COLD
VENGEANCE

DOUGLAS PRESTON AND
LINCOLN CHILD

GRAND CENTRAL
PUBLISHING

NEW YORK   BOSTON

While most towns and other locations in *Cold Vengeance* are imaginary, we have in a few instances employed our own version of existing places such as Scotland, New York City, New Orleans, and Baton Rouge. In such cases, we have not hesitated to alter geography, topology, history, and other details to suit the needs of the story.

All persons, locales, police departments, corporations, institutions, museums, and governmental agencies mentioned in this novel are either fictions or used fictitiously.

Grand Central Publishing
Hachette Book Group
237 Park Avenue
New York, NY 10017
www.HachetteBookGroup.com

Grand Central Publishing is a division of Hachette Book Group, Inc. The Grand Central Publishing name and logo is a trademark of Hachette Book Group, Inc.

The publisher is not responsible for websites (or their content) that are not owned by the publisher.

Printed in the United States of America

Originally published in hardcover by Hachette Book Group
First trade edition: August 2011
First international mass market edition: February 2012
First oversize mass market edition: February 2012

10 9 8 7 6 5 4 3 2 1

*Lincoln Child dedicates this book to his
daughter, Veronica*

*Douglas Preston dedicates this book to
Marguerite, Laura, and Oliver Preston*

CHAPTER 1

Cairn Barrow, Scotland

Aₛ ᴛʜᴇʏ ᴍᴏᴜɴᴛᴇᴅ ᴛʜᴇ ʙᴀʀʀᴇɴ sʜᴏᴜʟᴅᴇʀ of Beinn
Dearg, the great stone lodge of Kilchurn vanished into
the darkness, leaving only the soft yellow glow of its
windows tingeing the misty air. Attaining the ridge,
Judson Esterhazy and Special Agent Aloysius Pendergast paused and switched off their flashlights to listen. It was five o'clock in the morning, the cusp of first
light: almost time for the stags to begin roaring.

Neither man spoke. The wind whispered through
the grasses and moaned about the frost-fractured rocks
while they waited. But nothing stirred.

"We're early," said Esterhazy at last.

"Perhaps," murmured Pendergast.

Still they waited as the faintest gray light crept into
the easternmost horizon, silhouetting the desolate peaks
of the Grampian Mountains and casting a dreary pall
over the surroundings. Slowly, the landscape around
them began to materialize out of the darkness. The hunting lodge stood far behind them, turrets and ramparts
of stone streaked with damp, surrounded by black fir
trees, heavy and silent. Ahead rose the granite ramparts

of Beinn Dearg itself, disappearing into the darkness above. A burn tumbled down its flanks, dropping into a series of waterfalls as it made its way to the black waters of Loch Duin, a thousand feet below, barely visible in the faint light. To their right and below lay the beginning of the great moorlands known as the Foulmire, overspread by rising tendrils of mist, which carried upward the faint smell of decomposition and swamp gas mingled with the sickly scent of overblooming heather.

Without a word, Pendergast reshouldered his rifle and began walking along the contour of the shoulder, heading slightly uphill. Esterhazy followed, his face shadowed and inscrutable under his deerstalker cap. As they climbed higher, the Foulmire came into direct view, the treacherous moors stretching to the horizon, bounded to the west by the vast black-sheeted waters of the great Inish Marshes.

After a few minutes, Pendergast halted and held up a hand.

"What is it?" Esterhazy asked.

The answer came, not from Pendergast, but in a strange sound echoing up from a hidden glen, alien and dreadful: the roar of a red stag in rut. It throbbed and bellowed, the echo resounding over the mountains and marshlands like the lost cry of the damned. It was a sound full of rage and aggression, as the stags roamed the fells and moorlands fighting one another, often to the death, over possession of a harem of hinds.

The roar was answered by a second, closer in, which came boiling up from the shores of the loch, and then yet another cry rose from a distant fold of land. The scattered bellowings, one after another, shook the landscape. The two listened in silence, noting each sound, marking its direction, timbre, and vigor.

Finally Esterhazy spoke, his voice barely audible over the wind. "The one in the glen, he's a monster."

No response from Pendergast.

"I say we go after him."

"The one in the Mire," murmured Pendergast, "is even larger."

A silence. "Surely you know the rules of the lodge regarding entrance into the Mire."

Pendergast made a short, dismissive gesture with a pale hand. "I am not one who is concerned with rules. Are you?"

Esterhazy compressed his lips, saying nothing.

They waited as a gray dawn bled suddenly red into the eastern sky and the light continued to creep over the stark Highland landscape. Far below, the Mire was now a wasteland of black pools and ribbons of marshy water, quaking bogs and heaving quickmire, interspersed among deceptive grassy meadows and tors of broken rock. Pendergast extracted a small spyglass from his pocket, pulled it open, and scanned the Mire. After a long moment, he passed the glass to Esterhazy. "He's between the second and third tor, half a mile in. A rogue stag. No harem."

Esterhazy peered intently. "Looks like a twelve-point rack on him."

"Thirteen," murmured Pendergast.

"The one in the glen would be much easier to stalk. Better cover for us. I'm not sure we have even the ghost of a chance of bagging the one in the Mire. Aside from the, ah, risks of going in there, it'll see us a mile away."

"We approach on a line of sight that passes through that second tor, keeping it between us and the stag. The wind is in our favor."

"Even so, that's treacherous ground in there."

Pendergast turned to Esterhazy, gazing for a few awkward seconds into the high-domed, well-bred face. "Are you afraid, Judson?"

Esterhazy, momentarily taken aback, brushed off the comment with a forced chuckle. "Of course not. It's just that I'm thinking of our chances of success. Why waste time in a fruitless pursuit all over the Mire when we have an equally fine stag waiting for us down there in the glen?"

Without responding, Pendergast delved into his pocket and extracted a one-pound coin. "Call it."

"Heads," said Esterhazy reluctantly.

Pendergast flipped the coin, caught it, slapped it on his sleeve. "Tails. The first shot is mine."

Pendergast led the way down the shoulder of Beinn Dearg. There was no trail, only broken rock, short grass, tiny wildflowers, and lichen. As night gave way to morning, the mists thickened over the Mire, eddying about the low areas and streaming up the hillocks and tors.

They moved silently and stealthily down toward the verge of the Mire. When they reached a small hollow, a corrie, at the base of the Beinn, Pendergast gestured for them to halt. Red deer had an extremely acute suite of senses, and the men had to take exquisite care not to be seen, heard, or scented.

Creeping to the brow of the corrie, Pendergast peered over the top.

The stag was about a thousand yards off, moving slowly into the Mire. As if on cue, he raised his head, snuffled the air, and let out another ear-shattering roar, which echoed and died among the stones, then shook his mane and went back to sniffing the ground and taking odd snatches of grass.

"My God," whispered Esterhazy. "He's a monster."

"We must move quickly," murmured Pendergast. "He's heading deeper into the Mire."

They swung around below the rim of the corrie, keeping out of sight, until they had lined up the stag with a small tor. Turning, they approached the animal using the hummock as cover. The edges of the Mire, after the long summer, had firmed up, and they moved quickly and silently, the soft hillocks of grass acting as stepping-stones. They came up in the lee of the hill, then hunkered down behind it. The wind was still in their favor and they heard the stag roar again, a sign he was unaware of their presence. Pendergast shivered; the end of the roar sounded uncannily like that of a lion. Motioning Esterhazy to remain behind, he crept up to the hill's edge, cautiously peering through a tumble of boulders.

The stag stood a thousand yards off, nose in the air, moving restlessly. He shook his mane again, the polished antlers gleaming. He raised his head and roared once again. Thirteen points: at least five hundred inches of antler. Strange that this late in the rutting season, he had not accumulated a sizable harem. Some stags, it seemed, were just born loners.

They were still too distant for a reliable shot. A good shot wasn't good enough; one could never chance wounding an animal of this caliber. It had to be a certain kill.

He crept back down the side of the hill and rejoined Esterhazy. "He's a thousand yards off—too far."

"That's exactly what I was afraid of."

"He's awfully sure of himself," said Pendergast. "Since nobody hunts in the Foulmire, he's not as alert as he should be. The wind's in our faces, he's moving away from us—I think we can chance an open stalk."

Esterhazy shook his head. "There's some treacherous-looking ground ahead."

Pendergast pointed to a sandy area adjacent to their hiding spot, where the track of the stag could be seen. "We'll follow his track. If anyone knows the way through the Mire, he does."

Esterhazy held out a palm. "Lead the way."

They unshipped their rifles and crept out from behind the tor, moving toward the stag. The animal was indeed distracted, focused on scenting the air coming from the north, paying little attention to what lay behind him. His snuffling and roaring covered the sounds of their approach.

They advanced with the utmost care, pausing whenever the animal hesitated or turned. Slowly, they began to overtake him. The stag continued to ramble deeper into the Mire, apparently following an airborne scent. They continued in utter silence, unable to speak, keeping low, their Highland camouflage perfectly adapted to the moorland environment. The trail of the stag followed almost invisible rivels of firmer ground, the path snaking among treacly pools, shivering morass, and grassy flats. Whether from the untrustworthy ground, the hunt, or some other reason, the tension in the air seemed to increase.

Gradually, they moved into shooting range: three hundred yards. The stag paused yet again, turning sideways, nosing the air. With the faintest of hand gestures, Pendergast indicated a halt and carefully sank into a prone position. Pulling his H&H .300 forward, he fitted the scope to his eye and carefully aimed the rifle. Esterhazy remained ten yards behind, crouching, as motionless as a rock.

Peering through the scope, Pendergast settled the crosshairs on a spot just forward the shoulder of the animal, took a breath, and began to squeeze the trigger.

As he did so, he felt the cold touch of steel against the back of his head.

"Sorry, old boy," said Esterhazy. "Hold your rifle out with one hand and lay it down. Slow and easy."

Pendergast laid down the rifle.

"Stand up. Slowly."

Pendergast complied.

Esterhazy backed away, covering the FBI agent with his hunting rifle. He suddenly laughed, the harsh sound echoing over the moorlands. Out of the corner of his eye, Pendergast saw the stag startle and bound away, disappearing into the mists.

"I'd hoped it wouldn't come to this," said Esterhazy. "After a dozen years, it's a bloody tragedy you didn't leave well enough alone."

Pendergast said nothing.

"You're probably wondering what this is all about."

"In fact, I am not," said Pendergast, his voice flat.

"I'm the man you've been looking for: the unknown

man at Project Aves. The one Charles Slade refused to
name for you."

No reaction.

"I'd give you a fuller explanation, but what's the
point? I'm sorry to do this. You realize it's nothing
personal."

Still no reaction.

"Say your prayers, brother."

Esterhazy raised the rifle, aimed, and pulled the
trigger.

CHAPTER 2

A FAINT CLICK SOUNDED IN THE DAMP AIR.

"Christ!" Esterhazy said through clenched teeth, shooting open the bolt, ejecting the bad round and slamming a new one in place.

Click.

In a flash Pendergast leapt to his feet, scooping up his rifle and leveling it at Esterhazy. "Your not-so-clever stratagem failed. I've suspected it since your ham-handed letter asking which firearms I'd be bringing with me. I'm afraid the ammunition in your rifle is doctored. And so the thing goes full circle: from the blanks you put in Helen's rifle to the blanks now in your own."

Esterhazy kept working the bolt, frantically ejecting the bad rounds with one hand while delving into his musette bag with another, scooping out fresh rounds.

"Stop or I'll kill you," said Pendergast.

Ignoring him, Esterhazy ejected the last round and rammed a fresh one into the receiver, then slammed the bolt into place.

"Very well. This one's for Helen." Pendergast pulled the trigger.

A dull *thunk* sounded.

Instantly realizing the situation, Pendergast threw himself back, diving for cover behind an outcropping of rock as Esterhazy fired. The live shot ricocheted off the outcropping, spraying chips. Pendergast rolled farther behind cover, ditching his rifle and pulling out the Colt .32 he had brought as a backup. He rose, aimed, and fired, but Esterhazy had already taken cover himself around the other side of the small hill, and his return fire smacked into the rocks just in front of Pendergast.

Now they were both behind cover, on either side of the tor. Esterhazy's laugh once again cut across the land. "Looks like *your* not-so-clever stratagem has also failed. Did you think I'd let you out here with a working rifle? Sorry, old boy, I removed the firing pin."

Pendergast lay on his side, hugging the rock, breathing hard. It was a standoff—they were on either side of the same small hill. That meant whoever got to the top first…

Leaping to his feet, Pendergast scrambled spider-like up the side of the tor. He arrived at the summit at the very moment as Esterhazy did and they came together in a violent embrace, grappling on the high point of the hill before toppling off, rolling down the rocky face in a desperate clinch. Shoving Esterhazy back, Pendergast swung his .32 around, but Esterhazy slashed at it with the barrel of his rifle, the two weapons clashing like swords, both going off simultaneously. Pendergast seized the barrel of Esterhazy's rifle with one hand and they struggled over it, Pendergast dropping his pistol in an attempt to wrest away Esterhazy's weapon with both hands.

The *mano a mano* continued, all four hands on the same rifle, twisting and thrashing, each trying to shake the other off. Pendergast bent forward and sank his teeth into Esterhazy's hand, ripping into the flesh. With a roar Esterhazy head-butted him, knocking the FBI agent back, and kicked him fiercely in his side. The clash brought both of them down onto the frost-split rocks again, their camouflage ripping and tearing.

Getting his hand on the trigger, yanking and twisting, Pendergast fired it again and again to empty the magazine. He let go and drove his fist into Esterhazy's skull just as the man swung the rifle around, club-like, slamming Pendergast in the chest. Seizing the stock, Pendergast tried to wrench it free again but in a surprise move Esterhazy jerked the agent forward while delivering a savage kick to his face, almost breaking his nose in the process. Blood spurted everywhere and Pendergast fell back, shaking his head, trying to clear it as Esterhazy fell on top of him, slamming his face again with the rifle stock. Through the fog and blood he could see Esterhazy scrabbling fresh rounds out of his bag, shoving them into the rifle.

He kicked up the muzzle and threw himself sideways as a shot rang out, seized his own handgun from where he had dropped it, rolled and returned fire. But Esterhazy had already scrambled for cover behind the tor.

Taking advantage of the temporary lull, Pendergast leapt up and raced down the hill, turning to fire several times, keeping Esterhazy pinned down while he sprinted away. Reaching the bottom of the hill, he darted into the Mire, heading for a hollow, where he was quickly enveloped in a swirl of dense fog.

There he paused, surrounded by quaking mud. The ground under his feet shook strangely, like gelatin. He probed ahead with the toe of his boot, locating firmer ground, and headed deeper into the Foulmire, stepping from hillock to hillock, stone to stone, trying to keep clear of the sucking pools of quicksand while putting as much distance as possible between himself and Esterhazy. As he moved, he heard a series of shots from the direction of the tor, but they went wild; Esterhazy was firing at shadows.

Making a thirty-degree turn, Pendergast slackened his pace. There was little cover on the Mire beyond the odd tumulus of broken rock; the fog would be his only protection. That meant keeping low.

He continued on, moving as swiftly as prudence would allow, often pausing to probe with his foot. He knew Esterhazy would be following; the man had no choice. And he was a superb tracker, perhaps even superior to Pendergast himself. As he walked, he slipped a kerchief out of his bag and pressed it to his nose, trying to stem the flow of blood. He could feel the grating of a broken rib in his chest, a result of the fierce struggle. He silently reproached himself for not checking his rifle immediately before their departure. The rifles had been locked in the lodge's gun room, as the rules required; Esterhazy must have used some ploy to get at his weapon. It only took a minute or two to remove a firing pin. He had underestimated his adversary; he would not do so again.

Suddenly he paused, examining the ground: there, in a gravelly patch, was the track of the stag they had spooked. He listened intently, peering behind from whence he had come. The mists were rising from the Mire in tattered columns, momentarily obscuring and disclosing views of the endless moors and distant mountains. The tor on which they had fought was wreathed in mist, and his pursuer was nowhere to be seen. A deep gray light lay over all, with a darkness looming to the north, occasionally shot through with flickers of lightning—an approaching storm.

Reloading his Colt, Pendergast headed still deeper into the Mire, following the faint track of the stag as it picked its way along an invisible path known only to itself, threading ingeniously between quaking bogs and sucking pools.

It wasn't over. Esterhazy was in hot pursuit. There could be only one outcome: one of them would not return.

CHAPTER 3

PENDERGAST FOLLOWED THE FAINT TRACK of the stag as it meandered through the shivering fens of the Mire, keeping to firm ground. As the storm moved in, the sky grew darker and distant thunder rolled over the moors. He moved swiftly, pausing only long enough to examine the ground for signs of the stag's passage. The Mire was especially treacherous this time of year, when the long summer had allowed green grass to overspread many of the pools of quaking bog, leaving a deceptive crust that would break under the weight of a man.

Lightning flashed and rain started down, heavy drops whirling out of the leaden sky. The wind rose, rustling over the heather, carrying up a miasmic smell from the Inish Marshes to the west: a vast, sheeted surface of water covered with patches of reeds and cattails, swaying in the wind. For more than a mile, he followed the stag's trail. It gradually led to higher and firmer ground, and then—through a sudden gap in the mists—Pendergast spied a ruin ahead. Silhouetted against the sky at the top of a rise stood an old stone corral and shepherd's hut, fitfully illuminated by the flickering lightning. Beyond the hill lay the ragged edges of the marshes. Examining the broken furze, Pendergast noted that the stag had passed through the ruins and continued toward the vast swamp on the far side.

He mounted the hill and quickly explored the ruin. The hut was unroofed, the stone walls broken and covered with lichen, the wind moaning and whistling through the tumbled remains. Beyond, the hill fell away to a swamp that lay hidden in a murk of rising vapors.

The ruin, commanding the high ground, offered an ideal defensible position, with unobstructed views in all directions: a perfect place from which to ambush a pursuer or stand against an attack. For those reasons, Pendergast passed it by and continued down the hill toward the Inish Marshes. Again he picked up the track of the stag and was momentarily puzzled; the stag seemed to be heading into a dead end. The animal must have felt harried by Pendergast's pursuit.

Circling back along the verge of the marsh, Pendergast came to an area of thick reeds where an esker of cobbled ground ambled out into water. A string of glaciated rocks provided a small but obvious cover; he paused, removed a white handkerchief, wrapped it around a stone, and placed it in a precise location behind the boulders. He then passed by. Beyond the finger of cobbled ground, he found what he had been looking for: a flattish rock just under the surface of the water, surrounded by reeds. He could see that the stag had also gone this way, heading into the marshes.

The natural blind was an unlikely place to take cover and an even more unlikely place to attempt a defense. For those reasons, it would suffice.

Wading out to the stone, being careful to avoid the morass on either side, Pendergast took a position among the reeds, well hidden from view. There he crouched, waiting. A spur of lightning split the sky, followed by the crash of thunder; more fog came rolling in from the marshes, temporarily obscuring the ruins on top of the hill. No doubt Esterhazy would arrive soon. The end was in sight.

Judson Esterhazy paused to examine the ground, reaching down and fingering some gravel that had been pushed aside by the passage of the stag. Pendergast's footprint was much less obvious, but he could see it in the form of pressed earth and flattened stems of grass nearby. The man was taking no chances, continuing to follow the stag on its winding course through the Foulmire. Clever. No one would dare venture in here without a guide, but a stag was as good a guide as any. As the storm rolled in, the fogs thickened; it became dark enough that he was glad to have the flashlight— carefully shielded—to examine the trail.

Pendergast clearly intended to lure Esterhazy out into the Mire to kill him. For all his pretensions to southern gentility, Pendergast was the most implacable man he had ever met, and a dirty bastard of a fighter.

A bolt of lightning illuminated the desolate moors and he saw, through a break in the mist, the ragged outline of a ruin standing on a rise a quarter mile away. He paused. That would be a logical place for Pendergast to go to ground and await his arrival. He would approach the ruin accordingly; ambush the ambusher...But even as his practiced eye roamed over the site, he considered that Pendergast was too subtle a man to take the obvious course of action.

Esterhazy could assume nothing.

There was very little cover in this barren landscape, but by timing his movements he could take advantage of the heavy fogs coming in from the marshes to provide the cover he needed. As if on cue, a new bank of mist rolled in and he was enveloped in a colorless world of nothing. He scurried up the hill toward the ruins, able to move fast on the harder ground. About a hundred yards below the summit, he circled the hill so as to approach from an unexpected direction. The rain came down, heavier now, while the rumblings of thunder marched away over the moors.

He crouched and took cover as the fogs cleared for a moment, allowing him a glimpse of the ruins above. No sign of Pendergast. As the fog rolled back in he moved up the side of the hill, rifle in hand, until he reached the stone wall surrounding an old corral. He moved along it, keeping low, until another break in the mist allowed him to peer through a gap in the rocks.

The corral was vacant. But beyond it stood the roofless hut.

He approached the structure from along the perimeter of the corral, keeping below the wall. In a moment he had flattened himself against its rear wall. Creeping up to a broken window, he waited for another gap in the fog. The wind picked up, sighing through the stones and covering the faint sounds of his own movement as he readied himself: and then, as the air cleared a little, he swung around into the window and swept his rifle across the inside of the hut, covering it from corner to corner.

Empty.

Vaulting over the sill, he crouched inside the hut, thinking furiously. As he suspected, Pendergast had avoided the obvious. He had not occupied the strategic high ground. But where had he gone? He muttered a curse; with Pendergast, only the unexpected could be expected.

Another bank of fog rolled in and Esterhazy took the opportunity to examine the area around the hut, looking for Pendergast's track. He found it with difficulty: it was quickly disappearing in the heavy rains. Continuing down the far side of the hill toward the marshlands below, he could glimpse the lay of the land through gaps in the mists. It was a dead end of sorts— beyond lay only the Inish Marshes. So Pendergast must have taken cover somewhere along the marsh edge. He felt a low-grade panic take hold. Through the breaking mists, he scanned the area; surely the man wouldn't be hiding in the reeds or cattails. But there was a finger of land that extended into the marshes; he pulled out his spyglass and noted a scattering of glacial boulders that provided just enough cover to hide a man. And by God, there he was: a patch of white, just visible behind one of the rocks.

That was it, then: he had taken the only cover there was, and was waiting in ambush for Esterhazy to pass as he followed Pendergast's trail along the edge of the marsh.

Once again: the unobvious thing. And Esterhazy saw just the way to thwart him.

The welcoming fog returned; he started down the hill and was soon back among the treacherous bogs of the Mire, following the double track of Pendergast and the stag. As he approached the verge of the marshes, he found himself stepping from one hillock to another over quivering sheets of morass. He regained firmer ground, moving off the trail, toward a position where he would have a clear line of fire to the area behind the rocks concealing Pendergast. Taking up a position, he crouched behind a hillock, waiting for the mists to part so he could take a shot.

A minute passed; a gap appeared in the mists. He could see the little bit of white from Pendergast's hidden position; it appeared to be part of his shirt and it offered enough of a view to accept a bullet. He raised his rifle...

"Stand up ever so slowly," came the disembodied voice from behind him, almost as if from the marsh water itself.

CHAPTER 4

ESTERHAZY FROZE AT THE SOUND OF THE VOICE.

"As you rise, hold your rifle in your left hand, extended away from your body."

Still, Esterhazy found himself unable to move. How was it possible?

Whing! The round smacked into the ground between his feet, kicking up a spray of dirt. "I won't ask again."

Holding his rifle out by his left hand, Esterhazy stood up.

"Drop the rifle and turn around."

He allowed the rifle to fall, then turned. There was Pendergast, twenty yards away, pistol in hand, himself rising from a clump of reeds apparently standing in water—but Esterhazy could now see there was a small meandering path of glacially deposited rocks at the water's surface, surrounded on both sides by quickmire.

"I just have one question," said Pendergast, his voice thin in the moaning wind. "How could you murder your own sister?"

Esterhazy stared at him.

"I require an answer."

Esterhazy couldn't quite bring himself to speak. Looking into Pendergast's face, he knew he was a dead man. He felt the unutterably cold fear of death fall upon him like a sodden cloak, mingling with horror, regret, and relief. There was nothing he could do. He would not, at least, give Pendergast the satisfaction of an undignified exit. Even with his death, there would be pain enough for Pendergast in the months ahead. "Just get it over with," he said.

"No explanations, then?" asked Pendergast. "No whining justifications, no abject pleading for understanding? How disappointing." The finger tightened on the trigger. Esterhazy closed his eyes.

And then it happened: a sudden, overpowering crash of sound. Esterhazy saw an explosion of reddish fur, the flash of antlers—and the stag burst through the reeds, one antler swiping Pendergast, catching his gun and sending it flying into the water. As the stag bounded away, Pendergast staggered and thrashed—and Esterhazy realized he had been thrown into a pool of mire with only a skimming of water covering its surface.

Seizing his own rifle from the ground, Esterhazy aimed and fired. The round caught Pendergast in the chest, slamming him backward into the pool. Esterhazy aimed, preparing to fire again, then paused. A second shot, a second bullet, would be impossible to explain— if the body was found.

He lowered the rifle. Pendergast was struggling, held fast now in the mire, his strength already ebbing. A dark stain was spreading across his chest. The shot had struck him off center but was sufficient to do catastrophic damage. The man looked a sight: clothing torn and bloody, pale hair streaked with mud and darkened by rain. He coughed, and blood came burbling from his lips.

That was it: as a doctor, Esterhazy knew the shot was fatal. It had punctured a lung, creating a sucking wound, and its placement left a good possibility it had torn up the left subclavian artery, which was rapidly filling the lungs with blood. Even if he wasn't sinking irretrievably into quicksand, Pendergast would be a dead man in a few minutes.

Already up to his waist in the quaking bog, Pendergast stopped struggling and stared up at his assassin. The icy glitter in the pale gray eyes spoke more eloquently of his hatred and despair than any words he might have spoken, and it shook Esterhazy to the core.

"You want an answer to your question?" Esterhazy asked. "Here it is. I never did murder Helen. She's still alive."

He couldn't bear to wait for the end. He turned and walked away.

CHAPTER 5

THE LODGE LOOMED UP, THE WINDOWS CASTING a blurry yellow light into the driving rain. Judson Esterhazy grasped the heavy iron door ring, heaved it open, and staggered into the entry hall, lined with suits of armor and huge racks of antlers.

"Help!" he cried. "Help me!"

The guests were standing around a roaring fire in the great hall, drinking noontime coffee, tea, and small glasses of malt. They turned and looked at him, astonished.

"My friend's been shot!"

A boom of thunder temporarily drowned him out, rattling the leaded windows.

"Shot!" Esterhazy repeated, collapsing to the floor. "I need help!"

After a moment of frozen horror, several people rushed over. On the floor, his eyes closed, Esterhazy felt them crowding around, heard the low babble of voices.

"Step back," came the stern Scottish voice of Cromarty, the lodgekeeper. "Give him air. Step back, please."

A glass of whisky was pressed to his mouth. He took a swallow, opened his eyes, struggled to sit up.

"What happened? What are you saying?"

Cromarty's face loomed over him: neatly trimmed beard, wire spectacles, sandy hair, angular jaw. The deception was easy enough; Esterhazy was genuinely horror-struck, chilled to the bone, barely able to walk. He took another swallow of whisky, the peaty malt like a fire in his throat, reviving him.

"My brother-in-law...we were stalking a stag in the Mire—"

"The Mire?" said Cromarty, his voice suddenly sharp.

"A real giant..." Esterhazy swallowed, tried to pull himself together.

"Come to the fire." Taking his arm, Cromarty helped him up. Robbie Grant, the old gamekeeper, bustled into the room and took Esterhazy's other arm. Together they helped him shuck off his saturated camouflage jacket and led him to an armchair by the hearth.

Esterhazy sank down.

"Speak," said Cromarty. The other guests stood around, faces white with shock.

"Up on Beinn Dearg," he said. "We spotted a stag. Down in the Foulmire."

"But you know the rules!"

Esterhazy shook his head. "I know, but he was a monster. Thirteen points. My brother-in-law insisted. We tracked him deep into the Mire. Down to the marshes. Then we split up—"

"Are you bloody daft, man?" It was the gamekeeper,

Robbie Grant, speaking in a shrill tenor. "You split up?"

"We had to corner him. Drive him against the marshes. The fogs were coming in, visibility was poor, he broke cover... I saw movement, fired..." He paused, heaved a breath. "Hit my brother-in-law square in the chest..." He gasped, covered his face.

"You left an injured man on the moors?" Cromarty demanded angrily.

"Oh, God." Esterhazy broke into racking sobs, hiding his face in his hands. "He fell into the bogs... Got sucked down..."

"Hold on," said Cromarty, the tone of his voice as cold as ice. He spoke slowly, quietly, enunciating every word. "You're telling me, sir, that you went out into the Mire; that you accidentally shot your brother-in-law; and that he fell into a bog? Is that what you're telling me?"

Esterhazy nodded wordlessly, still hiding his face.

"Christ Jesus. Is there any chance he's still alive?"

Esterhazy shook his head.

"Are you absolutely sure of that?"

"I'm sure," Esterhazy choked out. "He went down. I'm... I'm so sorry!" he suddenly wailed. "I've killed my brother-in-law!" He began rocking back and forth, head in his hands. "God forgive me!"

A stunned silence.

"He's out of his head," the gamekeeper muttered. "As clear a case of moor fever as I've ever seen."

"Get these people out of here," Cromarty rumbled, gesturing at the guests. He turned to the gamekeeper. "Robbie, call the police." He swung on Esterhazy. "Is that the rifle you shot him with?" He gestured roughly at the rifle Esterhazy had carried in, now lying on the floor.

He nodded miserably.

"Nobody touch it."

The guests left in murmuring groups, speaking in hushed tones, shaking their heads. The lightning flashed, a boom of thunder following. Rain lashed the windows. Esterhazy sat in the chair, slowly lowering his hands from his face, feeling the welcome warmth of the fire creeping through his wet clothing. An equally marvelous warmth crept into his inner being, slowly displacing the horror; he felt a sense of release washing over him, even elation. It was over, over, *over*. He had nothing more to fear from Pendergast. The genie was back in the bottle. The man was dead. As for his partner, D'Agosta, and that other New York City cop, Hayward—killing Pendergast had cut the head off that snake. This was truly the end. And by all appearances, these Scottish dunces were buying the story. There was nothing that could come to light to contradict anything he'd said. He had gone back, collected all the shells except the one he wanted them to find. Pendergast's rifle and the shells from their fight he had deposited in a bog on his way back, and they'd never find that. That would be the only mystery—the missing rifle. Nothing strange in that: a rifle could easily get permanently lost once sunk in the Mire. They knew nothing about his handgun, and Esterhazy had made that disappear as well. The stag's tracks, if they survived the storm, would be fully consistent with his story.

"Bloody hell," muttered Cromarty, going to the

mantelpiece, grabbing a bottle of scotch and pouring himself a tumblerful. He drank it in small gulps, pacing before the fire, ignoring Esterhazy.

Grant came back in. "The police are on their way from Inverness, sir. Along with a Northern Constabulary Special Services team—with grapnels."

Cromarty turned, downed the glass, poured himself another, and glared at Esterhazy. "You stay put till they get here, you bloody damned fool."

Another peal of thunder shook the old stone lodge, and the wind howled across the moors.

CHAPTER 6

T HE POLICE ARRIVED MORE THAN AN HOUR LATER, their flashing lights striping the gravel drive. The storm had passed, leaving a leaden sky of swift-moving clouds. They were dressed up in blue slickers, boots, and waterproof hats, tramping across the stone entryway, looking self-important. Esterhazy watched them from the chair, reassured by their unimaginative stolidity.

The last one to enter was the man in charge, and the only one not in uniform. Esterhazy examined him surreptitiously; he was at least six foot five, bald with a fringe of pale hair; he had a narrow face and blade-thin nose and carried himself tilted forward, as if cutting his way through life. His nose was just red enough to compromise the appearance of seriousness, and he occasionally dabbed at it with a handkerchief. He was dressed in old shooting clothes: tin oil pants, a tight twill sweater, and a scuffed Barbour jacket, unzipped.

"Hullo, Cromarty," he said, extending an easy hand as Cromarty bustled over. They huddled at the far end of the hall, speaking in low tones, occasionally glancing in Esterhazy's direction.

Then the officer came over and took the wing chair next to Esterhazy. "Chief Inspector Balfour of the Northern Constabulary," he said quietly, not offering his hand, but leaning forward, elbows on his knees. "And you are Judson Esterhazy?"

"That's right."

He slipped out a small steno pad. "All right, Dr. Esterhazy. Tell me what happened."

Esterhazy went through the story from beginning to end, pausing frequently to collect himself or choke back tears, while Balfour took notes. When he was done, Balfour shut the pad. "We're going to the scene of the accident. You're coming with us."

"I'm not sure . . ." Esterhazy swallowed. ". . . that I'm up to it."

"I'm quite sure you are," said Balfour crisply. "We've two bloodhounds. And Mr. Grant will be coming with us as well. He knows the byways of the Mire." He stood up, consulting a large marine watch. "We've five hours of daylight left."

Esterhazy got up with a long, mournful face and a show of reluctance. Outside, the team was gearing up with packs, ropes, and other equipment. At the end of the graveled drive, a dog handler was exercising two leashed bloodhounds around the greensward.

An hour later, they had tramped over the side of Beinn Dearg and arrived at the edge of the Foulmire, the boggy ground marked by a ragged line of boulders. A mist lay over the moors. The sun was already sinking in the sky, the endless landscape disappearing into gray nothingness, the dark pools lying motionless in the heavy air. There was a faint smell of vegetal decay.

"Dr. Esterhazy?" Balfour looked at him, frowning, arms folded over his chest. "Which way?"

Esterhazy glanced around, his face a blank. "It all looks the same." No point in giving them too much help.

Balfour shook his head sadly.

"The dogs have a scent over here, Inspector." The thick brogue of the gamekeeper drifted through the mist. "And I see a bit of sign."

"Is that where you went into the Mire?" Balfour asked.

"I think so."

"All right. The dogs will lead the way. Mr. Grant, you stay with them up front. The rest of you follow. Dr. Esterhazy and I will come last. Mr. Grant knows the good ground; follow in his footsteps at all times." The inspector took a moment to remove a pipe, which had been pre-packed, and lit it. "If anyone gets mired, don't the rest of you rush in like damn fools and get mired yourself. The team has ropes, lifesaver rings, and telescoping hooks for retrieving any who get stuck in quicksand."

He puffed away, looking around. "Mr. Grant, do you have anything to add?"

"I do," said the small, wizened man, leaning on his walking stick, his voice almost as high as a girl's. "If you do get caught in it, don't struggle. Lean back into it gently, let your body float up." He fixed a bushy eye on Esterhazy, glaring. "I've got a question for Dr. Esterhazy: when you were traipsing over the Mire after that stag, did ye see any landmarks?"

"Like what?" Esterhazy said, his voice confused and uncertain. "It seemed awfully empty to me."

"There's ruins, cairns, and standing stones."

"Ruins...yes, it seems we passed by some ruins."

"What'd they look like?"

"If I remember correctly—" Esterhazy frowned in mock recollection—"they appeared to be a stone corral and a shelter on a sort of hill, with the marshes beyond and to the left."

"Aye. The old Coombe Hut." Without another word the gamekeeper turned and began tramping through the grass, moss, and heather, the bloodhounds with their handler hurrying to keep up. He walked fast with his head down, his short legs churning, walking stick swinging, his shaggy hair like a white halo around a tweed cap perched on top.

For a quarter of an hour they moved in silence, interrupted only by the snuffling and whining of the dogs and the murmured instructions of their handler. As the clouds thickened again and a premature gloaming fell over the moors, some of the men took out powerful flashlights and switched them on. The beams lanced through the cold mists. Esterhazy, who had been feigning ignorance and confusion, began to wonder if they hadn't gotten lost for real. Everything looked strange and he recognized nothing.

As they descended into yet another lonely hollow, the dogs suddenly stopped, snuffled all around in circles, and then charged forward on a scent, straining their leashes.

"Easy, now," the handler said, pulling back, but the dogs were too excited and began to bay, a deep-throated sound that echoed over the moors.

"What's with them?" Balfour said sharply.

"I don't know. Back. Back!"

"For God's sake," shrilled Grant, "pull them back!"

"Bloody *hell*!" The handler pulled on the leashes but the dogs responded by lunging forward, in full throat.

"Watch out, there!" cried Grant.

With a scream of pure terror the handler suddenly went down into a quagmire, breaking through a crust of sphagnum, slopping and struggling, and one of the dogs went in with him, the baying turning into a shriek. The dog churned, his head held up in terror.

"Stop your struggling!" Grant hollered at the handler, his voice mingling with the cries of the dog. "Lean back!"

But the handler was in too much of a panic to pay attention. "Help me!" he screamed, flailing away, splattering mud.

"Bring the hook!" commanded Balfour.

A member of the Special Services team had already dropped his pack and was untying a rod with a large rounded handle on one end and a broad loop of rope on the other. He snapped it out like a telescope and knelt at the edge of the bog, wrapped the rope around his waist, and extended the end with the handle.

The dog yelped and paddled.

"Help me!" the trapped man cried.

"Grab hold, ye damn fool!" cried Grant.

The high-pitched voice seemed to have penetrated and the man grasped its meaning. He reached out and grabbed the handle at the end of the rod.

"Pull!"

The rescuer leaned back, using his body to leverage the man out. The handler clung on desperately, his body emerging slowly with a sucking noise, and was dragged onto firmer ground, where he lay shivering and gasping for breath, covered with clinging muck.

Meanwhile the dog was shrieking like a banshee, churning and slapping the bog with his front legs.

"Lasso his front quarters!" shouted Grant.

One of the men already had his rope out and was fashioning it into a loop. He tossed it toward the dog, but it fell short. The dog struggled and screamed, his eyes rolling white.

"Again!"

The man tossed it again, and this time it fell over the dog.

"Tighten and pull!"

He pulled but the dog, feeling the rope around his neck, twisted and struggled to avoid it, letting it slip off.

Esterhazy watched in mingled horror and fascination.

"He's going under!" said the handler, who was slowly recovering from his fright.

Another man readied a loop, this one tied with a slipknot, lasso-style, and he crouched at the bank, giving it a gentle toss. It missed. He pulled it in, loosened the noose, prepared to toss it again.

But the dog was going down fast. Now only his neck was above the muck, every tendon popping, the mouth like a pink cavern from which came a sound that went beyond a scream into something not of this world.

"Do something, for the love of God!" cried the handler.

Ooowooo! Ooowooo! came the sound, horribly loud.

"Again! Toss it again!"

Again the man tossed the lasso; again he missed.

And suddenly, without even a gurgle, there was silence. The sound of the dog's last smothered cry echoed across the moorlands and died away. The muck closed up and its surface smoothed. A faint tremor shook the bog, and then it went still.

The handler, who had risen to his feet, now sank to his knees. "My dog! Oh, great Christ!"

Balfour fixed him with a stare and spoke quietly but with great force. "I'm very sorry. But we have to continue."

"You can't just *leave* him!"

Balfour turned to the gamekeeper. "Mr. Grant, lead on to the Coombe Hut. And you, sir, bring that other bloodhound. We still need him."

Without further ado they continued on, the dog handler, dripping with mud, his feet squelching, leading the remaining bloodhound, who was shaking and trembling, useless for work. Grant was once again walking like a demon on stubby legs, swinging his stick, stopping only occasionally to viciously stab the end of it at the ground with grunts of dissatisfaction.

To Esterhazy's surprise, they weren't lost after all. The land began to rise and, against the faint light, he made out the ruins of the corral and hut.

"Which way?" said Grant to him.

"We passed through and went down the other side."

They climbed the hill and passed the ruins.

"Here, I think, is where we split up," said Esterhazy, indicating the place where he had departed from Pendergast's trail in the effort to flank him.

After examining the ground, the gamekeeper grunted, nodded.

"Lead on," said Balfour.

Esterhazy took the lead, with Grant right behind, holding a powerful electric torch. The yellow beam cut through the mist, illuminating the rushes and cattails along the edge of the marsh.

"Here," Esterhazy said, halting. "That's...that's where he went down." He pointed to the broad, still pool at the verge of the marsh. His voice broke, he covered his face, and a sob escaped. "It was like a nightmare. God forgive me!"

"Everyone stay back," said Balfour, motioning the team with his hand. "We're going to set up lights. You, Dr. Esterhazy, are going to show us exactly what happened. The forensic team will examine the ground, and then we'll drag the pool."

"Drag the pool?" Esterhazy asked.

Balfour glared at him. "That's right. To recover the body."

CHAPTER 7

ESTERHAZY WAITED BEHIND THE YELLOW TAPE laid on
the ground as the forensic team, bent over like crones,
finished combing the area for evidence under a battery
of harsh lights that cast a ghastly illumination over the
stark landscape.

He had followed the evidence gathering with growing satisfaction. All was in order. They had found the
one brass casing he'd deliberately left behind, and
despite the heavy rains they managed to find some faint
tracks of the stag, as well as to map some of the crushed
marks in the heather made by himself and Pendergast.
In addition, they had managed to confirm where the
stag had burst through the reeds. Everything was consistent with the story he'd told.

"All right, men," Balfour called. "Pack away your
kits and let's drag the pool."

Esterhazy felt a shiver of both anticipation and
revulsion. Gruesome as it was, it would be a relief to
see his adversary's corpse dragged up from the muck; it
would provide that final act of closure, an epilogue to
a titanic struggle.

On a piece of graph paper, Balfour had sketched out the dimensions of the pool—a small area twelve feet by eighteen—and drawn a scheme of how it would be dragged. In the glare of the lights, the team clipped a claw-like grapnel to a rope, the long steel tines gleaming evilly, and then fixed a lead weight to the eye. Two men stood back, holding the coil of rope, while a third balanced himself on the pool's edge. With Balfour consulting his drawing and murmuring directions, the third man gave the hook a toss over the shivering bog. It landed in the muck on the far side, the weight carrying it down. When it finally came to rest on the bottom, the other two behind began hauling it back in. As the grapnel inched through the bog, the rope straining and tightening, Esterhazy tensed involuntarily.

A minute later the grapnel surfaced, trailing muck and weeds. Balfour, clipboard in hand, examined the tines with a latex-gloved hand, then shook his head.

They moved eighteen inches along the shore and gave another toss, another pull. More weeds. They moved again, repeated the process.

Esterhazy watched every emergence of the muck-coated grapnel, a knot of tension growing in the pit of his stomach. He ached all over, and his bitten hand throbbed. The men were approaching the spot where Pendergast had gone down. Finally the grapnel was tossed over the very spot, and the team began to retract it.

It halted, arrested by a submerged object.

"Got something," one of the men said.

Esterhazy held his breath.

"Easy, now," said Balfour, leaning forward, his body tense as bowed steel. "Slow and steady."

Another man joined the rope-line and they began to haul it in, hand over hand, with Balfour hovering over them and urging them not to rush things.

"It's coming," grunted one.

The surface of the bog swelled, the muck running to the sides as a long, log-like object emerged—mud-coated, misshapen.

"Take it slow," Balfour warned.

As if they were landing a huge fish, the men held the corpse at the surface while they ran nylon straps and webbing under it.

"All right. Bring it in."

With additional effort, they eased the corpse up, sliding it onto a plastic tarp laid on the ground. Mud drained away in thick rivers from it and a hideous stench of rotting meat suddenly washed over Esterhazy, propelling him a step back.

"What in blazes?" murmured Balfour. He bent over the corpse, felt it with his gloved hand. Then he gestured at one of the team members. "Rinse this off."

One of the forensic team came over. Together they bent over the misshapen head of the carcass, the man washing the quicksand off with a squeeze bottle.

The stench was hideous, and Esterhazy felt the bile rise in his throat. Several of the men were hastily lighting cigars or pipes.

Balfour abruptly straightened up. "It's a sheep," he said matter-of-factly. "Drag it off to the side, rinse this area down, and let's continue."

The men worked in silence, and soon the grappling hook was back in the water. Again and again they dragged the pool; again and again the claws of the hook emerged from the muck with nothing more than weeds. The reek of the suppurating sheep, lying behind them, covered the scene like a pall. Esterhazy found the tension becoming unbearable. Why weren't they finding the body?

They reached the far end of the pool. Balfour called a discussion, the team conferring at one side in low tones. Then Balfour approached Esterhazy. "Are you sure this is where your brother-in-law went down?"

"Of course I'm sure," Esterhazy said, trying to control his voice, which was on the edge of breaking.

"We don't seem to be finding anything."

"He's down there!" Esterhazy raised his voice. "You yourself found the shell from my shot, found the marks in the grass—you *know* this is the right place."

Balfour looked at him curiously. "It certainly seems so, but…" His voice trailed off.

"You've got to find him! Drag it again, for God's sake!"

"We intend to, but you saw how thorough a job we made of it. If a body was down there…"

"The currents," said Esterhazy. "Maybe the currents took him away."

"There are no currents."

Esterhazy took a deep breath, desperately trying to master himself. He tried to speak calmly, but could not quite get the tremor out of his voice. "Look, Mr. Balfour. I know the body's there. *I saw him go down.*"

A sharp nod and Balfour turned to the men. "Drag it again—at right angles this time."

A murmur of protests. But soon the process began all over again, the grappling hook being tossed in from another side of the pool, while Esterhazy watched, the bile cooking in his throat. As the last of the light drained from the sky, the mists thickened, the sodium lamps casting ghastly bars of white in which shadowy figures moved about, indistinct, throwing bizarre shadows, like the damned milling about in the lowest circle of hell. It was impossible, Esterhazy thought. There was absolutely no way Pendergast could have survived and gotten away. No way.

He should have stayed. He should have waited to the bitter end...He turned to Balfour. "Look, is it at all possible someone could manage to get out—extract themselves from this kind of mire?"

The man's blade-like face turned to him. "But you saw him go down. Am I correct?"

"Yes, yes! But I was so upset, and the fogs were so thick...Maybe he could have gotten out."

"Highly doubtful," said Balfour, staring at him with narrowed eyes. "Unless, of course, you left him while he was still struggling."

"No, no, I tried to rescue him, just as I said. But the thing is, my brother-in-law's incredibly resourceful. Just maybe—" He tried to inject a hopeful tone into his voice, to cover up his panic. "Just maybe he got out. I *want* to think he got out."

"Dr. Esterhazy," said Balfour, not unsympathetically, "I'm afraid there isn't much hope. But you're right, we need to give that possibility serious consideration. Unfortunately the remaining bloodhound is too traumatized to work, but we have two experts who can help." He turned. "Mr. Grant? Mr. Chase?"

The gamekeeper came over, with another man whom

Esterhazy recognized as the head of the forensic team. "Yes, sir?"

"I'd like you both to examine the larger area around the bog here. I want you to look for any evidence—any at all—that the victim might have extracted himself and gone off. Search everywhere and cut for sign."

"Yes, sir." They disappeared into the darkness, just the beams of their flashlights remaining visible, stabbing about in the murk.

Esterhazy waited in silence, the mists congealing into fog. Finally, the two men returned. "There's no sign, sir," Chase said. "Of course, we've had very heavy rains that would have destroyed anything subtle. But a wounded man, shot, perhaps crawling, bleeding profusely, covered with mud—he would have left some evidence. It's not possible the man escaped the Mire."

Balfour turned to Esterhazy. "There you have your answer." Then he added: "I think we'll be winding up here. Dr. Esterhazy, I'm afraid I'm going to have to ask you to remain in the area until the inquest." He removed a handkerchief, dabbed at his running nose, put it away. "Do you understand?"

"Don't worry," said Esterhazy fervently. "I fully intend to remain here until I learn *exactly* what happened to my...my dear brother-in-law."

CHAPTER 8

New York City

Dr. John Felder followed the police van as it jounced its way down the one-lane road that traversed Little Governor's Island. It was warm for an evening in early October, and the swampy marshland on either side was dotted with pools of mist. The trip south from Bedford Hills had taken just under an hour, and their destination now lay directly ahead.

The van turned into a lane of long-dead chestnut trees, and Felder followed. Through the trees, he could see the East River and the numberless silhouetted buildings of Manhattan's East Side. So near, and yet so very, very far.

The van slowed, then stopped outside a tall wrought-iron gate. A guard stepped out of the security booth beside it and walked up to the driver. He glanced at a clipboard the driver handed him, then nodded, returned to his booth, and opened the gate with the press of a button. As the two vehicles entered the compound, Felder glanced at a bronze plaque on the gate: MOUNT MERCY HOSPITAL FOR THE CRIMINALLY INSANE. There had been some effort recently to change the name to something more modern, less stigmatizing, but the massive plaque looked like it was there to stay.

The van pulled into a small, cobbled parking area, and Felder stopped his Volvo beside it. He got out and stared up at the vast gothic pile, its grand old windows now covered by bars. It had to be the most picturesque— not to mention unusual—asylum in all America. It had taken him a great deal of time and paperwork to arrange for the transfer, and he was not a little irritated that the man who had promised to "reveal all" about the prisoner in return for this favor seemed to have disappeared from the face of the earth.

His gaze quickly shifted from the building to the police van. A prison guard had gotten out of the passenger seat and walked to the rear doors, unlocking them with a key on a large key ring. A moment later, the doors opened and a police officer, uniformed and armed with a shotgun, stepped out. While he waited, gun at the ready, the prison guard reached into the van to help out the other occupant.

As Felder watched, a young woman in her early twenties stepped out into the evening air. She had dark hair, cut in a short, stylish bob, and her voice—when she thanked the orderly for his assistance—was low and even, its cadence reserved and antique. She was dressed in a prison uniform, and her wrists were handcuffed before her, but as she was led toward the entrance her head was held high, and she walked with grace and dignity, her carriage erect.

Felder joined the little group as they walked by.

"Dr. Felder," she said, nodding gravely at him. "A pleasure to see you again."

"Likewise, Constance," he replied.

As they approached the front door, it was unlocked from within and opened by a fastidious-looking man wearing a white medical jacket over an expensive suit. "Good evening, Miss Greene," he said in a calm, quiet voice, as if speaking to a child. "We've been expecting you."

Constance gave a faint curtsy.

"I'm Dr. Ostrom, and I'll be your attending physician here at Mount Mercy."

The young woman inclined her head. "A pleasure to make your acquaintance, Doctor. Please call me Constance."

They stepped into the waiting area. The air was warm and smelled faintly of disinfectant. "I know your, ah, guardian, Aloysius Pendergast," Dr. Ostrom went on. "I'm very sorry we couldn't have brought you here sooner, but it took longer than expected to get the necessary paperwork cleared."

As Ostrom said this, his gaze briefly met Felder's. Felder knew that the room Constance was assigned at Mount Mercy had—after a thorough search—been very carefully cleaned, first with bleach, then antiseptic, and then repainted with three coats of oil-based paint. These measures were deemed necessary because the room's prior occupant had been notorious in her fondness for poisons.

"I'm most grateful for your attentions, Doctor," Constance said primly.

There was a brief wait while Dr. Ostrom signed the forms handed him by the prison guard. "You can remove the handcuffs now," Ostrom said as he returned the clipboard.

The guard complied. An orderly let the guard and police officer out and locked the front door carefully behind them. "Very good," Ostrom said, rubbing his hands together lightly as if pleased by the transaction. "Now Dr. Felder and I will show you to your room. I think you'll find it quite nice."

"I have no doubt that I will, Dr. Ostrom," Constance replied. "You're very kind."

They made their way down a long, echoing corridor, Dr. Ostrom explaining the rules at Mount Mercy and expressing hope that Constance would find herself comfortable with them. Felder shot a private glance at Constance. Anyone would find her an unusual woman, of course: the old-fashioned diction, the unreadable eyes that seemed somehow older than the face they were set in. And yet there was nothing about her looks or her manner that could prepare one for the truth: that Constance Greene was deeply insane. Her presentation was unique in Felder's experience. She claimed to have been born in the 1870s, to a family long gone and forgotten, save for scattered traces in public records. Most recently, she had returned by ship from England. During the voyage, she had—by her own admission—thrown her infant son overboard because, she'd insisted, he was the embodiment of evil.

In the two months since he'd become involved with her case, Felder had—first at Bellevue, then at the Bedford Hills Correctional Facility—continued his analysis of Constance. And while his fascination with the case had only sharpened, he had to admit that he'd made no progress at understanding either her or her illness.

They waited while an orderly unlocked a heavy metal

door, then they turned down another echoing passage, at last stopping before an unmarked door. The orderly unlocked this in turn, and Dr. Ostrom ushered them into a small room, windowless and sparsely furnished. All the furniture—bed, table, single chair—was bolted securely to the floor. A bookcase was fixed to one wall, containing half a dozen volumes. A small plastic flowerpot with daffodils from the hospital's garden sat on the table.

"Well?" Ostrom asked. "What do you think, Constance?"

The young woman looked around, taking in everything. "Perfectly satisfactory, thank you."

"I'm pleased to hear that. Dr. Felder and I will give you some time to settle in. I'll send a matron by with more appropriate attire."

"I'm much obliged to you." Constance's gaze settled on the bookcase. "My goodness. Cotton Mather's *Magnalia Christi Americana*. Benjamin Franklin's *Autobiography*. Richardson's *Clarissa*. Aren't these Great-Aunt Cornelia's books?"

Dr. Ostrom nodded. "New copies of them. This used to be her room, you see, and your guardian asked us to purchase the books for you."

"Ah." For a moment, Constance flushed with what appeared to be pleasure. "It's almost like coming home." She turned to Felder. "So nice to carry on the family tradition here."

Despite the warmth of the room, Felder felt a cold thrill of dismay course down his spine.

CHAPTER 9

LIEUTENANT VINCENT D'AGOSTA STARED DOWN at his desk, trying not to feel depressed. Ever since he'd come off sick leave, his boss, Captain Singleton, had placed him on modified duty. All he seemed to do was push paper from one side of the desk to the other. He glanced out the door into the squad room. There, people were busily coming and going; phones were ringing; criminals were being processed. Stuff was *happening*. He sighed, glanced back down at the desk. D'Agosta hated paperwork. But the fact was, Singleton had done it for his own good. After all, just half a year ago he'd been lying in a hospital bed in Baton Rouge, fighting for his life, a bullet having nicked his heart. He was lucky to be alive at all, let alone vertical and back at work. Anyway, desk duty wouldn't last forever. He just had to fully recover his old strength.

Besides, he told himself, he should be looking on the bright side. His relationship with Laura Hayward had never been better. Almost losing him had changed her somehow, softened her, made her more affectionate and demonstrative. In fact, once he was back to one hundred percent he was seriously thinking of proposing. He didn't think the average relationship counselor would recommend getting shot in the chest, but it had sure worked for him...

He realized somebody was standing in his office doorway and glanced up to see a young woman staring back at him. She was maybe nineteen or twenty, petite, dressed in jeans and an aging Ramones T-shirt. A black leather bag, studded with small metal points, hung from one arm. Her hair was dyed a severe black and he could see a tattoo on her upper arm peeking out from beneath her shirt, which he recognized as an M. C. Escher design.

A Goth.

"Can I help you, ma'am?" he asked. Where was the damn secretary to screen these people?

"Do I look like a ma'am to you?" came the reply.

D'Agosta sighed. "What can I do for you?"

"You're Vincent D'Agosta, right?"

He nodded.

She stepped into the office. "He mentioned you a few times. I'm usually bad with names, but I remembered that one because it was so Italian."

"So Italian," D'Agosta repeated.

"I don't mean that in a bad way. It's just that where I come from, in Kansas, nobody has a name like that."

"The Italians never made it that far inland," D'Agosta replied dryly. "Now, who's this 'he' you mentioned?"

"Agent Pendergast."

"Pendergast?" D'Agosta couldn't keep the surprise out of his voice.

"Yup. I was his assistant out in Medicine Creek, Kansas. The 'Still Life' serial murders?"

D'Agosta stared. Pendergast's assistant? The girl was delusional.

"He must have mentioned me. I'm Corrie Swanson."

D'Agosta frowned. "I'm vaguely familiar with the Still Life killings, but I don't recall him mentioning your name."

"He never talks about his cases. I drove him around, helped him scope out the town. With that black suit and all he stuck out like a sore thumb—he needed an insider like me."

D'Agosta was surprised to hear this but realized she was probably telling the truth—if exaggerated. Assistant? He found his irritation give way to a darker emotion. "Come in," he said belatedly. "Have a seat."

She sat down, metal jingling, and swept back her raven hair, revealing a streak of purple and another of yellow. D'Agosta leaned back in his chair, carefully disguising his reaction. "So. What's up?"

"I'm in New York for the year. Got here in September. I'm a sophomore, and I've just transferred to the John Jay College of Criminal Justice."

"Go on," D'Agosta said. The John Jay part impressed him. She was no idiot, although she was doing her damnedest to look like one.

"I'm taking a class called Case Studies in Deviance and Social Control."

"Deviance and Social Control," D'Agosta repeated. Sounded like a course Laura might have taken—she'd been big on sociology.

"As part of this, we're supposed to do a case study

ourselves and write a paper. I chose the Still Life killings."

"I'm not sure Pendergast would approve," D'Agosta said carefully.

"But he *did* approve. That's the problem. Back when I first arrived, I set up a lunch with him. It was supposed to be for yesterday. He never showed. Then I went to his apartment at the Dakota—nothing, all I got was the runaround from a doorman. He's got my cell number, but he never called me to cancel or anything. It's like the guy vanished into thin air."

"That seems odd. Perhaps you got the appointment wrong?"

She fished in her little bag, pulled out an envelope, and handed it over.

D'Agosta extracted a letter from the envelope and began to read.

The Dakota
1 West 72nd Street
New York, NY 10023

5 September

Ms. Corrie Swanson
844 Amsterdam Avenue, Apt. 30B
New York, NY 10025

My dear Corrie,

I'm pleased to hear that your studies are going well. I approve of your choice of courses. I believe you will find the Introduction to Forensic Chemistry to be most interesting. I've given some thought to your project and agree to take part, provided I may vet the final product and that you agree not to reveal certain minor details in your paper.

By all means let's get together for lunch. I will be out of the country later this month, but I should be back by mid-October. October 19 agrees with my calendar. Allow me to suggest Le Bernardin on West 51st Street at 1 PM. The reservation will be in my name.

I look forward to seeing you then.

Kind regards,
A. Pendergast

D'Agosta read the letter twice. It's true he hadn't heard from Pendergast in a month or two, but that in itself wasn't especially unusual. The agent frequently disappeared for long periods of time. But Pendergast was a stickler about keeping his word; not showing up for lunch, after making plans, was out of character.

He handed the letter back. "Was there a reservation?"

"Yes. It had been made the day after he sent the letter. He never called to cancel."

D'Agosta nodded, covering up his own growing concern.

"I was hoping you might know something about his whereabouts. I'm worried. This isn't like him."

D'Agosta cleared his throat. "I haven't spoken to Pendergast in a while but I'm sure there's an explanation. He's probably deep in a case." He ventured a reassuring smile. "I'll check into it, get back to you."

"Here's my cell number." Pulling a pad of paper across the desk toward her, she scribbled a number onto it.

"I'll let you know, Ms. Swanson."

"Thank you. And it's Corrie."

"Fine. Corrie." The more D'Agosta thought about it, the more worried he became. He almost didn't notice her picking up her bag and heading out the door.

CHAPTER 10

Cairn Barrow

THE HIGH STREET RAN THROUGH THE CENTER of the village, crooking slightly east at the square and running down into the green folds of the hills surrounding Loch Lanark. The shops and houses were of identical earth-colored stone, with steeply gabled roofs of weathered slate. Primroses and daffodils peeked out from freshly painted window boxes. The bells in the squat belfry of the Wee Kirk o' the Loch sleepily tolled ten AM.

It was, even to Chief Inspector Balfour's jaundiced eye, an almost impossibly picturesque scene.

He walked quickly down the street. A dozen cars were parked in front of the town pub, The Old Thistle—practically a traffic jam this late in the season, long after the summer day-trippers and the foreign tourists had departed. He stepped inside, nodding to Phillip, the publican, then pushed through the door beside the telephone box and mounted the creaking wooden stairs to the Common Room. The largest public space for twenty miles around, it was now filled almost to capacity with men and women—witnesses and curious spectators—sitting on long benches, all facing the rear wall, where a large oak table had been placed. Behind the table sat Dr. Ainslie, the local coroner, dressed in somber black, his dry old face with its deeply scored frown lines betraying perpetual dismay at the world and its doings. Beside him, at a much smaller table, sat Judson Esterhazy.

Ainslie nodded curtly to Balfour as the inspector took a seat. Then, glancing around, he cleared his throat.

"This court of inquiry has been summoned to establish the facts surrounding the disappearance and possible demise of Mr. Aloysius X. L. Pendergast. I say 'possible' due to the fact that no body has been recovered. The only witness to Mr. Pendergast's death is the person who may have killed him—Judson Esterhazy, his brother-in-law." Ainslie's scowl deepened, his face so desiccated it almost looked as if it might flake off from the effort. "Since Mr. Pendergast has no living relations, one could say that Judson Esterhazy appears here not only as the person responsible for Mr. Pendergast's accident but as his family representative, as well. As a result, this proceeding is not—and cannot be—a standard inquest, because in this case there is no body and the fact of death remains to be established. We shall, however, follow the form of an inquest. Our purpose then is to establish the facts of the disappearance as well as the proximate circumstances, and to rule, if the facts allow, on whether a death has or has not occurred. We will hear testimony from all concerned, then make a determination."

Ainslie turned to Esterhazy. "Dr. Esterhazy, do you agree that you are a properly interested person in this matter?"

Esterhazy nodded. "I do."

"And you have declined, of your own free will, to retain a solicitor?"

"That is correct."

"Very well. Before we begin, let me remind all present of Coroner's Rule 36: an inquest is not a gathering in which any civil or criminal liability can be assigned—although we can determine if the circumstances meet certain legal definitions of culpability. The determination of culpability is a matter to be taken up separately by the courts, if warranted. Are there any questions?"

When the room remained silent, Ainslie nodded. "Then let us proceed to the evidence. We shall begin with a statement from Ian Cromarty."

Inspector Balfour listened as the lodgekeeper spoke at some length of Pendergast and Esterhazy—of his initial impressions of them, of how they had shared dinner together the night before, of how Esterhazy had burst in the following morning crying that he had shot his brother-in-law. Next, Ainslie questioned a few of the Kilchurn Lodge guests who had witnessed Esterhazy's frantic, disheveled return. Then he turned to Grant, the gamekeeper. As the proceedings continued, Ainslie's face remained an astringent mask of disapproval and suspicion.

"You're Robert Grant, correct?"

"Aye, sir," the wizened old man replied.

"How long have you been gamekeeper at Kilchurn?"

"Going on thirty-five years, sir."

At Ainslie's request, Grant described in detail the trek to the site of the accident and the death of the search dog.

"How common is it for hunters from your lodge to venture into the Foulmire?"

"Common? It isnae common. It's agin the rules."

"So Pendergast and Dr. Esterhazy here violated those rules."

"That they did."

Balfour could see Esterhazy stirring uncomfortably at this.

"Such behavior signals a lack of judgment. Why did you let them go out on their own?"

"Because I recalled them from before."

"Go on."

"The pair of them were here once, some ten, twelve years back. I took them out meself, I did. Bloody good shots, knew exactly what they were doing, especially Dr. Esterhazy here." Grant nodded in the doctor's direction. "If I couldna vouch for that myself I'd never have let them out without a guide."

Balfour sat up in his seat. He'd known that Pendergast and Esterhazy had hunted at Kilchurn before, of course—Esterhazy had mentioned as much in one of the interrogation sessions—but the fact that Grant had taken them out and could vouch for Esterhazy's being an excellent shot was news to him. Esterhazy had always played down his skill. Balfour cursed himself for not having discovered this nugget on his own.

Next, it was his own turn to speak. Balfour described his arrival at the lodge; Esterhazy's emotional state; the search for the body and the dragging of the pool; and the subsequent fruitless search of the moors and surrounding hamlets for any sign of a body. He spoke slowly and carefully. Ainslie listened intently, interrupting only infrequently with questions.

When he was done, Ainslie peered about. "And in

the ten days since the shooting was reported," he said, "the police have continued their searches?"

"That is correct," Balfour replied. "We dragged the pool not once, but twice, and then a third and fourth time. We also dragged the surrounding pools. We used bloodhounds to try to pick up a trail from the accident scene. They found no trace, although to be sure there had been very heavy rains."

"So," said Ainslie, "you have found no independent evidence Pendergast is dead, nor any evidence he is still alive. Is that correct?"

"Correct. We did not recover his body or any personal effects, including his rifle."

"Inspector," Ainslie said, "have you found Dr. Esterhazy to be cooperative in this matter?"

"For the most part, yes. Although he describes his shooting skills rather differently than Mr. Grant."

"And how does Dr. Esterhazy describe his shooting abilities?"

"He calls himself inexperienced."

"Have his actions and statements corresponded to those of a person responsible for such an egregious accident?"

"So far as I have seen, yes." Balfour, despite all, had not been able to put his finger on a single thing in Esterhazy's actions that was inconsistent with shame, grief, and self-blame.

"Would you say he can be considered a reliable and competent witness to these events?"

Balfour hesitated. "I would say that nothing we've found to date has in any way disagreed with his statements."

The coroner seemed to consider this a moment. "Thank you, Inspector."

Next to speak was Esterhazy himself. In the ten days since the shooting, he had regained a good measure of composure, although a faintly haggard look of anxiety seemed to have deepened about him. His voice was steady, earnest, and low. He spoke of his friendship with Pendergast, which started when his sister married the FBI agent. He briefly mentioned her shocking death in the jaws of a man-eating lion, which elicited audible gasps from the audience. And then—at the gentle prodding of the coroner—he talked about the events leading up to Pendergast's death: the hunt on the moors; the discussion of which stag to try for; the stalking on the Foulmire; the rising fog; his own disorientation; the sudden, bounding entrance of the stag and his instinctive shooting; the frantic attempt to rescue his former brother-in-law; and the man's sinking into the quickmire. As Esterhazy spoke of these last events, and of his desperate trek back to Kilchurn Lodge, his veneer of calm broke and he became visibly upset, his voice cracking. The onlookers shook their heads, clearly moved and sympathetic. Ainslie's face, Balfour noted with approval, remained as mournfully skeptical as always. He had a few questions about minor particulars—the timing of certain events, Esterhazy's medical opinion of Pendergast's wound—but beyond that, nothing. Esterhazy's testimony was over in fifteen minutes. All in all, a remarkable performance.

Performance. Now, why had he chosen that word?

Because, despite everything, Balfour continued to find himself deeply suspicious of Esterhazy. It was nothing he could put his finger on. All the evidence added up. But if Balfour had wanted to kill someone, and make it look like an accident, he would have gone about it precisely as Esterhazy had.

His mind was occupied with these thoughts while a string of minor witnesses cycled through. He glanced at Esterhazy. The man had taken great pains to come across as ingenuous, frank, simple to a fault—the typical bumbling American. But he wasn't bumbling, and he clearly wasn't stupid. He had both a medical degree and a doctorate—Balfour had checked.

Ainslie's dry voice went on. "As I mentioned earlier, the purpose of this inquest is to establish if there was a death. The evidence is as follows. It is the testimony of Dr. Esterhazy that he accidentally shot Aloysius Pendergast; that in his medical opinion the wound was mortal; and that he witnessed, with his own eyes, Pendergast's submergence in the mire. It is the testimony of Inspector Balfour and others that the scene of the accident was fully investigated, and that the scant evidence found on the site was consistent with Dr. Esterhazy's testimony. The inspector also testified that no body or effects were recovered either from the mire or from the surrounding moorlands. It is Inspector Balfour's further testimony that, despite an exhaustive search of the neighboring villages, no trace of Mr. Pendergast has been found, and no witnesses to either his living or dead person have come to light."

He glanced around the common room. "Under the circumstances, there are two possible verdicts that could be delivered consistent with the facts presented: involuntary culpable homicide, or an open verdict.

Involuntary culpable homicide is adjudged to be homicide, save for the fact that the *mens rea* for murder is not present. An open verdict is a verdict in which the cause and circumstances of death, or in this case even the fact of death, cannot be established at the present time."

He paused and scoured the courtroom again with a pair of cynical eyes. "Based on the testimony and evidence presented here today, I declare an open verdict in this case."

"Excuse me, sir!" Balfour found that he was suddenly on his feet. "I must protest that verdict."

Ainslie looked toward him, frowning. "Inspector?"

"While—" Balfour hesitated, tried to collect himself. "While the act in question may not have been murder, it was nevertheless caused by improper conduct. That argues strongly for a verdict of involuntary culpable homicide. We have Dr. Esterhazy's own testimony to support that verdict. Negligence was clearly the overwhelming factor in this death. There isn't a scrap of evidence the victim survived the shooting and overwhelming evidence he did not."

"We do have that testimony," Ainslie said. "But let me remind you, Inspector: we have no body. We have no corroborative evidence. All we have is the statement of a single eyewitness. And thus we have no independent evidence that anyone was actually killed. Therefore, this inquest has no choice but to render an open verdict."

Balfour remained standing. "If there's an open verdict, I have no legal recourse for keeping Dr. Esterhazy in Scotland."

"If there is an objection," the coroner went on, "you can always request a judicial review in divisional court."

A low muttering began to rise from the assembly. Balfour shot another glance at Esterhazy. There was nothing he could do.

"If that is all," Ainslie said, looking around sternly, "I declare this inquest to be concluded."

CHAPTER 11

Inverkirkton, Scotland

THE LONE BICYCLIST PEDALED WITH EVIDENT effort up the narrow, winding road. The black three-speed was fitted with a special rack over the rear fender, and it currently held leather panniers, kept in place with bungee cords. The rider was dressed in a dark gray windcheater and dove-colored corduroy trousers, and together with the black bicycle he formed a curiously monochromatic figure, set against the gorse and heather of the Scottish hills.

At the top of the hill, where a series of weathered boulders reared fang-like from the green furze, the road divided at a T-intersection. Here the rider stopped, dismounted, and—by all indications grateful for the rest—pulled a map from beneath his jacket, smoothed it over the seat, and began to study it leisurely.

But inside, Judson Esterhazy felt anything but leisurely. He had lost his appetite; it was an effort to force down food. He constantly had to fight the urge to look over his shoulder. He couldn't sleep nights: every time he closed his eyes he saw Pendergast, mortally wounded, staring up at him from the mire, eyes glittering with implacable intensity.

For the thousandth time he bitterly reproached himself for leaving the FBI agent in the Foulmire. He should have waited until the muck had totally consumed him. Why hadn't he? It was those eyes; he couldn't bear to look into those narrow silver eyes for one more second, staring back at him with the intensity of a scalpel. A pathetic and inexcusable weakness had overwhelmed him at the very moment of truth. Esterhazy knew that Pendergast was transcendentally resourceful. *You have no idea—and I mean no idea—how dangerous this man Pendergast is.* Hadn't those been his very own words half a year earlier? *He's tenacious and clever. This time around he's motivated*—uniquely *motivated.* All Esterhazy's careful planning—and still no real closure.

What a curse it was not knowing.

As he stood there beside the bicycle, pretending to regard the map, the chill damp breeze tugging at his trouser cuffs, he reminded himself that the wound was fatal—it had to be. Even if Pendergast had somehow managed to extricate himself from the mire, they should have discovered his corpse in their days and nights of careful searching. The most likely reason dragging the mire had failed was because Pendergast had somehow escaped the first mire, only to die in some thicket or get sucked down into another, distant bog.

But he didn't know—not for sure, and that was driving him mad. He *had* to learn the truth. The alternative—a lifetime of fear and paranoia—was simply not acceptable.

After the inquest he had departed Scotland—in as high-profile a manner as he could manage, being driven to Glasgow by a disgruntled Inspector Balfour himself.

Now, a week later, he was back. He'd cut his hair short and dyed it black; he was wearing thick tortoiseshell glasses; he'd purchased a high-quality stage mustache. In the unlikely event that he ran into Balfour or any of his men, the chance of being recognized was virtually nil. He was simply another American tourist, enjoying a late-year bicycle tour of the Highlands.

Nearly three weeks had passed since the shooting. The trail, if there ever was one, was now cold. But it couldn't be helped: before the inquest he'd been kept under close observation, prevented from making private inquiries. He'd have to move as quickly as he could now, make sure no time was wasted. He had to prove to his own satisfaction that Pendergast had not survived, had not crawled out of the Mire. If he could do that, then perhaps he could find peace.

At last he turned his attention to the map. He located his own position; located the peak of Beinn Dearg and the Foulmire; located Cairn Barrow, the largest village of the region. With a fingertip on the spot where he'd shot Pendergast, he examined the surrounding area closely. The nearest village was Inverkirkton, about three miles from the shooting site. Besides Kilchurn Lodge, no other habitation was closer. If Pendergast had survived—if he'd gone anywhere—it would have been Inverkirkton. That's where he would start.

Esterhazy folded up the map and glanced down the far side of the hill. From his vantage spot, he could just make out Inverkirkton. He cleared his throat, got back on the bicycle. A moment later he was coasting eastward down the hill, the afternoon sun on his back, taking no notice of the sweet smell of heather drifting in the air.

Inverkirkton was a clustering of well-tended buildings at a bend in the road, but it had the two things every Scottish settlement seemed to have: a pub and an inn. He wheeled up to the inn, climbed off the bike, leaned it against the whitewashed stone. Then, plucking a handkerchief from his pocket, he stepped inside.

The small lobby was cheerfully decorated, with framed photos of Inverness and the Mull of Kintyre beside tartans and a local map. It was empty save for a man in his early sixties, evidently the innkeeper, who was standing behind a counter of polished wood, reading a newspaper. He glanced up as Esterhazy stepped in, his bright blue eyes inquisitive. Esterhazy made a show of mopping his face with the handkerchief and blowing hard. Word of the shooting would have been news in this tiny local hamlet, and Esterhazy was relieved that there was no sign of recognition in the man's gaze.

"Good afternoon to you," the man said with a deep burr.

"Afternoon," Esterhazy replied after seeming to recover some of his breath.

The innkeeper glanced over Esterhazy's shoulder, where the front wheel of the bicycle was just visible through the door. "On holiday, are we?"

Esterhazy nodded. "I'd like a room, if one's available."

"Aye, one is. What might your name be, sir?"

"Edmund Draper." He took another series of shuddering breaths, wiped his face again with the handkerchief.

The innkeeper hefted down a large ledger from a shelf behind him. "You seem a bit fagged, laddie."

Esterhazy nodded again. "Cycled here from Fraserburgh."

The innkeeper stopped in the act of opening the ledger. "Fraserburgh? But that's close to forty miles—a good bit of it over mountains."

"I know. I found that out the hard way. It's only my second day of vacation, and I guess I overdid it. That's the way I am."

The innkeeper shook his head. "Well, all I can say is that you'll sleep well tonight. You'd best take it easy tomorrow."

"I don't think I'll have a choice." Another pause for breath. "By the way, I saw the pub next door—I assume it serves dinner?"

"Aye, and a fine one. And if you don't mind I'd like to suggest the local malt, Glen—"

The man stopped talking. Esterhazy's face had assumed a worried, pained expression.

"Is anything the matter?" the innkeeper asked.

"I don't know," Esterhazy replied. He allowed his voice to become strained. "I've got this sudden pressure—pain—in my chest."

A look of concern crossed the other man's face. Bustling out from behind the counter, he led Esterhazy to a small adjoining parlor and eased him into an overstuffed chair.

"It's shooting down my arm now...oh, God, it hurts." Esterhazy gritted his teeth, clutched at his chest with his right hand.

"Would you like me to get you a drink, then?" the innkeeper said, bending over him solicitously.

"No...call for a doctor. Quickly..." And then, slumping over, Esterhazy closed his eyes.

CHAPTER 12

New York City

THE DRIVE LEADING UP TO THE PORTE COCHERE of 891 Riverside Drive looked a lot better than the first time D'Agosta had seen it. Back then, it had been filled with drifting trash, the surrounding ailanthus and sumac bushes dead or dying; the Beaux-Arts mansion itself had been shuttered and covered with gang graffiti. Now the property was clean and orderly, the four-story stone structure completely restored, its mansard roof, towers, and widow's walk returned to period condition. And yet—as D'Agosta stared at it from the carriageway—there was something cold and strangely empty about the place.

He wasn't sure why he was here, exactly. More than once he'd told himself to stop being paranoid, to stop acting like an old woman. But something about the visit from Corrie Swanson had stuck with him. And this time, when the impulse to stop by Pendergast's mansion had risen yet again, he'd decided to act on it.

He stood for a minute, catching his breath. He'd taken the number 1 train to 137th Street and walked toward the river, but even that short journey had winded him.

He hated this long convalescence; hated how the gunshot wound, the pig valve replacement, the subsequent gradual recovery, had sapped him of strength. The only good thing about it was that he'd initially lost weight, but now he was gaining it back, in spades. And unable for the time being to exercise it off.

After a few moments, he walked down the carriageway and stepped up to the oaken front door. He seized the brass knocker, gave it a stout rap.

Silence.

He waited a minute, then two. Nothing. He leaned in toward the door, listening, but the house was too well built for any sound to escape. He knocked a second time. What with Constance Greene in an asylum, maybe the place really was as deserted as it looked. But that made no sense—he knew Pendergast employed help both here and at the Dakota.

There was a whisper of a key turning in well-oiled tumblers, then the massive door slowly opened. The entranceway was dimly lit, but D'Agosta could make out the features of Proctor, Pendergast's chauffeur and sometime butler. Normally expressionless and imperturbable, today Proctor looked dour, almost forbidding.

"Mr. D'Agosta, sir," he said. "Won't you please come in?"

D'Agosta stepped inside, and Proctor carefully locked the door behind him. "Would you care to step into the library?" the man asked.

D'Agosta had the creepy sensation he had been expected. He followed Proctor down the long, echoing gallery and into the reception hall, its dome of Wedgwood blue soaring overhead, the dim light illuminating the dozens of rippled-glass display cases and their curious contents. "Is Pendergast in?" he asked.

Proctor paused and turned back. "I am very sorry to say he is not, sir."

"Where is he?"

The chauffeur's cold look only wavered slightly. "He's dead, sir."

D'Agosta felt the room reel. "*Dead?* How?"

"He was on a hunting expedition, to Scotland. With Dr. Esterhazy."

"Judson Esterhazy? His brother-in-law?"

"There was an accident. Out on the moors, while they were hunting a stag. Dr. Esterhazy shot Mr. Aloysius. He sank in the mire."

This couldn't be real. He had misheard. "What the hell are you talking about?"

"Nearly three weeks ago."

"So what about the funeral preparations? Where's Esterhazy? Why wasn't I informed?"

"There's no body, sir. And Dr. Esterhazy has disappeared."

"Oh, my God. You're telling me Esterhazy accidentally *shot* Pendergast and there's no body and then Esterhazy just *disappeared*?" He realized he was yelling and didn't care.

Proctor's face remained unreadable. "The local constabulary searched for days, dragging the mire, looking everywhere. No body was recovered."

"Then why do you say he's dead?"

"Because of Dr. Esterhazy's own testimony at the inquest. He testified that he shot him in the chest. He saw him sink and disappear into the quicksand."

D'Agosta felt short of breath. "Esterhazy told you this himself?"

"I learned this from a telephone call from the inspector investigating the shooting. He wanted to ask me a few questions about Mr. Aloysius."

"And you've heard from nobody else?"

"Nobody, sir."

"Where was this, exactly?"

"At Kilchurn Lodge. In the Scottish Highlands."

D'Agosta clenched his jaw. "People don't just disappear. Something about this whole story stinks."

"I'm sorry, sir, that's all I know."

D'Agosta took a few deep, shuddering breaths. "Jesus. Okay. Thank you, Proctor. I'm sorry I'm talking like this. I'm just upset."

"I understand. Would you care to step into the library for a glass of sherry before you go?"

"Are you kidding? I've got to do something about this."

Proctor looked at him. "And what might that be?"

"I don't know yet. But you can bet your ass I'm going to do something."

CHAPTER 13

Inverkirkton

JUDSON ESTERHAZY SAT AT THE SCUFFED BAR of the Half Moon Pub, nursing a pint of Guinness. The pub was tiny, befitting the size of the hamlet: three seats at the bar, four booths, two each built into opposite walls. Currently it was empty save for him and old MacFlecknoe, the barkeep, but it was almost five PM and that would change very soon.

He drained his glass, and MacFlecknoe bustled over. "Will you be having another, sir?" he asked.

Esterhazy made a show of considering this. "Why not?" he said after a moment. "I don't suppose Dr. Roscommon will mind."

The barkeep chuckled. "Sure, and it'll be our secret."

As if on cue, Esterhazy saw the doctor through the large round window in the front door of the pub. Roscommon walked briskly down the street, stopping at the door of his practice, which he unlocked with a deft turn of his wrist. Esterhazy watched as the man disappeared inside the building, closing the door after him.

While pretending to have a heart attack the day before, Esterhazy had a clear image in his mind of what the local doctor would look like: bluff and red-faced, aging but muscular, as accustomed to grappling with sick cows and horses as with people. But Roscommon had proved a surprise. He was thin and fortyish, with bright alert eyes and an intelligent expression. He had examined his new patient with a cool, relaxed professionalism that Esterhazy could only admire. Quickly determining that the chest pains were nothing serious, Roscommon nevertheless recommended a few days of rest. Esterhazy had expected this, and in fact welcomed it: now he had an excuse to hang around the village. And he had met the local doctor: his main purpose. He'd hoped to befriend the doctor and extract some information from him, but the man had proven the very picture of Scottish reserve, with little to say beyond what was necessary for medical advice. That might be his nature—or he might be hiding something.

As he sipped the fresh Guinness, Esterhazy wondered again what a man like Roscommon was doing in a one-horse town like Inverkirkton. He clearly had the ability to open a lucrative practice in a bigger city. If Pendergast, against all odds, had survived the mire, Roscommon was the man he'd have gone to; he was the only game in town.

The door to the pub opened and a woman came in—Jennie Prothero. Already, Esterhazy felt like he'd met practically the whole damn town. Mrs. Prothero ran the village's curio-and-souvenir shop and—since that business wasn't exactly lucrative—took in laundry on the side. She was plump and amiable, with a face almost as red as a lobster. Despite the mild October day, her neck was heavily swathed in a wool scarf.

"Hullo, then, Paulie," she said to the bartender, settling onto one of the two free bar stools as demurely as her two hundred pounds would allow.

"Afternoon, Jennie," MacFlecknoe replied, dutifully wiping the scarred wooden counter in front of her, drawing a pint of bitter, and placing it on a coaster.

The woman turned to Esterhazy. "And how are you today, Mr. Draper?"

Esterhazy smiled. "I'm quite better, thanks. Just a pulled muscle, it would seem."

She nodded knowingly. "I'm glad to hear that."

"I have your Dr. Roscommon to thank."

"He's a fine one, and no mistake," the bartender said. "We're lucky to have him."

"Yes, he seems like an excellent doctor."

MacFlecknoe nodded. "London trained, and all."

"Frankly, I'm surprised there's enough here to keep him occupied."

"Well, he's the only medical fellow for twenty miles 'round," Prothero said. "At least, since old Crastner passed away last spring."

"So he's quite busy?" Esterhazy asked, taking a casual pull from his pint.

"That he is," said MacFlecknoe. "Takes callers at all hours."

"All hours? I'm surprised to hear that. I mean, with a country practice."

"Well, we have emergencies here, just like everywhere else," the bartender replied. He nodded across the street toward the doctor's practice. "Sometimes you'll see every light in his house ablaze, well after midnight."

"You don't say," Esterhazy replied. "When was the last time that happened?"

MacFlecknoe thought. "Oh, maybe three weeks back. Maybe more. Can't say for sure. It isn't all that common. I remember that time, though, because his car came and went twice. Late it was—past nine."

"It might have been poor Mrs. Bloor," Jennie Prothero said. "She's been poorly these past few months."

"No, he didn't head toward Hithe," the bartender said. "I heard the car going west."

"West?" the woman said. "There's nothing that way but the Mire."

"Maybe it was one of the guests up the lodge," said MacFlecknoe.

The woman took a pull of bitter. "Now that you mention it, there were some linens from the doctor's practice sent in for laundry around then. Bloody as you please, they were."

"Really?" Esterhazy asked, his heart quickening. "What kind of linens?"

"Oh, the usual. Dressings, sheets."

"Well, Jennie, that's not uncommon," said the barkeep. "Farmers 'round these parts are always having accidents."

"Yes," said Esterhazy, speaking more to himself than the others. "But not in the middle of the night."

"What was that, Mr. Draper?" Jennie Prothero asked.

"Oh, nothing." Esterhazy drained his pint.

"Would you care for another, then?" the barkeep asked.

"No, thank you. But please let me set one up for yourself and Mrs. Prothero."

"I'll do that, sir, and thank you most kindly."

Esterhazy nodded, but he didn't glance toward the barkeep. His eyes were trained on the circular window in the pub door, and the cream-colored office of Dr. Roscommon that lay across the street.

CHAPTER 14

Malfourche, Mississippi

NED BETTERTON PULLED UP BEFORE THE GRIMY plate-glass storefront of the Ideal Café, stepped into the bacon-and onion-perfumed interior, and ordered himself a cup of coffee, sweet and light. The Ideal wasn't much of a café, but then Malfourche wasn't much of a town: dirt-poor and half deserted, its fabric slowly crumbling into ruin. The kids with any talent obviously got their asses out of town just as fast as they could, running for bigger and more exciting cities, leaving the losers behind. Four generations of that and look what you got, a town like Malfourche. Hell, he'd grown up in a place just like it. Problem was, he hadn't run far enough. Scratch that: he was still running, running like hell, but getting nowhere.

At least the coffee was halfway decent and once inside, it felt like home. He had to admit, he liked hard-scrabble joints like this, with the gut-solid waitresses, truckers bellying up to the counters, greasy burgers, orders conveyed full throat, and strong fresh coffee.

He was the first in his family to graduate high school, not to mention college. A small and scrappy child, he'd been raised by his mother, just the two of them, his father doing time for robbing a Coca-Cola bottling plant. Twenty years, thanks to a careerist prosecutor and pitiless judge. His father died of cancer in the slammer, and Betterton knew it was despair that caused the cancer that killed him. And in turn, his father's death had killed his mother.

As a result, Betterton was inclined to assume that anyone in a position of authority was a lying, self-interested son of a bitch. For that reason he'd gravitated toward journalism, where he figured he could fight those people with real weapons. Problem was, with his state college degree in communications all he could land was a job at the *Ezerville Bee*, and he'd been there for the past five years, trying to move up to a bigger paper. The *Bee* was a throwaway, an excuse for advertising mailed free to all residents and stacked a foot high at gas stations and supermarkets. The owner, editor, and publisher, Zeke Kranston, was mortally afraid of offending anyone if there was even a microscopic chance of hustling them for ad space. So: no investigative stories, no exposés, no hard-hitting political pieces. "The job of the *Ezerville Bee* is to sell advertising," Kranston would say, after removing the sodden toothpick that always seemed to be hanging from his lower lip. "Don't try to dig up another Watergate. You'll only alienate readers—and businesses." As a result, Betterton's clipping book looked like something out of *Woman's World*: all service pieces, rescued dogs, and reports from church bake sales, high-school football games, and ice-cream socials. With a book like that, no wonder he couldn't get an interview at a real newspaper.

Betterton shook his head. He sure as hell wasn't going to stay in Ezerville the rest of his life, and the only way to get out of Ezerville was to find that scoop. It didn't matter if it was crime, a public interest story, or aliens with ray guns. One story with legs—that's all he needed.

He drained his cup, paid, then stepped out into the morning sunlight. There was a breeze coming in off the Black Brake swamp, uncomfortably warm and malodorous. Betterton got into the car and started the engine, putting the A/C on full blast. But he didn't go anywhere—not yet. Before he got into this story, he wanted to think it out. With great difficulty and many promises, he had persuaded Kranston to let him cover it. It was a curious human interest story and it could become the first real journalism clip in his book. He intended to exploit the opportunity to the max.

Betterton sat in the cooling car, going over what he'd say, what questions he'd ask, trying to anticipate the objections he was sure to hear. After five minutes, he was ready. He recombed his limp hair and mopped the sweat off his brow. He glanced down at the Internet map he'd printed, then shifted into drive, making a U-turn and heading back down the ramshackle street toward the outskirts of town.

Even covering the fluff, he had learned to pay attention to the slightest crumb of rumor or gossip, no matter how trivial. He'd heard rumors about the mysterious couple: about their disappearance years ago and their sudden reappearance a few months back, and a fake suicide somewhere along the way. A visit to the local parish police station earlier that morning had confirmed that the rumor was, in fact, true. And the police report, perfunctory as hell, had raised more questions than it answered.

He glanced down at the map, then at the rows of sad-looking clapboard houses that lined both sides of the potholed street. There it was: a small bungalow, painted white and bracketed by magnolias.

He nosed his car to the curb, killed the engine, and spent another minute psyching himself up. Then he got out, straightened his sports jacket, and marched with determined step up to the door. There was no doorbell, just a knocker, and he grasped it and gave an authoritative knock.

Betterton could hear it echoing through the house. For a moment, nothing. Then the sound of approaching feet. The door opened and a tall, svelte woman appeared in the entrance. "Yes?"

Betterton hadn't known what to expect, of course, but the last thing he'd anticipated was that she would be beautiful. Not young, of course, but exceedingly handsome.

"Mrs. Brodie? June Brodie?"

The woman looked him up and down with cool blue eyes. "That's correct."

"My name's Betterton. I'm from the *Ezerville Bee*. Please, could I have a few minutes of your time?"

"Who is it, June?" came a man's high-pitched voice from within the house. *Good*, Betterton thought. *They're both in*.

"We have nothing to say to the press," June Brodie said. She took a step back and began to close the door.

Betterton wedged a desperate foot between the door

and the sill. "Please, Mrs. Brodie," he said. "I already know almost everything. I've been to the police, it's a matter of public record. I'm going to run the story, regardless. I just thought you'd like the opportunity to have your own voice heard."

She looked at him a minute. Her intelligent gaze seemed to bore right through him. "What story are you talking about?"

"About how you staged your own suicide and disappeared without a trace for a dozen years."

There was a brief silence. "June?" Betterton could hear the male voice call again.

Mrs. Brodie opened the door and stepped to one side.

Quickly, before she could change her mind, Betterton went in. Directly ahead lay a tidy living room that smelled faintly of mothballs and floor polish. The room was almost empty: a couch, two chairs, a side table on a small Persian rug. His footsteps echoed hollowly as he trod the wooden floor. It felt like a house that had just been moved into. A moment later he realized that was, in fact, the case.

A small man, pale and slightly built, emerged from a darkened hallway, holding a plate in one hand and a dish towel in the other. "Who was that—" he began, then stopped when he caught sight of Betterton.

June Brodie turned toward him. "This is Mr. Betterton. He's a newspaper reporter."

The small man looked from his wife to Betterton and back again, face suddenly hostile. "What does he want?"

"He's doing a story on us. On our return." There

was an edge of something—not quite scorn, not quite irony—in her voice that made Betterton a little nervous.

Carefully, the man set the plate down on the side table. He was as frumpy as his wife was elegant.

"You're Carlton Brodie?" Betterton asked.

The man nodded.

"Why don't you tell us what you know—or think you know?" June Brodie said. She had pointedly not offered him a seat or refreshment of any kind.

Betterton licked his lips. "I know that your vehicle was left on the Archer Bridge more than twelve years ago. Inside was a suicide note in your handwriting that read: *Can't take it anymore. All my fault. Forgive me.* The river was dragged but no body was ever found. A few weeks later, the police paid a follow-up visit to your husband, Carlton, only to find that he had left on a trip of indefinite duration to an unknown location. That was the last anyone ever heard of the Brodies—until you suddenly reappeared here, out of nowhere, a few months ago."

"That would seem to sum things up," June Brodie said. "Not much of a story, is it?"

"On the contrary, Mrs. Brodie—it's a fascinating story, and I think the readers of the *Bee* would feel the same way. What would lead a woman to do such a thing? Where has she been all this time? And why—after more than a decade—would she return?"

June Brodie frowned but said nothing. There was a brief, frosty silence.

After a moment, Mr. Brodie sighed. "Look, young man. I'm afraid it isn't as interesting as you think."

"Carlton, don't bother to humor him," June Brodie said.

"No, dear, I think it's better if we get it said," Mr. Brodie told her. "Say it once, then refuse to speak of it again. We'll only prolong the story if we don't cooperate." He turned to Betterton. "We were going through a difficult time with our marriage."

Betterton nodded.

"Things were bad," Mr. Brodie went on. "Then June's employer died in a fire and she lost her job with Longitude Pharmaceuticals when the company went bankrupt. She was at her wit's end, half crazy. She had to get away—away from everything. And so did I. It was a foolish thing for her to do, staging a suicide, but at the time there seemed like no other choice. Later I went to her. We decided to travel. Stopped at a B and B, loved it at first sight, found it was up for sale, bought it and ran it for years. But…well, we're older and wiser now, and things are less raw, so we decided to come home. That's all."

"That's all," Betterton repeated, hollowly.

"If you read the police report, you know that already. There was an investigation, naturally. Everything happened a long time ago; no fraud was involved; there was no escape from debt, no insurance scam, no laws broken. So the matter was dropped. And now we just want to live here, in peace and quiet."

Betterton considered this for a moment. The police report had mentioned the B&B but included no details. "Where was this B and B?"

"Mexico."

"Where in Mexico?"

A brief hesitation. "San Miguel de Allende. We fell in love with the place at first sight. It's a city of artists in the mountains of Central Mexico."

"What was the name of the B and B?"

"Casa Magnolia. A beautiful place. Within walking distance of the Mercado de Artesanias."

Betterton took a deep breath. He could think of no other questions. And the man's frank ingenuousness left him with nothing to follow up on. "Well, I thank you for being candid."

In reply, Brodie nodded, picked up the dish and the dish towel.

"May I call you? If I have any further questions, that is?"

"You may not," June Brodie said crisply. "Good morning."

Outside, walking to his car, Betterton's step grew jauntier. It was still a good story. All right, not the scoop of a lifetime, but it would make people sit up and take notice and it would look good among his clips. A woman who faked her suicide, got her husband to join her in exile, then returned home after a dozen years: a human interest story with a twist. With a little bit of luck, the wire services might get wind of it.

"Ned, you rascal," he said as he opened the car door. "Okay, so it isn't Watergate, but it just might get your sorry ass out of Ezerville."

June Brodie watched through the window, face impassive, cold blue eyes unblinking, until the car receded into the distance. Then she turned toward her husband. "Do you think he bought it?"

Carlton Brodie was polishing the china plate. "The police bought it—didn't they?"

"We had no choice about that. But now it's public."

"It was already public."

"Not *newspaper* public."

Brodie chuckled. "You're giving the *Ezerville Bee* too much credit." Then he stopped and looked at her. "What is it?"

"Don't you remember what Charles said? How frightened he always was? 'We must stay hidden,' he'd insist. 'Stay secret. *They* can't know we're alive. *They* would come for us.'"

"So?"

"So what if 'they' read the paper?"

Brodie chuckled again. "June, please. There is no 'they.' Slade was old. Old, sick, mentally ill, and paranoid as hell. Trust me, this is for the better. Get it said, and said our way—without a lot of rumor and speculation. Nip it in the bud." And he walked back toward the kitchen, still wiping the plate.

CHAPTER 15

Cairn Barrow

D'AGOSTA SAT IN THE DRIVER'S SEAT of the rented Ford, looking disconsolately out at the endless gray-green moorlands. From the height of land on which he'd parked, they seemed to stretch into a misty infinity. And for all the luck he'd had, they might as well go on forever, cloaking their dark secrets for all time to come.

He was wearier than he'd ever been in his life. Even now, seven months later, the gunshot wound was still kicking his ass: here he was, winded by something as simple as climbing a set of stairs or walking through an airport terminal. These last three days in Scotland had driven it home with a vengeance. Thanks to a solicitous and competent Chief Inspector Balfour, he'd seen everything there was to see. He'd read all the official transcripts, depositions, evidence reports. He'd been to the scene of the shooting. He'd spoken to the employees of Kilchurn Lodge. He'd visited all the houses, farms, barns, stone huts, mires, tors, dingles, dells, and every other damn thing within a twenty-mile radius of this godforsaken place—all without success. It had proven exhausting. Beyond exhausting.

And the cold, drizzly Scottish environment hadn't exactly helped. He knew the British Isles could be damp, but he hadn't seen the sun since he left New York. The food was lousy, not a plate of pasta within a hundred miles. He'd been persuaded to eat a dish called haggis the evening he'd arrived and his digestive system hadn't been the same since. Kilchurn Lodge itself was elegant enough, but it was drafty, and the cold worked its way into his bones and caused his old wound to ache.

He took another glance out the window, fetched a sigh. The last thing he felt like doing was going out onto that moor again. But in the pub the evening before, he'd heard by chance of an old couple—mad, or just a little touched, depending on whom you talked to—who lived in a stone house out in the Mire, not far from the Inish Marshes; they raised their own sheep and grew much of their own food, and almost never came into town. There was no road to their place, he was told, only a small footpath marked by rock cairns. It was in the middle of nowhere, well off the road and twelve miles from where the shooting had taken place. It was impossible, D'Agosta knew, that a gravely wounded Pendergast could have reached it across all that distance. But nevertheless he owed it to both himself and his old friend to check this one last lead before heading back to New York.

He took a last look at the topographic map he had bought, folded it up, and shoved it in his pocket. He'd better get started—the sky was lowering, and threatening clouds were gathering in the west. He hesitated a moment longer. Then, with a grunt of effort, he opened the door and heaved himself out of the car. He pulled the waterproof tight around himself and started out.

The trail was clear enough: a gravelly path that wound among tussocks of grass and patches of heather. He spied the first cairn—not the usual pile of rocks but a tall, narrow slab of granite sunk into the ground. As he approached, he noticed that something had been carved into its face:

GLIMSHOLM
4 MI.

That was it, the name of the cottage they'd mentioned in the pub. He grunted with satisfaction. *Four miles.* It would take maybe two hours if he took it easy. He set off, his newly purchased walking shoes crunching on the gravel, the keen edge of the wind in his face. But he was well bundled against the cold, and he had a good seven hours of daylight.

For the first mile or so, the trail remained on solid ground, following a faint elevation that extended into the Mire. D'Agosta breathed deeply, surprised and more than a little pleased that all his traipsing around these past few days seemed to have left him a bit stronger, despite his weariness and the ache of his injury. The trail was well marked, with long, narrow pieces of granite stuck into the ground like pikes to guide the way.

Deeper into the Mire the trail itself grew fainter, but the markers were still visible for hundreds of yards; at each one he paused, searched the landscape ahead, located the next, and continued on. Even though the ground seemed relatively flat and open, as he proceeded he realized there were many folds and gentle rises that made it difficult and deceptive to get the lay of the land and maintain a straight course.

As eleven o'clock neared, the trail began to descend, ever so slightly, toward lower, more boggy moorlands. In the vast distance on his right, he could see a dark line that, according to his map, marked the border of the Inish Marshes. The air became still, the wind dying to nothing, the mists collecting in the hollows and rising in tendrils over dark bogs. The sky darkened and clouds rolled in.

Hell, thought D'Agosta, looking upward. That damn Scottish drizzle was starting. Again.

He soldiered on. Suddenly the drizzle was interrupted by a terrific gust of wind. He heard it coming before it arrived—a humming noise across the moors, the heather flattened in its wake—and then it buffeted him, flapping his raincoat and tugging at his hat. And now heavier drops of rain began to patter over the ground. The mists that had settled in the low areas seemed to jump out and become clouds tumbling across the moors, or maybe the leaden sky itself had lowered to the ground.

D'Agosta checked his watch. Almost noon.

He stopped to rest on a boulder. There had been no more signs for Glims Holm, but he figured he'd gone at least three miles. One more to go. He searched the landscape ahead; he could see nothing that might be a distant cottage. Another gust of wind swept across him, the cold raindrops stinging his face.

Son of a bitch. He heaved himself up, checked his

map, but it was pretty much useless as there weren't any distinct landmarks visible by which he could measure his progress.

Ridiculous that someone lived way out here. They were clearly more than "touched"—they must be stark raving mad. And this was a fool's errand: no way in hell Pendergast could have gotten as far as the cottage.

The rain continued, hard and steady. It kept growing darker, to the point that it almost felt as if night were coming on. The trail became fainter, the bogs pressing in on either side, and in places the trail crossed watery areas on corduroys or lines of flat stones. With the mists, rain, and darkness, D'Agosta began finding it difficult to locate each next cairn, peering into the murk for a long time before spying it.

How much farther? He checked his watch. Twelve thirty. He'd been walking two and a half hours. He should be practically on top of the cottage. But ahead he could see only gray moorlands emerging helter-skelter from mist and rain.

He hoped to hell he would find someone at the cottage and that there would be a fire going and hot coffee, or at least tea. He was starting to feel a cold, penetrating chill as the water worked its way into his clothing. This had been a mistake; the ache of the injury was now joined by the occasional shooting pain down his leg. He wondered if he should rest again, decided against it now that he was almost there. A rest might stiffen him up and make him even colder.

He stopped. The trail had ended in a broad, quaking pool of muck. He looked around for cairns that might lead through it and saw none. Hell, he hadn't been paying attention. He turned, looking back over the trail on which he had come. Now that he looked at it, it didn't look like a trail—more a linked series of dirt patches. He started to retrace his steps, then stopped: there seemed to be two ways he could have come in, two wandering paths. Examining them both closely, he couldn't see his footprints in the hard surface, now puddled with rain. He straightened up and scanned the horizon, looking for a telltale spike of granite. But no matter how hard he stared, he could see nothing but gray boggy swamp and tatters of mist.

He took a deep breath. The cairns were placed a couple of hundred yards apart. He couldn't be more than a hundred yards from the last. All he had to do was go slow, take it easy, stay calm, and get his ass back to the previous cairn.

He took the right-hand path and moved slowly, stopping every now and then to peer ahead for the cairn. After going about fifty yards, he concluded that this could not be the way he'd come—the cairn would have been visible by now. Fine; he would take the other path. He turned back and retraced his steps about fifty yards, but for some reason it didn't return to the fork in the trail that had puzzled him previously. He went a little farther, thinking he had misjudged the distance— only to find the trail dead-ending at another bog.

He stopped, controlled his breathing. All right: he was lost. But he wasn't *that* lost. He still couldn't be more than one or two hundred yards from the last cairn. What he had to do was look around. He would not move until he had oriented himself and knew where he was going.

The rain gusted, and he could feel a cold trickle down his back. Ignoring the sensation, he took stock. He seemed to be in a bowl-like depression. The horizon was perhaps a mile away on all sides, but it was hard to tell with the incessantly moving mists. He started to take out his map and then shoved it back into his pocket. What good would that do? He cursed himself for not bringing a compass. At least with a compass, he could have known his general direction. He looked at his watch: one thirty. About three hours to sunset.

"Damn," he said aloud, and then, louder: "*Damn!*"

That made him feel better. He picked a point on the horizon and began to scrutinize it for a cairn. And there it was—a distant vertical scratch in the shifting mists.

He worked his way toward it, stepping from one gravelly patch to the next. But the bogs conspired to block his every turn: he kept having to go first one way, then another, and then retrace, until it seemed he was stuck on some sort of snake-like island in the middle of the bogs. Christ, he could see the stupid cairn not two hundred yards away!

Coming to a narrow stretch of bog, he spied the trail itself running along the other side, a sandy piece of ground winding off toward the cairn. He experienced a huge feeling of relief. Probing this way and that, he looked for a way across the narrow bog. At first, he could find no clear passage. But then he noticed that at one point the bog was interspersed with hillocks, close enough together to allow him to step across. Taking a deep breath, he stepped out onto the first hillock, tested it, put his weight down, and brought his other foot over. Doing the same with the next, he stepped across the bog from hillock to hillock, the black muck quaking below, sometimes bubbling up with marsh gas disturbed by the vibrations of his footfalls.

He was almost there. He reached his foot across one large gap, placed it on a hillock, pushed off with the other foot—and lost his balance. With an involuntary yell he tried to leap over the last piece of mire to hard ground, came up short, and landed in the bog with a heavy smack.

As the clammy muck settled around his thighs, pure, hysterical panic took over. With another yell he tried to wrench one leg free, but the movement only pulled the rest of him in deeper. His panic spiked. Yanking the other leg had the same effect; struggling just sucked his body deeper into the icy pressure of the mud, the effort releasing bursts of bubbles that broke all around him, enveloping him in the stench of swamp rot.

"Help!" he cried, the small part of his brain not yet in panic mode registering how stupid the cry was. "Help me!" The muck was now above his waist; his arms flailed instinctively, trying to push himself out, but this merely anchored both his arms and drew him in deeper. It was as if he were fastened in a straitjacket. He thrashed, trying to get at least one arm free, but he was powerless, like a fly in honey, sinking slowly and helplessly into the mire.

"Help me, for God's sake!" D'Agosta screamed, his voice echoing over the empty moors.

You idiot, that small rational part of his brain told him, *stop moving*. Every movement was driving him farther under. With a superhuman effort, he willed his panic into submission.

Take a deep breath. Wait. Don't move.

It was hard to breathe with the pressure of the mud encircling his chest. It was up to the tops of his shoulders, but by not moving, by remaining absolutely still, he almost seemed to have stopped sinking. He waited, trying to overcome the panicky sensation of the mud creeping up toward his neck, slower now. Finally it stopped. He waited in the driving rain until he realized that he had, in fact, stopped sinking; he was stable, in equilibrium.

Not only that, he now realized he was only five feet from the trail on the other side.

With exquisite slowness he began to raise one arm, keeping his fingers straight, extracting it slowly from the muck, avoiding any suction, giving the mud time to flow around it as he drew it out.

A miracle. His arm was free. Keeping it buoyed above the surface, he ever so slowly leaned forward. There was a huge moment of panic as he felt the mud creep up his neck, but by immersing more of his upper body he could feel a buoyancy effect on his lower extremities, and his feet felt like they might have risen just a little. As he leaned forward more, his feet rose in response. Gingerly, he immersed part of his head in the muck, which increased the effect and brought his legs up still more, tilting his body toward the embankment of the bog. Keeping as relaxed as possible, moving with agonizing slowness, he continued leaning forward and—just as the mud came up to his nose—he managed to reach out and grasp a branch of heather.

With slow, easy pressure, he drew his body toward the embankment until his chin rested on the grass.

Then he extracted his other arm—slowly, very slowly—and reached out with it as well, grasping another bush and pulling himself out onto firm ground.

He lay there, feeling a wash of infinite relief. Slowly the pounding of his heart subsided. The heavy rain began to rinse the mud from him.

After a minute or two, he managed to stand up. He was chilled to the very bone, dripping with foul-smelling mud, his teeth chattering. He held up his wrist and let the rain wash the mud from his watch: four o'clock.

Four o'clock! No wonder it was getting so dark. The sun set early in October in these northern climes.

He felt himself shivering uncontrollably. The wind was gusting, the rain was lashing down, and he could hear rumbles of thunder. He didn't even have a flashlight or a lighter. This was insane—he was risking hypothermia. Thank God he had found the trail. Squinting into the gloom, he saw the cairn ahead that he had been trying so hard to reach.

After shaking off as much mud as he could, he started cautiously toward it. As he approached, however, it began to look wrong somehow. Too thin. And then when he came up to it, he saw what it really was—a small dead tree trunk, stripped and silvered and scoured by the wind.

D'Agosta stared in pure disbelief. A freakish dead tree trunk, here in the middle of nowhere, miles from any live trees. If he had passed this before he would surely have noticed.

But wasn't he on the trail...?

As he looked around in the gathering gloom, scrutinizing the trail, he began to realize that what he'd thought was a path was just a collection of random patches of sand and gravel interspersed among the bogs.

Now it was really getting dark. And the cold was deepening. It might even go below freezing.

His colossal stupidity in venturing alone out on the moors began to sink home. He was still in a weakened condition. No flashlight, no compass, his solitary sandwich long-since eaten. His concern for Pendergast had led him to take foolish risks and push himself to the edge . . . and then over it.

What the hell now? It was already so dark that trying to continue would be stupid. The landscape had dissolved into a dim, mottled gray and there was no hope of identifying any cairn now. God, he'd never been so cold in his life. It felt like the cold was hardening the very marrow of his bones.

He would have to spend the night on the moors.

He looked about and saw, not far off, a pair of boulders. Shivering, teeth chattering hard, he went over and hunkered down between them, out of the wind. He tried to make himself as small as possible, curling up into a fetal position, forcing his hands under his arms. The rain pounded on his back, creeping in rivulets around his neck and down his face. And then he realized it was no longer raining but sleeting, the heavy drops of slush splattering on his mac and sliding down its surface.

Just as he was thinking he couldn't stand the cold anymore, he began to feel a creeping warmth. Unbelievable—the strategy was working, his body was responding. Adjusting to the intense cold. The warmth began at his very core and slowly, slowly, radiated outward.

He felt sleepy and strangely peaceful. He grew calmer. He might just be able to weather this night after all. And in the morning the sun might be up, it would be warmer, and he could start afresh and pick up the trail.

Now he was feeling quite warm and his mood soared. This was going to be a piece of cake. Even the ache of his injury was gone.

Darkness had fallen and he felt unbelievably sleepy. It would be good to get some sleep, the night would pass a lot faster. As the darkness became complete, the sleet tapered off. More good luck. No—it was now snowing. Well, at least the wind had died down. God, he was sleepy.

And then in adjusting his position, he glimpsed it: a faint light in the fields of blackness—yellow, wavering. D'Agosta stared. Was he seeing things? It had to be Glims Holm—what else could it be? And it wasn't all that far off. He should go there.

But no; he was so wonderfully sleepy he'd spend the night here, and go in the morning. Good to know it was close by. Now he could go to sleep in peace. He drifted off into a deliciously warm sea of nothingness . . .

CHAPTER 16

Antigua, Guatemala

THE MAN IN THE LINEN SUIT AND WHITE STRAW FEDORA sat at a small table in the front courtyard of the restaurant, eating a late breakfast of *huevos rancheros* with sour cream and jalapeño sauce. From his vantage point he could see the Parque Central, fringed with green, tourists and children gathered around the rebuilt fountain at its center. Beyond lay the Arco de Santa Catalina, the rich deep yellow of its arch and bell tower more suited to Venice than Central America. And still farther— beyond the pastel-colored buildings and brown roofs— rose huge volcanic peaks, their dark crowns smoked by banks of cloud.

Even at this hour, music echoed faintly from open windows. Cars passed in the street, stirring up occasional bits of trash.

It was a warm morning, and the man removed the fedora and placed it on the table. He was tall and imposing, and the linen suit could not fully hide the massive, sculpted physique of a bodybuilder. His movements were slow, almost studied, but his pale eyes were alert, taking in everything, missing nothing. His deeply tanned skin was in marked contrast to the full head of pure white hair, and it had an unusual suppleness, almost a silkiness, that made it hard to guess his age: perhaps forty, perhaps fifty.

The waitress took away his plate, and he thanked her in fluent Spanish. Glancing around once more, he reached down into a worn briefcase that stood between his feet and pulled out a thin folder. He took a sip of the iced espresso, lit a cigarillo with a gold lighter, then opened the folder, wondering at the urgency of its delivery. Normally, these things went through channels, using remailing services or encrypted files stored in a high-security Internet cloud. But this had arrived by hand, via bonded courier, one of very few the organization employed.

It was, he mused, the only way they could be positive—one hundred percent positive—that it reached him personally.

He took another sip of espresso, placed the cigarillo in a glass ashtray, then plucked a silk handkerchief from the pocket of his jacket and mopped his brow. Despite his years living in tropical climes, he had never grown accustomed to the heat. He frequently had dreams—strange dreams—of his childhood summers in the old hunting lodge outside Königswinter, with its rambling corridors and its views of the Siebengebirge hills and the Rhine Valley.

Stuffing the handkerchief back in his pocket, he opened the folder. It contained a single newspaper clipping, printed on the tawdriest grade of newsprint. Although the article was dated only a few days before, it was already yellowing. An American newspaper with a ludicrous name: the *Ezerville Bee*. His eye turned to the headline and opening paragraphs:

Mystery Couple Surfaces After Years in Hiding

By Ned Betterton

MALFOURCHE, MISSISSIPPI—Twelve years ago, a woman named June Brodie, despondent after losing her job as executive secretary at Longitude Pharmaceuticals, apparently took her own life by jumping off the Archer Bridge, leaving a suicide note in her car...

The man lowered the clipping with nerveless fingers. "*Scheisse*," he muttered under his breath. Raising the clipping again, he read it in its entirety twice. Folding the article and placing it on the table, he glanced carefully around the square. Then he pulled the lighter from his pocket, lit one edge of the article, and dropped it in the ashtray. He watched it carefully, making sure it burned to a cinder, then crushed the ashes with the end of his cigarillo. He took a deep drag, pulled a cell phone from his pocket, and dialed a long string of numbers.

The call was picked up after one ring. "*Ja?*" said the voice.

"Klaus?" the man said.

He could hear the voice on the other end of the line stiffen as his own was recognized. "*Buenos dias*, Señor Fischer," said the voice.

Fischer continued in Spanish. "Klaus, I have a job for you."

"Of course, sir."

"There will be two phases to the job. The first is investigative. The second will involve wet work. You are to begin immediately."

"I am at your command."

"Good. I will call you tonight from Guatemala City. You will receive detailed orders then."

Although the line was secure, Klaus's next question was coded. "What color is the flag on this job?"

"Blue."

The voice stiffened further. "Consider it already a success, Señor Fischer."

"I know I can count on you," Fischer said, and hung up.

CHAPTER 17

The Foulmire, Scotland

D'AGOSTA SEEMED TO BE SHROUDED IN GREAT DEPTHS of comfort, drifting on a tide of warmth. But even as he was suspended in a quasi-dream-state, that small, rational part of his brain spoke again. A single word: *hypothermia*.

What did he care?

You're dying.

The voice was like an annoying person who wouldn't stop talking, wouldn't let you change the subject. But it was just loud enough, and scary enough, that he felt himself swimming back to reality. *Hypothermia*. He had all the symptoms: extreme cold followed by unexpected warmth, irresistible desire to sleep, lack of caring.

Christ, he was just accepting it.

You're dying, idiot.

With an inarticulate roar and an almost superhuman effort, he staggered to his feet, slapping, almost beating his body. He whacked his face twice, hard, and felt a tingle of cold. He hit himself so hard he staggered and fell, rose again, thrashing about like a wounded animal.

He could hardly stand, he was so weak. Pain shot up his legs. His head practically exploded with pain, his injured shoulder throbbing. He started stamping around in circles, alternately hugging himself and smacking his arms against his trunk, shedding snow, yelling as loud as he could, hollering, welcoming the pain. Pain meant survival. Clarity of mind began to return, bit by bit. He jumped, jumped again. All the while he kept his eyes on that yellow light, wavering in the darkness. How to get there? He staggered forward and fell yet again, his face inches from the edge of a bog.

He cupped his hands and yelled. "Help! Help me!"

His voice echoed over the dead moorlands.

"I'm lost! I'm trying to find Glims Holm!"

The yelling helped tremendously. He felt the blood recirculating, his heart pumping.

"Please help me!"

And then he saw it: a second light beside the first, brighter. It seemed to be moving in the darkness, coming his way.

"Over here!" he cried.

The light moved toward him. He realized it was farther off than he'd initially thought: it wandered about, sometimes disappearing and then reappearing. Then it disappeared again and D'Agosta waited.

"Over here!" he cried in a panic. Had they heard him or was it coincidence? Was he seeing things?

"I'm over here!" Why hadn't they called back? Had they gone down in the mire?

And suddenly there was the light, directly in front of him. The person carrying the light shone it in his face, then placed it on the ground, and in its glow he saw a strange woman with pendulous lips, bundled up in a mackintosh and boots, scarf, gloves, and hat, with a nest of white hair peeking out, a hooked nose, and two wild blue eyes. In the mist and swirling dark, she looked like an apparition.

"What in the devil's name . . . ?" she asked in a sharp voice.

"I'm looking for Glims Holm."

"Ye found it," she said, and then added, sarcastically, "almost." She picked up the lamp and turned around. "Watch your step."

D'Agosta stumbled after her. Ten minutes later, the lamp disclosed the dim outlines of a cottage, its mortared stones once whitewashed but now almost completely covered with lichen and moss, with a gray slate roof and chimney.

She pushed open the door and D'Agosta followed into the astonishing warmth of a cozy cottage, with a fire blazing on a giant hearth, an old-fashioned enameled stove, comfortable sofas and chairs, braided rugs on the floor, walls covered with books and odd pictures, along with a row of mounted stags' antlers, all illuminated by kerosene lanterns.

The heat was the most wonderful thing D'Agosta had felt in his entire life.

"Strip," the white-haired woman said sharply, moving to the fire.

"I—"

"*Strip*, blast your eyes." She went into a corner and dragged out a big wicker basket. "Clothes in there."

D'Agosta removed his raincoat, dropped it into the

basket. This was followed by his sodden sweater, shoes, socks, shirt, tank top, and pants. He stood there in muddy boxers.

"Breeks as well," said the woman. She busied herself at the stove, removing a large kettle from the hob, pouring water into a galvanized washbasin and setting it near the fire, placing a washcloth and towel beside it.

D'Agosta waited until her back was turned before taking off his boxers. The heat from the fire was exquisite.

"What's your name?" she demanded.

"D'Agosta. Vincent D'Agosta."

"Wash. I'll bring ye some fresh clothes. Yer a bit stout to fit into the mister's clothes but we'll find something." She disappeared up a narrow flight of stairs, and he heard her moving about. He heard coughing and the querulous voice of an old man, who did not sound pleased.

She returned with an armful of clothes while he was sponging himself off. He tried to turn and found her staring at him, her eyes not on his face. "Now *that's* a sight for an old woman's eyes." With a cackle she placed the clothes down and turned back to the fire, dropping a few pieces of wood on it, and then busied herself at the stove again.

Feeling sheepish, D'Agosta finished washing off the mud, toweled himself dry, then put on the clothes. They were for a taller, thinner man, but he managed to get them on fairly well, except he wasn't able to button the pants. He used a belt to keep them up. The old woman had been stirring a pot, and the unbearably delicious smell of lamb stew reached his nostrils.

"Sit down." She brought over a large bowl of the stew, tore a few pieces of bread from a rough loaf, and put the stew and bread before him. "Eat."

D'Agosta took a greedy spoonful, burned his mouth. "This stew is wonderful," he said. "I don't know how to thank—"

She cut him off. "You found Glims Holm. What's your business, then?"

"I'm looking for a friend."

She stared at him keenly.

"Almost four weeks ago, a good friend of mine disappeared down by the Inish Marshes, over by what they call the Coombe Hut. You know that area?"

"Aye."

"My friend's American, like me. He was on a stalk from Kilchurn Lodge when he disappeared. He was injured—accidentally shot. They dragged the Mire for his body but couldn't find it, and, knowing him, I thought he might have somehow gotten away."

Her face creased with suspicion. The old woman might be touched, but nevertheless she obviously had plenty of innate cunning.

"Coombe Hut is twelve mile off, across the marshes."

"I know—but this was my last hope."

"Hain't seen him nor anyone else."

Even though he had known it was a long shot, D'Agosta felt almost crushed by disappointment. "Perhaps your husband might have seen—?"

"Nowt goes out. Invalid."

"Maybe you've seen someone in the distance, someone moving—"

"Hain't seen a soul these many weeks now."

He heard a quavering, irritated voice calling from upstairs, with such a thick brogue he couldn't quite make out the words. The woman scowled and trudged back up the stairs. He heard the old man's muffled, complaining voice and her sharp retorts. She came back down, still scowling. "Time for bed. I sleep down by the stove. You'll have to sleep in the loft with the mister. Blanket's on the floor."

"Thank you, I'm grateful for the help."

"Don't disturb the mister, he's poorly."

"I'll be quiet."

A sharp nod. "Well, good night now."

D'Agosta mounted the creaking staircase, so steep it was almost a ladder. He came into a low room with a peaked ceiling, illuminated by a small kerosene lantern. A wooden bed stood at the far end, under the eaves, and in it he could see the rumpled form of the husband, a scarecrow with a bulbous red nose and bushy white hair. He stared at D'Agosta with a single good eye, which contained a certain malevolence.

"Um, hello," said D'Agosta, unsure of what to say. "Sorry to disturb you."

"Aye, me too," came the growled reply. "Dinnae make noise." The old man turned over roughly, showing D'Agosta his back.

Relieved, D'Agosta took off the borrowed shirt and pants and crawled under a blanket that had been set out on a primitive wooden cot. He blew out the kerosene lantern and lay in the dark. It was wonderfully warm in the loft, and the sounds of the storm outside, the howling wind, were oddly comforting. He fell asleep almost immediately.

• • •

An indeterminate time later, he awoke. It was pitch black and he'd been so sound asleep that it took him a moment of fright to remember where he was. When he did, he realized the storm had died down and the cottage was very, very silent. His heart was pounding. He had the distinct impression that someone, or something, was standing over him in the dark.

He lay there in utter darkness, trying to calm himself. It had just been a dream. But he couldn't shake the sensation that some person was standing, maybe even leaning, over him.

The floor beside his cot creaked softly.

Jesus. Should he shout out? Who could it be? Surely not the old man. Had someone come in the night?

The floor creaked again—and then he felt a hand grasp his arm in a grip of steel.

CHAPTER 18

"My dear Vincent," came the whispered voice. "While I am touched at your concern, I am nevertheless exceedingly displeased to see you here."

D'Agosta felt almost paralyzed with shock. He was surely dreaming. He heard the whisper of a match, a sudden glow, and the lantern was lit. The old man stood over him, misshapen, clearly ill. D'Agosta stared at the sallow, wrinkled skin; the sparse beard and greasy shoulder-length white hair; the bulbous reddened nose. And yet the voice, faint as it was—and the silvery glint the rheumy eye could not fully conceal—these belonged unmistakably to the man he was searching for.

"Pendergast?" D'Agosta finally managed to choke out.

"You shouldn't have come," Pendergast said in the same whispery voice.

"What—how—?"

"Allow me to get back in my bed. I'm not strong enough to stand for long."

D'Agosta sat up and watched the old man hang the lantern and shuffle painfully back to the bed.

"Pull up a chair, my friend."

D'Agosta rose, put on the borrowed clothes, and took a chair down from a hook on the wall. He sat next to the old man who bore such remarkably little resemblance to the FBI agent. "God, I'm so glad to find you alive. I thought…" D'Agosta found himself choking up, unable to speak, overwhelmed with emotion.

"Vincent," said Pendergast. "Your heart is as big as ever. But let us not become maudlin. I have much to say to you."

"You were shot," said D'Agosta, finally finding his voice. "What the hell are you doing way out here? You need medical attention, a hospital."

Pendergast put out a restraining hand. "No, Vincent. I have received excellent medical attention, but I must remain hidden."

"Why? What the hell's going on?"

"If I tell you, Vincent, you must promise me you'll return to New York at your earliest opportunity—and not breathe a word of this to anybody."

"You need help. I'm not going to leave you. I'm your partner, damn it."

With obvious effort, Pendergast rose slightly from the bed. "You *must*. I need to recover. And then I'm going to find my would-be killer." He sank back slowly onto the pillow.

D'Agosta exhaled. "So the bastard really did try to kill you."

"And not just me. I believe he was the one who shot you as we were leaving Penumbra. And he was also the one who tried to kill Laura Hayward, on our way to visit you in the hospital at Bastrop. He's the missing

link. The mysterious other person involved in Project
Aves."

"Unbelievable. So he's your wife's killer? Her own
brother?"

A sudden silence. "No. He didn't kill Helen."

"Then who did?"

"Helen's alive."

D'Agosta could hardly believe it. In fact, he didn't
believe it. He couldn't find anything to say.

A hand reached out, the steel fingers gripping him
once again. "As I was shot and sinking into the quickmire, Judson told me Helen was still alive."

"But didn't you see her die? You took the ring off
her severed hand. You *showed* it to me."

For a long moment, the little room was silent. Then
D'Agosta spoke again. "The scumbag said it to torture
you." He looked at the figure in the bed, the glitter in
the man's silvery eyes. In it, he could see an undeniable
desire: to *believe.*

"So what's your, ah, plan?"

"I'm going to find him. I'm going to put a gun to his
head. And I'm going to make him take me to Helen."

D'Agosta was filled with dismay. The obsessive timbre of the voice, the desperation of it, was very unlike
his old friend.

"And if he doesn't do as you say?"

"He will, Vincent. Trust me: I will make sure of
that."

D'Agosta decided not to ask Pendergast how. Instead
he changed the subject. "When you were shot...how
did you get away?"

"When the impact of the bullet knocked me into

the bog, I began to sink. After a moment I realized I wasn't sinking farther—that my feet had come to rest on something only a few feet beneath the surface. Something soft and buoyant, a carcass I believe. It kept me from going down. To give the illusion of sinking, I slowly lowered myself into a crouch. It was my great good fortune that Judson left the scene without waiting until I was fully...immersed."

"Great good fortune," D'Agosta muttered.

"I waited four, maybe five minutes," Pendergast said. "I was bleeding too badly to wait any longer. Then I rose again and—using the carcass as leverage—extricated myself from the mire. I improvised a compression bandage as best I could. I was miles from anywhere—miles from the nearest village or the lodge."

Pendergast fell silent a minute or two. When he began again, his voice was a little stronger. "Judson and I had hunted here before, a decade ago. On that trip, I made the acquaintance of a local doctor named Roscommon. We had some similar interests. His practice was in the village of Inverkirkton, about three miles away. It happened to be the closest point as the crow flies from where I was shot."

"How did you do it?" D'Agosta asked after a moment. "Reach him without leaving any tracks?"

"The improvised dressing stopped my leaving any blood spoor," Pendergast said. "I moved with great care. The rain took care of the rest."

"You traveled three miles in the rain, with a sucking chest wound, to the doctor's house?"

Pendergast fixed him with his gaze. "Yes."

"Jesus Christ, *how*...?"

"I suddenly had something to live for."

D'Agosta shook his head.

"Roscommon is an unusually intelligent and subtle man. He quickly understood my situation. Two things were in my favor: the bullet had missed my subclavian artery by a hair, and it had passed all the way through, so an operation wasn't necessary to extract it. Roscommon re-inflated the lung and managed to control the hemorrhaging. Under cover of darkness, he brought me out to this cottage. And his aunt has looked after me ever since."

"His aunt?"

Pendergast nodded. "Looking after her well-being is the only thing that keeps him in this part of Scotland, rather than in a lucrative Harley Street practice. He knew I would be safe with her."

"And you've been here for the past month."

"And I'll be here a little longer still—until I'm sufficiently recovered to finish the job."

"You need me," said D'Agosta.

"No," Pendergast said with great vehemence. "*No*. The sooner you go home, the better. For God's sakes, Vincent, you may already have led the wolf to the door with this ill-timed discovery."

D'Agosta fell silent.

"Your mere presence imperils me. Judson is undoubtedly still around. He's in high panic. He doesn't know if I'm alive or dead. But if he sees you, particularly in the vicinity of this cottage . . ."

"I can help you in other ways."

"Absolutely not. I almost got you killed once. Captain Hayward would never forgive me if I let it happen again. The best thing you can do for me, the *only* thing, is to return to New York, go back to your job, and not breathe a word of this to anyone. What I must do, *I must do alone.* Say nothing to no one, not Proctor, not Constance, not Hayward. Do you understand? I need to recover my strength before I can get Judson. And I *will* get him. If he doesn't get me first."

D'Agosta felt the sting of this last comment. He stared at Pendergast, lying in the cot, so weak in body, so fierce in mind. Once again, he was struck by the fanatical obsession lurking in those eyes. God, he must have loved that woman.

"All right," he said with huge reluctance. "I'll do what you say. Except that I've got to tell Laura. I swore I'd never deceive her again."

"Very well. Who knows of your efforts to find me here?"

"The inspector, Balfour. Quite a few others. I've been asking around."

"Then Esterhazy knows. We can turn this to our advantage. Tell everyone your search was fruitless, that you're now convinced I'm dead. Go home, show all the outward signs of mourning."

"If that's really what you want."

Pendergast's eyes slid toward him. "It's what I *insist.*"

CHAPTER 19

New York City

Dr. John Felder walked down the echoing hallway of Mount Mercy Hospital, a slim folder under one arm and the physician in charge, Dr. Ostrom, at his side.

"Thank you for allowing this visitation, Dr. Ostrom," Felder said.

"Not at all. I take it your interest in her will be ongoing?"

"Yes. Her condition is ... unique."

"Many things involving the Pendergast family are unique." Ostrom started to say more and then fell silent, as if he'd already said too much on the matter.

"Where is Pendergast, her guardian?" Felder asked. "I've been trying to get in touch with him."

"He's a cipher to me, I'm afraid—comes and goes at the oddest times, makes demands and then vanishes. I've found him a somewhat difficult person to deal with."

"I see. So you have no objections to my continuing visits to the patient?"

"None at all. I'll be glad to share my observations with you, if you wish."

"Thank you, Doctor."

They reached the door, and Ostrom knocked lightly. "Please come in," came the response from the other side.

Ostrom unlocked the door and ushered Felder in ahead of him. The room looked similar to the last time he'd seen it, except that there were more books in it—many more books. The bookcase that before had held only half a dozen volumes now had several times that many. Glancing at the titles, Felder noticed *The Complete Poetry of John Keats*, Jung's *Symbols of Transformation*, the Marquis de Sade's *120 Days of Sodom*, Eliot's *Four Quartets*, Thomas Carlyle's *Sartor Resartus*. No doubt these were from the Mount Mercy library; Felder found himself mildly shocked that certain of these titles were allowed to circulate.

There was another difference, too: the room's single table was now covered with sheets of foolscap, which were filled with dense lines of writing, punctuated by elaborate sketches, profiles, still lifes, equations, and Leonardo-like diagrams. And there, on the far side of the desk, sat Constance. She was in the act of writing, a quill pen in one hand, a bottle of blue-black ink on the desk beside her.

She glanced up at the two men as they entered. "Good morning, Dr. Ostrom. Good morning, Dr. Felder." She stacked the sheets one on top of the other, then turned the top sheet over the rest.

"Good morning, Constance," Ostrom said. "Did you sleep well?"

"Very well, thank you."

"Then I'll leave you two. Dr. Felder, I'll have

someone outside the door. Just knock when you're ready to leave." Ostrom stepped out. A moment later, Felder heard a key turning smoothly in the lock.

He turned to see Constance regarding him with her strange eyes. "Please have a seat, Dr. Felder."

"Thank you." Felder sat in the only vacant chair in the room, a plastic chair with steel legs bolted to the floor. He was curious about her writings but decided to address that issue another time. He placed the folder on his knees and nodded at the quill. "Interesting choice of writing instrument."

"It was either this or crayons." She paused. "I did not expect to see you again so soon."

"I hope you don't find our conversations disagreeable."

"On the contrary."

Felder shifted in the chair. "Constance, if you don't mind, I wanted to speak with you again, briefly, about—about your childhood."

Constance sat up slightly.

"First, let me make sure I understand. You state that you were born on Water Street in the 1870s, though you are unsure of the exact year. Your parents died of tuberculosis, and both your brother and older sister died within a few years as well. That would make you…" He paused to calculate. "More than one hundred and thirty years old."

For a moment, Constance did not reply. She just regarded him calmly. Once again, Felder was struck by her beauty: her intelligent expression, her bob of auburn hair. She had far more self-possession than was natural for a woman who looked only twenty-two or -three.

"Doctor," she said at last, "I've much to thank you for. You've treated me with kindness and respect. But if you're here to humor me, I'm afraid my good opinion of you will suffer."

"I'm not here to humor you," Felder said, with sincerity. "I'm here to help you. But I need to understand you better first."

"I've told you the truth. Either you believe me or you don't."

"I want to believe you, Constance. But put yourself in my place. It's a biological impossibility that you're a hundred and thirty years old. And so I seek other explanations."

Again she paused briefly. "A biological impossibility? Doctor, you are a man of science. Do you believe that the human heart can be transplanted from one person to another?"

"Of course."

"Do you believe that X-ray radiographs and MRI machines can take pictures of the internal structure of the body, without resorting to invasive procedures?"

"Naturally."

"Around the time of my birth, such things would have been thought 'a biological impossibility.' Is it really 'impossible' that medicine could retard aging and prolong a life span beyond its natural length?"

"Well...perhaps prolong a life span. But to keep a girl in her early twenties for more than a century? No, I'm sorry, it's just not possible." As he spoke, Felder felt his own convictions wavering. "Are you saying that's what happened to you? You were the subject of some kind of medical procedure to prolong your life?"

Constance did not reply. Felder felt he was getting somewhere, all of a sudden.

"How did it happen? What brought it about? Who performed this procedure?"

"To say anything more would be to betray a confidence." Constance smoothed the front of her dress. "I've already said more than I should have. The only reason I tell you this is I sense you have a sincere desire to help me. But I can say nothing more. What you choose to believe is entirely up to you, Doctor."

"So it is. I thank you for sharing this with me." Felder hesitated. "I wonder if you would do me a favor."

"Certainly."

"I'd like you to think back to your childhood on Water Street. Your earliest memories of the neighborhood."

She looked at him very carefully, as if searching his face for any sign of coyness or deception. After a moment, she nodded.

"Do you remember Water Street with any clarity?"

"I remember it well."

"Very good. As I recall, you have said your home was at Sixteen Water Street."

"Yes."

"And you were roughly five years of age when your parents died."

"Yes."

"Tell me about the immediate surroundings— around your residence, I mean."

For a moment, Constance's alert eyes seemed to go far away. "There was a tobacconist next door. I remember the smell of Cavendish and Latakia drifting into the front window of our flat. On the other side of us was a fishmonger's. The neighborhood cats liked to congregate on the brick wall of its back garden."

"Do you remember anything else?"

"Across the street was a haberdasher. London Town, they called it. I recall the model displayed over the signboard. And down the street was a chemist's shop—Huddell's. I remember it because my father took us inside once for a penny bag of chocolates." Her face shone briefly at the memory.

Felder found the answers more than a little disturbing.

"What about schooling? Did you go to school on Water Street?"

"There was a school, down at the corner, but I didn't go. My parents couldn't afford it. Universal free public education didn't exist then. And I told you—I'm self-educated." She paused. "Why are you asking me these questions, Dr. Felder?"

"I'm curious to see how clear your early memories are."

"Why—in order to satisfy yourself they are delusional?"

"Not at all." His heart was beating fast, and he tried to conceal his excitement and confusion.

Constance met his gaze with her own and seemed to see into him. "If you don't mind, Doctor, I'm tired."

He took up the folder with both hands and rose. "Thank you again, Constance," he said. "I appreciate your candor."

"You're welcome."

"And for what it's worth—" he said suddenly—"I believe you. I don't begin to understand it, but I believe you."

Her expression softened. Very faintly, she inclined her head.

He turned and knocked on the door. What had possessed him to make such an impulsive statement? A moment later, the key turned and an orderly appeared.

Outside in the corridor, as the orderly relocked the door, Felder opened the folder he'd been carrying. Inside was an article from that morning's *New York Times*. It described a historical find that had just been announced that very day: the diary of a young man, Whitfield Speed, who had lived on Catherine Street from 1869 to his untimely death under the wheels of a carriage in 1883. Speed, an enthusiastic New Yorker, had apparently been very taken with Stow's *Survey of London* and was hoping to write a similarly fine-grained account of the streets and shops of Manhattan. He had only managed to fill a single journal with observations before his death. The journal had remained locked in an attic trunk with his few possessions, unknown since his death, and had only just been rediscovered. It was being hailed as an important addition to the history of the city, as it gave very specific information about the composition of his neighborhood— information unobtainable from any other source.

Speed's Catherine Street residence had been just around the corner from Water Street. And on an inside page, the *Times* had printed one of the elaborate pencil sketches from Speed's journal-in-progress—a sketch that included a detailed neighborhood map of two streets, Catherine and the adjoining Water. Until this very morning, nobody alive knew precisely, on a building-by-building basis, what shops those streets had consisted of during the 1870s.

The moment Felder had read the article at the breakfast table earlier that morning, he'd been struck with an idea. It seemed crazy, of course—he was really doing little more than indulging Constance, encouraging her delusions—but here was a perfect opportunity to check on her information. In the face of truth—the *real* layout of 1870s Water Street—perhaps Constance could be persuaded to begin leaving her fantasy-world behind.

Standing in the corridor, Felder scrutinized the image in the newspaper carefully, struggling to parse the antique handwriting scrawled across the diagram. Then he went rigid. There was the tobacconist. And two buildings away, Huddell's Chemists. Across the street was the haberdasher London Town, and on the corner, Mrs. Sarratt's Academy for Young Children.

He closed the folder slowly. The explanation was obvious, of course. Constance had already seen today's paper. A mind as inquisitive as hers would want to know what was going on in the world. He set off down the hall toward reception.

As he drew close to the receiving station, he noticed Ostrom standing in an open doorway, speaking with a nurse.

"Doctor?" Felder asked, with some hurry.

Ostrom glanced back at him, eyebrows raised in inquiry.

"Constance has seen the morning paper, right? The *Times*?"

Ostrom shook his head.

Felder froze. "No? You're sure about that?"

"I'm positive. The only newspapers, radios, and

televisions that are patient-accessible are in the library. And Constance has been in her room all morning."

"Nobody has seen her? No staff, no nurses?"

"Nobody. Her door hasn't been unlocked since last night. The log states it quite clearly." He frowned. "Is something the matter?"

Felder realized he'd been holding his breath. He exhaled slowly. "Nothing. Thank you."

And he walked out of the lobby, into bright sunlight.

CHAPTER 20

CORRIE SWANSON HAD PUT OUT A ROUTINE Google alert for "Aloysius Pendergast." At two AM, as she fired up her laptop and collected her e-mail, she saw she'd gotten a rare hit. It was an obscure document, a transcript of an inquest held in a place called Cairn Barrow, Scotland. The inquest was dated some weeks before, but it had just been posted online today.

As she read the dry, legalistic language, a sense of complete disbelief took hold. Without commentary or analysis or even a conclusion, the transcript was nothing more than a record of the testimony of various witnesses relating to a shooting incident on some Highland moor. A terrible, utterly unbelievable incident.

She read through it again, and again, and yet again, each time feeling an increase in the sense of unreality. Clearly, this strange tale was only the tip of some iceberg, with the real story submerged beneath the surface. None of it made sense. She felt her emotions morphing—from disbelief, to unreality, to desperate anxiety. Pendergast, shot dead in a hunting accident? Impossible.

Hands trembling slightly, she fished out her notebook and looked up a telephone number, hesitated, then swore softly to herself and dialed the number. It was D'Agosta's home number and he wouldn't be happy getting a call at this hour, but screw it, the cop had never called her back, never followed through on his promise to look into it.

She swore out loud again, this time louder, as her fingers misdialed and she had to start over.

It rang about five times and then a female voice answered. "Hello?"

"I want to talk to Vincent D'Agosta." She could hear the tremor in her own voice.

A silence. "Who is this?"

Corrie took a deep breath. If she didn't want to get hung up on, she'd better cool her jets. "This is Corrie Swanson. I'd like to speak to Lieutenant D'Agosta."

"The lieutenant isn't here," came the chilly response. "Perhaps I could take a message?"

"Tell him to call me. Corrie Swanson. He has my number."

"And this is in reference to—?"

She took a deep breath. Getting mad at D'Agosta's wife or girlfriend or whoever wouldn't help. "Agent Pendergast. I'm trying to find out about Pendergast," she said, and added, "I worked with him on a case."

"Agent Pendergast is dead. I'm sorry."

Just hearing it seemed to strike her dumb. She swallowed, tried to find her voice. "How?"

"A shooting accident in Scotland."

There it was. Confirmation. She tried to think of something more to say, but her mind was blank. Why hadn't D'Agosta called her? But there was no point in talking further with this person. "Look, have the lieutenant call me. ASAP."

"I'll pass on the message," was the cool response.

The phone went dead.

She slumped in her chair, staring at the computer screen. This was crazy. What was she going to do? She felt suddenly bereft, as if she had lost her father. And there was no one to talk to, no one to grieve with. Her own father was a hundred miles away, in Allentown, Pennsylvania. She felt suddenly, desperately alone.

Staring at the computer screen, she clicked on the link to the website about Pendergast she had been lovingly maintaining:

www.agentpendergast.com

Working quickly, almost automatically, she created a frame with a thick black border and began to write within it.

> I've just learned that Agent P.—Special Agent A. X. L. Pendergast—has passed away in a bizarre and tragic accident. This is awful. I can hardly believe it to be true. I can't believe the world can keep spinning without him on it.
>
> It happened during a hunting trip to Scotland...

But even as she wrote the eulogy, fighting back tears, the surreal aspects of the story began to reassert themselves in her mind. And in the end, as she finished and posted it, she wondered if she even believed what she had just written.

CHAPTER 21

The Foulmire

JUDSON ESTERHAZY PAUSED TO CATCH HIS BREATH. It was an uncharacteristically sunny morning, and the boggy moorlands that surrounded him on all sides shone in rich browns and greens. In the distance, he could see the dark line of the Inish Marshes. And between the hillocks ahead of him, a few hundred yards away, stood the small stone cottage known as Glims Holm.

Esterhazy had heard tell of it but had initially dismissed it as being too many miles from the site of the shooting and far too primitive for Pendergast to have received the kind of medical attention he would have needed. But then he'd learned D'Agosta had been in Inverkirkton, asking around for Pendergast, and from there he'd discovered that Glims Holm was the last place D'Agosta had visited before returning to America, disappointed.

But was he truly disappointed? The more he thought about it, the more it began to seem—perversely— the kind of place Pendergast would have chosen to recuperate.

And then—accidentally, in the course of background research into the official records of the Shire of Sutherland—Esterhazy had learned the nugget that convinced him: the strange old woman who lived in the stone cottage in front of him was Dr. Roscommon's aunt. This was a fact that Roscommon—all too clearly a man of habitual restraint—had kept concealed from the good folk of Inverkirkton.

Positioning himself behind a thicket of gorse, Esterhazy took out his binoculars and observed the cottage. He could see the old woman through the downstairs window, laboring over a stove and moving about. After a while she removed something from the stove, and he watched as she walked past the window and out of sight. For a moment she was gone...and then he saw her figure pass by the second-story window, carrying what looked like a mug. He could just barely see her figure inside the attic space, leaning over what seemed to be a sickly person in a bed, helping him sit up and giving him the mug to drink.

Esterhazy's heart quickened. Digging his walking stick into the soft ground, he made a circuit of the cottage, ending up on the far side. There was a small back door, of rough wood, that connected to a small kitchen garden; a shed; and a stone sheep pen. There were no windows on the back side of the house.

He glanced around carefully. Nobody was to be seen; the infinitude of moor and mire on all sides was devoid of life. He pulled the small handgun from his pocket, ensured there was a round in the chamber. With great care, he approached the cottage from its blind side.

Soon he was crouched by the back door. With a

single finger he made a small scratching noise on the wood and waited.

Sure enough, the sharp-eared old crone heard it; he listened to her footsteps and unintelligible imprecations as she approached. A bolt shot back and the door opened. The woman looked out.

A muttered oath.

With one swift, economical movement Esterhazy rose, clamped his hand over her mouth, and dragged her one-armed from the doorway. He gave her a solid tap on the back of the head with the butt of the gun, then laid her unconscious body on the turf. A moment later he had noiselessly slipped into the cottage. The ground floor was a single large room; he looked around quickly, taking in the enameled stove, the worn chairs, the antlers on the walls, the steep staircase rising to the loft overhead. A loud, stertorous breathing could be heard coming from above. It continued undisturbed.

He moved around the small room with infinite care, placing each foot with fanatical caution, checking the commode, the single closet, satisfying himself that nobody was in hiding. Then, keeping tight hold of the gun, he moved over to the staircase. It was built of thick pegged planks, which might or might not creak.

He waited at the bottom of the stairs, listening. The breathing continued, somewhat labored, and once he heard the man upstairs shift in his bed and grunt with what sounded like discomfort. Esterhazy waited, letting a full five minutes pass. All seemed normal.

He raised a leg and placed one foot on the lower stair, began to put pressure on it, bit by bit, until his full weight was applied. No creak of wood. He placed his next foot on the higher tread, performing the same excruciating operation, and again there was no creak. With maddening slowness he ascended the staircase in this fashion, consuming minutes of time, until he was almost at the top. The foot of a primitive bed was visible five feet away. He raised himself ever so slowly and peered over the top into the bed. A figure lay in it: back to him, covered, sleeping, his breathing labored but regular. He was a gaunt old man in a heavy night-dress, with white hair almost as wild and rumpled as the crone's. Or so it appeared.

Esterhazy knew better.

An extra pillow had been draped over the head-board. Putting his gun away, Esterhazy took hold of the pillow and, keeping his eyes fixed on the man in the bed, picked it up. Tensing, gripping the pillow in both hands, he crouched like a tiger—then suddenly pounced, landing on the bed, bringing the pillow down on the man's face and leaning into it with all his strength.

A muffled cry came from below and a hand flew up, scratching and flailing at Esterhazy, but there was no weapon in the hand and he knew his attack had been a complete and total surprise. He drove the pillow down even harder, the muffled sounds cut off, and now the weakened man struggled silently, his flapping hands plucking at his shirt. The body heaved below him, sur-prisingly strong for one so recently gravely wounded. One large spidery hand grasped the covers, yanking them this way and that, as if mistaking the covers for his assailant's own clothing. With a final heave of hands and legs the covers came off, exposing his upper body, but Pendergast was rapidly weakening and the end would come soon.

Then something gave Esterhazy pause: the man's gnarly old hands. He stared in the dim light at the man's lower body, his spindly legs, the parchment skin, the varicose veins. There was no mistaking it—this was the body of an old man. Nobody could create such an effective disguise. But more than that was the absolute lack of bandages, scar, or anything remotely like a month-old gunshot wound on the heaving torso.

His mind worked furiously to overcome the shock and rage. He had been so sure, so very sure...

He quickly released the pillow, exposing the old man's distorted face, his tongue protruding, his eyes popping with terror. He coughed once, twice, gasping for breath, his sunken chest heaving with the effort.

In a blind panic, Esterhazy threw the pillow aside and stumbled down the stairs; the old crone was just staggering into the back door, blood running down her face.

"You devil!" she shrieked, grasping at him with bony fingers as he ran past, flinging open the front door and running back over the wide, empty moorlands.

CHAPTER 22

Malfourche

THE MILD NIGHT AIR, SIGHING IN THROUGH the open window, stirred the muslin curtains of the living room. Feeling the breeze on her face, June Brodie looked up from the Mississippi Board of Nursing forms she was filling out. Except for the low susurrus of wind, the night was quiet. She glanced at her watch: nearly two in the morning. Faintly, from the den, she could hear the sound of a deep-voiced narrator droning from the television: no doubt Carlton was watching one of the military history shows he was so passionate about.

She took a sip from the bottle of Coke that sat at her elbow. She had always loved Coke out of glass bottles; it reminded her of her childhood and the old-fashioned vending machines where you opened the narrow glass window and pulled the bottles out by their necks. She was convinced it tasted different in a bottle. But for the last decade, out in the swamp, she'd had to content herself with aluminum cans. Charles Slade hadn't been able to bear the way that light glinted off glass, and almost no exposed glass had been allowed on Spanish Island. Even the syringe barrels had been plastic.

She replaced the bottle on its coaster. There were other benefits of returning to a normal life. Carlton could watch his television programs without having to wear headphones. Blinds could be opened wide, allowing light and fresh air. She could decorate the house with fresh flowers—roses and gardenias and her favorite, calla lilies—without fear that their scent would provoke a desperate protest. She'd kept herself trim, she liked fine clothes and fashionable hairstyles; now she would have a chance to wear them where others could see. It's true, they'd had to endure more than their share of stares from neighboring townsfolk—some suspicious, some merely curious—but already people were getting used to their being back. The police investigation was over and done with. The annoying reporter from the *Ezerville Bee* hadn't returned. And while his story had been picked up as a small item in a Houston paper, it didn't seem to have spread any farther. After Slade's death, they had taken their time—almost five months— to make sure nobody would ever know how they had been living, what they had been doing. Only then had they made a public reappearance. The secret of their lives in the swamp would remain just that—a secret.

June Brodie shook her head a little wistfully. Despite telling herself all this, there were still times—times like this, in the quiet of the night—when she missed Charles Slade so much it was almost a physical pain. It's true, all those years of tending to his wasted body, to a mind ravaged by disease and a toxic sensitivity to any kind of sensory stimulus, had dulled her love. And yet she had once loved him so fiercely. She'd known it was wrong, utterly unfair to her husband. But as CEO of

Longitude, Slade had been so powerful, so handsome, so charismatic—and in his own way, so very kind to her...She had been willing, so much more than willing, to give up her job as an RN and devote herself to him, by day and—quite frequently—by night as well.

The den had gone silent. Carlton must have turned off the TV in favor of his other passion: crossword puzzles from the London *Times*.

She sighed, glanced down at the papers in her lap. Speaking of her job, she'd better get these things filled out. Her license as an advanced practice registered nurse had expired prior to 2004, and under Mississippi law reinstatement required that she...

Quite abruptly she looked up. Carlton was standing in the doorway, a very odd look on his face.

"Carlton?" she said. "What is it? What—"

At that moment another figure loomed into view out of the darkness behind her husband. She caught her breath. It was a man, tall and lean, and dressed in a dark, expensive-looking trench coat. A black leather cap was pulled down low over eyes that looked at her with calm detachment. In one of his gloved hands was a gun, which was aimed at the base of her husband's skull. Its barrel seemed strangely long until she realized it had been fitted with a silencer.

"Sit down," the man said, and half prodded, half pushed her husband into a love seat beside her. Despite the rush of adrenaline that animated her limbs and the sudden pounding of her heart, June Brodie picked up on the foreign tang in the voice. It was European, maybe Dutch, more likely German.

The man glanced around the room, noticed the

open window, shut it, and closed the curtains. He took off the trench coat and draped it over a nearby chair. Pulling the chair up in front of the couple, he sat down and crossed his legs. The handgun drooped easily at his side. He hitched up the knees of his trousers and casually shot his cuffs, as if he were wearing a thousand-dollar suit instead of a cat burglar's outfit. He leaned toward her, a long, thin, worm-like mole growing out below one eye. She had the sudden ridiculous thought: *Why doesn't he get that thing removed?*

"I wonder," he said in a pleasant voice, "if you could clear something up for me."

June Brodie glanced covertly at her husband.

"Can you tell me, please, what is a moon pie?"

The room remained silent. June wondered if she'd misheard.

"Local foods and delicacies interest me," the man continued. "I've been in this curious part of your country for a day now. I've learned the difference between crawfish and crayfish—that is, none. I've tasted grits and—what are they called again?—hush puppies. But I can't seem to find out what kind of a pie a moon pie is."

"It's not a pie," Carlton said, in a high, strained voice. "It's a large cookie. Made of marshmallow and graham cracker. And, um, chocolate."

"I see. Thank you." The man paused to look at them in turn. "And now, perhaps you will be good enough to tell me where you both have been the last twelve years?"

June Brodie took a deep breath. When she spoke, she was surprised at the evenness of her own voice. "It's no secret. It was in the papers. We ran a B and B in San Miguel, Mexico. It's called Casa Magnolia, and—"

With a single economical move, the man lifted his weapon and—with a muffled *thunk*—shot off Carlton Brodie's left kneecap. Brodie jerked as if touched with a cattle prod, doubling over with a roar of surprise and pain, the blood pouring out between the fingers clutching at his knee.

"If you are not immediately silent," the man told him coolly, "the next shot will be in your brainpan."

Carlton took the fist that was not clutching his knee and put it in his mouth. Tears streamed from his eyes. June had jumped up to go to him, but a jerk of the gun made her sink back into the chair.

"Lying to me is insulting," the man said. "Don't do it again."

The room was silent. The man tugged at his gloves, first one, then the other. He pushed the leather cap back on his head, revealing fine aquiline features: a thin nose, high cheekbones, blond hair cut short, narrow chin, cold blue eyes, lips that turned down at the edges. The man looked from one to the other, the weapon once again lolling at his side. "We know, Mrs. Brodie, that your family owns a hunting lodge in Black Brake swamp, a place not far from here. The lodge is known as Spanish Island."

June Brodie stared at him. Her heart was now beating painfully in her breast. On the love seat, her husband moaned and shivered, clutching his ruined knee.

"Not too long ago—shortly before you reappeared—a man named Michael Ventura was found dead in the swamp, shot, not far from Spanish Island. He was once chief of security for Longitude Pharmaceuticals. He is a person of interest to us. Would you know anything about that?"

We know, he'd said. *Of interest to us.* June Brodie thought of the words the invalid Slade used to whisper, so often, with such apparent urgency: *Stay secret. They can't know we're alive. They would come for us.* Was it possible—was it remotely possible—that those weren't, after all, the ravings of a paranoid, half-lunatic man?

She swallowed. "No, we don't," she said aloud. "Spanish Island went bankrupt decades ago, it's been shuttered and vacant since—"

The man raised the handgun again and casually shot Carlton Brodie in the groin. Blood, matter, and body fluids gushed over the love seat. Brodie howled in agony, doubled over again, fell out of his chair and writhed on the ground.

"All right!" June cried. "All right, *all right, for the love of God stop it, please!*" The words tumbled out.

"Shut him up," the man said, "or I'll have to."

June rose and rushed over to her husband, doubled up and crying out in pain. She put a hand over his shoulder. Blood was running freely from his knee, between his legs. With an ugly gushing noise he vomited all over his trousers and shoes.

"Talk," said the man, still casual.

"We were out there," she said, almost spitting the words in her fright. "Out in the swamp. At Spanish Island."

"For how long?"

"Since the fire."

The man frowned. "The fire at Longitude?"

She nodded almost eagerly.

"What were you doing out there in the swamp?"

"Taking care of him."

"Him?"

"Charles. Charles Slade."

For the first time, the man's mask of calm unconcern fell away. Surprise and disbelief bloomed on his fine features. "Impossible. Slade died in the fire..." He stopped talking and his eyes widened slightly, gleaming as if in comprehension.

"No. That fire was a setup."

The man looked at her and spoke sharply. "Why? To destroy evidence of the lab?"

She shook her head. "I don't know why. Most of the lab work was done at Spanish Island."

Another look of surprise. June stared at her husband, who was moaning and shivering uncontrollably. He seemed to be passing out. Maybe dying. She sobbed, choked, tried to control herself. "Please..."

"Why were you hiding there?" the man asked. His tone was disinterested, but the gleam had not left his eyes.

"Charles got sick. He caught the avian flu. It... *changed* him."

The man nodded. "And he kept you and your husband on to look after him?"

"Yes. Out in the swamp. Where he wouldn't be found. Where he could work and then—when his disease got worse—where he could be taken care of." She was almost choking with terror. The man was brutal—but if she told him everything, everything, maybe he would let them go. And she could get her husband to the hospital.

"Who else knew about Spanish Island?"

"Just Mike. Mike Ventura. He brought supplies, made sure we had everything we needed."

The man hesitated. "But Ventura is dead."

"*He* killed him," June Brodie said.

"Who? Who killed him?"

"Agent Pendergast. FBI."

"The FBI?" For the first time, the man raised his voice perceptibly.

"Yes. Along with a captain in the NYPD. A woman. Hayward."

"What did they want?"

"The FBI agent was looking for the person who killed his wife. It had something to do with Project Aves—the secret avian flu team at Longitude... Slade had her killed. Years ago."

"Ah," the man said, as if understanding something new. He paused to inspect the fingernails of his left hand. "Did the FBI agent know about Slade's still being alive?"

"No. Not until... Not until he got to Spanish Island and Slade revealed himself."

"And then what? Did this FBI agent kill Slade, as well?"

"In a way. Slade died."

"Why wasn't any of this in the news?"

"The FBI agent wanted to let the whole thing die in the swamp."

"When was this?"

"More than six months ago. March."

The man thought for a moment. "What else?"

"That's all I know. *Please.* I've told you everything. I need to help my husband. *Please* let us go!"

"Everything?" the man said, the slightest tinge of skepticism in his voice.

"Everything." What else could there be? She'd told him about Slade, about Spanish Island, about Project Aves. There was nothing else.

"I see." The man looked at her for a moment. Then he lifted his gun and shot Carlton Brodie between the eyes.

"God, *no!*" June felt the body jump in her arms. She screamed.

The man slowly lowered the gun.

"Oh, no!" June said, weeping. "*Carlton!*" She could feel her husband's body slowly relaxing in her arms, a low, bellows-like sigh escaping his lungs. Blood was now coursing in regular rivulets from the back of his head, blackening the fabric of the love seat.

"Think very carefully," the man said. "Are you sure you've told me everything?"

"Yes," she sobbed, still cradling the body. "Everything."

"Very well." The man sat still for a moment. He chuckled to himself. "Moon pie. How vile." Then he rose, and—still moving slowly—walked toward the chair where June had been working on the nursing forms. He hovered over it, glanced down at the paperwork for a moment as he snugged the gun into his waistband. Then he picked up her half-finished bottle of Coke, poured the contents into a nearby flowerpot, and—with a sharp rap to the side of the table—broke off its mouth.

He turned toward her, bottle held forward, at hip level. June stared at the sharp edges of the broken neck, the glass glinting in the lamplight.

"But I've told you everything," she whispered.

"I understand," he said, nodding sympathetically. "Yet one must be sure."

CHAPTER 23

Inverkirkton

"AFTERNOON, MR. DRAPER. And a fine afternoon it is, too."

"Indeed it is, Robbie."

"Did you have a good morning's ride, then?"

"I did. Cycled as far as Fenkirk and back."

"That's a wee distance."

"I wanted to take advantage of the good weather. I'll be off in the morning."

"I'll hate to lose your trade, Mr. Draper. But I figured you'd be on your way soon. Lucky to have had you this long."

"If you would just prepare the bill for me, I'll square accounts."

"Right away, sir."

"You've been very hospitable. I think I'll go up to my room and wash up, then pop over to the Half Moon for one last bite of steak-and-kidney pudding."

"Very good, sir."

Upstairs, Esterhazy washed his hands in the sink and dried them on a towel. For the first time in weeks, he felt a tremendous relief. All this time, he'd been unable to convince himself that Pendergast was dead. His search for Pendergast had developed into an obsession, consuming his waking thoughts, tormenting his dreams. But somehow, the visit to Glims Holm had—at long last—convinced him that Pendergast was dead. If the FBI agent were still alive, he'd have found some trace of him in his long, exhaustive search. If he were alive, Roscommon would have let slip some morsel of information during Esterhazy's three visits to his clinic. If he were alive, Esterhazy would have found him at the stone cottage that morning. He felt as if a huge weight had been lifted from his shoulders. He could go home and pick up his life from the point it had been upended when Pendergast and D'Agosta had first shown up on his doorstep.

Whistling, he closed the door to his room and descended the stairs. He was not concerned the old lady would venture into town to announce the assault, and even if she did the village so clearly thought her touched that her story would never be believed. The bicycle ride, and the eight-mile hike across the moors and back, had sharpened his appetite, and for the first time in weeks that appetite was not dulled by anxiety.

He entered the dark and fragrant confines of the Half Moon and settled onto a bar stool with satisfaction. Jennie Prothero and MacFlecknoe, the barkeep, were there in their usual positions: one before the bar, one behind.

"Afternoon, Mr. Draper, sir," said MacFlecknoe as he drew a pint of the usual for Esterhazy.

"Afternoon, Paulie. Jennie." Numerous rounds purchased by Esterhazy over the last week had earned him the considerable right of calling them by their Christian names.

Mrs. Prothero nodded and smiled. "Hello, luv."

MacFlecknoe set the pint before Esterhazy, then turned back to Jennie Prothero. "Odd we haven't seen him around before," he said.

"Well, he did say he'd been over at the Braes of Glenlivet." The old woman sipped her bitter. "Think he ever went to the constable about it?"

"Nae. What's to tell? Besides, last thing he'd want would be to get mixed up in something, on vacation and all."

Esterhazy pricked up his ears. "Have I missed something?"

MacFlecknoe and the shopkeeper-*cum*-laundress exchanged glances. "Clergyman," the barkeep said. "You just missed him. Stopped in for a dram."

"Several drams," said Jennie, with a knowing wink.

"Nice old fellow, he was," said MacFlecknoe. "For a Welshman. Has a little church down in Anglesey. He's been up here in the Highlands the last month."

"Gravestone rubbing," said Jennie Prothero, shaking her head.

"Now, Jennie," said the barkeep. "It's a respectable pastime enough, especially for a man of the cloth."

"Perhaps," the old woman replied. "Said he was an aquarium, he did."

"Antiquarian," MacFlecknoe corrected.

Esterhazy gently interrupted. "I'll have the steak-and-kidney pudding, please, Paulie." He added, in his most disinterested tone: "What's this about the constable?"

MacFlecknoe hesitated. "Well, now, Mr. Draper, sir,

I don't know as I should say. He'd already had three whiskies by the time he told us the tale, you know."

"Oh, don't be daft, Paulie!" Jennie Prothero scolded. "Mr. Draper here's a good sort. He's not going to go making any trouble for the old fellow."

The barkeep considered this. "Right, then. It was some weeks back. The priest had just come into the area and was on his way to Auchindown. He spotted the churchyard of Ballbridge chapel—it's a bit of a ruin, hard by the Inish Marshes—and stopped to examine the gravestones. Well, no sooner was he inside the churchyard when a man came out of the mists. Drunk and sick he was, shivering, blood and muck all over."

"The poor cleric felt sure he was a fugitive," said the shopkeeper, putting one finger to her nose. "Running from the law."

Esterhazy knew of the ruined chapel—it was situated between the Foulmire and Inverkirkton. "What did the man look like?" he asked, his heart suddenly rattling in his chest like a rat caught in a tin can.

MacFlecknoe thought a moment. "Well, now, he didn't say. He was desperate, though, raving about something. The cleric thought the man wanted to make a confession, and so he listened. He said the chap was nearly out of his wits. Trembling all over, teeth chattering. He told the man some sort of story and needed to know the way around the marshes. The vicar drew him a bit of a map. Made the vicar promise not to whisper anything about the encounter to a soul. The poor old priest went back to his car to get a spare blanket from the boot. But by the time he got back to the churchyard, the fellow had vanished again."

"I'll be locking my door tonight, and all," said Jennie Prothero.

"What story did the man tell the priest, exactly?" Esterhazy asked.

"Now, Mr. Draper, you know how the clergy are," the barkeep said. "Sanctity of the confessional, and all."

"And you said his parish was in Anglesey," Esterhazy said. "Was he on his way back?"

"No. He still had a few days left of his holidays. Said he was going to stop over at Lochmoray."

"A wee bit of a village over west," said MacFlecknoe, his tone implying that Inverkirkton was a metropolis by comparison.

"Plenty of old gravestones to rub at St. Muns," Jennie Prothero added, with another shake of her head.

"St. Muns," Esterhazy repeated, slowly, as if to himself.

CHAPTER 24

Lochmoray, Scotland

JUDSON ESTERHAZY BICYCLED UPHILL, leaving the little town far behind. As the road wound back into the granite hills, all signs of civilization dropped away, and in another ninety minutes a gray stone steeple appeared in the distance, just poking above the folded landscape.

That could only be the chapel of St. Muns, with its historic churchyard, where—with any luck—he would find the priest.

He stared at the long, winding road, caught his breath, and began the ascent.

The road went up through pines and firs before curving around the shoulder of the hill, dropping into a glen, and then climbing one last leg toward the isolated chapel. A cold wind blew and clouds scudded across the sky as he paused at the shoulder to examine the approach.

Sure enough: the priest was in the churchyard, all alone, dressed not in black but tweeds, with only a clerical collar to mark his calling. The man's bicycle was propped against a gravestone, and the cleric himself was bent over a table-type tomb, involved in making a rubbing. Although he felt a little foolish, Esterhazy probed the reassuring lump of his pistol, assuring himself it was readily accessible, and then he remounted his bicycle and coasted down.

It was amazing. The bastard Pendergast was still making trouble for him, even from beyond the grave. It must have been Pendergast this priest bumped into, out there on the moors. He would have been weak from loss of blood, half mad with pain, just minutes from death. What had he told the man? Esterhazy could not leave Scotland without knowing.

The churchman rose awkwardly as Esterhazy approached, brushing twigs and grass off his knees. A large sheet of rice paper lay on the tomb; the rubbing was half complete. A portfolio of other rubbings lay nearby, spread out on a piece of canvas with crayons, pastels, and charcoal.

"*Ouf!*" muttered the priest, adjusting his clothes and patting himself back into order. "Afternoon to you." He had a picturesque Welsh accent, and his face was red and veined.

Esterhazy's habitual caution evaporated as the priest extended his hand. His grasp was unpleasantly damp and not altogether clean.

"You must be the priest up from Anglesey," Esterhazy said.

"That's right." The man's smile gave way to a look of confusion. "And how might you be knowing that?"

"I've just come from the pub at Inverkirkton. They mentioned you were in the neighborhood. Making rubbings of gravestones." Esterhazy nodded toward the tomb.

The old man beamed. "Quite right! Quite right!"

"What a coincidence running into you like this. My name's Wickham."

"Delighted to make your acquaintance."

They stood a moment in amiable silence.

"They also mentioned you told them quite a story," Esterhazy went on. "About a rather desperate fellow you encountered on the moor."

"And so I did!" The eagerness in the priest's face told Esterhazy he was one of those men who avidly sought to give advice on any and all subjects.

Esterhazy glanced around, feigning disinterest. "I'd be curious to hear about it."

An eager nod. "Yes, indeed. Indeed. It was...let's see...early October."

Esterhazy waited impatiently, trying not to press the priest too hard.

"I ran into a man. Lurching across the moors."

"His appearance?"

"Dreadful. He was sick, or at least that's what he said...I think he might have been drunk, or more likely on the run from the law. Must have fallen on the rocks, too—his face was bloody. He was very pale, muddy...soaked to the bone. It had rained heavily that afternoon, as I recall. Yes, I do recall that rain. Fortunately, I had brought along my double waterproof—"

"But his exact appearance? Hair color?"

The clergyman paused, as if thinking of something for the first time. "What's your interest in this, if you don't mind my asking?"

"I—I write mysteries. I'm always looking for ideas."

"Oh. Well, in *that* case, let me see: pale hair, pale face, tall. Dressed in hunting tweeds." The priest shook his head and gave a bird-like cluck. "The poor fellow was in a state, and no mistake."

"And did he say anything?"

"Well, yes. But I can't really talk about that, you understand. A man's confessions to God are a sacred secret."

The priest was speaking so slowly, so deliberately, that Esterhazy felt he might go mad. "What a fascinating story. Is there anything else you can tell me?"

"He asked me the way around the marshes. I told him it was several miles." The priest puckered his lips. "But he insisted, so I drew him a little map."

"A map?"

"Well, yes, it was the least I could do. I had to draw him the route. It's terribly treacherous, bogs everywhere."

"But you're up from Anglesey. How do you know this area?"

The priest chuckled. "I've been coming here for years. Decades! I've wandered all over these moors. I've visited every kirkyard between here and Loch Linnhe! This is a very historic area, you see. I've rubbed hundreds of tombstones, including those of the lairds of—"

"Yes, yes. But tell me about the map you drew. Can you draw the same map for me?"

"Of course! Delighted! You see, I sent him around the marshes because the way by Kilchurn Lodge is even more dangerous. I honestly don't know how he got out there in the first place." He clucked again as he drew a crude map, with atrocious draftsmanship, cramped and small. "Here is where we were," he said, poking at an *X*.

Esterhazy was forced to bend down to see better. "Where?"

"*Here.*"

Even before Esterhazy could comprehend what was happening, he felt a ferocious jerk. Then he was forced to the ground and pinned, his arm twisted behind his back, his face pressed into the turf—and the cold barrel of a pistol was jammed so hard into his ear canal that it cut his flesh, drawing blood.

"Talk," said the clergyman.

The voice was that of Pendergast.

Esterhazy struggled, his mind wild, but the barrel jammed in relentlessly. He felt a wave of horror and terror. Just when he was sure the devil was dead and gone, he reappeared. This was the end. Pendergast had finally won. The enormity of it sank in like poison.

"You said Helen was alive," came the voice, almost a whisper. "Now tell me the rest. All of it."

Esterhazy struggled to bring his mind into order, to overcome his shock, to consider what he would say and how he would say it. The smell of turf filled his nostrils, gagging him. "Just a moment," he gasped. "Let me explain from the beginning. Please, let me up."

"No. Stay down. We have plenty of time. And I have no compunctions about forcing you to talk. You *will* talk. But if you lie to me, even once, I'll kill you. No warning."

Esterhazy grappled with an almost overwhelming fear. "But then...then you'll never know."

"Wrong. Now that I know she's alive, I'll find her regardless. But you could spare me a lot of time and trouble. I repeat: truth or die."

Esterhazy heard the soft click of the safety being thumbed off.

"Yes, I understand..." He tried once again to collect his thoughts, calm himself down. "You have no idea," he gasped, "no idea what's involved here. It goes back, before Longitude." He heaved, struggling for air in the dew-laden grass. "It goes back even before we were born."

"I'm listening."

Esterhazy took a heaving breath. This was harder than he ever imagined. The truth was so very, very awful...

"Start at the beginning."

"That would be April 1945..."

The pressure of the gun abruptly vanished. "My dear fellow, that was a nasty fall! Let me help you up." Pendergast's voice had changed, and the Welsh accent was back in force.

For a moment Esterhazy was utterly confused.

"You've cut your ear! Oh, dear!" Pendergast dabbed at the ear and Esterhazy felt the gun, now in Pendergast's pocket, pressing into his side. At the same time he heard a car door slam, then voices—a chorus of voices. He looked up from the earth, blinking. A jolly group of men and women approached, with walking sticks, waterproofs, notebooks, cameras, and pens. The van in which they had arrived was parked just beyond the old stone wall enclosing the kirkyard. Neither of them had heard it come, so intense was their confrontation.

"Hallo!" said their leader, a short, fat, vigorous man, who came stumping toward them waving a furled umbrella. "Are you all right?"

"Just a little fall," said Pendergast, helping Esterhazy to his feet but at the same time gripping him with a hand of steel, the gun barrel rammed like a pike into his kidneys.

"Fancy meeting other people in this forgotten corner of Scotland! And you here by bicycle, no less! What brings you to these wild climes?"

"Tomb iconography," said Pendergast, with remarkable calmness. His eyes, however, were anything but calm.

Esterhazy made a huge effort to pull himself together. Pendergast was temporarily stymied, but he could be sure the agent wouldn't miss even the slightest opportunity to finish what he'd started.

"We on the other hand are genealogists!" said the man. "And our interest is in names." He stuck out his hand. "Rory Monckton, Scottish Genealogical Society."

Esterhazy saw his chance. As the man pumped Pendergast's unwilling hand, thus temporarily occupying it, Pendergast was forced to release Esterhazy's arm for a moment.

"Nice to make your acquaintance," Pendergast began, "but I fear we really must be on our way—"

Esterhazy slammed his arm back against the lump of the gun and twisted away from it with sudden violence, dropping down; Pendergast fired but was a millisecond too late, and by then Esterhazy had his own weapon out.

"Mother of God!" The portly man threw himself down on the grass.

The group, which had started to deploy about the headstones, now fell into hysteria, some taking cover, others scattering like partridge in the direction of the hills.

A second shot tore through the flap of Esterhazy's coat while he simultaneously got off a shot at Pendergast. Tumbling behind a tombstone, Pendergast fired again, and missed; he was not in good form, obviously still weakened by his injury.

Esterhazy fired twice, forcing Pendergast back behind the tombstone, and then ran like hell for the van, going around the far side and leaping in, keeping low.

The keys were in the ignition.

A bullet slammed through the side windows, showering him with glass. He returned fire.

Starting the van, Esterhazy continued firing with one hand out the now-shattered window, over the heads of the genealogists and between the gravestones, preventing Pendergast from getting in a good shot. Screams pealed from the churchyard as Esterhazy threw the van into reverse, scattering pebbles like shotgun pellets. He heard bullets striking the rear of the van as he slewed about, jamming his foot on the accelerator and taking off.

Another round struck the van before he sped over the shoulder of the hill and was out of range. He couldn't believe his good fortune. He considered that the chapel of St. Muns was twelve miles from Lochmoray. There was no cell coverage. And no car, only two old bicycles.

He had two hours, perhaps a little less, to get to an airport.

CHAPTER 25

Edinburgh, Scotland

Y OU MAY PUT YOUR SHIRT BACK ON NOW, Mr. Pendergast."
The elderly doctor replaced his tools in the worn Gladstone bag, one by one, with fussy, precise movements: stethoscope, blood pressure monitor, otoscope, penlight, ophthalmoscope, portable EKG monitor. Closing up the bag, the man looked around the luxurious hotel suite, then fixed his disapproving gaze once more upon Pendergast. "The wound has healed badly."

"Yes, I know. The recuperative conditions were... less than ideal."

The doctor hesitated. "That wound was clearly inflicted by a bullet."

"Indeed." Pendergast buttoned his white shirt, then slipped into a silk dressing gown of a muted paisley pattern. "A hunting accident."

"Such accidents have to be reported, you know."

"Thank you, the authorities know all that is necessary."

The doctor's frown deepened. "You are still in a considerably weakened state. Anemia is quite pronounced, and bradycardia is present. I would recommend at least two weeks' bed rest, preferably in hospital."

"I appreciate your diagnosis, Doctor, and will take it under advisement. Now if you could please provide me with a report of my vital signs, along with the EKG readout, I will be happy to attend to your bill."

Five minutes later, the doctor left the suite, closing the door softly behind him. Pendergast washed his hands in the bathroom sink, then went to the telephone.

"Yes, Mr. Pendergast, how can I be of service?"

"Please have a setup delivered to my suite. Old Raj gin and Noilly Prat. Lemon."

"Very good, sir."

Pendergast hung up the phone, walked into the living room, opened the set of glass doors, and stepped out onto the small terrace. The hum of the city rose to meet him. It was a cool evening; below, on Princes Street, several cabs were idling at the hotel entrance, and a lorry went trundling past. Travelers were streaming into Waverly Station. Pendergast raised his gaze over the Old Town toward the sprawling, sand-colored bulk of Edinburgh Castle, ablaze with light, framed against the purple glow of sunset.

There was a knock, then the door to the suite opened. A uniformed valet entered with a silver tray containing glasses, ice, a shaker, a small dish of lemon peels, and two bottles.

"Thank you," Pendergast said, stepping in from the terrace and pressing a bill into his hand.

"My pleasure, sir."

The valet left. Pendergast filled the shaker with ice, then poured in several fingers of gin and a dash of vermouth. He shook the mixture for sixty seconds, then strained it into one of the glasses and pinched in a zest of lemon. He took the drink back onto the patio, sat down in one of the chairs, and fell into deep thought.

An hour passed. Pendergast refilled the drink, returned to the patio, and sat again—motionless—another hour. Then at last he drained the glass, plucked a cell phone from his pocket, and dialed.

It rang several times before a sleepy voice answered. "D'Agosta."

"Hello, Vincent."

"Pendergast?"

"Yes."

"Where are you?" The voice was instantly alert.

"The Balmoral Hotel, Edinburgh."

"How's your health?"

"As good as can be expected."

"And Esterhazy—what's happened to him?"

"He managed to slip from my grasp."

"Jesus. How?"

"The details aren't important. Suffice to say that even the best-laid plans can fall victim to circumstance."

"Where is he now?"

"In midair. On an international flight."

"How can you be sure of that?"

"Because a van he stole was found parked on a service road outside the Edinburgh airport."

"When?"

"This afternoon."

"Good. So his plane hasn't landed yet. Tell me where the son of a bitch is headed and I'll have a welcoming committee waiting for him."

"I'm afraid I can't do that."

"Why the hell not? Don't tell me you're just going to let him go."

"It isn't that. I've already checked with immigration and passport control. There's no record of a Judson Esterhazy leaving Scotland. Hundreds of other Americans, yes, but no Judson."

"Well then, that abandoned van was just a ruse. He's still holed up somewhere over there."

"No, Vincent—I've thought this thing through from every conceivable angle. He has definitely fled the country, probably for the United States."

"How the hell can he do that without going through passport control?"

"After the inquest, Esterhazy made a big show of leaving Scotland. Passport control has a record of the date and the flight number. But they have no record of him coming *back* into Scotland—although we both know that he did."

"That isn't possible—not with airport security the way it is these days."

"It's possible if you're using a false passport."

"A false passport?"

"He must have procured one back in the States, when he returned after the inquest."

There was a brief pause. "It's virtually impossible to fake a U.S. passport these days. There's got to be another explanation."

"There isn't. He has a fake passport—which I find deeply troubling."

"He can't hide. We'll put the dogs on him."

"He now knows I'm still alive and most eager to catch up with him. Therefore, he'll go to ground.

Searching for him, in the short term, is pointless. He's clearly had some professional help. And so my investigation must proceed along a different course."

"Yeah? And what course is that?"

"I must discover the whereabouts of my wife on my own."

This was greeted by another, longer pause. "Um, Pendergast...I'm sorry, but you know where your wife is. In the family plot."

"No, Vincent. Helen is alive. I'm as sure about that as I've ever been about anything in my life."

D'Agosta gave an audible sigh. "Don't let him do this to you. Can't you see what's happening? He knows how much she meant to you. He *knows* you'd give anything, do anything, to get her back. He's messing with you—for his own sadistic reasons."

When Pendergast did not reply, D'Agosta swore under his breath. "I suppose this means you're not in hiding anymore."

"There's no longer any point. However, I'm still planning to operate under the radar for the foreseeable future. No reason to telegraph my moves."

"Anything I can do to help? From this end?"

"You can look in on Constance at Mount Mercy Hospital for me. Make sure she wants for nothing."

"You got it. And you? What'll you do next?"

"It's as I told you. I'm going to find my wife." And with that, Pendergast rang off.

CHAPTER 26

Bangor, Maine

He had cleared customs and retrieved his bags without incident. And yet Judson Esterhazy couldn't get up the nerve to leave baggage claim. He remained seated in the last seat of a bank of molded plastic chairs, nervously scanning the face of everyone who passed. Bangor, Maine, had the most obscure international airport in the country. And Esterhazy had changed planes twice—first in Shannon, and then in Quebec—in the hope of muddying his trail, frustrating Pendergast's pursuit.

A man sat down heavily beside him, and Esterhazy turned suspiciously. But the traveler weighed close to three hundred pounds, and not even Pendergast could have duplicated the way the man's adipose tissue bulged around his waistband. Esterhazy turned back to the faces of the people passing by. Pendergast could easily be among them. Or, with his FBI credentials, he could be in some security office nearby, watching him on a closed-circuit monitor. Or he could be parked outside Esterhazy's Savannah house. Or even worse, waiting inside, in the den.

The ambush in Scotland had scared the living shit out of him. Once again, he felt blind panic wash over him, mingling with rage. All these years of covering his tracks, of being so very careful...and now Pendergast was undoing it all. The FBI agent had no idea how big a Pandora's box he was prying open. Once *they* stepped in...He felt mercilessly squeezed between Pendergast on one side, and the Covenant on the other.

Gasping, tugging at his collar, he fought back the panic. He could handle this. He had the intelligence, he had the wherewithal. Pendergast wasn't invincible. There had to be some way for him to handle this himself. He would hide; he would bury himself deep, give himself time to think.

But what place was too remote, too obscure, for Pendergast to find? And even if he did hunker down in some remote backwater, he couldn't go on living in fear, year after year, like Slade and the Brodies.

The Brodies. He'd read in the paper about their ghastly deaths. No doubt they'd been discovered by the Covenant. It was a dreadful shock—but really, he should have expected it. June Brodie hadn't known the half of what she'd been involved in—what he and Charles Slade had involved her in. If she had, she'd never have emerged from that swamp. Amazing that Slade, even in all his craziness and decline, had never betrayed the one, central, all-important secret.

In that moment of fear and desperation Esterhazy finally realized what he had to do. There was one answer—only one. He couldn't go it alone. With Pendergast on the rampage, he needed that last resort. He had to contact the Covenant, quickly, *proactively.* It would be far more dangerous if he didn't tell them, if they found out what was going on in some other way. He had to be seen as cooperative. Trustworthy. Even if it meant putting himself once again fully in their power.

Yes: the more he thought of what he had to do, the more inevitable it became. This way he could control what information they received, withhold the facts they could never be allowed to learn. And if he placed himself under their protection, Pendergast would be powerless to hurt him. In fact, if he could convince them Pendergast was a threat, then even the FBI agent, with all his wiles, would be as good as dead. And his secret would remain safe.

With this decision came a small sense of relief.

He looked around once more, scrutinizing each face. Then, rising and picking up his bags, he strode out of the baggage claim area to the taxi stand. There were several cabs idling: good.

He went to the fourth cab in line, leaned in the open passenger window. "You far into your shift?" he asked.

The cabbie shook his head. "The night's young, buddy."

Esterhazy opened the rear door, threw his bags in, and ducked in after them. "Take me to Boston, please."

The man stared into the rearview mirror. "Boston?"

"Back Bay, Copley Square." Esterhazy dug into his pocket, dropped a few hundreds in the man's lap. "That's a starter. I'll make it worth your while."

"Whatever you say, mister." And putting the taxi in gear, the driver nosed out of the waiting line and drove off into the night.

CHAPTER 27

N ED BETTERTON LOOKED BOTH WAYS, THEN CROSSED the wide and dusty expanse of Main Street, a white paper bag in one hand and two cans of diet soda in the other. A beat-up Chevy Impala was idling at the curb outside Della's Launderette. Walking around its hood, Betterton got into the passenger seat. A short and muscular man sat behind the wheel. He wore dark glasses and a faded baseball cap.

"Hey, Jack," said Betterton.

"Hey, yourself," came the reply.

Betterton handed the man a soda, then fished inside the paper bag, bringing out a sandwich wrapped in butcher's paper. "Crawfish po'boy with rémoulade, hold the lettuce. Just like you ordered." He passed it over to the driver, then reached into the bag again and brought out his own lunch: a massive meatball Parmesan sandwich.

"Thanks," said his companion.

"No problem." Betterton took a bite of his sandwich. He was famished. "What's the latest with our boys in blue?" he mumbled through the meatballs.

"Pogie's chewing everybody out again."

"Again? What's eating the chief this time?"

"Maybe his midnight ass is acting up."

Betterton chuckled, took another bite. *Midnight ass* was cop lingo for "hemorrhoids," an all-too-common complaint among officers who sat in cars for hours at a time.

"So," Betterton said. "What can you tell me about the Brodie killings?"

"Nothing."

"Come on. I bought you lunch."

"I *said*, thanks. A free lunch isn't worth a pink slip."

"That's not going to happen. You know I'd never write anything that could come back to haunt you. I just want to know the real dope."

The man named Jack scowled. "Just because we used to be neighbors, you think you can hit me up for all your leads."

Betterton tried to look hurt. "Come on, that's not true. You're my friend, you want me to turn in a good story."

"You're my friend—you should think more of keeping me out of hot water. Besides, I don't know any more than you do."

Betterton took another bite. "Bull."

"It's basically true. The thing's too big for us, they've brought in the state boys, even a homicide squad all the way from Jackson. We've been cut out."

The journalist thought a moment. "Look, all I know is that the husband and wife—the couple I interviewed not so long ago—were brutally murdered. You've got to have more information than that."

The man behind the wheel sighed. "They know it wasn't a robbery. Nothing was taken. And they know it wasn't anybody local."

"How do they know that?" Betterton mumbled through a huge bite of meatball.

"Because nobody local would do this." The man reached into a folder at the side of his seat, pulled out an eight-by-ten color glossy, and handed it over. "And I didn't show this to you."

Betterton took a look at the scene-of-crime photo. The color drained from his face. His chewing slowed, then stopped. And then, quite deliberately, he opened the car door and spat the mouthful into the gutter.

The driver shook his head. "Nice."

Betterton handed the photo back without looking at it again. He wiped his mouth with the back of a hand. "Oh, my God," he said huskily.

"Get the idea?"

"Oh, my God," Betterton repeated. His mighty hunger had vanished.

"Now you know all I know," the cop said, finishing his po'boy and licking his fingers. "Oh, except one thing—we don't have anything even remotely like a lead on this. The crime scene was clean. A professional job the likes of which we just don't see around here."

Betterton didn't reply.

The man glanced over, eyed the half-eaten remains of the meatball sandwich. "You going to eat that?"

CHAPTER 28

New York City

CORRIE SWANSON SAT ON A BENCH on Central Park West, with a McDonald's bag next to her, pretending to read a book. It was a pleasant morning, the glorious color in the park behind her just starting to fade, the sky patched with cumulus, everyone out on the streets enjoying the Indian summer. Everyone except Corrie. Her entire attention was focused across the street on the façade of the Dakota and its entrance, around the corner on Seventy-Second Street.

Then she saw it: the silver Rolls-Royce coming up Central Park West. It was a familiar car to her—unforgettable even. She grabbed the McDonald's bag and leapt up from the bench, her book tumbling to the ground, then ran across the street against the light, dodging traffic. She paused at the corner of Central Park West and Seventy-Second, waiting to see if the Rolls turned in.

It did. The driver—whom she could not see—moved into the left-hand lane and put on his blinker, slowing as he approached the corner. Corrie jogged down Seventy-Second to the Dakota, reaching it a few moments before the Rolls arrived. As it began to turn slowly into the entrance, she stepped out in front of the car. The Rolls stopped and she stared at the driver through the windshield.

It wasn't Pendergast. But it damn sure was his car: there couldn't be another vintage Rolls like it in the whole country.

She waited. The driver's-side window went down and a head poked out, a man with a chiseled face and bull neck.

"Excuse me, miss," he said, his voice calm and pleasant. "Would you mind...?" His voice trailed off and the question mark dangled in the air.

"I *do* mind," she said.

The head continued to look at her. "You're blocking the driveway."

"How inconvenient for you." She took a step forward. "Who are you and why are you driving Pendergast's car?"

The head stared at her for a moment and disappeared, and then the door opened and a man got out, the pleasant smile almost, but not quite, gone. He was powerfully built, with the shoulders of a swimmer and the torso of a weight lifter. "And you are?"

"None of your business," said Corrie. "I want to know who *you* are and why you're driving his car."

"My name is Proctor and I work for Mr. Pendergast," he said.

"How nice for you. I notice you just used the present tense."

"Excuse me?"

"You said, 'I work for Mr. Pendergast.' How can that be, if he's dead? You know something I don't?"

"Listen, miss, I don't know who you are, but I'm sure we could discuss this more comfortably somewhere else."

"We're going to discuss it right *here*, as *un*comfortably as possible, blocking the driveway. I'm sick of getting the runaround."

The Dakota attendant emerged from his brass pillbox. "Is there a problem?" he asked, his Adam's apple bobbing.

"Yeah," said Corrie. "A big problem. I'm not moving until this man tells me what he knows about the owner of this car, and if that's a problem maybe you'd better call the cops and report a disturbance of the peace. Because that's what's going to happen if I don't get some answers."

"That won't be necessary, Charles," the man named Proctor said calmly. "We're just going to settle this quickly and be out of your way."

The attendant frowned doubtfully.

"You may go back to your post," Proctor said. "I've got this under control." His voice remained quiet, but it managed to project an unmistakable air of command. The attendant obeyed.

He turned back to her. "Are you an acquaintance of Mr. Pendergast?"

"You bet I am. I worked with him out in Kansas. The Still Life killings."

"Then you must be Corrie Swanson."

She was taken aback, but recovered quickly. "So *you* know me, anyway. Good. What's this about Pendergast being dead?"

"I regret to say he—"

"Don't give me any more bullshit!" Corrie cried. "I've been thinking about it, and that hunting accident story stinks worse than Brad Hazen's jockstraps. You tell me the truth or I can just feel that disturbance of the peace coming on."

"There's no need to get excited, Miss Swanson. Just what is your purpose in wanting to contact—"

"Enough!" Corrie removed the ball-peen hammer she had been carrying in the McDonald's bag and raised it above the windshield.

"Miss Swanson," said Proctor, "don't do anything rash." He began to take a step toward her.

"Halt!" She raised her arm.

"This is no way to go about getting information—"

She brought the hammer down smartly on the windshield. A star pattern of cracks burst into the sunlight.

"My God," Proctor said in disbelief, "do you have any idea how—?"

"Is he alive or dead?" She raised her arm again. As Proctor tensed to approach her, she yelled, "Touch me and I'll scream rape."

Charles stood in his pillbox, bug-eyed.

Proctor froze in position. "Just a minute. I'll have an answer for you—but you'll have to be patient. Any more violence and you'll get nothing."

There was a brief moment of stasis. Then, slowly, Corrie lowered the hammer.

Proctor took out a cell phone, held it up so she could see. Then he began to dial.

"You'd better be quick. Maybe Charles is calling the cops."

"I doubt it." Proctor spoke into the phone, in a low voice, for about a minute. Then he held it out to her.

"Who is it?"

Instead of replying, Proctor simply continued to hold out the phone, looking at her through narrowed eyes.

She took it. "Yeah?"

"My dear Corrie," came the silky voice she knew so well, "I'm terribly sorry to have missed our lunch at Le Bernardin."

"They're saying you're dead!" Corrie gasped, chagrined at feeling tears spring into her eyes. "They—"

"The reports of my death," came the droll voice, "are greatly exaggerated. I've just emerged from deep cover. This ruckus you're causing is rather inconvenient."

"Jesus, you could have *told* me. I've been worried sick." Her flood of relief began to turn to anger.

"Perhaps I should have. I'd forgotten how resourceful you are. Poor Proctor, he had no idea what he was up against. You'll have a very difficult time getting back into his good graces, I fear. Did you have to break the windscreen on my Rolls to get his attention?"

"Sorry. It was the only way." She felt her face flush. "You let me think you were *dead*! How could you?"

"Corrie, I'm under no obligation to account to you for my whereabouts."

"So what's this case?"

"I can't speak of it. It's strictly private, unofficial, and—if you'll pardon the jargon—*freelance*. I'm alive, I've just returned to the United States, but I'm operating on my own and I need no help. None whatsoever. You can rest assured I will make good on our lunch,

but it may not be for some time. Until then, please continue with your studies. This is an exceedingly dangerous case and you must *not* become involved in any way.
Do you understand?"

"But—"

"Thank you. By the way, I was touched by what you
wrote on your website. A rather nice eulogy, I thought.
Like Alfred Nobel, I have had the curious experience
of reading my own obituary. Now: do I have a solemn
promise from you to do absolutely nothing?"

Corrie hesitated. "Yes. But are you supposed to be
dead? What should I say?"

"The need for that fiction has recently passed. I'm
back in circulation—although I'm maintaining a low
profile. Once again, my apologies for any discomfort
you've experienced."

The phone went dead even as she was saying good-
bye. She stared at it for a moment and then handed it
back to Proctor, who pocketed it, eyeing her coolly.

"I hope," he said, his voice edging below freezing,
"that we won't be seeing you around here again."

"No problem," said Corrie, putting the hammer
back into the bag. "But if I were you, I'd ease off on the
bench-pressing. You've got a rack that would do Dolly
Parton proud." She turned on her heel and walked
back toward the park. The obituary *was* rather nice, she
thought. Maybe she'd leave it up on the website for a
while longer, just for fun.

Chapter 29

Plankwood, Louisiana

MARCELLUS JENNINGS, DIRECTOR OF THE OFFICE of Public Health for the parish of St. Charles, sat in tranquil contemplation behind his commodious desk. Everything was in order, as he liked it. Not a single memorandum was out of place in the old-fashioned inbox; not a speck of dust or stray paper clip was to be seen. Four pencils, freshly sharpened, lay in a neat line beside the leather-cornered blotter. A computer sat on the right side of the desk, powered down. Three official commendations hung on the wall, lined up with a straightedge and carpenter's level: all for perfect attendance at Louisiana state conferences. A small bookshelf behind him held a collection of regulatory manuals and guidebooks, carefully dusted and only rarely opened.

There was a light rap on the office door.

"Come in," Jennings said.

The door opened and Midge, his secretary, poked her head in. "A Mr. Pendergast to see you, sir."

Even though it was his only official appointment of the morning, Jennings opened a drawer of his desk, pulled out his calendar, and consulted it. Punctual, very punctual. Jennings admired punctuality. "You may show him in," he said, putting the calendar away.

A moment later, the visitor entered. Jennings rose to greet him, then froze in surprise. The man looked as if he were at death's door. Gaunt, unsmiling, pale as a waxwork dummy. Dressed in a suit of unrelieved black, he reminded Jennings of nothing so much as the grim reaper. All that was missing was the scythe. He had begun to put out his hand for a shake but quickly diverted it into a wave toward the row of chairs before his desk. "Please, have a seat."

Jennings watched as the man stepped forward and slowly, painfully sat down. Pendergast, Pendergast... The name rang a bell—he wasn't sure why. He leaned forward, putting his elbows on the desk and crossing his capacious forearms. "Pleasant day," he observed.

The man named Pendergast did not directly acknowledge this pleasantry.

"Well." He cleared his throat. "Now, just what can I do for you, Mr. Pendergast?"

In reply, Pendergast plucked a small leather wallet from his suit jacket, opened it, and placed it on the desk.

Jennings peered at it. "FBI. Is this, ah, official business of some sort?"

"No." The voice was faint, yet melodious, with mellow accents of New Orleans gentry. "It is a personal matter." And yet the FBI shield lay there on the desk, like some charm or totem.

"I see." Jennings waited.

"I'm here about an exhumation."

"I see," Jennings repeated. "Is this in reference to

an exhumation that has already been completed or a request in process?"

"A new exhumation order."

Jennings removed his elbows from the desk, sat back, took off his glasses, and began to polish them with the fat end of his polyester tie. "Just who is it you would like exhumed?"

"My wife. Helen Esterhazy Pendergast."

The polishing stopped for a moment. Then it resumed at a slower pace. "And you say this is not a question of a court order? A police request to determine cause of death?"

Pendergast shook his head. "As I said, it's personal."

Jennings raised a hand to his mouth and coughed politely. "You must understand, Mr. Pendergast, that these things have to be done through proper channels. There are rules in place, and they have been enacted with good reason. Exhumation of interred remains is not an act to be taken lightly."

When Pendergast said nothing, Jennings, encouraged by the sound of his own voice, went on. "If we're not dealing with a court order or some other officially sanctioned request—such as a forensic autopsy due to suspicions about cause of death—there is really only one circumstance under which an application for exhumation can be approved—"

"If the family of the deceased wishes to move the remains to another burial spot," Pendergast finished.

"Well, ah, yes, that is it precisely," Jennings said. The interjection had caught him off guard, and he struggled for a moment to find his rhythm again. "Is that the case?"

"It is."

"Well then, I think we can get the application process started." He turned to a filing cabinet that stood beside the bookcase, opened a drawer, pulled out a form, and placed it on his desk blotter. He examined it for a moment. "You realize there are certain, ah, prerequisites. For example, we would need a copy of the death certificate of... of your late wife."

Reaching into his jacket again, Pendergast produced a folded piece of paper, unfolded it, and placed it on the desk beside his shield.

Leaning forward, Jennings examined it. "Ah. Very good. But what is this? I see the originating cemetery is Saint-Savin. That's clear on the other side of the parish. I'm afraid you'll have to take this request over to the west parish office."

He found the silvery eyes staring into his. "You also have jurisdiction—technically speaking."

"Yes, but as a matter of protocol, Saint-Savin is handled only through the west parish branch."

"I picked you, Mr. Jennings, for a very particular reason. Only *you* can do this for me—no one else."

"I'm flattered, I'm sure." Jennings felt a flush of pleasure at the declaration of confidence. "I suppose we could make an exception. Moving on, then, to the matter of the application fee ..."

Once again, the pale, slender hand disappeared into the suit jacket. Once again, it reappeared, this time with a check, dated and signed, made out in the correct amount.

"Well, well," Jennings said, looking at it. "And then there is the form of consent, naturally, from the management of the cemetery where the remains are currently interred."

Another form was produced and laid on the desk.

"And the form of consent from the cemetery to which the body is being transferred."

Still another form was placed, slowly and deliberately, on the polished wood.

Jennings stared at the row of paper in front of him. "Well, aren't we organized today!" He attempted a smile but was discouraged by the grim look on the man's face. "I, ah, believe that is everything we need. Oh—except the form from the transport company in charge of moving the remains from the old burial site to the new."

"That won't be necessary, Mr. Jennings."

Jennings blinked in surprise at the apparition on the far side of his desk. "I don't quite understand."

"If you take a closer look at the two forms of consent, I think all will become clear."

Jennings put his glasses back on his nose and peered at the two documents for a moment. Then he looked up quickly. "But these cemeteries are one and the same!"

"That is correct. So as you can see, there will be no need for transportation. Cemetery management will be in charge of transferring the body."

"Is there something wrong with the current burial spot of the deceased?"

"The current spot is fine. I chose it myself."

"Is it a question of new construction? Must the body be moved because of changes being done at the cemetery?"

"I selected Saint-Savin Cemetery specifically because nothing will ever change there—and no new families are being accepted for burial."

Jennings leaned forward slightly. "Then may I ask why are you moving the body?"

"Because, Mr. Jennings, moving the body is the only way I can get temporary access to it."

Jennings licked his lips. "Access?"

"A medical examiner will be standing by, fully licensed and accredited by the State of Louisiana, during the exhumation. An examination of the remains will be performed in a mobile forensic lab, parked on cemetery grounds. Then the body will be reburied—in a grave directly adjoining the one in which it had previously lain, within the Pendergast family plot. It is all spelled out in the application."

"Examination?" Jennings said. "Is this related to some sort of...question of inheritance?"

"No. It's strictly a private matter."

"This is irregular, Mr. Pendergast—most irregular. I can't say I've ever had such a request before. I'm sorry, but this is not something I can approve. You'll have to go through the courts."

Pendergast regarded him for a moment. "Is that your final word on the subject?"

"The guidelines on exhumations are quite clear. I can do nothing." Jennings spread his hands.

"I see." Pendergast picked up the shield and replaced it in his suit jacket. He left the paperwork where it was. "Would you mind coming with me for a moment?"

"But where—?"

"It will only take a minute."

Reluctantly, Jennings rose out of his seat.

"I wish to show you," Pendergast said, "why I chose you in particular for this request."

They walked through the outer office, down the main corridor of the public building, and out the main entrance. Pendergast stopped on the wide front steps.

Jennings looked around at the bustling thoroughfare. "Like I said, pleasant day," he observed with excessive cheer, trying to make small talk.

"Pleasant day indeed," came the reply.

"That's what I love about this part of Louisiana. The sun just seems to shine more brightly than anywhere else."

"Yes. It lends a curious gilding effect to everything it touches. Take that plaque, for instance." And Pendergast gestured toward an old brass plaque that had been set into the brick façade of the building.

Jennings peered at the plaque. He passed it every morning, of course, on the way to his office, but it had been many years since he had bothered to examine it.

THIS CITY HALL OF PLANKWOOD, LOUISIANA,
WAS ERECTED WITH FUNDS GENEROUSLY
DONATED BY
COMSTOCK ERASMUS PENDERGAST IN THE
YEAR OF OUR LORD 1892

"Comstock Pendergast," Jennings murmured under his breath. No wonder the name seemed vaguely familiar.

"My great-grand-uncle. The Pendergast family, you see, has long had a tradition of supporting certain towns in the parishes of both New Orleans and St. Charles, places where various branches of our family lived these past centuries. While we may no longer be around in many of these towns, our legacy lives on."

"Of course," Jennings said, still staring at the plaque. He began to conceive a rather unpleasant notion as to why Pendergast had been so particular in selecting his office for the request.

"We don't advertise it. But the fact is, the various Pendergast trusts and charities continue to make benefactions to several towns—including Plankwood."

Jennings looked from the plaque to Pendergast. "Plankwood?"

Pendergast nodded. "Our trusts provide scholarships to graduating seniors, help maintain the police auxiliary fund, buy books for the library—and support the good work of your very own public health office. It would be a shame to see this support falter...or, perhaps, cease entirely."

"Cease?" Jennings repeated.

"Programs might be cut." Pendergast's gaunt features assumed a sorrowful cast. "Salaries reduced. Jobs lost." He placed a certain emphasis on this last phrase as his gray eyes affixed Jennings.

Jennings raised a hand to his chin, rubbed it thoughtfully. "On second thought, Mr. Pendergast, I feel certain your request might be reviewed favorably—if you can assure me that it is of great importance."

"I can, Mr. Jennings."

"In that case, I'll get the application process started." He glanced back at the plaque. "I could even go so far as to promise you that the paperwork will be put through in a rush. In ten days, perhaps as little as a week, we can have this order approved—"

"I'll stop by for it tomorrow afternoon, thank you," Pendergast said.

"What?" Jennings removed his glasses, blinked in the sunlight. "Oh, of course. Tomorrow afternoon."

CHAPTER 30

Boston, Massachusetts

THE MAN WITH THE SUNKEN EYES AND FIVE O'CLOCK shadow shuffled across Copley Square, in the shadow of the John Hancock Tower. Except for brief glances at the passing traffic, his head hung dejectedly; his hands were deep in the pockets of his grimy raincoat.

He walked down Dartmouth Street and entered the Copley subway station. Passing the line of people buying CharlieCards, he slouched down the cement staircase and stopped, looking around. A row of benches was set against the tiled wall to his right, and he made his way toward them, sitting down at the far end. There he lounged, unmoving, hands still buried in the pockets of his raincoat, staring at nothing.

A few minutes later, another man strolled up. He could not have looked more different. He was thin and tall, dressed in a well-tailored suit and a Burberry trench coat. In one hand he held a copy of *The Boston Globe*, neatly folded; in the other was a crisply rolled black umbrella. A large gray fedora kept his face in shadow. The only distinguishing mark was an odd-looking mole underneath his right eye. Sitting down beside the derelict, he opened the paper wide and began perusing the inside stories.

When a Green Line train squealed its way into the station, the man in the fedora began to speak. He spoke quietly, under the noise of the train, and he kept his gaze on the newspaper.

"State the nature of the problem," he said in accented English.

The derelict let his head hang as he replied. "It's this fellow Pendergast. My brother-in-law. He's found out the truth."

"The truth? All of it?"

"Not yet. But he will. He's an extremely competent and dangerous man."

"What does he know, exactly?"

"He knows that what happened in Africa, the lion killing, was murder. He knows all about Project Aves. And he knows..." Esterhazy hesitated. "He knows about Slade, and Longitude Pharmaceuticals, the Doane family—and Spanish Island."

"Ah yes, Spanish Island," said the man. "This is something *we* have just learned. We now are aware Charles Slade's death twelve years ago was an elaborate hoax and that he was still alive until some seven months ago. This is most unfortunate news. Why didn't you tell us these things?"

"I had no idea, either," Esterhazy lied as forcefully as he could. "I swear to you, I didn't know anything about it." He just *had* to put the genie back in the bottle, once and for all, or he was as good as dead. He found his voice moving up a notch and brought it back down. "It was Pendergast who figured it all out. And what he doesn't know yet—he will."

"Pendergast." The man in the fedora's tone became tinged with skepticism. "Why haven't you killed him? You promised us you would."

"I've tried—on several occasions."

The man in the fedora did not reply. Instead he turned the page of the newspaper and continued reading.

After several minutes, he spoke again. "We're disappointed in you, Judson."

"I'm sorry." Esterhazy felt the blood infuse his face.

"Don't ever forget your origins. You owe us *everything*."

He nodded mutely, face burning in shame—shame at his fear, his submission, his dependence, his failure.

"Does this Pendergast know of the existence of our organization?"

"Not yet. But he's like a pit bull. He doesn't give up. You've got to take him out. We can't afford to leave him on the loose. I'm telling you, we've got to kill him."

"*You* can't afford to leave him on the loose," the man replied. "*You* must deal with him—decisively."

"God knows, I've tried!"

"Not hard enough. How tiresome of you to think you can drop the problem in our lap. Everyone has a weak spot. Find his and attack it."

Esterhazy felt himself shaking with frustration. "You're asking the impossible. Please, I need your help."

"Naturally, you can rely on us for whatever assistance you need. We helped you with that passport—we'll help you again. Money, weapons, safe houses. And we've got the *Vergeltung*. But you have to deal with this man yourself. In fact, taking care of this—quickly and completely—would go a long way toward restoring yourself to our good graces."

Esterhazy was silent a moment, letting this sink in. "Where's the *Vergeltung* docked?"

"Manhattan. The Seventy-Ninth Street Boat Basin." The man paused. "New York...That's where Agent Pendergast lives, is it not?"

This was enough of a surprise that Esterhazy could not help lifting his eyes to the man for a moment.

The man returned to his newspaper with an air of finality. After a minute, Esterhazy rose to go. As he did so, the man spoke once more. "Did you hear what happened to the Brodies?"

"Yes," Esterhazy replied in a low voice. He wondered if the question was an implied threat.

"Don't worry, Judson," the man went on. "We'll take good care of you. Just as we always have."

And as another train came shrieking into the station, he turned back to his paper and did not speak again.

CHAPTER 31

Malfourche

NED BETTERTON DROVE HIS DENTED NISSAN down the main street—the only street, really—of Malfourche. Although it was technically part of his beat, for the most part Betterton avoided the town: too much of that deep-bayou mentality. But the Brodies had lived here. *Had*...Grudgingly, Kranston was letting him follow up, only because the horrific double murder was so big it would have seemed strange if the *Bee* pretended it hadn't happened. "Let's get it over with," Kranston had grumbled. "Quickly. Then we move on."

Though Betterton had nodded agreeably, he'd no intention of getting it over with. Instead, he'd done something he should have done earlier—double-check the story the Brodies told him. Right away it fell apart. A few phone calls revealed that, while there was a B&B in San Miguel named Casa Magnolia, the Brodies had never run it, never owned it. They had only stayed there once, years ago.

It had been a bald-faced lie.

And now they'd been murdered—the biggest killing in the area in a generation—and Betterton was sure it was somehow connected to their strange disappearance and even stranger reappearance. Drugs, industrial espionage, gun-running—it might be anything.

Betterton was convinced that Malfourche was the nexus of this mystery. Malfourche was where the Brodies reappeared—and where they had been brutally killed. Furthermore, he'd heard rumors of strange business in town, some months before the Brodies resurfaced. There'd been an explosion at Tiny's, the local and somewhat notorious bait-and-bar emporium. A leaking propane tank—that was the official story—but there were whispered hints of something else a lot more interesting.

He passed the Brodies' little house, where not so long ago he'd interviewed them. Now crime-scene tape covered the front door and a sheriff's vehicle sat by the curb.

Main Street made a gentle bend to the west and the edge of the Black Brake swamp hove into view, its thick fringe of green and brown like a low dark cloud in an otherwise sunny afternoon. He drove on into the sad business district, sullen-looking shopfronts and peeling signboards. He pulled up beside the docks, killed the engine. Where Tiny's had been, the skeleton of a new building was beginning to rise from the wreckage of the old. A pile of half-burned two-by-fours and creosote pilings were stacked near the docks. Out in front, adjoining the street, the new front steps of the building had been completed and half a dozen scruffy-looking men were seated on them, loafing around and drinking beer out of paper bags.

Betterton got out of the car and approached them. "Afternoon, all of y'all," he said.

The men fell silent and watched him approach with suspicion.

"Afternoon," one finally replied grudgingly.

"Ned Betterton. *Ezerville Bee*," he said. "Hot day. Anybody care for a cold one?"

An uneasy shifting. "In return for what?"

"What else? I'm a reporter. I want information."

This was greeted by silence.

"Got some frosties in the trunk." Betterton moseyed back to his car—you didn't want to move too fast around people like this—popped the trunk, hauled out a large Styrofoam cooler, lugged it over, and set it down on the stairs. He reached in, pulled one out, popped it open, and took a long pull. Soon a number of hands were reaching in, sliding cans out of the melting ice.

Betterton leaned back with a sigh. "I'm doing a story on the Brodie murders. Any idea who killed them?"

"Might be gators," someone offered, drawing hoots of derisive laughter.

"The *po*lice done asked us about them already," said a skinny man in a tank top, his cheeks sporting about five days' worth of stubble. "We don't know nothing."

"I think that FBI feller killed 'em," one old, almost toothless man slurred, already drunk. "That sumbitch was crazy."

"FBI?" Betterton asked immediately. This was new.

"The one come down here with that New York City policewoman."

"What did they want?" Betterton realized he sounded way too interested. He covered it up by taking another slug of beer.

"Wanted directions to Spanish Island," the toothless man answered.

"Spanish Island?" Betterton had never heard of the place.

"Yeah. Kinda coincidental that…" The voice trailed off.

"Coincidental? What's coincidental?"

A round of uneasy glances. No one said anything. *Holy mackerel*, thought Betterton: his digging had almost reached the mother lode.

"You shut up," the skinny one snapped, glaring at the old drunk.

"Why, hell, Larry, I ain't said nothing."

This was so easy. He could tell right away they were hiding something big. The whole damn brainless group. And he was going to know it in a moment.

At that moment, a large shadow fell over him. A huge man had emerged from the gloom of the unfinished building. His pink head was shaven, and a ring of fat the size of a small life preserver bulged around the rear of his neck, bristling with little blond hairs. One cheek bulged with what appeared to be a cud of chewing tobacco. He folded one hamhock arm over the other and stared, first at the seated group, then at Betterton.

Betterton realized this could only be Tiny himself. The man was a local legend, a bayou warlord. And suddenly he wondered if that mother lode was a little farther off than he'd anticipated.

"Fuck you want?" Tiny asked in a pleasant tone.

Instinctively, Betterton took a stab. "I'm here about the FBI agent."

The look that came over Tiny's face wasn't so pleasant. "Pendergast?"

Pendergast. So that was his name. And it was familiar—wasn't it?—the name of one of those wealthy, decaying antebellum families down New Orleans way.

Tiny's little pig eyes grew smaller still. "You a friend of that peckerwood?"

"I'm with the *Bee*. Looking into the Brodie killings."

"A reporter." Tiny's face grew dark. For the first time, Betterton noticed an inflamed scar on one side of the man's neck. It bulged in time to the pulsing of a vein beneath.

Tiny looked around the group. "What you talking to a reporter for?" He spat out a ropy brown stream of tobacco. The audience stood up, one by one, and several started to shuffle off—but not before scooping out additional beers.

"A reporter," Tiny repeated.

Betterton saw the explosion coming but wasn't quick enough to get away. Tiny lashed out and grabbed Betterton's collar, twisting it roughly. "You can tell that mother for me," he said, "that if I ever catch his skinny, black-suited, albino ass around these parts again, I'm gonna bust him up so bad he'll be shitting teeth for a week."

As he spoke, he twisted Betterton's collar tighter and tighter until the reporter could no longer breathe. Then, with a rough jerk of his arm, he threw Betterton to the ground.

Betterton sprawled in the dust. Waited a moment. Stood up.

Tiny stood there, his hands balled, waiting for a fight.

Betterton was small. When he was young, bigger kids had often felt free to knock him around, figuring the risk was nil. It started in kindergarten and didn't end until his first year of high school.

"Hey," said Betterton, his voice high and whiny. "I'm leaving, I'm leaving! For chrissakes, you don't have to hurt me!"

Tiny relaxed.

Betterton put on his best cowering, cringing face and, scrambling a little closer to Tiny, ducked his head as if to grovel. "I'm not looking for a fight. Really."

"That's what I like to hear—"

Betterton rose abruptly and used his upward momentum to propel an uppercut directly into Tiny's jaw. The man went down like a hopper of soft butter dropped on cement.

The lesson Ned learned as a high-school freshman was that, whoever it was, no matter how big, you responded. Or it would just happen again, and worse. Tiny rolled in the dirt, cursing, but he was too stunned to get up and pursue. Betterton walked quickly to his car, passing the men who were still standing around, their mouths agape.

"Enjoy the rest of the beer, gents."

As he drove off, his hand throbbing, he remembered he was supposed to be covering the Women's Auxiliary Bake-Off in half an hour. Hell with it. No more bake-offs for him.

CHAPTER 32

St. Charles Parish, Louisiana

Dr. PETER LEE BEAUFORT FOLLOWED THE MOBILE forensic lab—painted a discreet gray—as it turned in at the side gate of Saint-Savin Cemetery. A groundskeeper swung the gate shut behind them, locking it securely. The two vehicles, his own station wagon and the mobile lab, moved slowly down the narrow graveled lane, flanked by graceful dogwoods and magnolia trees. Saint-Savin was one of the oldest incorporated cemeteries in Louisiana, its plots and glades impeccably manicured. Over the last two hundred years, some of New Orleans's most illustrious names had been buried here.

They would be most surprised, Beaufort mused, if they knew the nature of the procedure the cemetery was about to host.

The lane forked, then forked again. Now, ahead of the mobile lab, Beaufort could see a small cluster of cars: official vehicles, a vintage Rolls-Royce, a Saint-Savin van. The lab pulled into a narrow shoulder behind them and Beaufort followed suit, glancing at his watch as he did so.

It was ten minutes after six and the sun was just

climbing the horizon, casting a golden hue over the greensward and marble. To ensure maximum privacy, exhumations were always done as early in the morning as possible.

Beaufort got out of the car. As he approached the family plot, he could see workers in protective clothing erecting screens around one of the graves. It was an unusually cool day, even for early November, and for that he was profoundly thankful. Hot-day exhumations were invariably unpleasant.

Considering the wealth and long history of the Pendergast family, the actual plot had very few graves. Beaufort, who had known the family for decades, was well aware that most members had preferred to be buried in the family plot at Penumbra Plantation. But some had a curious aversion to that mist-shrouded, overgrown burial ground—or the vaults beneath—and preferred a more traditional interment.

He stepped around the privacy screens and over the low cast-iron fencing surrounding the plot. Besides the technicians, he saw the gravediggers, Saint-Savin's funeral director, the manager of Saint-Savin, and a portly, nervous-looking fellow whom Beaufort assumed was Jennings, the health officer. At the far end stood Aloysius Pendergast himself, unmoving and silent, black and white, a monochromatic specter. Beaufort looked at him with curiosity. He had not seen the FBI agent since he was a young man. Although his face had changed little, he was gaunter than ever. Over his black suit he wore a long, cream-colored coat that looked like camel's hair, but—given its silky sheen—Beaufort decided was more likely vicuña.

Beaufort had first encountered the Pendergast family as a young pathologist in St. Charles Parish, when he was called to Penumbra Plantation after a serial poisoning by the mad old aunt—what was her name, Cordelia? No, Cornelia. He shuddered at the memory. Aloysius had been a boy then, spending his summers at Penumbra. Despite the awful circumstances of Beaufort's visit, the young Aloysius had latched onto him like a limpet, following him around, fascinated with forensic pathology. For several summers after, he haunted Beaufort's laboratory in the basement of the hospital. The boy was an exceptionally quick study and possessed of a rare and powerful curiosity. *Too* powerful, and disturbingly morbid. Of course, the boy's morbidity had paled in comparison with his brother's . . . But this reflection was too distressing and Beaufort forced it away.

On cue, Pendergast looked up, caught his eye. He came gliding over and took Beaufort's hand. "My dear Beaufort," he said. "Thank you for coming." Pendergast had always had—even as a boy—the habit of calling him by his last name only.

"My pleasure, Aloysius. How good to see you again after all these years—but I'm sorry it had to be under these particular circumstances."

"Yet if it hadn't been for death, we should never have known each other—would we?"

Those penetrating silver eyes turned on him and Beaufort, as he parsed the thought, felt a small shiver travel down his spine. He had never before known Aloysius Pendergast to be tense or agitated. Nevertheless, despite a veneer of calm, the man seemed so today.

The privacy screens were pulled into place around

COLD VENGEANCE   191

the plot, and Beaufort turned his attention to the goings-on. Jennings had been glancing at his watch and plucking at his collar. "Let us begin," he said in a high, nervous voice. "May I have the exhumation license, please?"

Pendergast pulled it from inside his coat and handed it over. The health official glanced at it, nodded, handed it back. "Recall that at all times, our primary responsibility is to protect the public health and to ensure the dignity and respect of the deceased."

He glanced down at the gravestone, which read, simply:

HELEN ESTERHAZY PENDERGAST

"Are we all in agreement on the correctness of the grave?"

There was a general nodding of heads.

Jennings stepped back. "Very well. The exhumation may proceed."

Two gravediggers, wearing gloves and respiratory face masks in addition to their protective clothing, began by cutting a rectangle in the thick green sod and, with expert finesse, neatly detaching and rolling it up in strips, setting them carefully aside. An operator stood by with a tiny cemetery backhoe.

The sod up, the two gravediggers set to work with square-bladed shovels, aiming sharp alternating blows into the black earth, piling it neatly on a plastic sheet laid to one side. The hole took shape, the diggers blading the walls to crisp angles and planes. And then they stepped back while the backhoe inched forward, its miniature bucket plunging into the dark ground.

The backhoe and the two diggers alternated work, the diggers trimming the hole while the bucket took out the dirt. The assembled group watched in almost liturgical silence. As the hole deepened, the air became charged with its scent; loamy and oddly fragrant, like the smell of the deep woods. The open grave smoked faintly in the early-morning air. Jennings, the health officer, dipped a hand into his coat, pulled out a face mask, and put it on.

Beaufort shot a private glance at the FBI agent. He was staring at the deepening hole as if transfixed, an intense expression on his face that was, at least to Beaufort, unreadable. Pendergast had been evasive about why he wanted his wife's body dug up—only that he wanted the mobile forensic van to be prepared for any and all tests of identity. Even for a family as notably eccentric as the Pendergasts, it seemed disturbing and inexplicable.

The digging continued for fifteen minutes, then thirty. The two men in masks and protective clothing stopped for a brief rest, then returned to work. A few minutes later, one of the shovels hit a heavy object with a loud, hollow *thunk*.

The men surrounding the open grave glanced at one another. All except Pendergast, whose eyes remained riveted on the yawning hole at his feet.

More carefully now, the diggers evened out the walls of the grave, then continued down, slowly exposing the standard cement container in which the coffin rested. The backhoe, fitted with straps, lifted the concrete lid, exposing the coffin inside. It was made of mahogany, even blacker than the surrounding soil, trimmed with brass handles, corners, and rails. A new scent was introduced to the already charged atmosphere: a faint odor of decomposition.

Four more men now appeared at the graveside, carrying the "shell"—a new casket to hold both the old casket and its exhumed remains. Placing it on the ground, they stepped forward to help the diggers. As the group watched silently, new webbing was lowered into the grave and slid beneath the coffin. Together— slowly, carefully, by hand—the six men strained to lift the coffin from its resting place.

Beaufort watched. At first, the coffin seemed to resist being disturbed. And then, with a faint groan, it came free and began to rise.

As the witnesses stepped back to give them room, the Saint-Savin workers lifted the coffin out of the grave and placed it on the ground beside the shell. Jennings came forward, pulling on latex gloves. Kneeling at the head of the coffin, he bent forward to inspect the nameplate.

"Helen Esterhazy Pendergast," he read through the mask. "Let the record show the name on the casket conforms with the name on the exhumation license."

Now the shell was opened. Beaufort saw that its interior consisted of a tarred zinc liner, covered with a plastic membrane and sealed with isopon. All standard. At a nod from Jennings—who had backed quickly away—the cemetery workers once again lifted Helen Pendergast's coffin by the webbing, carried it to the open shell, and placed it inside. Pendergast watched as if frozen, his face pale, his eyes hooded. He had not moved a muscle, save to blink, since the exhumation process started.

With the coffin safely inside the shell, the lid was closed and fastened. The cemetery manager came forward with a small brass nameplate. As the workers removed the disposable protective clothing and washed their hands with disinfectant, he hammered the nameplate into the surface of the shell.

Beaufort stirred. It was almost time for his own work to begin. The workers lifted the shell by its railings and he led them to the rear of the mobile forensic lab, parked on the gravel nearby. It sat in the shade of the magnolias, generator rumbling quietly. His assistant opened the rear doors and helped the cemetery workers lift the shell up and slide it inside.

Beaufort waited until the doors were shut again, then he followed the workers back to the screened-off plot. The group was still assembled, and would remain there until the procedure was complete. Some of the workers began filling in the old grave, while others, with the help of the backhoe, began opening a fresh one beside it: when his work on the remains was complete, they would be re-interred in the new grave. Beaufort knew that moving her body—even so slight a distance as this—was the only way Pendergast had been able to get the exhumation approved. And even then he wondered what pressure had been brought to bear on the nervous, sweating Jennings.

At last Pendergast stirred, glancing his way. The anticipation, the tense watchfulness, had deepened in his pale features.

Beaufort came up to him and spoke in a low voice. "We're ready. Now, exactly what tests would you like done?"

The FBI agent looked at him. "DNA, hair samples, fingerprints if possible, dental X-rays. Everything."

Beaufort tried to think of the most tactful way to say it. "It would help if I knew what the purpose of all this was."

A long moment passed before Pendergast replied. "The body in the coffin is not that of my wife."

Beaufort absorbed this. "What leads you to believe there's been a . . . a mistake?"

"Just perform the tests, if you please," said Pendergast quietly. His white hand emerged from under his suit; in it was a hairbrush in a ziplock bag. "You'll need a sample of her DNA."

Beaufort took the bag, wondering at a man who would keep his wife's hairbrush untouched for more than ten years after her death. He cleared his throat. "And if the body is hers?"

When there was no reply to this question, Beaufort asked another. "Would you, ah, care to be present when we open the coffin?"

The agent's haunted eyes seemed to freeze Beaufort. "It's a matter of indifference to me."

He turned back to the grave and said no more.

CHAPTER 33

New York City

THE FOOD LINE AT THE BOWERY STREET MISSION snaked slowly past the front row of refectory-style tables toward the steam trays.

"Shit," said the man directly ahead. "Not chicken and dumplings again."

Distractedly, Esterhazy picked up a tray, helped himself to corn bread, shuffled forward in the line.

He had been staying below the radar. Way below. He'd taken a bus down from Boston and stopped using credit cards and withdrawing cash from ATMs. He went by the name on the false passport and bought a new cell phone under that assumed name. His lodgings were a cheap SRO on Second Street that preferred dealing in cash. Whenever possible he was subsisting on handouts such as this. He had a goodly supply of cash left over from his trip to Scotland, so for the time being money wasn't a concern, but he would need to make it last. Pendergast's resources were frighteningly exhaustive—he wasn't about to take any chances. Besides, he knew *they* would always give him more.

"Goddamn green Jell-O," the man in front of him

continued to complain. He was perhaps forty years old, sported a wispy goatee, and wore a faded lumberjack shirt. His grimy, pale face was seamed with every manner of vice, self-gratification, and corruption. "Why can't we ever get red Jell-O?"

The banality of evil, thought Esterhazy as he slid an entrée onto his plastic tray without even looking at it. This was no way to live. He had to stop running and get back on the offensive. Pendergast had to die. He'd tried to kill Pendergast twice. Third time's the charm, as the saying went.

Everyone has a weak spot. Find his and attack it.

Carrying the tray, he walked over to a nearby table and sat down at the only empty place, next to the goateed man. He lifted his fork, picked absently at the food, put the fork down again.

Now that he thought about it, Esterhazy realized how little he really knew about Pendergast. The man had been married to his sister. And yet, though they'd been on friendly terms, he'd always remained distant, cool, a cipher. He had failed to kill Pendergast partly because he hadn't really understood him. He needed to learn more about the man: his movements, his likes, his dislikes, his attachments. What made him tick, what he cared about.

We'll take good care of you. Just as we always have.

Esterhazy could hardly swallow his food with that phrase echoing in his mind. He put down his fork and turned to the goateed vagrant sitting next to him. He stared at the man until he stopped eating and looked up.

"Got a problem?"

"As a matter of fact, yes." Esterhazy bestowed a friendly smile on the man. "May I ask you a question?"

"What about?" The man was instantly suspicious.

"Someone's pursuing me," said Esterhazy. "Threatening my life. I can't shake him."

"Kill the mother," said the man, resuming slurping up his Jell-O.

"That's just it. I can't get near enough to kill him. What would you do?"

The man's deep-set eyes glittered with malice, and he put down his spoon. This was a problem he understood. "You get to someone close to him. Someone weak. Helpless. A bitch."

"A bitch," Esterhazy repeated.

"Not just any bitch, *his* bitch. You get to a man through his bitch."

"That makes sense."

"No shit it makes sense. I had a beef with this dealer, man, wanted to bust a cap in his ass, but he always had his crew around him. Well, he had this little sister, real juicy…"

The story went on for a long time. But Esterhazy wasn't listening. He had fallen into pensive thought.

His bitch…

CHAPTER 34

Savannah, Georgia

THE ELEGANT TOWN HOUSE DOZED IN THE FRAGRANT cool of a fall evening. Outside, in Habersham Street, and beyond in Whitfield Square, passersby chatted animatedly and tourists snapped pictures of the park's gingerbread cupola and the historic brick structures surrounding it. But within the town house, all was still.

Until, with a faint rustle of metal against metal, the lock turned and the back door was teased open.

Special Agent Pendergast slipped into the kitchen, barely a shadow in the fading light. He closed and locked the door behind him, then turned and leaned against it, listening. The house was vacant, but he paused in the silence anyway. The air smelled stale and the blinds were all drawn. This was a building that had not been entered in some time.

He recalled the last time he had been in this house, several months before, under very different circumstances. Esterhazy had since gone to ground, and done it very well. But there would be traces. Clues. And of any place, this house was the most likely to contain that information—because nobody could disappear without a trace.

Except perhaps Helen.

Pendergast raked the kitchen with his pale eyes. It was almost obsessively neat and, like the rest of the house, decidedly masculine in its choice of furnishings: the heavy oak breakfast table, the oversize slab of butcher block studded with massive knives, the dark cherry cabinets and black granite countertops.

He made his way out of the kitchen, through the hall, and up the stairs to the second floor. The doors off the landing were closed, and he opened each one in turn. One led to an attic staircase, which he climbed to an unfinished, peaked-ceilinged space smelling of mothballs and dust. He pulled a string hanging beside a bare bulb, bathing the room in harsh light. There were a number of boxes and trunks here, neatly arranged against the walls, all locked. In one corner stood a full-length mirror, dull and cobwebbed.

Pendergast withdrew a pearl-handled switchblade from his jacket pocket and flicked it open. Methodically, without hurry, he slit open the boxes and sorted through them, resealing them with fresh packing tape when he was done. The steamer trunks came next: locks picked, searched, and relocked, everything left as before.

As he moved toward the stairs, he paused before the mirror, and then, with the sleeve of his black suit, polished the mirror clean in one area and gazed into it. The face that looked back at him seemed almost alien; he turned away.

Turning off the light, he descended to the second

floor, which consisted of two bathrooms, Esterhazy's bedroom, a study, and a guest bedroom. Pendergast went to the bathrooms first, opening the medicine cabinets and examining the contents. He squirted tubes of toothpaste, cans of shaving cream, and containers of talcum into the toilets to make sure they were genuine and not containers for hiding valuables, returning the flattened and emptied containers to their proper places. The guest bedroom came next. Nothing of interest.

Pendergast's breathing quickened slightly.

He then passed into Esterhazy's own bedroom. It was as meticulously neat as the rest of the house: hardcover novels and biographies were carefully stacked on their shelves, antique Wedgwood and Quimper ceramics arranged in small niches.

Pendergast pulled the covers from the bed and examined the mattress, sliding it off the bed and palpating it, pulling the fabric aside and examining the springs. He felt the pillows and examined the bed frame, and then remade the bed. Opening the clothes closet, he systematically felt through every item of clothing, looking for anything concealed within. He pulled every drawer from the old Duncan Phyfe armoire and examined the contents, no longer being overly careful to replace them in order. He plucked the books off the shelves one at a time, flipped through them, and shoved them back out of order. His movements became more rapid, verging on the brusque.

Next came the study. Pendergast walked over to the lone filing cabinet, jimmied the lock with a savage twist of the switchblade, and opened each drawer, removing the folders inside, examining them closely, and then dropping them back in place. It took almost an hour to go through all the bills, tax forms, correspondence, financial ledgers, and other documents—interesting in the light they threw on Esterhazy but of no obvious significance. Next came the heavy shelves of reference books and medical texts. The contents of the desk followed. A laptop sat atop the desk; taking a screwdriver from his pocket, Pendergast opened its base, plucked out the hard disk, and slipped it into his pocket. The walls were covered with framed commendations and awards; these were removed, their backs inspected, then rehung indifferently.

He paused in the doorway before proceeding downstairs. The contents of the study—and indeed the house—remained more or less neat and regular; no one would know that every millimeter had been invaded, scrutinized, violated . . . except Judson. He would know.

Gliding down the stairs, Pendergast examined the dining room just as thoroughly as he had the upstairs, followed by the den. There he noted a safe in the wall, hidden behind a diploma. This was saved for later exploration. He opened and searched the gun case, finding nothing of note.

He finally moved into the living room, the most exquisite room in the house, with burnished mahogany wainscoting, antique wallpaper, and a number of lovely eighteenth- and nineteenth-century paintings. But the pièce de résistance sat against one wall: a heavy Louis XV breakfront displaying a collection of ancient Greek red-figure pottery.

He searched the room, ending at the breakfront. A quick twist and the lock was broken. He swung open the doors and examined the contents. He had long known of the collection, but once again he was struck by just how extraordinary it was, perhaps the finest small collection of its kind in the world. It consisted of only six pieces, each one a priceless, irreplaceable example of the work of an ancient Greek artist: Exekias; the Brygos Painter; Euphronios; the Meidias Painter; Makron; the Achilles Painter. His eye traveled over the vases, bowls, kylixes, and kraters, each an incomparable masterpiece, a testament to the highest and most rarefied artistic genius. This was not a collection assembled for show or prestige: these pieces had been painstakingly collected at astonishing cost by a person with a faultless eye and a profound appreciation. Only someone who truly and deeply loved the work could have amassed a collection so perfect, the loss of which would impoverish the world.

The sound of ragged breathing gradually filled the room.

With a sudden, violent movement of his arm, Pendergast swept the collection off the shelves, the heavy ceramics tumbling to the oak floor and shattering into hundreds of pieces, the fragments skittering and bouncing everywhere. Gasping with effort, possessed by an explosion of fury, he smashed the pieces underfoot into smaller and smaller ones, eventually grinding them into grit.

And then, except for the sound of heavy breathing, all was silent once more. Pendergast was still weak from his ordeal in Scotland, and it took some time for his breathing to return to normal. After a long while, he brushed some pottery dust off his suit and moved stiffly toward the basement door. Forcing it open, he descended and conducted a careful inspection of the cellar.

It was mostly empty save for a furnace and plumbing. But off in an alcove stood a door that, when forced, revealed a large wine cellar, lined in cork, with temperature and humidity controls mounted on one wall. He stepped inside and examined the bottles. Esterhazy had an exceptional cellar, mostly French, and favoring the Pauillacs. Pendergast ran his eye over the long columns of bottles: Lafite Rothschild, Lynch-Bages, Pichon-Longueville Comtesse de Lalande, Romanée-Conti. He noted that—while his own wine holdings at the Dakota and Penumbra were far more extensive— Esterhazy had a first-class collection of Château Latour, including several bottles from the very greatest vintages that were missing from his own cellars.

Pendergast frowned.

Selecting the best vintages—the 1892, 1923, 1934, the fabled 1945, 1955, 1961, half a dozen others—he pulled them from their niches and placed them carefully on the floor. He chose no wine younger than thirty years. It took four trips to gently carry them all up to the den.

Leaving them on a side table, he fetched a corkscrew, decanter, and oversize wineglass from the kitchen. Back in the den he opened each bottle of wine in turn, letting them air upon the sideboard while he rested from his exertions. It was dark outside now, a pale moon hanging over the palmetto trees of the square. He glanced at the moon for a moment, recalling—almost against his will—that other moon: the first moonrise he and Helen had shared. It had been only two weeks after they'd first met. It was the night on which their love for each other had been so passionately revealed. Fifteen years ago—and yet so vivid was the memory that it could have been yesterday.

Pendergast held the memory briefly, like a precious jewel, then let it fade away. Turning from the window, he let his eye roam around the room, taking in the African sculptures, the beautiful mahogany furniture, the jades, and the bookshelves laden with gold-stamped tomes. He did not know when Esterhazy would return, but he wished he could be there to appreciate the homecoming.

He let the wines rest for half an hour—a longer rest would be risky with the older vintages—and then began his tasting. Starting with the 1892, he poured no more than a mouthful into the decanter and swirled it slowly, examining the color in the light. Then he poured it into the glass, inhaled the aroma, and—eventually—took a generous sip. Placing the bottle on the windowsill, uncorked, he moved on to the next younger.

The entire process took another hour, and by the end his equanimity was fully restored.

At last, he put the decanter and glass aside and rose from the chair. He finally addressed his attention to the small safe he had earlier discovered behind one of the diplomas hanging on the wall. It resisted Pendergast's advances quite valiantly, yielding only after ten minutes of delicate work.

Just as he was opening its door, Pendergast's cell phone rang. He examined the incoming number before answering. "Yes?"

"Aloysius? It's Peter Beaufort. I hope I'm not inter-rupting anything."

A sudden silence, and then Pendergast said, "I was just enjoying a quiet glass of wine."

"The results are in."

"And?"

"I think I'd rather tell you in person."

"I would like to know now."

"I won't tell you over the phone. Get here as quickly as you can."

"I'm in Savannah. I'll catch a late-night flight and meet you in your office tomorrow morning. At nine."

Pendergast returned the phone to his pocket and returned his attention to the safe. It contained the usual items: jewelry, some stock certificates, the deed to the house, a last will and testament, and a variety of miscellaneous papers including what appeared to be some old bills from a nursing home in Camden, Maine, concerning a patient named Emma Grolier. Pendergast swept up the documents and put them in his pocket for later examination. Then he sat down at the roll-top desk, took a sheet of blank linen paper, and wrote a short note.

My dear Judson,

I thought you'd be interested in the results of my vertical wine tasting of your Latours. I found the 1918 sadly faded, and the 1949 was to my mind overrated: it ended worse than it started, with tan-nic overtones. The 1958 was, alas, corked. But the rest were quite delightful. And the '45 was superlative— still rich and surpassingly elegant, with an aroma of currants and mushrooms and a long, sweet finish. Pity you only had a single bottle.

My apologies for what happened to your collection of old pots. I've left you a little something to compensate.

P.

Pendergast placed the letter on top of the desk. Reaching into his pocket, he extracted a five-dollar bill from his wallet and put it alongside.

He had reached the doorway before a thought struck him. Turning back, he walked over to the windowsill and picked up the 1945 bottle of Château Latour. Corking it carefully, he took it with him, making his way from the den to the kitchen and out into the fragrant night air.

CHAPTER 35

Armadillo Crossing, Mississippi

BETTERTON WAS OUT FOR AN EARLY-MORNING cup of coffee when the idea hit him. It was a long shot, but not so much that it wasn't worth a ten-mile detour to check on.

He turned his Nissan around and headed once again in the direction of Malfourche, stopping a few miles short at the sorry-looking fork in the road known locally as Armadillo Crossing. The story was, someone had run over an armadillo here years ago, the smashed carcass remaining long enough to give the fork its name. The only house at the fork consisted of a tar-paper shack, the residence of one Billy B. "Grass" Hopper.

Betterton pulled up in front of the old Hopper place, almost indistinguishable beneath a thick covering of kudzu. His hand was throbbing like a son of a bitch. Grabbing a pack of cigarettes from the glove compartment, he got out of the car and walked toward the porch in the rising light. He could make out Billy B., rocking lazily. Despite the early hour, a Bud was in one gnarled hand. When a hurricane had blown down the sign indicating the Malfourche turnoff some years ago, Billy B., inevitably manning his rocking chair, would almost always be consulted by strangers as to which road led into town.

Betterton mounted the old, creaking steps. "Hiya, Grass," he said.

The man peered at him out of sunken eyes. "Well, Ned. How are you, son?"

"Good, good. Mind if I take a load off?"

Billy B. pointed at the top step. "Suit yourself."

"Thanks." Betterton sat down gingerly, then raised the pack of cigarettes and shook one loose. "Coffin nail?"

Billy B. plucked the cigarette from the pack; Betterton lit it for him, then snugged the pack back into his shirt pocket. He did not smoke himself.

For the next few minutes, as Grass smoked his cigarette, the two chatted idly about local matters. Finally, Betterton worked around to the real purpose of his visit.

"Any strangers been around lately, Grass?" he asked casually.

Billy B. took a last deep drag on the cigarette, plucked it from his mouth, examined the filter, then mashed it out in a nearby kudzu vine. "Couple," he said.

"Yeah? Tell me about them."

"Let's see now." Billy B. screwed his face up in thought. "Jehovah's Witness. Tried to give me one of her little magazines when she asked which way to Malfourche. I told her to take a right."

Betterton forced a chuckle at this misdirection.

"Then there was that foreign fella."

Betterton said, as casually as possible: "A foreign fella?"

"Had an accent."

"What country you suppose he was from?"

"Europe."

"I'll be doggone." Betterton shook his head. "When-abouts was this?"

"I know exactly when it was." The man counted on his fingers. "Eight days ago."

"How can you be so sure?"

Billy B. nodded sagely. "It was the day before they discovered them Brodie folk murdered."

This was more than Betterton had hoped for in his wildest dreams. Was this all there was to being an investigative reporter? "What did the fellow look like?"

"Tall. Skinny. Blond hair, ugly little mole under one eye. He was wearing a fancy raincoat, like you see in those spy movies."

"You remember what kind of car he was driving?"

"Ford Fusion. Dark blue."

Betterton stroked his chin thoughtfully. He knew that Ford Fusions were very commonly used as rental cars. "Did you tell any of this to the police, Grass?"

A truculent look stole over the man's features. "Never asked me."

It was all Betterton could do not to leap off the porch and race to his car. Instead he forced himself to stay, make a little more conversation. "The Brodies," he said. "Bad business."

Billy B. obliged that it was.

"Lot of excitement around these parts recently," Betterton went on. "What with that accident at Tiny's and all."

Billy B. spat thoughtfully into the dirt. "That wasn't no accident."

"What do you mean?"

"That FBI feller. Blew the place up."

"Blew it up?" Betterton repeated.

"Put a bullet in the propane tank. Blew everything to hell. Shotgunned a bunch of boats, too."

"Well, I'll be...Why did he do that?" This was stupendous news.

"Seems Tiny and his pals bothered him and his lady partner."

"They bother lots of folks around here." Betterton thought for a moment. "What did the FBI want down here?"

"No idea. Now you know everything I know." He opened a fresh beer.

The last sentence was the signal that Billy B. was tired of chatting. This time, Betterton stood up.

"Drop by again," Billy B. said.

"I'll do that." Betterton walked down the steps. Then he stopped, reached into his pocket, pulled out the cigarettes.

"Keep the pack," he said. He tossed it gently into Billy B.'s lap and made for his Nissan with as much gravity as he could manage.

He'd driven out on a hunch and now he was returning with a story that *Vanity Fair* or *Rolling Stone* would kill for. A couple who had faked their own deaths—only to be savagely murdered. A blown-up bait shop. A mysterious place known as Spanish Island. A foreign fella. And above all, a crazy FBI agent named Pendergast.

His hand still throbbed, but now he hardly felt it. This was shaping up to be a very good day.

CHAPTER 36

New Orleans, Louisiana

Peter Beaufort's consultation room looked more like a wealthy professor's study than a doctor's office. The bookcases were filled with leather-bound folio volumes. Beautiful landscapes in oils decorated the walls. Every piece of furniture was antique, lovingly polished and maintained: there was no hint of steel or chrome anywhere, let alone linoleum. There were no eye charts, no anatomical engravings, no treatises on medicine, no articulated skeletons hanging from hooks. Dr. Beaufort himself wore a tastefully tailored suit, *sans* lab coat and dangling stethoscope. In dress, manner, and appearance he avoided all suggestion of the medical man.

Pendergast eased himself into the visitor's chair. In his youth he had spent many hours here, peppering the doctor with questions of anatomy and physiology, discussing the mysteries of diagnosis and treatment.

"Beaufort," he said, "thank you for seeing me so early."

The M.E. smiled. "You called me Beaufort as a youth," he replied. "Do you think perhaps you're old enough now to address me as Peter?"

Pendergast inclined his head. The doctor's tone was light, almost courtly. And yet Pendergast knew him well enough to see the man was ill at ease.

A manila folder lay closed on the desktop. Beaufort opened it, put on a pair of eyeglasses, examined the pages within. "Aloysius…" His voice faltered, and he cleared his throat.

"There is no need for tact in this matter," Pendergast said.

"I see." Beaufort hesitated. "I'll be blunt, then. The evidence is incontrovertible. The body in that grave was that of Helen Pendergast."

When Pendergast did not speak, Beaufort went on. "We have matches on multiple levels. For starters, the DNA on the brush matched the DNA of the remains."

"How closely?"

"Beyond any shadow of mathematical doubt. I ordered half a dozen tests on each of four samples from the hairbrush and the remains. But it isn't just the DNA. The dental X-rays matched, as well, showing just the single small cavity in number two—the upper right second molar. Your wife still had beautiful teeth, despite the passage of time…"

"Fingerprints?"

Beaufort cleared his throat again. "With the heat and humidity in this part of the country…well, I was able to recover only a few partial prints, but what I did recover also matches." Beaufort turned a page. "My forensic analysis shows the corpse was definitely partially consumed by a lion. In addition to the, ah, perimortem physical evidence—teeth marks and so forth on the bones—*Leo pantera* DNA was found. Lion."

"You said the fingerprints were only partials. That isn't adequate."

"Aloysius, the DNA evidence is conclusive. The body was that of your wife."

"That cannot be, since Helen is still alive."

A long silence ensued. Beaufort spread his hands in a gesture of futility. "If you don't mind me saying so, this is very unlike you. The science tells us otherwise, and you of all people respect the science."

"The science is wrong." Pendergast put a hand on the arm of the chair, prepared to rise. But then he caught the look on Beaufort's face and paused. It was obvious from the M.E.'s expression that he had more to say.

"Leaving aside that question," Beaufort said, "there's something else you should know. It may be nothing." He tried to make light of it but Pendergast sensed otherwise. "Are you familiar with the science of mitochondrial DNA?"

"In general terms, as a forensic tool."

Beaufort removed his eyeglasses, polished them, put them back on his nose. He seemed oddly embarrassed. "Forgive me if I repeat what you already know, then. Mitochondrial DNA is completely separate from a person's regular DNA. It's a bit of genetic material residing in the mitochondria of every cell in the body, and it is inherited unchanged from generation to generation, through the female line. That means all the descendants—male and female—of a particular woman will have identical mitochondrial DNA, which we call mtDNA. This kind of DNA is extremely useful in forensic work, and separate databases are kept of it."

"What of it?"

"As part of the battery of tests I performed on your wife's remains, I ran both the DNA and mtDNA through a consortium of some thirty-five linked medical databases. In addition to confirming Helen's DNA, there was a hit in one of the ... more unusual databases. Regarding her mtDNA."

Pendergast waited.

Beaufort's embarrassment seemed to deepen. "It was in a database maintained by the DTG."

"The DTG?"

"Doctors' Trial Group."

"The Nazi-hunting organization?"

Beaufort nodded. "Correct. Founded to pursue justice against the Nazi doctors of the Third Reich who aided and abetted the Holocaust. It grew out of the so-called Doctors' Trials at Nuremberg after the war. A lot of doctors escaped Germany after the war and went to South America, and the DTG has been hunting them ever since. Theirs is a scientifically impeccable database of genetic information on those doctors."

When Pendergast spoke again, his voice was very quiet. "What kind of a hit did you find—exactly?"

The M.E. took another sheet from the file. "With a Dr. Wolfgang Faust. Born in Ravensbrück, Germany, in 1908."

"And what, exactly, does this mean?"

Beaufort took a deep breath. "Faust was an SS doctor at Dachau in the last years of World War II. He disappeared after the war. In 1985, the Doctors' Trial Group finally tracked him down. But it was too late to bring him to justice—he'd already died of natural causes in 1978. The DTG found his grave and exhumed his remains to test them. That is how Faust's mtDNA became part of the DTG database."

"Dachau," Pendergast breathed. He fixed Beaufort with his gaze. "And what was the relation between this doctor and Helen?"

"Only that they are both descended from the same female ancestor. It could be one generation back, or a hundred."

"Do you have any more information about this doctor?"

"As you might expect, the DTG is a rather secretive organization connected, so they say, to Mossad. Except for the public database, their files are sealed. The record on Faust is thin and I haven't followed up with any research."

"The implications?"

"Only genealogical research can determine the relationship between Helen and Dr. Faust. Such genealogical research would have to explore your wife's ancestry in the female line—mother, maternal grandmother, maternal great-grandmother, and so forth. And the same for Faust. All this means is that this Nazi doctor and your wife shared a direct female ancestor. It could be some woman who lived in the Middle Ages, for all we know."

Pendergast hesitated for a moment. "Would my wife have known of Faust?"

"Only she could have told you that."

"In that case," Pendergast said, almost to himself, "I shall have to ask her when I see her."

There was a long silence. And then Beaufort spoke.

"Helen is dead. This...quixotic belief of yours concerns me."

Pendergast rose, his face betraying nothing. "Thank you, Beaufort, you've been most helpful."

"Please consider what I just said. Think about your family history..." Beaufort's voice trailed off.

Pendergast managed a cold smile. "Your further assistance is unnecessary. I wish you good day."

CHAPTER 37

New York City

Laura Hayward cut into the rare, juicy meat, separated it from the bone, and placed a forkful in her mouth. She closed her eyes. "Vinnie, it's perfection."

"I just threw it together, but thanks." D'Agosta waved a dismissive hand, but he turned his attention to his own dinner to hide the pleased look he knew was settling over his face.

D'Agosta had always enjoyed cooking, in a casual, nondemanding bachelor way: meat loaf and barbecue and roast chicken, with the occasional Italian specialty of his grandmother's thrown in. But since moving in with Laura Hayward, he'd become a much more serious chef. It had started out as a kind of guilt, a way to offset his living in her apartment while not being allowed to contribute to the rent. Later—when Hayward finally acquiesced about splitting the rent—his interest in cooking continued. Part of it was Hayward herself, no slouch when it came to preparing varied and interesting dishes. And part of it, no doubt, was the influence of Agent Pendergast's unrelievedly gourmet tastes. But another part of it had to do with his relationship with Laura. There was something he found loving about the act and art of cooking, a way for him to express his feelings for her, something more meaningful than flowers or even jewelry. He'd branched out from southern Italy into French cuisine, which had taught him the basic techniques for many noble dishes as well as a fascination for the mother sauces and their countless variations. He'd grown interested in various regional American cuisines. Hayward tended to work longer hours than he did, allowing him time to unwind in the kitchen of an evening, cookbook propped open, working on some new dish, which he would present to her when she arrived, an offering. And the more he did it, the more accomplished he became: his knifework improved; dishes were assembled more quickly and more deftly; he grew increasingly confident in his own variations on master recipes. And so tonight, in which he'd served rack of lamb with a burgundy-pomegranate persillade, he could say, with more than a little truth, that it had been almost effortless.

For a few minutes they ate in silence, enjoying the time together. Then Hayward dabbed at her mouth with her napkin, took a sip of Pellegrino, and spoke with friendly irony. "So: what happened at the office today, dear?"

D'Agosta laughed. "Singleton's launching yet another of his departmental morale campaigns."

Hayward shook her head. "That Singleton. Always with the cop-psychology theory *du jour.*"

D'Agosta took a bite of *épinards à la crème.* "Corrie Swanson stopped by to see me. Again."

"This is the third time she's come to bug you."

"At first she was a pain, but now we've sort of become friends. She keeps asking about Pendergast, what he's up to, when he's coming back."

Hayward frowned. Almost any mention of Pendergast, it seemed, was sufficient to rub her the wrong way, even after their informal partnership earlier that year. "What do you tell her?"

"The truth. That I wish I knew myself."

"You haven't heard anything more from him?"

"Not since that call from Edinburgh. When he said he didn't want my help."

"Pendergast scares me," said Hayward. "You know, he gives the impression of being in icy control. But underneath . . . he's like a maniac."

"A maniac who solves cases."

"Vinnie, a case isn't exactly solved if the suspect ends up dead. When was the last time Pendergast actually took a case to trial? And now this business about his wife being alive—"

D'Agosta laid down his fork, his appetite gone. "I'd rather you didn't talk that way about Pendergast. Even if—"

"Even if I'm right?"

D'Agosta didn't respond. She had touched a nerve; never had he been so worried about his friend.

There was a moment of silence. And then—with some surprise—D'Agosta felt Hayward's hand close over his.

"I love your loyalty," she said. "And your integrity. I want you to know I've come to respect Pendergast more than I used to, even if I abhor his methods. But you know what? He's right to shut you out of this one. That man is poison to a career in law enforcement. *Your* career. So I'm glad you're following his advice and leaving well enough alone." She smiled, squeezed his hand. "Now come and help me wash up."

CHAPTER 38

Fort Meade, Maryland

Aloysius Pendergast strolled into the lobby of an unremarkable building on the campus of the National Security Agency. He checked his weapon and shield with a waiting soldier, walked through a metal detector, stepped up to the reception desk. "The name is Pendergast. I have an appointment to see General Galusha at ten thirty."

"Just a moment." The secretary made a call, then filled out a temporary ID badge. She nodded and another soldier with a sidearm came over.

"Follow me, sir."

Pinning the ID to the breast pocket of his jacket, Pendergast followed the soldier to a bank of elevators, where they descended a number of levels. The doors opened into a bleak maze of cinder-block corridors that eventually brought them to a nondescript door marked only Gen. Galusha.

The guard knocked politely and a voice within said, "Enter."

The guard opened the door and Pendergast went in, the guard closing the door after him, prepared to wait outside until the appointment was over.

Galusha was a neat, soldierly looking man in casual military fatigues, the single black star Velcroed to his chest patch the only evidence of rank. "Please sit down," he said. His demeanor was cool.

Pendergast seated himself.

"I have to tell you up front, Agent Pendergast, that I can't respond to your request until you and your FBI superiors go through the usual channels. And I don't see how, exactly, I could be of help to you in any case."

For a moment, Pendergast did not respond. Then he cleared his throat. "As one of the, ah, gatekeepers of M-LOGOS, you could be a great deal of help to me, General."

Galusha went very still. "And just what do you know of M-LOGOS, Agent Pendergast...assuming such a thing exists?"

"I know quite a bit about it. For example, I know that it is the most powerful computer yet built by humankind—and that it is located in a hardened bunker beneath this building. I know that it is a massively parallel processing system, running a special AI known as StutterLogic, and that it has been designed for a single purpose: to data-mine information on potential threats to national security. The threats could be of any kind: terrorism, industrial espionage, domestic hate group activity, market manipulation, tax evasion, even the emergence of pandemics."

He crossed one leg delicately over the other. "In pursuit of this objective, M-LOGOS maintains a database containing all kinds of information: from cell phone records and e-mails to the tracking of highway tolls, medical and legal records, social networking sites, and university research databases. The database is said to contain names and information on virtually one hundred percent of all individuals within U.S. borders, all cross-referenced and cross-linked. I don't know what the percentage is for individuals outside America, but I think it's safe to say that M-LOGOS possesses all the information that exists in digital form about most human beings in the industrialized world."

Throughout this, the general had remained silent and motionless. Now he spoke. "That was quite a little speech, Agent Pendergast. And just how have you come by such information?"

Pendergast shrugged. "My work at the FBI has taken me into several—shall we say—exotic areas of investigation. But let me answer a question with a question: if Americans had any idea how thorough, comprehensive, and well organized the M-LOGOS database was—and how much information the government possessed on American citizens in good standing—what do you think the response would be?"

"But they won't know, will they? Because such a revelation would be a treasonous act."

Pendergast inclined his head. "I'm not interested in revelations. I'm interested in a single person."

"I see. And I take it that you'd like us to find this individual in the M-LOGOS database."

Pendergast crossed his legs and leveled his gaze at General Galusha. He said nothing.

"Since you know so much, you must also know that access to M-LOGOS is highly restricted. I just can't open it up to any agent who walks in…even one as intrepid as you seem to be."

Still Pendergast did not speak. His sudden silence, after such an extended soliloquy, seemed to irritate Galusha.

"I'm a busy man," he said.

Pendergast recrossed his legs. "General, please confirm that you have the authorization to grant—or not grant—my request without involving others."

"I do, but I'm not going to play games with you. There's no way in hell I'm going to grant such a request."

Again Pendergast let the silence build, until Galusha frowned again. "I don't mean to be rude, but I think we're done here."

"No," said Pendergast simply.

Galusha's eyebrows went up. "No?"

With a smooth motion, Pendergast removed a document from his suit jacket and laid it on the desk.

Galusha looked at it. "What the hell—this is my résumé!"

"Yes. Very impressive."

Galusha stared at him with narrowed eyes.

"General, I can see that you are basically a good officer, loyal to his country, who has served with real distinction. For that reason I truly regret what I am about to do."

"Are you threatening me?"

"I'd like you to answer another question: why did you feel the need to lie?"

A long silence.

"You served in Vietnam. You won a Silver Star, a Bronze Star, and two Purple Hearts. You rose through the ranks by ability alone—nobody helped you. And yet it's all built on a lie, because you never matriculated from the University of Texas as you state on your résumé. You don't have a college degree. You dropped out the last semester of your senior year. Which means you weren't eligible for OCS. Astonishing that no one checked this before. How did you do it? Get into OCS, I mean."

Galusha rose, his face almost purple. "You're a low-life bastard."

"I'm not a bastard. But I am an exceedingly desperate man who will do anything to get what he wants."

"And what is it you want?"

"I fear to ask. Because now, having met you, I sense you are a man with enough integrity to resist succumbing to the blackmail scheme I had in mind. I believe you will probably go down in flames rather than provide me access to that database."

A long silence. "You're damn right about that."

Pendergast could see that Galusha was already mastering himself, adjusting to the awful news, steeling himself for what was to come. It was his bad luck to find a man like Galusha in this position.

"Very well. But before I leave, I'm going to tell you why I'm here. Ten years ago, my wife died most horribly. Or so I thought. But now I've learned she is alive. I have no idea why she hasn't revealed herself to me. Perhaps she's being coerced, held against her will. Perhaps she is otherwise kept in thrall. Whatever the case, I *must* find her. And M-LOGOS is the best way."

"Do your worst, Mr. Pendergast, but I will never give you access to that database."

"I'm not asking you to. I'm asking you to check it yourself. If you find her, just let me know. That's all.

I want no confidential information. Just a name and location."

"Or you will expose me."

"Or I will expose you."

"I won't do it."

"Consider this decision with great care, General. I've already researched the probable outcome: you will lose your position, be busted down a grade, and very likely discharged. Your distinguished military career will be reduced to a lie. Your honorable career will become an uncomfortable subject in your family, never to be discussed. You will return to civilian life too late for any real redemption or second career, and many of the avenues open to retired army officers will now be closed to you. You will be forever defined by that lie. It's terribly unfair: we're all liars, and you're a far better man than most. The world is an ugly place. Long ago I stopped struggling against that fact and accepted I was part of that ugliness. It made everything so much easier. If you don't do what I ask, which will harm no one and will help another human being, you will quickly discover just how ugly the world can be."

Galusha stared at Pendergast, and there was so much sadness and self-reproach in those eyes the agent almost winced. Here was a man who had already seen a great deal of life's underbelly.

When the general spoke again, his voice was barely a whisper. "I'll need your wife's personal information to conduct the search."

"I've brought a wealth of information." Pendergast removed a folder from his jacket. "In here you will find DNA data, handwriting samples, medical history,

dental X-rays, distinguishing marks, physical characteristics, and more. She's alive somewhere in the world—
please find her for me."

Galusha reached out to the file, as if it were something loathsome, but he could not quite bring himself to take it. The hand remained poised in midair,
trembling.

"I have an incentive for you, as well," Pendergast
went on. "A certain acquaintance of mine possesses
unusual computer skills. He will adjust the files at the
University of Texas to give you that BA, cum laude,
which you would have been awarded had your father
not died, forcing you to drop out in your last semester."

Galusha bowed his head. Finally his veined hand
grasped the file.

"How long?" Pendergast said, his voice almost a
whisper.

"Four hours, maybe less. Wait here. Speak to no
one. I'll handle this myself."

Three and a half hours later the general returned. His
face was gray, collapsed. He laid the file on the table
and took a seat, the chair scraping slowly, moving like
an old man. Pendergast remained very still, watching
him.

"Your wife is dead," said Galusha wearily. "She must
be. Because all trace of her vanished ten years ago.
After..." He raised his tired eyes to Pendergast. "After
she was killed by that lion in Africa."

"It's not possible."

"I'm afraid it's not only possible but almost inevitable. Unless she's living in North Korea or certain

parts of Africa, Papua New Guinea, or one of a very few other highly isolated places in the world. I know all about her now—and about you, Dr. Pendergast. All records pertaining to her, all threads, all lines of evidence, come to an end in Africa. She is dead."

"You're mistaken."

"M-LOGOS doesn't make mistakes." Galusha pushed the folder back at Pendergast. "I know you well enough now to be confident you'll keep your end of the bargain." He took a deep breath. "So the only thing left to say is good-bye."

CHAPTER 39

Black Brake swamp, Louisiana

NED BETTERTON TOOK THE HANDKERCHIEF from his pocket and wiped his forehead for what seemed the hundredth time. He was wearing a loose T-shirt and Bermuda shorts, but he hadn't expected the swamp air to be this suffocating so late in the year. And the tight gauze bandage around his bruised knuckles felt as hot as a damn rotisserie chicken.

Hiram—the old, almost toothless man he'd spoken to on the front stoop of Tiny's—was at the wheel of the battered airboat, a shapeless cap pulled down around his ears. He leaned over the gunwale, spat a brown rope of tobacco-laced saliva into the water, then straightened again and returned his gaze to the narrow logging channel that led ahead into a green fastness.

An hour of research in the records office at the county seat was all it had taken for Betterton to discover that Spanish Island was a former fishing and hunting camp deep in Black Brake swamp—owned by June Brodie's family. Upon learning this, he immediately turned his attention to tracking down Hiram. It had taken a great deal of wheedling and cajoling to convince the old geezer to take him out to Spanish Island. Ultimately a hundred-dollar bill and the brandishing of a quart bottle of Old Grand-Dad had done the trick—but even then, Hiram insisted on their meeting up at the far northwestern corner of Lake End, away from the prying eyes of Tiny and the rest of the crowd.

When they first started out, Hiram had been morose, nervous, and uncommunicative. The journalist had known better than to force the man to speak. Instead he'd left the Old Grand-Dad within easy reach, and now—two hours and many pulls later—Hiram's tongue had begun to loosen.

"How much farther?" Betterton asked, once again plying the handkerchief.

"Fifteen minutes," Hiram said, sending another thoughtful jet of saliva over the side. "Maybe twenty. We're getting into the thick stuff now."

He's not kidding, Betterton thought. The cypress trees were closing in on either side, and overhead the braided green and brown of jungle-like vegetation blotted out the sun. The air was so thick and humid, it felt as if they were underwater. Birds and insects chattered and droned, and now and then there was a heavy splash as a gator slid into the water.

"You think that FBI man actually made it as far as Spanish Island?" Betterton asked.

"Don't know," Hiram replied. "He didn't say."

Betterton had spent a most entertaining couple of days looking into Pendergast's background. It hadn't been easy, and he could just as well have spent a whole week at it. Maybe even a month. The man was in fact one of the New Orleans Pendergasts, a strange old family of French and English ancestry. The word *eccentric* didn't even begin to describe them—they were scientists, explorers, medical quacks, hucksters, magicians, con men...and killers. Yes, killers. A great-aunt had poisoned her entire family and been shut up in an insane asylum. An uncle several times great had been a famous magician and Houdini's teacher. Pendergast himself had a brother, who had apparently vanished in Italy, about whom there were many strange rumors but few answers.

But it was the fire that intrigued Betterton most of all. When Pendergast was a child, a mob in New Orleans had burned down the family mansion on Dauphine Street. The ensuing investigation had not been able to clarify exactly why. Although nobody admitted to being part of the mob, various people questioned by police gave different and conflicting reasons as to why the mansion was torched: that the family was practicing voodoo; that the son had been killing local pets; that the family was plotting to poison the water supply. But when Betterton had sorted through all the conflicting information, he sensed something else behind the mob action: a carefully crafted and highly subtle disinformation campaign by a person or persons unknown, aimed at destroying the Pendergast family.

It appeared the family had a powerful, hidden enemy...

The airboat bumped over a particularly shallow mud bank, and Hiram gunned the engine. Ahead, the vegetation-choked channel forked. Hiram slowed to a virtual standstill. To Betterton, the two channels looked identical: dark and gloomy, with vines and cypress branches hanging down like smokehouse sausages. Hiram rubbed his chin quizzically, then glanced upward as if to get a celestial fix from the braided ceiling overhead.

"We're not lost, are we?" Betterton asked. He realized that trusting himself to this aged rummy might not have been a prudent move. If anything happened way out here, he'd be dead meat. There was not a chance in hell of his finding his way out of this swampy labyrinth.

"Naw," Hiram said. He took another pull at the bottle and abruptly gunned the airboat into the left-hand passage.

The channel narrowed still further, choked with duckweed and water hyacinth. The hooting and chattering of invisible creatures grew louder. They maneuvered around an ancient cypress stump, sticking up out of the muck like a broken statue. Hiram slowed again to negotiate a sharp bend in the channel, peering through a thick curtain of hanging moss that blocked the view ahead.

"Should be right up yonder," he said.

Goosing the engine gently, he carefully nosed the airboat through the dark, slime-choked passage. Betterton ducked as they pushed through the curtain of moss, then rose again, peering intently ahead. The ferns and tall grasses appeared to be giving way to a gloomy clearing. Betterton stared—then abruptly drew in his breath.

The swamp opened into a small, roughly circular stand of muddy ground, ringed by ancient cypresses. The entire open region was scorched, as if it had been

234 DOUGLAS PRESTON & LINCOLN CHILD

bombed with napalm. The remains of dozens of fat creosote pilings rose, burnt and blackened, thrusting toward the sky like teeth. Charred pieces of wood lay strewn everywhere, along with twisted bits of metal and debris. A damp, acrid, burnt odor hung over the place like a fog.

"This is Spanish Island?" Betterton asked in disbelief.

"What's left of it, I reckon," Hiram replied.

The airboat moved forward into a slackwater bayou, sliding up onto a muddy shore, and Betterton stepped out. He walked forward gingerly over the rise of land, pushing debris around with his foot. The rubble was spread out over at least an acre, and it contained a riot of things: metal desktops, bedsprings, cutlery, the burned-out remains of sofas, antlers, melted glass, the spines of books, and—to his vast surprise—the blackened remains of machines of unknown function, smashed and twisted. He knelt before one, picked it up. Despite the intense heat it had been subjected to, he could tell it was a metering device of some kind: brushed metal, with a needle gauge measuring something in milliliters. In one corner was a small, stamped logo: PRECISION MEDICAL EQUIPMENT, FALL RIVER, MASS.

What the hell had happened here?

He heard Hiram's voice from over his shoulder, high-pitched, tense. "Mebbe we should be getting back."

Suddenly Betterton became aware of the silence. Unlike the rest of the bayou, here the birds and insects had fallen still. There was something awful about the listening quiet. He stared down again at the confusion of debris, at the strange burnt pieces of metal, at the twisted equipment of unknown function. This place felt dead.

Worse than that—it felt haunted.

All at once Betterton realized that he wanted nothing more than to get away from this creepy place. He turned and began picking his way back to the boat. Hiram, apparently possessed by the same thought, was already halfway there. They gunned out of the slackwater bayou, heading back through the narrow, twisting channels that led to Lake End.

Once—just once—Betterton glanced over his shoulder into the dense green fastness behind him, shadow-woven, mysterious, braided around and above by tree limbs and kudzu vines. What secrets it held—what dreadful event had transpired at Spanish Island—he couldn't say. But he was sure of one thing. One way or another, this shady bastard Pendergast was at the center of everything.

CHAPTER 40

River Pointe, Ohio

IN THE MIDDLE-CLASS CLEVELAND SUBURB, the bell in the tower of St. Paul's Episcopal Church tolled midnight. The wide streets were drowsy and quiet. Dead leaves skittered in the gutters, rustled along by a gentle night breeze, and somewhere in the distance a dog barked.

Only a single second-story window was illuminated in the white clapboard house that stood on the corner of Church Street and Sycamore Terrace. Beyond the window—locked, nailed shut, and covered by two layers of heavy curtain—lay a room whose every corner was stuffed full of instrumentation. One floor-to-ceiling rack held tier-one, high-density blade servers; numerous layer-three, forty-eight-port gigabit Ethernet switches; and several NAS devices configured as RAID-2 arrays. Another rack held passive and active monitoring devices, packet sniffers, police and civilian scanner-interceptors. Every horizontal surface was littered with keyboards, wireless signal boosters, digital infrared thermometers, network testers, Molex extractors. An ancient modem with an acoustic coupler sat on a high shelf, apparently still in use. The air was heavy with the smell of dust and menthol. The only light came from LCD screens and countless front-panel displays.

In the middle of the room sat a shrunken figure in a wheelchair. He was dressed in faded pajamas and a terry-cloth bathrobe. He moved slowly from terminal to terminal, checking readouts, peering at lines of cryptic code, occasionally firing off a machine-gun-like series of typed commands on one of the wireless keyboards. One of the man's hands was withered, the fingers malformed and shrunken, yet he typed with amazing facility.

Suddenly he paused. A yellow light had appeared on a small device situated over the central monitor.

The figure quickly rolled himself to the main terminal and typed in a volley of commands. Instantly the monitor dissolved into a chessboard-like grid of black-and-white images: incoming feeds from two dozen security cameras placed in and around the perimeter of the house.

He quickly scanned the various camera feeds. Nothing.

Panic—which had flared up in an instant—ebbed again. His security was first-rate and doubly redundant: if there had been a breach, he would have been alerted by half a dozen movement sensors and proximity triggers. It had to be a glitch, nothing more. He'd run a diagnostic in the morning—this was one subsystem that could not be allowed to...

Suddenly a red light winked on beside the yellow one, and a low alarm began to bleat.

Fear and disbelief washed over him like a tidal wave.

A full-scale breach, with hardly any warning? It was impossible, unthinkable...The withered hand reached toward a small metal box fixed to one arm of his wheelchair, flicked away the safety toggle covering the kill switch. One crooked finger hovered over the switch. When it was pressed, several things would happen very quickly: 911 calls would go out to police, fire officials, and emergency paramedic units; sodium vapor lights would come on throughout the house and grounds; alarms in the attic and basement would emit earsplitting shrieks; magnetic media degaussers placed strategically throughout the room would generate targeted magnetic fields for fifteen seconds, wiping all data from the hard disks; and finally, an EMP shock pulse generator would fire, completely disrupting all the microprocessor circuitry and electronics in the second-floor room.

The finger settled onto the button.

"Good evening, Mime," came the unmistakable voice from the darkness of the hallway.

The finger jerked away. "Pendergast?"

The special agent nodded and stepped into the room.

For a moment, the man in the wheelchair was nonplussed. "How did you get in here? My security system is state-of-the-art."

"Indeed it is. After all, I paid for its design and installation."

The man wrapped the bathrobe more closely around his narrow frame. His composure was quick to return. "We had a rule. We were never to meet face-to-face again."

"I'm aware of that. And I deeply regret having to break it. But I have a request to make—and I felt that, by making it in person, you would better understand its urgency."

A cynical smile slowly broke over Mime's pale features. "I see. The Secret Agent Man has a request. Another request, I should say, of the long-suffering Mime."

"Our relationship has always proceeded on a—how shall I put it?—symbiotic basis. After all, wasn't it only a few months back that I arranged for a dedicated fiber-optic line to be installed here?"

"Yes, indeedy. Allowing one to bask in three hundred Mbps goodness. No more purloined sips from the T-3 soda straw for me."

"And I was instrumental in having those troublesome charges against you dropped. You'll recall, the ones from the Department of Defense alleging—"

"Okay, Secret Agent Man, I haven't forgotten. So: what can I do for you this fine evening? Mime's Cyber-Emporium is open for all your hacking needs. No firewall too thick, no encryption algorithm too strong."

"I need information on a certain person. Ideally, her whereabouts. But anything will do: medical files, legal issues, movement. Starting from the time of her presumed death and going forward."

Mime's sunken, strangely child-like visage perked up at this. "Her presumed death?"

"Yes. I am convinced the woman is alive. However, there is a one hundred percent certainty she is using an assumed name."

"But you know her real name, I assume?"

Pendergast did not answer for a moment. "Helen Esterhazy Pendergast."

"Helen Esterhazy Pendergast." Mime's expression grew more interested still. "Well, dust my broom." He thought for a moment. "Naturally, I'll need as much personal data as you can provide if I'm to fashion a sufficiently girthy search avatar of your...of your..."

"Wife." And Pendergast passed over a thick folder.

Mime reached for it eagerly, turned over the pages with his withered hand. "It would appear you've been holding out on me," he said.

Pendergast did not reply directly. Instead, he said, "Searches through official channels have turned up nothing."

"Ah. So M-LOGOS came up dry, did it?" When Pendergast did not answer, Mime chuckled. "And now Secret Agent Man wants me to try it from the other side of the cyber-street. Lift up the virtual carpet and check what's beneath. Probe the seamy underbelly of the information superhighway."

"An unfortunate mix of metaphors, but yes, that is the general idea."

"Well, this may take a while. Sorry there isn't a chair—feel free to bring one in from the next room. Just don't turn on any lights, please." Mime gestured toward a large insulated food container that sat in one corner. "Twinkie?"

"Thank you, no."

"Suit yourself."

For the next ninety minutes, not a single word was spoken. Pendergast sat in a darkened corner, motionless as a Buddha, while Mime wheeled himself from terminal to terminal, sometimes typing in a rapid-fire volley of commands, other times poring over lengthy readouts scrolling down one of the innumerable LCD monitors. As the minutes slowly passed, the figure in the wheelchair grew more sunken and discomposed. Sighs grew more frequent. Now and then, a hand slapped against a keyboard in irritation.

Finally, Mime wheeled back from the central terminal in disgust. "Sorry, Agent Pendergast," he said in a tone that sounded almost contrite.

Pendergast glanced toward the hacker, but Mime was facing the other way, his back to the agent. "Nothing?"

"Oh, there's a great deal—but all before that trip to Africa. Her work at Doctors With Wings, school records, medical evaluations, SAT scores, books borrowed from a dozen different libraries...even a poem she wrote in college while babysitting some kid."

"'To a Child, Upon Losing His First Tooth,'" Pendergast murmured.

"That's the one. But after the lion attack—zip." Mime hesitated. "And that usually means only one thing."

"Yes, Mime," Pendergast said. "Thank you." He thought for a moment. "You mentioned school records and medical evaluations. Did you come across anything unusual—anything at all? Something that perhaps struck you as strange or out of place?"

"No. She was the picture of health. But then, you must have known that. And she seems to have been a good student. Decent grades in high school, excellent grades in college. Did well as far back as elementary school, in fact—which is surprising, considering."

"Considering what?"

"Well, that she spoke no English."

Pendergast rose slowly out of his chair. "What?"

"You didn't know? It's right here." Mime wheeled himself back to the keyboard, typed rapidly. An image came onto the screen: a transcript of some kind, typed on a manual typewriter, with handwritten notations at the bottom.

"The Maine Department of Education digitized all its old records a few years back," Mime explained. "See the notation here, attached to Helen Esterhazy's second-grade report card." He leaned toward the screen, quoted: " 'Considering that Helen immigrated to the United States in the middle of last year as a native Portuguese speaker with no English, her progress at school, and her growing command of the language, have been impressive.' "

Pendergast came forward, glanced at the scanned image himself, a look of pure astonishment on his face. Then he straightened up, mastering the expression. "Just one other thing."

"What is it, Secret Agent Man?"

"I'd like you to access the University of Texas database and make a correction to their records. One Frederick Galusha is reported as having left college his senior year, before graduation. The records should show that he graduated, cum laude."

"Piece of cake. But why cum laude? I'll make him summa cum laude, Phi Beta Kappa, for just a dollar more."

"Cum laude will be sufficient." Pendergast inclined his head. "And make sure he gets all the course credits he needs to make his record consistent. I'll see myself out."

"Righteous. Remember: no more surprise visits. And please don't forget to reset anything you may have disabled on your way in."

As Pendergast turned to go, the figure calling himself Mime spoke again. "Hey, Pendergast?"

The agent glanced back.

"Just one thing. Esterhazy is a Hungarian name."

"Indeed."

He scratched his neck. "So how come her native language was Portuguese?"

But when he looked up he was speaking to an empty doorway. Pendergast had already vanished.

CHAPTER 41

New York City

As Judson Esterhazy stepped out of the taxi, he glanced up at the oppressive stone canyons of Lower Manhattan before retrieving his leather briefcase and paying the cabbie. He walked across the narrow sidewalk, smoothing his tie, his step measured and confident, and disappeared into the low-ceilinged lobby of the New York City Department of Health.

It felt good to be wearing a suit again, even if he was still deep undercover. And it felt even better to be on the offensive, to be doing something other than just running. The fear and uncertainty that had been eating away at him were almost gone, replaced—after an initial period of knee-jerk panic—with a clear and decisive plan. One that would solve his Pendergast problem once and for all. But just as important, his plan satisfied *them. They* were going to help him. Finally.

You get to a man through his bitch.

Excellent advice, if rather crudely expressed. And finding the "bitch" had been easier than Esterhazy had hoped. The next challenge was to find a way to access said bitch.

Walking over to the building's directory, he noted that the Division of Mental Hygiene was located on the seventh floor. He stepped up to a bank of elevators, entered a waiting car, and pressed the button marked "7." The doors slid shut and he began to ascend.

His knowledge of medical databases had proven invaluable. In the end, it had taken only a few hits to get the information he needed, and from that to form the plan of attack. The first hit had been an involuntary commitment proceeding in which Pendergast had been called as an interested person but—perversely—elected not to appear. The second had been a paper by one Dr. Felder, not yet published but submitted to the medical community for peer review, about a most interesting case, temporarily incarcerated in the Bedford Hills Correctional Facility for Women but due for transfer to Mount Mercy Hospital. While the identity of the patient had of course been withheld, given the commitment proceedings it was a trivial matter to determine her identity.

Exiting the elevator, Esterhazy asked directions to the office of Dr. John Felder. The psychiatrist was at work in his neat and diminutive office, and he rose as Esterhazy entered. He was as small as his office, neatly dressed, with short mouse-colored hair and a trim Van Dyke beard.

"Dr. Poole?" he said, extending his hand.

"Dr. Felder," Esterhazy said, shaking the proffered hand. "A pleasure."

"The pleasure is mine," said Felder, waving his guest to an empty chair. "To meet someone with prior experience treating Constance is an unexpected boon to my work."

To my work. It was exactly as Esterhazy had figured. He glanced around the impersonal office, at the textbooks and studiously neutral paintings. From his own observations, it was clear that being a court-appointed psychiatrist must be a pretty thankless job. Half the patients one saw were run-of-the-mill sociopaths; the other half were faking symptoms in order to beat a rap. Esterhazy had gotten a strong whiff of Felder's aspirations just by reading the peer-review version of his paper: here was a case one could sink one's teeth into, perhaps even make one's career on. He was clearly a trusting fellow, eager, open, and, like many intelligent people, a bit naive. A perfect mark.

Even so, he had to plot his course with care. Any hint of his own true ignorance of the patient and the case would immediately arouse suspicion. The trick would be to twist that ignorance to his own advantage.

He waved a hand. "Hers is a unique presentation, at least in my experience. I was delighted to see your paper, because not only is this an interesting case, but I think it could be an important one. Perhaps even a benchmark. Although I myself have no interest in publication—my interests lie elsewhere."

Felder simply nodded his understanding, yet Esterhazy saw a brief glimmer of relief in the psychiatrist's eyes. It was important Felder realize his guest was no threat to his ambitions.

"How many times have you spoken with Constance?" Esterhazy asked.

"I've had four consultations so far."

"And has she manifested amnesia yet?"

Felder frowned. "No. Not at all."

"It was the part of her treatment that I found most challenging. I would complete a session with her, feeling that I had made progress in addressing some of her more dangerous delusions. But when I returned for the next session, I found that she retained absolutely no memory of the previous visit. Indeed, she claimed not to remember me at all."

Felder tented his fingers. "How odd. In my experience, her memory has been excellent."

"Interesting. The amnesia is both dissociative and lacunar."

Felder began taking notes.

"What I find most interesting is that there are strong indications that this may be a rare case of dissociative fugue."

"Which might explain, for example, the ocean voyage?" Felder was still writing.

"Exactly—as well as the inexplicable outburst of violence. Which is why, Dr. Felder, I termed this case unique. I think we have a chance—*you* have a chance—to substantially advance medical knowledge here."

Felder scribbled faster.

Esterhazy shifted in his chair. "I often wondered if her, ah, unusual personal relationships might have been a factor in her disorder."

"You mean, her guardian? This fellow Pendergast?"

"Well..." Esterhazy seemed to hesitate. "It is true that *guardian* is the term Pendergast uses. However—speaking as one doctor to another, you understand—the relationship has been a great deal more intimate than that term would suggest. Which may explain why

Pendergast—or so I understand—declined to show up at her competency hearing."

Dr. Felder stopped scribbling and looked up. Esterhazy nodded, slowly and significantly.

"That is very interesting," Felder said. "She denies it quite specifically."

"Naturally," Esterhazy replied in a low voice.

"You know—" Felder stopped a moment, as if considering something. "If there was some severe emotional trauma, sexual coercion or even abuse, it might not only explain that fugue state, but her strange ideas about her past."

"Strange ideas about the past?" Esterhazy said. "That must be a new development."

"Constance has been insisting to me that—well, not to put too fine a point to it, Dr. Poole—that she is roughly one hundred and forty years old."

It was all Esterhazy could do to keep a straight face. "Indeed?" he managed.

Felder nodded. "She maintains she was born in the 1870s. That she grew up on Water Street, just blocks from where we are now. That both her parents died when she was young and she lived for years and years in a mansion owned by a man named Leng."

Esterhazy quickly followed up this line. "That could be the other side of the coin of her dissociative amnesia and fugue state."

"The thing of it is, her knowledge of the past—at least the period in which she maintains she grew up—is remarkably vivid. And accurate."

What utter rubbish. "Constance is an unusually intelligent—if troubled—person."

Felder looked thoughtfully at his notes for a moment. Then he glanced at Esterhazy. "Doctor, could I ask you a favor?"

"Of course."

"Would you consider consulting with me on the case?"

"I would be delighted."

"I would welcome a second opinion. Your past experience with the patient and your observations would no doubt prove invaluable."

Esterhazy felt a shiver of joy. "I'm only in New York a week or two, up at Columbia—but I would be happy to lend what assistance I can."

For the first time, Dr. Felder smiled.

"Given the lacunar amnesia I mentioned," Esterhazy said, "it would be better to introduce me to her as if we have not met before. Then we can observe her response. It will be interesting to see if the amnesia has persisted through her fugue state."

"Interesting indeed."

"I understand she's currently in residence at Mount Mercy?"

"That is correct."

"And I assume you can arrange to get me the necessary consulting status there?"

"I believe so. Of course, I'll need your CV, institutional affiliation, the usual paperwork..." And here Felder's voice trailed off in embarrassment.

"Certainly! As it happens, I believe I have all the necessary paperwork here. I brought it along for the staff at Columbia." Opening his briefcase, he extracted a folder containing a beautifully forged set of accreditations and documents, compliments of the Covenant. There was indeed a real Dr. Poole in case Felder did a brief check, but given his trusting nature he didn't seem the type to make calls. "And here's a short breakdown— a brief summary—of my own work with Constance." He extracted a second folder, whose contents were designed more to whet Felder's curiosity than to provide any real information.

"Thank you." Felder opened the first folder, scanned through it quickly, then closed it and handed it back. As Esterhazy had hoped, this step had been merely a formality. "I should be able to give you an update by tomorrow."

"Here's my cell number." And Esterhazy passed a card across the table.

Felder slipped it into his jacket pocket. "I can't tell you how pleased I am, Dr. Poole, to have gained your assistance in this matter."

"Believe me, Doctor, the pleasure is all mine." And—rising—Esterhazy shook hands warmly with Felder, smiled into the earnest face, and showed himself out.

CHAPTER 42

Penumbra Plantation, St. Charles Parish

"WELCOME HOME, MR. PENDERGAST," SAID MAURICE, as if Pendergast had only been away a few minutes instead of two months, when he opened the front door. "Will you be wanting supper, sir?"

Pendergast entered the house, Maurice shutting the door against the chill fog of the winter air. "No, thank you. But a glass of amontillado in the second-floor parlor would be lovely, if you don't mind."

"The fire is laid."

"Marvelous." Pendergast climbed the stairs to the parlor, where a small fire blazed on the hearth, banishing the habitual dampness of the house. He took a seat in a wing chair beside it, and a moment later Maurice came in carrying a silver tray, with a small glass of sherry balanced on it.

"Thank you, Maurice."

As the white-haired servant turned to leave, Pendergast said, "I know you've been worried about me."

Maurice paused but did not respond.

"When I first discovered the circumstances of my wife's death," Pendergast continued, "I was not myself. I imagine you must have been alarmed."

"I was concerned," said Maurice.

"Thank you. I know you were. But I'm my own man once again, and there's no need to monitor my comings or goings or mention them to my brother-in-law..." He paused. "You were in contact with Judson about my situation, I assume?"

Maurice colored. "He is a doctor, sir, and he asked me to help, specifically with regard to your movements. He was fearful that you might do something rash. I thought, given the family history..." His voice trailed off.

"Quite so, quite so. However, it turns out that Judson may not have had my best interests in mind. We've had a bit of a falling-out, I'm afraid. And as I mentioned, I'm quite recovered. So you see there is no reason to share anything further with him."

"Of course. I hope my confidences to Dr. Esterhazy did not cause you any inconvenience?"

"None at all."

"Will there be anything else?"

"No, thank you. Good night, Maurice."

"Good night, sir."

One hour later, Pendergast sat motionless in a small space that had once been his mother's dressing room. The door was closed and locked. The heavy, old-fashioned furniture had been removed and replaced with a single wing chair, a mahogany table set before it. The elegant William Morris wallpaper had been stripped away and dark blue soundproofing installed in its place. There was nothing in the room to distract or to arouse interest. The only illumination in the windowless space came from a single beeswax taper placed on the small table, which cast a flickering light over the patternless walls. It was the most private and insular room in the mansion.

In the perfect silence, Pendergast turned his gaze to the candle flame, slowing both his respiration and pulse with great deliberation. Through the esoteric meditative discipline of Chongg Ran, which he had studied in the Himalayas many years before, he was preparing to enter the heightened mental state of *stong pa nyid*. Pendergast had combined this ancient Buddhist practice with the idea of the memory palace contained in Giordano Bruno's *Ars Memoria* to create his own unique form of mental concentration.

He stared at the flame and—slowly, very slowly—let his gaze pierce its flickering heart. As he sat, motionless, he allowed his consciousness to enter into the flame, to be consumed by it, to join with it first as an organic whole, and then—as the minutes passed—at an even more fundamental level, until it was as if the very molecules of his sentient being mingled with those of the flame.

The flickering heat grew to fill his mind's eye with endless, unquenchable fire. And then—quite suddenly—it winked out. Unrelieved blackness took its place.

Pendergast waited, in perfect equanimity, for his memory palace—the storehouse of knowledge and recollection to which he could retreat when in need of guidance—to appear. But the familiar marble walls did not rise up from the blackness. Instead, Pendergast found himself in a dim, closet-like area with a ceiling that sloped low over his head. Before him stood a latticed doorway looking out onto a service hallway; behind him was a wall covered with Rube Goldberg–

like diagrams and treasure maps, scrawled by youthful hands.

This was the hideout known as Plato's Cave, under the back stairs of the old house on Dauphine Street, where he and his brother, Diogenes, had gone to hatch childish schemes and plots...before the Event that sundered their comradeship forever.

This was the second time a memory crossing of Pendergast's had taken an unexpected turn to this place. With a sudden apprehension, he peered into the dark space at the rear of Plato's Cave. Sure enough: there was his brother, aged about nine or ten, wearing the navy blazer and shorts that were the uniform of Lusher, the school they attended. He was browsing through a book of Caravaggio's paintings. He glanced up at Pendergast, gave a sardonic smile, and returned to the book.

"It's you again," Diogenes said, the boy strangely speaking in the adult's voice. "Just in time. Maurice just saw a rabid dog running down the street near the Le Prêtres' house. Let's see if we can't goad it into entering the Convent of St. Maria, shall we? It's just noon, they're probably all assembled at mass."

When Pendergast did not reply, Diogenes turned over a page. "This is one of my favorites," he said. "*The Beheading of St. John the Baptist*. Notice how the woman on the left is lowering the basket to receive the head. How accommodating! And the nobleman standing over John, directing the proceedings—such an air of calm command! That's just how I want to look when I..." He abruptly fell silent and turned another page.

Still Pendergast did not speak.

"Let me guess," said Diogenes. "This has to do with your dear departed wife."

Pendergast nodded.

"I saw her once, you know," Diogenes continued, not looking up from the book. "You two were in the gazebo in the back garden, playing backgammon. I was watching from behind the wisteria bushes. Priapus in the shrubbery, and all that sort of thing. It was an idyllic scene. She had such poise, such elegance of movement. She reminded me of the Madonna in Murillo's *Immaculate Conception.*" He paused. "So you think she's still alive, *frater*?"

Pendergast spoke for the first time. "Judson told me so, and he had no motive to lie."

Diogenes did not look up from the book. "Motive? That's easy. He wanted to inflict the maximum amount of pain at the moment of your death. You have that effect on people." He turned another page. "I suppose you dug her up?"

"Yes."

"And?"

"The DNA matched."

"And yet you still think she's alive?" Another snicker.

"The dental records also matched."

"Was the corpse also missing a hand?"

A long pause. "Yes. But the fingerprint evidence was inconclusive."

"The body must've been in quite a state. How terrible for you to have that image lodged in your mind— your *last* image of her. Have you found the birth certificate yet?"

Pendergast paused, struck by the question. Now

that the subject came up, he did not recall ever having seen her birth certificate. It hadn't seemed important. He had always assumed she had been born in Maine, but that was now clearly a lie.

Diogenes tapped an image on the page: *Crucifixion of Saint Peter*. "I wonder how being hung upside down on a cross affects the continuity of one's thought processes." He looked up. "*Frater.* You're the one who was—not to put too fine a point on it—in possession of her loins. You were her soul mate, were you not?"

"I thought so."

"Well, sift your feelings. What do they tell you?"

"That she's alive."

Diogenes broke into a peal of laughter, his pink boyish mouth thrown back and open, the laugh grotesquely adult. Pendergast waited for it to subside. Finally Diogenes stopped, smoothed his hair, and laid the book aside. "This is so rich. Like the coming in of a foul tide, those bad old Pendergastian genes are finally rising to the fore in you. You now have a crazy obsession of your very own. Congratulations and welcome to the family!"

"It isn't an obsession if it's the truth."

"Oh, ho!"

"You're dead. What do you know?"

"Am I really dead? *Et in Arcadia ego!* The day will come when we shall, all of us Pendergasts, join hands in a great family reunion in the lowest circle of hell. What a party that will be! Ha ha ha—!"

With a sudden, violent burst of will, Pendergast sundered the memory crossing. Once again he was back in the old dressing room, sitting in the leather wing chair, with only the flickering candle for company.

CHAPTER 43

RETURNING TO THE SECOND-FLOOR PARLOR, Pendergast sipped his sherry in thoughtful silence. Although he'd told Maurice he was quite recovered, it was at heart a lie—and in no way was this clearer than in the oversight he now realized he had made.

In his earlier searches of Helen's papers, he had neglected to note the one important document that was missing: her birth certificate. He had everything else. The news that she had entered the second grade speaking only Portuguese had been so astonishing that he had completely failed to consider the vexing question it raised about her birth certificate—or lack thereof. She must have hidden it in a place that was accessible and yet secure. Which suggested it was still somewhere in the last house she'd inhabited.

He took another sip of sherry, pausing to examine its rich amber color. Penumbra was a large, rambling mansion, and there would be an almost limitless number of places to hide a single piece of paper. Helen was clever. He would have to think it out.

Slowly, he began eliminating potential hiding places.

It had to be in an area she spent time in, so that her presence there would not be considered unusual. A place she felt comfortable. A place where she would not be disturbed. And it would have to be in some corner, or within some piece of furniture, that would never be moved, emptied, dusted out, aired, or searched by someone else.

He remained in the parlor for several hours, deep in thought, mentally searching every room and corner of the mansion. Then—once he had definitively narrowed his search to a single room—he silently rose and descended the stairs to the library. He stood at its threshold, eyes traveling across the room, taking in the trophy heads, the great refectory table, the bookshelves and objets d'art, considering—then rejecting—dozens of possible hiding places in turn.

After thirty more minutes of thought, he had narrowed his mental search to a single piece of furniture.

The massive armoire that held the Audubon double elephant folio—Helen's favorite book—stood against the left-hand wall. He entered the library, shut the sliding doors, and walked over to the armoire. After staring at it for some time, he slid open the bottom drawer that held the two massive books of the folio. He carried each book to the refectory table in the middle of the room and laid them carefully side by side. Then he went back to the armoire, took the drawer all the way out, and turned it over.

Nothing.

Pendergast allowed himself the faintest of smiles. There were only two logical hiding places within the armoire. The first had been empty. That meant the birth certificate would definitely be hidden in the other.

He reached inside the empty space where the drawer had been and felt around, running his hand along the bottom of the shelf above, his fingers brushing against the wood in the very back of the deep armoire.

Again, nothing.

Pendergast jerked back from the armoire as if he had been burned. He stood up, staring at it. One hand rose to his lips, the tips of his fingers trembling slightly. Then—after a long moment—he turned away and glanced around the library with an unreadable expression.

Maurice was a habitual early riser. It was always his practice to be out of bed no later than six, tidying up, inspecting the grounds, preparing breakfast. But this morning he stayed in bed until well after eight.

He had hardly slept a wink. Maurice had heard, as he lay in bed, Pendergast making muffled sounds all night: traipsing up and down the stairs, moving things about, dropping things on the floor, shuffling items from one spot to another. He had listened, with mounting concern, while the bumping, scraping, thumping, dragging, and slamming had gone on and on, from attic to parlor to morning room to back bedrooms to basement, hour after hour. And now, although the sun was fully up and morning well under way, Maurice was almost afraid to leave his room and face the house. The mansion must be in a dreadful state of disarray.

Nevertheless, it could not be put off forever. And so, with a sigh, he pushed back the bedcovers and pulled himself up to a sitting position.

He rose and went softly to the door. The house was

intensely quiet. He put his hand on the knob, turned. The door creaked open. Gingerly—with mounting trepidation—he leaned his head out past the door frame.

The hallway was spotless.

Quietly, Maurice padded from one room to the next. Everything was in its place; Penumbra was in perfect order. And Pendergast was nowhere to be found.

CHAPTER 44

*Thirty-five thousand feet
over West Virginia*

"ANOTHER TOMATO JUICE, SIR?"

"No, thank you. There will be nothing else."

"Very good." And the cabin steward continued making her way down the plane's central aisle.

In the first-class compartment, Pendergast examined the yellowing document he had—after hours of exhaustive and exhausting search—finally retrieved from the queerest place: rolled up inside an old rifle barrel, proving once again how little he really knew his wife. His eye traveled once again down the document.

República Federativa do Brasil
Registro Civil Das Pessoas Naturais

Certidão de Nascimento

Nome
   Helen von Fuchs Esterházy

Local de Nacimento: Nova Godói, RIO GRANDE do SUL
   Filiação Pai: András Ferenc Esterházy
   Filiação Mãi: Leni Faust Schmid

Helen had been born in Brazil—in a place called Nova Godói. Nova Godói—*Nova G*. He recalled the name from the burnt scrap of paper he and Laura Hayward had come across in the ruins of the Longitude pharmacology laboratory.

Mime had said Helen's native language was Portuguese. Now it made sense.

Brazil. Pendergast thought for a moment. Helen had spent almost five months in Brazil before they were married, on a mission with Doctors With Wings. Or at least that was what she had said at the time. As he'd learned the hard way, no assumption about Helen was safe.

He glanced again at the birth certificate. At the very bottom was a box labeled OBSERVAÇÕES/AVERBAÇÕES—observations/annotations. He looked at it closely, and then removed a small magnifying glass from his pocket to examine it further.

Whatever had been in this box had not merely been blacked out: the paper itself had been excised and painstakingly replaced with an unmarked piece of paper with the same engraved background pattern, microscopically stitched together with the utmost craft. It was an exceedingly professional piece of work.

He finally accepted, at that moment, that he truly had not known his beloved wife. Like so many other fallible human beings, he had been blinded by love. He had not even begun to crack the ultimate mystery of her identity.

With care bordering on reverence, he refolded the birth certificate and placed it deep in a suit pocket.

CHAPTER 45

New York City

DR. JOHN FELDER SLOWLY CLIMBED THE STAIRS of the Forty-Second Street branch of the New York Public Library. It was late afternoon, and the broad steps were busy with students and camera-wielding tourists. Felder ignored them, passing between the marble lions that guarded the Beaux-Arts façade and pushing his way into the echoing entrance hall.

For years, Felder had used this main branch of the library as a kind of retreat. He loved the way it mixed a sense of elegance and wealth with scholarly research. He'd grown up bookish and poor, the son of a dry-goods salesman and a public-school teacher, and this had always been his haven away from the commotion of Jewel Avenue. Even now, with all the research materials available to him at the Department of Health, he nevertheless found himself returning to the library again and again. Just entering its book-perfumed confines was a comforting act, leaving the squalid world behind for a better place.

Except for today. Today felt different, somehow.

He climbed the two flights of stairs to the Main

Reading Room and made the long walk past dozens of long oaken tables to a far corner. Setting his case down on the scarred wooden surface, he pulled a nearby keyboard to him, then paused.

It had been half a year, roughly, since he'd first become involved with the case of Constance Greene. Originally it had been routine: another court-appointed interview with a criminal psychiatric patient. But it had quickly become more than that. She had been like no other patient he'd encountered. He'd found himself mystified, perplexed, intrigued—and aroused.

Aroused. Yes, that too. He'd finally come to admit it to himself. But it wasn't just her beauty—it was also her strange otherworldliness. There was something unique about Constance Greene, something that went beyond her evident madness. And it was this something that drove Felder on, that pushed him to understand her. In a way he did not quite understand, Felder felt a deep-seated need to help her, to *cure* her. This need was only sharpened by her apparent lack of interest in receiving help.

And it was into this strange tinderbox of emotion that Dr. Ernest Poole had just intruded. Felder was aware his feelings about Poole were mixed. He felt a certain proprietary interest in Constance, and the idea that another psychiatrist had previously studied her was oddly annoying. Yet Poole's own experience with Constance—quite unlike his own, apparently—promised perhaps the best chance yet of penetrating her mysteries. The fact that Poole's clinical evaluations were so different was both perplexing and encouraging. It could offer a uniquely three-dimensional vantage onto what would be—he felt increasingly certain—the case study of his career.

He put his fingers on the keyboard and paused again. *I was indeed born on Water Street in the '70s—the 1870s.* Funny: Constance's intensity of belief, coupled with her photographic, as-yet-unexplained knowledge of the old neighborhood, almost had him believing she was, in fact, a hundred and forty years old. But Poole's talk of her lacunar amnesia, her dissociative fugue, had brought him back to reality. Still, he felt he owed Constance enough benefit of doubt to undertake one final search.

Typing quickly, he brought up the library's database of periodicals. He would make one last search, this time of the *nineteen* seventies and later—the time frame during which Constance could reasonably be expected to have been born.

He moved the cursor down to the "search parameters" field, then paused, consulting his notes. *When my parents and sister died, I was orphaned and homeless. Mr. Pendergast's house at Eight Ninety-one Riverside Drive was then owned by a man named Leng. Eventually it became vacant. I lived there.*

He would search for three items: Greene, Water Street, and Leng. But he knew from past experience he'd better keep the terms of the search vague— scanned newspapers were notorious for typos. So he'd create a regular expression, using a logical AND query.

Typing once again, he entered the SQL-like search conditions:

```
SELECT WHERE (match) = = 'Green*' && 'Wat* St*' && 'Leng*'
```

Almost immediately, he got a response. There was a single hit: a three-year-old article in *The New York Times*

of all places. Another quick tapping of keys brought
it to the screen. He began reading—then caught his
breath in disbelief.

Newly-Discovered Letter Sheds Light on
19th-Century Killings

By WILLIAM SMITHBACK JR.

NEW YORK—October 8. A letter has been
found in the archives of the New York Museum of
Natural History that may help explain the grisly
charnel discovered in lower Manhattan early last
week.

In that discovery, workmen constructing a
residential tower at the corner of Henry and
Catherine Streets unearthed a basement tunnel
containing the remains of thirty-six young men
and women. Preliminary forensic analysis showed
that the victims had been dissected, or perhaps
autopsied, and subsequently dismembered. Preliminary dating of the site by an archaeologist,
Nora Kelly, of the New York Museum of Natural
History, indicated that the killings had occurred
between 1872 and 1881, when the corner was
occupied by a three-story building housing a private museum known as "J. C. Shottum's Cabinet of Natural Productions and Curiosities." The
cabinet burned in 1881, and Shottum died in the
fire.

In subsequent research, Dr. Kelly discovered
the letter, which was written by J. C. Shottum
himself. Written shortly before Shottum's death,

it describes his uncovering of the medical experiments of his lodger, a taxonomist and chemist by the name of Enoch Leng. In the letter, Shottum alleged that Leng was conducting surgical experiments on human subjects, in an attempt to prolong his own life.

The human remains were removed to the Medical Examiner's office and have been unavailable for examination. The basement tunnel was subsequently destroyed by Moegen-Fairhaven, Inc., the developer of the tower, during normal construction activities.

One article of clothing was preserved from the site, a dress, which was brought to the Museum for examination by Dr. Kelly. Sewn into the dress, Dr. Kelly found a piece of paper, possibly a note of self-identification, written by a young woman who apparently believed she had only a short time to live: "I am Mary Greene, agt [sic] 19 years, No. 16 Watter [sic] Street." Tests indicated the note had been written in human blood.

The Federal Bureau of Investigation has taken an interest in the case. Special Agent Pendergast, from the New Orleans office, has been observed on the scene. Neither the New York nor the New Orleans FBI offices would comment.

No. 16 Watter Street. Mary Greene had misspelled the street name—that was why he'd missed it before.

Felder read it once, then again, and then a third time. Then he sat back very slowly, gripping the arms of the chair so tightly that his knuckles hurt.

CHAPTER 46

NINE STORIES, AND EXACTLY ONE HUNDRED AND SIXTY FEET, below Dr. Felder's table in the Main Reading Room, Special Agent Aloysius Pendergast was listening intently to the ancient bibliophile researcher known as Wren. If Wren had a first name, nobody—including Pendergast—knew what it was. Wren's entire history—where he lived, where he'd come from, what exactly he did every night and most days in the deepest sublevels of the library—was a mystery. Years without sunlight had faded his skin to the color of parchment, and he smelled faintly of dust and binding paste. His hair stuck out from his head in a halo of white, and his eyes were as black and bright as a bird's. But for all his eccentric appearance, he had two assets Pendergast prized above all others: a unique gift for research, and a profound knowledge of the New York Public Library's seemingly inexhaustible holdings.

Now, perched upon a huge stack of papers like a scrawny Buddha, he spoke quickly and animatedly, punctuating his speech with sudden, sharp gestures. "I've traced her lineage," he was saying. "Traced it very carefully, *hypocrite lecteur*. And it was quite a job, too—the family seems to have been at pains to keep details of their bloodline private. Thank God for the Heiligenstadt Aggregation."

"The Heiligenstadt Aggregation?" Pendergast repeated.

Wren gave a short nod. "It's a world genealogy collection, given to the library in the early 1980s by a rather eccentric genealogist based in Heiligenstadt, Germany. The library didn't really want it, but when the collector also donated millions to, ah, 'endow' the collection, they accepted it. Needless to say it was immediately stuffed away in a deep, dark corner to languish. But you know me and deep, dark corners." He cackled and gave an affectionate pat to a four-foot stack of lined computer printouts sitting next to him. "It's especially comprehensive when it comes to German, Austrian, and Estonian families—which helped tremendously."

"Very interesting," Pendergast said with ill-concealed impatience. "Perhaps you will enlighten me as to your discoveries?"

"Of course. But—" and here the little man paused—"I'm afraid you're not going to like what I have to tell you."

Pendergast's eyes narrowed ever so slightly. "My preferences are irrelevant. Details, please."

"Certainly, certainly!" Wren, clearly having a marvelous time, rubbed his hands together. "One lives for details!" He gave the tower of computer printouts another fatherly pat. "Wolfgang Faust's mother was Helen's great-grandmother. The lineage goes like this. Helen's mother, Leni, married András Esterházy, who as it happens was also a doctor. Both Helen's parents have been dead for some time." He hesitated. "Did you know, by the way, that Esterhazy is a very ancient and noble Hungarian name? During the reign of the Habsburgs—"

"Shall we leave the Habsburgs for another time?"

"Very well." Wren began ticking off details on his long, yellow fingernails. "Helen's grandmother was Mathilde Schmid née von Fuchs. Wolfgang Faust was Mathilde's sister. The relative they shared was Helen's great-grandmother, Klara von Fuchs. Note the matrilineal succession."

"Go on," Pendergast said.

Wren spread his hands. "In other words, Dr. Wolfgang Faust, war criminal, SS doctor at Dachau, Nazi fugitive in South America...was your wife's great-uncle."

Pendergast did not appear to react.

"I've drawn up a little family tree."

Pendergast took the piece of paper, covered with scribbles, and folded it into his suit jacket without glancing at it.

"You know, Aloysius..." Wren's voice petered off.

"Yes?"

"Just this once, I almost wish that my research had been a failure."

CHAPTER 47

Coral Creek, Mississippi

NED BETTERTON PULLED INTO THE PARKING LOT of YouSave Rent-A-Car and sprang out of the driver's seat. He walked briskly toward the building, a broad smile on his face. For the last couple of days, fresh revelations had been practically tumbling into his lap. And one of those revelations was this: Ned Betterton was a damn good reporter. His years of covering Rotary luncheons, church socials, PTA meetings, funerals, and Memorial Day parades had been better training than two years at Columbia J School. Amazing. Kranston had started to scream bloody murder about the time he was spending on the story, but he'd temporarily shut the old man up by taking a vacation. There was nothing Kranston could do about it. The old bastard should have hired a second reporter years ago. It was his own fault if he was left covering everything himself.

He grasped the handle of the glass door, pulled it open. Now it was time to play another hunch—and see if his luck was still holding.

Inside, at one of the two red counters, Hugh Fourier

was just finishing up with a late-afternoon customer. Betterton had shared a dorm room with Fourier during their sophomore year at Jackson State, and now Fourier ran the only rent-a-car place within seventy miles of Malfourche—another nice coincidence that convinced Betterton he was still on a roll.

He waited as Fourier handed a set of keys and a folded sheaf of papers to the customer, then stepped up to the desk.

"Hiya, Ned!" Fourier said, the professional smile morphing into a far more genuine one as he recognized his old roommate. "How's tricks?"

"Getting on," Betterton said, shaking the proffered hand.

"Any breaking stories you'd care to share? A scoop on the spelling bee at the middle school, maybe?" Fourier chuckled at his own witticism.

Betterton laughed gamely. "How are things in the rental car game?"

"Busy. Really busy. And with Carol out sick today, I've been running around like a one-legged man at an ass-kicking contest."

Betterton forced himself to laugh at that one, too, remembering Hugh considered himself the class cut-up. He wasn't surprised to hear YouSave had been busy— with Gulfport-Biloxi International undergoing some major renovations, business at the local airport had picked up considerably.

"See any of the old crowd from Jackson?" Fourier asked as he stacked and squared a pile of paperwork.

They chatted about old times for a few minutes before Betterton got around to business. "Hey, Hugh," he said, bending forward over the counter. "I wonder if you could do me a favor."

"Sure. What do you want? I can get you a great weekly rate on a convertible." Fourier chuckled again.

"I was curious whether a certain individual might have rented a car from you."

Fourier's smile faded. "A certain individual? Why do you want to know?"

"I'm a reporter."

"Jesus, this isn't for a story, is it? Since when did you start doing hard news?"

Betterton shrugged as nonchalantly as he could. "It's just something I'm following up."

"You know I can't give you information about our clients."

"I'm not looking for a lot of information." Betterton leaned still closer. "Listen. I'll describe the guy. Tell you what he was driving. All I want to know is his name and where he flew in from."

Fourier frowned.

"I don't know about this . . ."

"I swear I'll keep you and YouSave out of the story completely."

"Man, this is asking a lot. Confidentiality is really big in our business—"

"The guy was foreign. Speaks with some kind of European accent. Tall, thin. He had a mole below one eye. Wore an expensive raincoat or trench coat. He'd have rented a dark blue Ford Fusion—probably on October twenty-eighth."

A look crossed Fourier's face, and Betterton immediately knew he'd struck gold. "You remember him. Right?"

"Ned—"

"Come on, Hugh."

"I can't."

"Look, you can see how much I know about the guy already. I just need this little bit more from you. Please."

Fourier hesitated. Then he sighed. "Yeah. I remember him. Just as you describe. A heavy accent, German."

"And this was the twenty-eighth?"

"Guess so. It was a week or two back."

"Can you check?" Betterton hoped that, if he could get Fourier to enter the information into his terminal, he might sneak a glance at the results.

But Fourier didn't bite. "No, I can't."

Oh, well. "And a name?"

Fourier hesitated again. "It was...Falkoner. Conrad Falkoner, I think. No—Klaus Falkoner."

"And where was he coming from?"

"Miami. Dixie Airlines."

"How do you know? Did you see the ticket?"

"We ask the customers to give us their arrival flight, so in the case of a delay we can hold the reservation."

Fourier's face had closed down and Betterton knew he'd get nothing more. "Okay, thanks, Hugh. I owe you one."

"Yes, you do." As another customer came in, Fourier turned away with evident relief.

Sitting in his Nissan in the YouSave parking lot, Betterton fired up his laptop, ensured his wireless connection was good, and then made a quick canvass of the Dixie Airlines website. He noticed they had only two flights into the local airport each day, one from Miami and another from New York. They arrived within an hour of each other.

He was wearing a fancy raincoat, like you see in those spy movies. That's what Billy B. had said.

Another quick check of the web informed him that October 28 had been a hot and sunny day in Miami. In New York, however, it had been cold with heavy rain.

So the man—Betterton was almost convinced he was the killer—had lied about where he'd come from. Not surprising. Of course, it was possible he'd lied about the airline as well, maybe given a phony name. But that seemed to be carrying paranoia too far.

Thoughtfully, he shut down his laptop. Falkoner had come from New York and Pendergast was living in New York. Were they in league? Pendergast sure as hell wasn't in Malfourche on official business, not with blowing up a bar and sinking a bunch of boats on his agenda. And this NYPD captain... New York City cops had a reputation for corruption and for being involved in the drug trade. He started to see the big picture: the Mississippi River, the burned-out lab in the swamp, the New York connection, the brutal and execution-style killing of the Brodies, corrupt law enforcement...

Damn if this wasn't about a major drug operation.

That did it: he was going to New York. He plucked his cell phone from his pocket, dialed.

"*Ezerville Bee*," came a shrill voice. "Janine speaking."

"Janine, it's Ned."

"Ned! How's the vacation going?"

"Educational, thanks."

"Are you going to be back at work tomorrow? Mr.

Kranston needs somebody to cover the rib-eating contest over at the—"

"Sorry, Janine, I'm going to extend my vacation by a couple of days."

A pause. "Well, when are you coming back?"

"Not sure. Maybe three days, maybe four. I'll let you know. I still have a week coming to me."

"Yeah, but I'm not sure Mr. Kranston sees it that way..." Her voice trailed off.

"See you." Betterton snapped the phone shut before she could say anything more.

CHAPTER 48

New York City

JUDSON ESTERHAZY—IN HIS ROLE AS DR. ERNEST POOLE—walked briskly down the corridor of Mount Mercy Hospital, Felder at his side. They were following a Dr. Ostrom, director of the hospital, who seemed polite, discreet, and extremely professional: excellent qualities for a man in his position.

"I believe you shall find this morning's consultation to be most interesting," Esterhazy told Ostrom. "As I've explained to Dr. Felder, the chances of her manifesting selective amnesia regarding any knowledge of me are high."

"I am eager to witness it," Ostrom said.

"And you've told her nothing about me, or prepared her in any way for this visit?"

"She's been told nothing."

"Excellent. We should probably keep the actual visit quite short: whatever she does or does not profess to know, the emotional strain will—though most likely unconscious in origin—no doubt be significant."

"A wise precaution," Felder agreed.

They turned a corner, waited for an orderly to

unlock a metal door. "She will almost certainly appear uncomfortable in my presence," Esterhazy went on. "This of course involves her own discomfort with her suppressed memories involving my earlier treatment."

Ostrom nodded.

"One last thing. At the close of the visit, I would appreciate a minute alone with her."

Ostrom slowed, glanced quizzically over his shoulder.

"I'm curious to learn whether her behavior, once you are out of the room, changes in any way, or if she will maintain the illusion of nonrecognition."

"I see no problem with that," Ostrom said. He stopped before a door—marked like the others only with a number—then knocked lightly.

"You may enter," came the voice from within.

Ostrom unlocked the door, then ushered Felder and Esterhazy into a small windowless room. The only furniture was a bed, table, bookcase, and single plastic chair. A young woman sat at the chair, reading a book. She gazed up as the three entered.

Esterhazy looked at her curiously. He had wondered what Pendergast's ward would look like—and was now well rewarded for his curiosity. Constance Greene was very—in fact extremely—attractive: thin and petite, with short dark mahogany hair and perfect porcelain skin and violet eyes that were alert and wise but oddly unfathomable. She looked from one man to the next. When she reached Esterhazy, she paused, but her expression did not change.

Esterhazy was not worried she might recognize him as Pendergast's brother-in-law. Pendergast was not the kind of man to keep family portraits around the house.

"Dr. Ostrom," she said, putting down her book and standing politely. Esterhazy noticed she had been reading Sartre's *Being and Nothingness*. "And Dr. Felder, how delightful to see you again."

Esterhazy was intrigued. Her movements, her pattern of speech, her very being seemed to echo an earlier, more dignified era. She could almost have been inviting them in for cucumber sandwiches and rose hip tea. She did not look at all like a crazed baby-killer locked in a mental ward.

"Please sit down, Constance," Dr. Ostrom said. "We'll only stay for a minute. Dr. Poole here happened to be in town and we thought you might like to see him."

"Dr. Poole," Constance repeated as she took her seat. She looked again at Esterhazy, a hint of curiosity kindling in her strange distant eyes.

"That's correct," said Felder.

"You have no recollection of me?" Esterhazy said, modulating his tone to one of benevolent concern.

Constance frowned slightly. "I've never had the pleasure of making your acquaintance, sir."

"Never, Constance?" Now Esterhazy added the faintest trace of disappointment and pity to his voice.

She shook her head.

Through the corner of his eye, Esterhazy noticed Ostrom and Felder exchange a brief, significant glance. It was working out just as he'd hoped.

Constance looked at him rather more searchingly. Then she turned toward Ostrom. "What gave you the impression that I would like to see this gentleman?"

Ostrom colored slightly, nodded to Esterhazy.

"You see, Constance," Esterhazy said, "I treated you once, years ago, at your, ah, guardian's request."

"You're lying," Constance said sharply, rising again. She turned to Ostrom once more, confusion and alarm now becoming evident in her expression. "Dr. Ostrom, I've never seen this man before in my life. And I would very much like you to remove him from the room."

"I'm very sorry for the confusion, Constance." Ostrom looked quizzically at Esterhazy. In return, Esterhazy indicated with a slight gesture that it was time to leave.

"We'll be going now, Constance," Felder added. "Dr. Poole has asked for a moment of your time alone. We'll be right outside."

"But—" Constance began, then fell silent. She shot a glance toward Esterhazy. He was momentarily taken aback by the hostility that freighted her gaze.

"Please be quick, Doctor," Ostrom said as he unlocked and opened the door. He slipped outside, followed by Felder. The door closed again.

Esterhazy took a step back from Constance, dropped his hands to his sides, and adopted as nonthreatening a stance as possible. There was something about this girl that set off warning bells in his head. He would have to be careful—consummately careful.

"You're right, Miss Greene," he said, his voice low. "You've never met me before in your life. I've never treated you. That was all a deception."

Constance just stared at him from behind the desk, suspicion radiating from her in tangible waves.

"My name is Judson Esterhazy. I'm Aloysius's brother-in-law."

"I don't believe you," Constance said. "He never mentioned your name." Her voice was low and utterly neutral.

"That's just like him, isn't it? Listen, Constance. Helen Esterhazy was my sister. Her death in the jaws of that lion was probably the worst thing that ever happened to him—except maybe the deaths of his parents in the New Orleans fire. You surely know him well enough to know he is not one to speak of his past—especially a painful one like this. But he asked me to help—because I'm the only one he can really trust."

Constance said nothing, merely staring at him from behind the desk.

"If you doubt me, here's my passport." He removed it, opened it for her. "Esterhazy's not a common name. I knew Great-Aunt Cornelia, the poisoner, who lived in this very room. I've been to the family plantation, Penumbra. I've gone shooting in Scotland with Aloysius. What more proof do you need?"

"Why are you here?"

"Aloysius sent me here to help get you out of this place."

"That makes no sense. He arranged for me to be here, and he knows I'm perfectly content."

"You don't understand. He didn't send me here to help you—he sent me here because *he* needs *your* help."

"My help?" Constance said.

Esterhazy nodded. "You see, he has made a terrible discovery. It seems his wife—my sister—didn't die accidentally."

Constance frowned.

Esterhazy knew that his best hope lay in keeping as

close to the truth as possible. "Helen's gun was loaded with blanks on the day of that lion hunt. And now Pendergast has embarked on a mission to find whoever was responsible. Only events have spiraled out of control. He can't do this alone. He needs the help of those he trusts the most. That means me—and you."

"What about Lieutenant D'Agosta?"

"The lieutenant was helping him. And got shot in the heart for his trouble. Not dead—but badly injured."

Constance started visibly.

"That's right. I told you events have spiraled out of control. Pendergast is in over his head, he's in terrible danger. So I took the only steps I could to contact you. I pretended to have knowledge of you and...your case. Obviously it was all a ruse."

Constance continued to stare at him. The hostility had largely disappeared, but uncertainty remained.

"I'm going to figure out a way to get you out of here. Meanwhile, please continue to deny knowing me. Or you could feign a growing recollection—whatever you feel more comfortable with. Just play along. All I ask is that you help me get you out of here. Because we're almost out of time. Pendergast needs your quick mind, your instincts, your research skills. And every hour counts. You can't imagine—and I haven't the time at present to explain—the forces that are now arrayed against him."

Constance continued staring, her face a mixture of suspicion, concern, and indecision. Better to leave her now, let her mull it all over. Esterhazy turned and rapped lightly on the door. "Dr. Ostrom? Dr. Felder? We can go now."

CHAPTER 49

Myrtle Beach, South Carolina

THE EIGHTEENTH HOLE AT PALMETTO SPRAY GOLF LINKS was one of the most infamous on the East Coast: a par-5 five-hundred-and-sixty-yard drive with a wicked dogleg and half a dozen wide bunkers tightly bracketing the fairway.

Meier Weiss rolled his wheelchair up to the tee, plucked the blanket from his ruined legs, grabbed the crutches that hung from his golf bag, and hoisted himself up to a standing position, locking the joints on his leg braces. "Mind if I give some more advice?"

Aloysius Pendergast slid his borrowed golf bag to the ground. "If you'd be so kind."

"It's a long hole, but we've got the wind to our backs. I usually try for a controlled fade. With luck, it puts you on the right of the fairway and sets you up for the green in two."

"I am, alas, a skeptic when it comes to the concept of 'luck.'"

The old man rubbed his sunburned forehead and chuckled. "I always like to play a round before getting down to any kind of business. Tells me all I need to know about my partner. Now, I've noticed improvement on your last few holes. Just remember to follow through on your swing, like I showed you."

Grabbing his driver, Weiss stumped over to the tee. Bracing himself on the crutches, he drew the club back, then swung it down in a perfect arc. The ball shot into the air with a *crack*, curving gracefully to the right and out of sight beyond the fringe of trees.

Pendergast watched, then turned to Weiss. "No 'luck' in that shot."

Weiss slapped the crutches and braces. "I've had plenty of years with these things to perfect it."

Pendergast stepped up to the tee, lined up his driver, and took the shot. The club impacted the ball with too open a face and what was meant as a fade turned into something more like a slice.

The older man shook his head, clucking in sympathy but hardly able to conceal his delight. "May have to go searching for that one."

Pendergast thought for a moment and then asked, "I suppose you wouldn't consider allowing me a mulligan?" He already knew the answer but was curious to hear Weiss's reaction.

"Mr. Pendergast, you surprise me. I wouldn't have pegged you for the mulligan type at all."

The ghost of a smile lingered on Pendergast's face as Weiss eased himself back into his wheelchair while unlocking the leg braces. His heavily muscled arms propelled him along, almost shooting him forward along the gravel path. It was a facet of the Nazi-hunter's forceful personality that he spurned the luxury of a golf cart, preferring to wheel himself over the course. It had been a long eighteen holes, but he showed no sign of fatigue.

As they made their way down the fairway and around the dogleg, their balls came into view: Weiss's lined up nicely for a shot to the green, Pendergast's in a sand trap beside the fringe.

Weiss shook his head again. "Your honor."

Pendergast took a calculating stroll around the bunker, then knelt beside the ball, estimating the trajectory to the pin. He waited for Weiss to issue his recommendation.

"If I were you, I'd choose the lob wedge," Weiss said after a moment. "It's more forgiving than the pitching wedge."

Pendergast rummaged through the set of Pings, took out the wedge, lined himself up gingerly, took a few practice swings, and then—with a huge spray of sand—hit the ball. The ball moved about two feet up the side of the bunker.

Weiss tut-tutted. "Don't think about it too much. Try to imagine the feel of the shot physically before you swing."

Pendergast lined himself up again. This time, he hit a more controlled chip shot that seemed to go long but, with heavy backspin, landed with barely a roll on the back side of the green.

"*Mazel tov!*" Weiss cried, beaming.

"Pure luck, I'm afraid," said Pendergast.

"Ah, but you said you didn't believe in luck. No— you followed my suggestion and now you see the excellent result." Selecting a seven iron, Weiss chipped his ball to within ten feet of the pin. Pendergast, at twenty feet, missed his first two putts, then holed out for a bogey. Weiss one-putted for a final eagle.

Pendergast marked it and handed the scorecard to Weiss. "You shot a sixty-nine. My congratulations."

"It's my home course. And I'm sure if you follow some of those tips I mentioned, you'd improve quickly. You have a natural golfer's physique. Now let us talk."

The formality of the game completed, they repaired to his house, just off the tee box of the fifteenth hole. The two men sat on the patio while Heidi, Weiss's wife, brought them a pitcher of mint juleps.

"And so to business," Weiss said, in a rare mood, pouring out the drinks and raising his glass. "So you have come to me about Wolfgang Faust."

Pendergast nodded.

"Then you have come to the right man, Mr. Pendergast. I made it my life's work to track down the Dachau Doctor. I was only stopped by *these*." And he gestured at the legs under the blanket. Putting down the drink, he reached for a thick folder that sat at one edge of the patio table. "A lifetime of work, Mr. Pendergast," he said, patting the folder. "Distilled between these covers. And I know it by heart." He took a deep sip of his julep. "Wolfgang Faust was born in Ravensbrück, Germany, in 1908 and attended the University of Munich, where he met and became the protégé of Josef Mengele, three years his senior. He worked as Mengele's assistant at the Institute for Hereditary Biology and Racial Hygiene in Frankfurt. In 1940, he received his medical degree and joined the Waffen-SS. Later, at Mengele's recommendation, he worked for Mengele in the clinic block at Auschwitz. You know the kind of 'work' Mengele was involved with?"

"I have an idea."

"Brutal, cruel, and inhuman surgeries—frequently done without anesthesia." Weiss's open and cheerful countenance had undergone a transformation into something hard, implacable. "Unnecessary amputations. Hideously painful and disfiguring medical 'experiments' performed on little children. Shock treatment. Sterilization. Brain surgery to alter one's perception of time. Injecting subjects with various poisons and diseases. Freezing people to death. Mengele was fascinated by anything unusual or abnormal: heterochromia, dwarfism, identical twins, polydactyly. Romas—Gypsies—were a favorite target. He infected a hundred of them with leprosy in an attempt to create a biological weapon. And when his fiendish experiments were complete, he would kill the sufferer—often with an injection of chloroform into the heart, to finish up with an autopsy to document the pathology—just like lab rats."

He took another slug of his drink. "Faust so distinguished himself at Auschwitz that he was sent to Dachau to set up his own facility. Not a great deal is known of the nature of his Dachau experiments—Faust was far more successful than Mengele at destroying his records and killing witnesses—but what we do know is as disturbing as Mengele's atrocities, if not more so. I will not speak of those details here; they are in this folder if you really want to know the true depths to which a man's depravity can lower him. Let us talk instead of what happened after the war. After the fall of Berlin, Faust went underground in Germany with the help of Nazi sympathizers, hidden in an attic—ironically, not that different from what happened to Anne Frank.

These sympathizers were well connected or well funded, or perhaps both."

"How do you know?"

"They had the ability to create—or procure—forged documents of a very high quality. Marriage licenses, identity papers, the like. These sympathizers gave Faust a phony passport in the name of Wolfgang Lanser. Sometime in the late 1940s—it is not known precisely when—he was smuggled out of the country and shipped off to South America. His first port of call was Uruguay. All this—what I have told you so far—took me ten years of work to uncover."

Pendergast inclined his head.

"He settled in a series of remote towns, earning money from doctoring the peasants, but it appears he was not long welcome in any one place; apparently his prices were extortionate, and at times he displayed a propensity for trying out various, ah, *cures* that often ended up killing instead."

"The inveterate experimenter," Pendergast murmured.

"By 1958, I had tracked him to Uruguay. Somehow, he learned I was on his trail. He changed identities again—this time to Willy Linden—had a facial operation, and moved to Brazil. But that's where the trail ends. Because around 1960, he vanished completely. I could turn up nothing, absolutely nothing further, on his whereabouts or his activities. In fact, it was only twenty-five years later, in 1985, that I came upon his grave site—and that itself was almost a coincidence, more a lucky break than the result of careful investigation. The remains were identified from dental, and later from DNA, records."

"When did he die?" Pendergast asked.

"As near as could be established, sometime in the late 1970s, 1978 or '79."

"And you have no idea what he was doing those last twenty years?"

Weiss shrugged. "I tried to find out. God knows, I tried." He finished the drink with one quick movement, his hand now trembling slightly.

For a few minutes, the two men remained in silence. Then Weiss looked over at Pendergast.

"Now tell me, Mr. Pendergast: what is your interest in Wolfgang Faust?"

"I have reason to believe he may have been...connected in some way to a death in my family."

"Ah, yes. Naturally. He 'touched' thousands of families in that way." Weiss paused. "After I came upon the remains, the case was basically closed. Other Nazi-hunters had little interest in filling in the gaps of Faust's life. The man was dead: why bother? But finding a body, or bringing someone to justice, just isn't enough. I believe we must know all there is to know about these monsters. It is our responsibility and our duty to understand. And there are so many unanswered questions about Faust. Why was he buried in the middle of nowhere in a plain pine box? Why did nobody in the area have any idea of who he was? Nobody I questioned in a twelve-mile radius of the grave site had ever seen or heard of the man named Willy Linden before. But after my accident...there was no one to take over for me. *Meier*, they said to me, *the man is dead. You found the man's grave. What more do you want?* I try not to be bitter."

Weiss suddenly put down the empty glass and pushed the file toward Pendergast. "You want to know more about the man, what he was doing in those last twenty years of his life? Then *you* do it. You carry on my work." He seized Pendergast's wrist. The man might have been wheelchair-bound, but despite his gentle mien he had the ferocity and tenacity of a lion.

Pendergast moved to free his arm but Weiss held on. "Carry on my work," he repeated. "Find out where that devil was, what he was doing. Then we can finally close the book on the Dachau Doctor." He stared into Pendergast's face. "Will you do this?"

"I'll do what I can," Pendergast replied.

After a moment, Weiss relaxed. He released his grip on Pendergast's wrist. "But be careful. Even today, such demons as Dr. Faust have their supporters... those who would guard the Nazi secrets, even beyond the grave." And he tapped the arm of his wheelchair significantly.

Pendergast nodded. "I shall be careful."

The passionate fit had passed, and Weiss's face was calm and gentle once again. "Then all that remains is for us to have another drink—if you're so inclined."

"I am indeed. Please tell your wife that she mixes an excellent julep."

"Coming from a man of the Deep South, that is a compliment indeed." And the older man lifted the pitcher and refilled their glasses.

CHAPTER 50

New York City

DR. OSTROM'S OFFICE AT MOUNT MERCY HAD ONCE BEEN—rather fittingly, Esterhazy thought—the consulting chamber of the hospital's "alienist." It still bore traces of the building's days as a private hospital for the wealthy: a large, rococo marble fireplace; elaborately carved moldings; leaded-glass windows, now fitted with steel bars. Esterhazy almost expected a butler in white tie to enter, sherry glasses balanced on a silver salver.

"So, Dr. Poole," Felder said, leaning forward in his chair and placing the palms of his hands on his knees. "What did you think of this evening's session?"

Esterhazy glanced back at the psychiatrist, taking in his eager, intelligent gaze. The man was so obsessed with Constance and the strange aspects of this case that it was blinding his professional objectivity and normally prudent nature. Esterhazy, on the other hand, couldn't care less about Constance or her perversities, beyond her use as a pawn in his game. And not caring gave him a huge advantage.

"I thought you handled her with great tact, Doctor,"

he said. "Refusing to address her delusions directly, but only within the context of a greater reality, is clearly a beneficial strategy." He paused. "I have to admit quite frankly, when I first approached you about this case, I had my doubts. You know the long-term prognosis of paranoid schizophrenia as well as or better than I do. And my earlier treatment of her was, as I've explained, less than satisfactory. But I'd be the first to admit that, where I once failed, you are now succeeding—to a degree I'd never thought possible."

Felder flushed slightly, nodded his thanks.

"Have you noticed that her selective amnesia has abated to some degree?"

Felder cleared his throat. "I have noticed that, yes."

Esterhazy smiled slightly. "And it's clear that this facility has played no small part in her progress. The welcoming and intellectually stimulating atmosphere of Mount Mercy has made a huge difference. In my opinion, it's helped turn a very guarded prognosis into a rather more optimistic one."

Ostrom, sitting in a nearby wing chair, inclined his head. He was more reserved than Felder, and—though clearly interested in the case—not obsessed with it. Esterhazy had to treat him with great care. But flattery was universally effective.

Esterhazy flipped through the chart Ostrom had provided, trying to pick out any nugget that might assist him. "I notice here that Constance seems to react to two activities with particular favor: library hours and recreational time spent on the grounds."

Ostrom nodded. "She seems to have an almost nine-teenth-century attraction to outdoor strolls."

"It's a positive sign, and one I believe we should foster." Esterhazy put the folder aside. "Have you thought of arranging a day trip away from Mount Mercy, such as a walk through the botanical gardens, perhaps?"

Ostrom glanced at him. "I must confess I haven't. Off-site trips normally require court approval."

"I understand. You say 'normally.' But I believe that, under the medical rules, if Constance is determined by Mount Mercy to be no danger to herself or others, and furthermore if the outing is deemed medically necessary, no court ruling is required."

"We rarely go that route," Ostrom replied. "The liability is too great."

"But think of the patient. The *good* of the patient."

Here Felder chimed in, as Esterhazy hoped he would. "I wholeheartedly agree with Dr. Poole. Constance has demonstrated not one iota of aggression or suicidal ideation. Nor is she an elopement risk: quite the contrary. Not only would this reinforce her interest in outdoor activity, but surely you'd agree that such an expression of confidence on our side would be highly beneficial in getting her to lower her defenses?"

Ostrom considered this.

"I think Dr. Felder is absolutely correct," said Esterhazy. "And on consideration I believe the Central Park Zoo would be an even better choice."

"Even if no ruling is required," Ostrom said, "because of her criminal conviction I would still have to get approval from a court officer."

"That shouldn't pose a serious impediment," Felder replied. "I can go through channels, using my position with the Board of Health."

"Excellent." Esterhazy beamed. "And how long do you expect that to take?"

"A day, perhaps two."

Ostrom took some time to answer. "I'd want you both to accompany her. And the outing should be limited to a single morning."

"Very prudent," Esterhazy replied. "Will you call me on my cell phone, Dr. Felder, once you've made the necessary arrangements?"

"With great pleasure."

"Thank you. Gentlemen, if you'll forgive me for the moment—time waits for no man." And, shaking their hands in turn, Esterhazy smiled and let himself out.

CHAPTER 51

THE MAN CALLING HIMSELF KLAUS FALKONER on the sky deck of the *Vergeltung*. It was another mild afternoon and the Seventy-Ninth Street Boat Basin was quiet, somnolent under a late-fall sun. On a small table beside him rested a pack of Gauloises and an unopened bottle of Cognac Roi de France Fine Champagne, along with a single brandy snifter.

Pulling a cigarette from the pack, Falkoner lit it with a gold Dunhill lighter, took a deep drag, then gazed at the bottle. With exquisite care, he pulled the old, original nineteenth-century wax from the neck of the bottle, crumpled it into a ball, and dropped it into a pewter ashtray. The cognac shone in the afternoon sun like liquid mahogany, a remarkably dark and rich color for such a spirit. There were a dozen more bottles just like it laid down in the wine cellar in the *Vergeltung*'s belly—a tiny percentage of the spoils plundered by Falkoner's predecessors during the occupation of France.

He exhaled, looking around with satisfaction. Another small percentage of those spoils—gold, jewelry, bank accounts, art, and antiques expropriated more than sixty years before—had paid for the *Vergeltung*. And a very special trideck motor yacht it was: one hundred and thirty feet LOA, twenty-six-foot beam, and six luxurious staterooms. The fuel capacity of fifty-four thousand gallons of diesel allowed the twin eighteen-hundred-horsepower Caterpillar engines to cross any ocean but the Pacific. This kind of independence, this ability to operate both beyond the law and below the radar, was critical to the work that Falkoner and his organization were engaged in.

He took another drag on the cigarette and crushed it out, only half smoked, in the ashtray. He was eager to sample the cognac. Very carefully, he poured out a measure into the tulip snifter, which—given the age and delicacy of the spirit—he'd chosen over the coarser balloon snifter. He gently swirled the glass, sampled the aroma, then—with delicious slowness—lifted it to his lips and took a tiny sip. The cognac bloomed on his palate with marvelous complexity, surprisingly robust for such an old bottle: the legendary "Comet" vintage of 1811. He closed his eyes, took a larger sip.

Quiet footsteps sounded on the teakwood floor, and then there was a deferential cough at his shoulder. Falkoner glanced over. It was Ruger, a member of the crew, standing in the shadows of the flying bridge. He held a phone in one hand.

"Telephone call for you, sir," he said in German.

Falkoner placed the snifter on the small table. "Unless it's Herr Fischer calling, I do not wish to be disturbed." *Herr Fischer.* Now there was a truly frightening man.

"It is the gentleman from Savannah, sir." Ruger held the phone at a discreet distance.

"*Verflucht*," Falkoner muttered under his breath as he took the proffered phone. "Yes?" he spoke into the mouthpiece. Irritation at having his ritual interrupted added an uncharacteristic harshness to his tone. This fellow was evolving from a nuisance into a problem.

"You asked me to deal with Pendergast decisively," came the voice on the other end of the phone. "I'm about to do just that."

"I don't want to hear what you're going to do. I want to hear what you've *done*."

"You offered me assistance. The *Vergeltung*."

"And?"

"I'm planning to bring a visitor on board."

"A visitor?"

"An unwilling visitor. Someone close to Pendergast."

"Am I to assume this is bait?"

"Yes. It will lure Pendergast on board, where he can be dealt with once and for all."

"This sounds risky."

"I've worked everything out to the last degree."

Falkoner expelled a thin stream of air. "I look forward to discussing this with you further. Not on the phone."

"Very well. But meanwhile, I'll need restraints—plastic cuffs, gags, rope, duct tape, the works."

"We keep that sort of thing at the safe house. I'll have to retrieve it. Come by this evening and we shall go over the details."

Falkoner hung up, handed the phone to the waiting crew member, and watched as the man receded out of sight. Then he once again picked up the tulip snifter, the look of contentment slowly settling back over his face.

CHAPTER 52

NED BETTERTON DROVE UP THE FDR DRIVE in his rented Chevy Aero, feeling more than a little disconsolate. He was due to return the rental car at the airport in about an hour, and that night he was flying back to Mississippi.

His little reportorial adventure was over.

It was hard to believe that—just a few days earlier—he had been on a roll. He'd gotten a bead on the "foreign fella." Using the social engineering strategy known as pretexting, he'd called Dixie Airlines and, posing as a cop, gotten the address of the Klaus Falkoner who'd flown to Mississippi almost two weeks before: 702 East End Avenue.

Easy. But then he'd hit a wall. First, there was no 702 East End Avenue. The street was barely ten blocks long, perched right on the edge of the East River, and the street numbers didn't go that high.

Next, he'd tracked Special Agent Pendergast to an apartment building called the Dakota. But it was a damn fortress, and gaining access proved impossible. There was always a doorman stationed in a pillbox outside the entrance, and more doormen and elevator men massed inside, politely but firmly rebuffing his every attempt and stratagem to enter the building or gain information.

Then he'd tried to get information on the NYPD captain. But there were several female captains and he couldn't seem to find out, no matter who he asked, which one had partnered with Pendergast or gone down to New Orleans—only that it must have been done off duty.

The basic problem was New York Freaking City. People were tight as shit with information and paranoid of their so-called privacy. He was a long way from the Deep South. He didn't know how things were done here, didn't even know the right way to approach people and ask questions. Even his accent was a problem, putting people off.

He had then returned his attention to Falkoner, and almost had a breakthrough. On the chance that Falkoner had used a fake house number on his real street—after all, East End Avenue was an odd choice for a false address—Betterton had canvassed the avenue from end to end, knocking on doors, stopping people in the street, asking if anyone knew of a tall, blond man living in the vicinity, with an ugly mole on his face, and who spoke with a German accent. Most people— typical New Yorkers—either refused to talk to him or told him to fuck off. But a few of the older residents he met were friendlier. And through them, Betterton learned that the area, known as Yorkville, had once been a German enclave. These elderly residents spoke wistfully of restaurants such as Die Lorelei and Café Mozart, about the marvelous pastries served at Kleine Konditorei, about the bright halls that offered polka dances every night of the week. Now that was all gone, replaced by anonymous delis and supermarkets and boutiques.

And, yes, several people did believe they had seen a man like that. One old fellow claimed he had noticed such a man going in and out of a shuttered building on East End Avenue between Ninety-First and Ninety-Second Streets, at the northern end of Carl Schurz Park.

Betterton had staked out the building. He quickly learned it was next to impossible to loiter around outside without attracting attention or causing suspicion. That had forced him to rent a car and make his observations from the street. He had spent three exhausting days watching the building. Hour after hour of surveillance—nobody in or out. He'd run out of money and his vacation clock was ticking. Worse, Kranston had begun calling him daily, wondering where the hell he was, even hinting about replacing him.

In this way, the time he had allotted to New York City came to an end. His flight home was on a nonrefundable ticket that would cost him four hundred dollars to change—money he didn't have.

And so now, at five o'clock in the evening, Betterton was driving up FDR Drive, on his way to the airport to catch his flight home. But when he saw the exit sign for East End Avenue, some perverse and irrepressible hope prompted him to swerve off. One more look—just one—and he would be on his way.

There was no place to park, and he had to drive around the block again and again. This was crazy: he was going to miss his flight. But as he came around the corner for the fourth time, he noticed that a taxi had stopped in front of the building. Intrigued, he pulled over and double-parked in front of the idling cab, pulling out a map and pretending to consult it while watching the shuttered building's entrance through his rearview mirror.

Five minutes passed, and then the front door opened. A figure stepped out, duffel bags in each hand—and Betterton caught his breath. Tall and thin and blond. Even at this distance, he could see the mole beneath his right eye.

"Holy mackerel," he muttered.

The man tossed the duffels into the taxi, climbed in after them, closed the door. A moment later, the vehicle nosed away from the curb and passed Betterton's Chevy. Betterton took a deep breath, wiped his palms on his shirt, put the map aside. And then—taking a fresh grip on the wheel—he began to follow the cab as it turned onto Ninety-First Street and headed west.

CHAPTER 53

D<small>R. J</small>OHN F<small>ELDER FELT LIKE A THIRD WHEEL</small> as Poole led Constance by the arm through the Central Park Zoo. They had visited the sea lions, the polar bears, and now Constance had asked to see the Japanese snow monkeys. She was more demonstrative than he'd ever seen her before—not excited, exactly, he couldn't imagine someone with such a phlegmatic disposition ever being excited, but she had definitely lowered her guard to a certain degree. Felder wasn't sure how he felt about the fact that Constance, who had seemed wary of Dr. Poole at first, had warmed to him significantly.

Perhaps a little too significantly, Felder thought sourly as he walked on her other side.

As they neared the outdoor snow monkey enclosure, he could hear the hoots and screams of the animals playing with one another, tumbling about their rock and water enclosure, raising a din.

He glanced at Constance. The wind had blown back her hair and raised a rosy blush on her normally pale cheeks. She watched the monkeys, smiling at the antics of one particular juvenile who, shrieking with delight, leapt off a rock and landed in the water, just as a child might do, then scampered back up to do it again.

"Curious they aren't cold," Constance said.

"Hence the name *snow monkeys*," replied Poole with a laugh. "They live in a snowy clime."

They watched for a while and Felder surreptitiously checked his watch. They still had half an hour left, but if the truth be told he was rather anxious to return Constance to Mount Mercy. This was proving too uncontrolled an environment, and he felt Dr. Poole was approaching, if not stepping over, the appropriate doctor-patient distance with his laughter, his witticisms, his arm-holding.

Constance murmured something to Poole, and he in turn glanced over at Felder. "I'm afraid we must visit the ladies' room. I believe it's over there, in the Tropic Zone building."

"Very well."

They made their way down the path and entered the Tropic Zone. The place was constructed like a tropical rain forest, with live animals and birds in their respective habitats. The restrooms were at the far end down a long corridor. Felder waited at the head of the corridor while Poole escorted Constance to the door of the ladies' room, opening it for her and then taking up a position outside.

A few minutes passed. Felder checked his watch again. Eleven forty. The outing was to end at noon. He glanced down the corridor to see Poole waiting by the door, arms crossed, a pensive look on his face.

A few more minutes went by, and Felder began to feel uneasy. He walked down the corridor. "Shall we check?" he murmured.

"We probably should." Poole leaned toward the door. "Constance?" he asked. "Are you all right?"

No answer from within.

"Constance!" He rapped on the door.

Still no answer. Poole glanced at Felder with alarm. "I'd better go in."

Felder, suppressing a sudden panic, nodded, and Poole pushed into the ladies' room, loudly announcing himself to anyone within. The door swung shut and Felder could hear him calling her name and opening and closing stalls.

He appeared again a moment later, his face ashen. "She's gone! And the back window's open!"

"Oh, my God," Felder said.

"She can't have gone far," said Poole, the words tumbling out in a rush. "We've got to find her. Let's go outside—you go left, I'll go to the right, we'll circle the building...and for God's sake, keep your eyes open!"

Felder sprinted toward the exit, burst out the door, and turned left, circling the building at a run and looking in all directions for the figure of Constance. Nothing.

He reached the rear of the building, where the restrooms were located. There was the bathroom window, standing open. But it was barred.

Barred?

He looked wildly around for Poole coming the other way, arriving from the opposite direction. But Poole didn't come. With a curse, Felder continued on around the building at a run, reaching the entrance sixty seconds later.

No Poole.

Felder forced his brain to slow down, to think

through the problem logically. How could she have gotten out a barred window? And where the hell was Poole? Was he in pursuit of her? That must be it. He recalled that the entire zoo was walled. There were only two exits: one at Sixty-Fourth and Fifth, the other at the south end of the zoo. He sprinted toward the southern exit, pushed through the turnstile, and stared out across the park—bare-branched trees, long promenades. There were few people walking around; given the time of day, the park seemed oddly deserted.

The striking figure of Constance was nowhere to be seen. Or that of Dr. Poole, either.

Clearly she was back in the zoo. Or maybe she had left by the other exit. Felder was suddenly seized with the direness of the situation: Constance was a murderer who had been judged insane. He had arranged for this outing himself, through his official position with the city. If she escaped while under his care, his career would be finished.

Should he call the police? Not yet. His head reeled as he imagined the headlines in the *Times*…

Get a grip. Poole must have found Constance. He must have. All Felder had to do was locate Poole.

He jogged around to the Sixty-Fourth Street entrance, reentered the zoo, and made his way back to the Tropic Zone. He searched the area thoroughly, inside and out, looking for Poole or Constance. Poole had her under control, he told himself. He'd caught up to her and was restraining her, somewhere nearby. He might need assistance.

Felder fumbled out his cell phone and dialed Poole's number, but it immediately rolled over to voice mail.

He went back to the ladies' room and barged inside. The window was still open, but it was clearly and visibly barred. Felder paused, staring at it, the full implications of that barred window suddenly sinking in.

He could swear he'd heard Poole opening and closing the stalls and calling out her name. But why would he do that if the window was barred, and there was no possibility of escape? He looked around the small, empty bathroom, but there was literally no place to hide.

And then—with a sudden, terrible clarity—Felder realized there could be only one explanation. Poole must have been in on the escape.

CHAPTER 54

CORRIE SWANSON HEARD THE FAINT RINGING of her cell phone, through her earpieces, as she lay on the bed in her dorm room listening to Nine Inch Nails. She scrambled up, plucked out the earbuds, sorted through the two-foot layer of clothes on her floor, and pulled out the phone.

A number she didn't recognize. "Yeah?"

"Hello?" came a voice. "Is this Corinne Swanson?"

"Corinne?" The man had an accent of the Deep South, not as refined and melodious as Pendergast's but not all that different, either. It instantly put her on alert. "Yeah, this is *Corinne*."

"Corinne, my name is Ned Betterton."

She waited.

"I'm a reporter."

"For who?"

A hesitation. "The *Ezerville Bee*."

At this, Corrie had to laugh. "Okay, who is this really and what's the joke? You a friend of Pendergast's?"

There was a silence on the other end. "This is no joke, but it happens that he's the reason I'm calling."

Corrie waited.

"My apologies for contacting you like this, but I understand you're the one who maintains the website on Special Agent Pendergast."

"Right," said Corrie warily.

"That's where I got your name," said the man. "I didn't realize you were in town until just today. I'm doing a story about a double murder that occurred down in Mississippi. I'd like to talk to you."

"Talk."

"Not on the phone. In person."

Corrie hesitated. Her instincts were to put him off, but she was curious about the Pendergast connection. "Where?"

"I don't really know New York well. How about, um, the Carnegie Deli?"

"I don't do pastrami."

"I heard they've got great cheesecake. How about in an hour? I'll be wearing a red scarf."

"Whatever."

There were about ten people in red scarves packing the deli, and by the time Corrie found Betterton she was in a foul mood. He rose as she approached and pulled out a chair for her.

"I can seat myself, thank you, I'm not some fainting southern belle," she said, pulling the chair from his solicitous grasp and sitting down.

He was in his late twenties, small but tough looking, ripped, old acne scars on an otherwise handsome face. He was dressed in a tacky sports jacket, with a Scotch

Pad of brown hair and a nose that looked like it had once been broken. Intriguing.

He ordered a slice of truffle torte cheesecake, and Corrie settled on a BLT. As the waitress walked away, Corrie crossed her arms and stared at Betterton. "Okay, so what's this all about?"

"Almost two weeks ago a couple, Carlton and June Brodie, were brutally murdered in Malfourche, Mississippi. Tortured and then killed, to be exact."

He was temporarily drowned out by the clattering of dishes and a waiter shouting an order.

"Go on," Corrie said.

"The crime's unsolved. But I've stumbled across some information that I'm following up on. Nothing definitive, you understand, but suggestive."

"Where does Pendergast come in?"

"I'll get to that in a moment. Here's the story. About ten years back, the Brodies disappeared. The wife faked suicide, then the husband vanished. A few months ago, they reappeared as if nothing had happened, moved back to Malfourche, and resumed life. She ascribed her fake suicide to marital and job difficulties, and they told everyone they'd been running a B and B in Mexico. Except that they hadn't been. It was a lie."

Corrie leaned forward. This was more interesting than she'd expected.

"Not long before their reappearance, Pendergast arrived in Malfourche with an NYPD captain—a woman—in tow."

Corrie nodded. That would be Hayward.

"No one can tell me what they were doing there, or why. It seems he was curious about a place deep in the adjoining swamp—a place called Spanish Island." He proceeded to tell Corrie about all he had learned and his suspicions that it involved a major drug refining and smuggling operation.

Corrie nodded. So this was what Pendergast was working on so secretly.

"Just short of two weeks ago, a man with a German accent showed up in Malfourche. The Brodies were brutally murdered. I traced the man back here to New York. He was using a fake address, but I managed to link him to a small brownstone at Four Twenty-eight East End Avenue. I did a little poking around. The building is in the heart of the old German-speaking area of Yorkville, and it's been owned by the same company since 1940. A real estate holding company. And it appears he's got a yacht moored at the Boat Basin—a huge one. I followed him from the brownstone to the yacht."

Another nod from Corrie. She wondered when he was going to want some information from her in return. "So?" she said.

"So I believe this Pendergast, whom you seem to know so much about, is the key to the whole thing."

"No doubt. This is the big case he's been working on."

An awkward pause. "That doesn't seem likely to me."

"What do you mean?"

"An FBI agent working a case doesn't blow up a bar and sink a bunch of boats, not to mention burn down a drug lab in the swamp. No—this is extracurricular."

"That's possible. He often investigates on a…free-lance basis."

"This was not an investigation. This was...retribution. Reckoning. This man Pendergast, I believe he's the mastermind behind the whole operation."

She stared at him. "Mastermind of what?"

"The Brodie killings. The drug smuggling operation—if that's what it is. Something big and highly illegal is going on here—that much is obvious."

"Now, hold on. You're calling Pendergast a drug lord, or maybe even a *murderer*?"

"Let us say I strongly suspect his involvement. Everything that's happened looks to me like drugs, and this FBI agent is up to his neck in it—"

Corrie stood up abruptly, her chair clattering to the floor. "Are you some kind of nutcase?" she said in a loud voice.

"Sit down, please—"

"I will *not* sit down! Pendergast, selling *drugs*?" Her tone of disgust and disbelief was turning heads in the crowded restaurant. She didn't care.

Betterton cringed under this outburst. "Will you be quiet—"

"Pendergast is one of the most honest men you'll ever meet. You aren't even fit to lick his shoes!"

She saw Betterton flushing with mortification. Now she had the riveted attention of the entire restaurant. Several waiters and waitresses were hurrying over. There was something almost gratifying about it.

Her long frustration at Pendergast's disappearance, her anger at being led to believe he was dead, seemed to coalesce and find a target in Betterton. "You call yourself a reporter?" she cried. "You couldn't report your way out of a douche bag! Pendergast saved my life! He's been putting me through college, for your information—and don't think there's anything between us, either, because he's the most decent man alive, you asswipe."

"Excuse me, miss!" A waiter was flapping his hands in a panic as if to wave her away by magic.

"Don't 'miss' me, I'm on my way out." She turned and looked at the horrified crowd in the restaurant. "What, you don't like foul language? Go back to Dubuque."

She flounced out of the restaurant, exited onto Seventh Avenue, and there, amid the lunchtime crowds, managed to regain her breath and her equilibrium.

This was serious. It seemed Pendergast was in some kind of trouble—maybe deep trouble. But he'd always handled trouble before, she knew. She had made him a promise—a promise to leave this alone—and she intended to keep it.

CHAPTER 55

CONSTANCE SAT IN THE REAR OF THE PRIVATE CAR speeding up Madison Avenue. She had been mildly surprised by an exchange in German between Dr. Poole and the driver of the vehicle, but Poole had given her no explanation of the plans he and Pendergast had put together for their reunion. She felt an almost overwhelming eagerness to see Pendergast and the inside of the Riverside Drive mansion again.

Judson Esterhazy, aka Dr. Poole, sat beside her, his tall, aristocratic frame and finely chiseled features set into sharp relief by the noontime sun. The escape had gone without a hitch, exactly as planned. She felt badly for Dr. Felder, of course, and realized this would be a blot on his career, but Pendergast's safety overshadowed all else.

She glanced at Esterhazy. Despite the family connection, there was something she didn't like about him. It was his body language, the arrogant look of triumph on his face. If the truth be told, she hadn't liked him from the start—there was some quality in his manner, his way of speaking, that aroused her instinctual suspicion.

No matter. She folded her hands, determined to help Pendergast in any way she could.

The car slowed. Through the smoked windows, she noticed them turning east on Ninety-Second Street.

"Where are we going?" she asked.

"Just a temporary stop while preparations for your, ah, final destination are completed."

Constance did not at all like his turn of phrase. "My final destination?"

"Yes." Esterhazy's arrogant smile widened. "Vengeance, you see, is where it will end."

"Excuse me?"

"I quite like the sound of that," Esterhazy said. "Yes: *vengeance* is where it will end."

She stiffened. "And Pendergast?"

"Never mind about Pendergast."

His brusqueness, the way he almost spat out the name, sent a prickle of alarm through Constance. "What are you talking about?"

Esterhazy laughed harshly. "Don't you realize it yet? You haven't been rescued—you've been kidnapped."

He turned to her in one smooth motion and, before she could react, she felt a hand clamp around her mouth and smelled the sudden, sweetish stench of chloroform.

Slowly, consciousness returned out of a drowsy fog. Constance waited while she recovered her wits. She was tied to a chair, blindfolded and gagged. Her ankles were bound, as well. Gradually, she became aware of her surroundings: the musty smell of the room, the faint sounds in the house. It was a small room, bare except for an empty bookshelf, a dusty table, a bed frame, and the chair she was tied to. Someone was moving around below—Esterhazy, no doubt—and she could hear traffic noises from outside.

The first thing she felt was a flood of self-recrimination. Foolishly, stupidly, and unforgivably, she'd allowed herself to be duped. She had cooperated in her own abduction.

Careful to keep her breathing under control, she began to take stock. She was tied—no, taped—to a chair. But when she wiggled her hands, she realized the tape wasn't particularly tight or secure. It was a hasty job, temporary. Esterhazy had even indicated as much. *Just a temporary stop while preparations for your final destination are completed.*

Your final destination...

She began to flex her arms and wrists, stretching and pulling at the tape. Slowly but steadily it began to loosen. She could hear Esterhazy moving around downstairs; at any moment he might come back up to retrieve her.

With a final burst of effort she managed to rip the tape free. Next, she pulled away the blindfold and gag and freed her ankles. She stood up and, as quietly as she could, went over to the door, tried to open it. Locked, of course—and very stout.

She went to the lone window in the room, which looked out onto a desolate garden. The window was locked and barred. She glanced out through the grimy glass. It was a typical Upper East Side backyard, the common rear gardens of the surrounding brownstones separated from one another by tall brick walls. The yard of her own prison-house was overgrown and empty, but in the next garden over she could see a red-haired woman in a yellow sweater, reading a book.

Constance tried waving, then knocked quietly on the window—but the woman was absorbed in her book.

She made a quick search of the room, pulling open drawers in the empty desk and cupboards—and found a carpenter's pencil in the back of one drawer.

An old book lay on the top bookshelf. She grabbed it, ripped out the flyleaf, and hurriedly scribbled a note on it. Then she folded it up and wrote a second note on the outside:

Please take this note immediately to
Dr. Felder, care of Mount Mercy Hospital,
Little Governor's Island. Please—IT'S A
MATTER OF LIFE OR DEATH.

After a moment, she added:

Felder will give you a monetary reward.

She went to the window. The woman was still reading. She rapped on the glass, but the woman didn't notice. Finally, feeling a rising desperation, she took up the book and rammed it into the window, edge first. The glass shattered and the woman in the next garden glanced up.

Immediately Constance could hear Esterhazy bounding up the stairs.

She placed the note inside the book to help weigh it down and then tossed it toward the next garden.

"Take the note!" she called down. "And go—please!" The woman stared at her as the book landed near her feet, and the last thing Constance saw was her bending down—she walked with a cane—and taking up the book.

Constance turned from the window just as Esterhazy burst in with a curse of surprise and rushed toward her. She raised a hand to claw at his eyes; he tried to bat it away but she managed to scratch two deep stripes down one cheek. He gasped in pain, but quickly recovered and tackled her. He fell atop her and they struggled, Esterhazy finally pinning her arms and pressing another chloroformed cloth over her mouth and nose. She felt consciousness slide away and blackness claim her once again.

Chapter 56

Camden, Maine

THE SITE OF THE FORMER NURSING HOME had been razed and condos erected in its place, a forlorn row of empty town houses with flapping banners advertising price reductions and incentives.

Strolling into the little sales office, Pendergast found it empty and rang a bell on the counter. A haggard-looking young woman appeared from a back room, seemingly almost startled to see him. She greeted him with a professional smile.

Pendergast sloughed off the bulky jacket and smoothed down his black suit, restoring it to linear perfection. "Good morning," he said.

"May I help you?"

"Yes, you may. I've been looking at real estate in the area."

This seemed like a new idea to the saleslady. Her eyebrows rose. "Are you interested in our condominiums?"

"Yes." Pendergast dumped the loathsome coat on a chair and settled himself down. "I'm from the South but looking for a cooler clime for my early retirement. The heat, you know."

"I don't know how they stand it down there," said the woman.

"Indeed, indeed. Now, tell me what you have available."

The woman bustled through a folder and brought out some brochures, fanning them out on the table and launching into an earnest sales pitch. "We've got one-, two-, and three-bedroom units, all with marble baths and top-of-the-line appliances: Sub-Zero refrigerators, Bosch dishwashers, Wolf stoves..."

As she droned on, Pendergast encouraged her with nods and approving murmurs. When she was done, he allowed her a brilliant smile. "Lovely. Only two hundred thousand for the two-bedroom? With a view of the sea?"

This elicited more talk, and Pendergast again waited for her to reach the end. Then he settled back in the chair and clasped his hands. "It somehow seems right for me to live here," he said. "After all, my mother was a resident some years ago."

At this the woman seemed confused. "How nice, but...well, we've only just opened—"

"Of course. I mean in the nursing home that was here before. The Bay Manor."

"Oh, that," she said. "Yes, the Bay Manor."

"Do you recall it?"

"Sure. I grew up here. It closed down when...well, that would have been about seven, eight years ago."

"There was a very nice aide who used to take care of my mother." Pendergast pursed his lips. "Did you know any of the people who worked there?"

"Sorry, no."

"Pity. She was such a lovely person. I was hoping to look her up while I was in town." He gave the woman a rather penetrating stare. "If I could see her name, I'm sure I'd recognize it. Can you help me?"

She practically jumped at the chance. "I can certainly try. Let me make a call or two."

"How kind of you. Meanwhile, I'll peruse these brochures." He flipped one open, reading assiduously and nodding with approval as she began working the phone.

Pendergast noted calls to her mother, an old teacher, and finally to a boyfriend's mother. "Well," the saleslady said, hanging up the phone with finality, "I did get some information. The Bay Manor was torn down years ago but I got the name of three people who worked there." She placed a piece of paper in front of him with a smile of triumph.

"Are any of them still around?"

"The first one, Maybelle Payson. She's still living in the area. The other two have passed away."

"Maybelle Payson...Why, I believe that is the very person who was so kind to my mother!" Pendergast beamed at her, taking up the paper.

"And now, if you like, I'd be happy to show you the model units—"

"Delighted! When I return with my wife we shall be glad to get a tour. You've been most kind." He scooped up the brochures, slipped them into his jacket, put on the puffy coat, and exited into the barbaric cold.

CHAPTER 57

MAYBELLE PAYSON LIVED IN A RUN-DOWN fourplex back from the water in a working-class part of town. This working class consisted almost entirely of lobstermen, their boats parked on their lawns, chocked, blocked, and braced, draped in plastic tarps, some even bigger than the trailers the owners lived in.

Trudging up the walk, Pendergast climbed up on the creaky porch, rang the bell, and waited. After a second ring, he could hear someone moving about, and eventually an owlish, wizened face appeared in the door pane, haloed in fine blue hair. The old woman looked at him with wide, almost child-like eyes.

"Mrs. Payson?" Pendergast said.

"Who?"

"Mrs. Payson? May I come in?"

"I can't hear you."

"My name is Pendergast. I'd like to speak to you."

"What about?" The watery eyes stared at him suspiciously.

Pendergast shouted into the door. "About the Bay

Manor. A relative of mine used to live there. She spoke highly of you, Mrs. Payson."

He heard the turnings of various locks, latches, and bolts. The door opened, and he followed the diminutive woman into a tiny parlor. The place was a mess and smelled of cats. She swept a cat off a chair and seated herself on the sofa. "Please sit down."

Pendergast eased himself into the chair, which was almost completely covered with white cat hair. It seemed to leap up onto his black suit, as if magnetized.

"Would you care for tea?"

"Oh, no, thank you," said Pendergast hastily. He removed a notebook. "I'm compiling a little family history and I wanted to speak to you about a relative of mine who was a resident at Bay Manor some years back."

"What was her name?"

"Emma Grolier."

A long silence.

"Do you remember her?"

Another long pause. The teakettle began to whistle in the kitchen, but the woman didn't seem to hear.

"Allow me," Pendergast said, rising to fetch the kettle. "What kind of tea, Mrs. Payson?"

"What?"

"Tea. What kind would you like?"

"Earl Grey. Black."

In the kitchen, Pendergast opened a tea box that sat on the counter, took out a bag, placed it in a mug, and poured in the boiling water. He brought it out with a smile and set it on the table next to the old woman.

"How very kind," she said, looking at him now with a much warmer expression. "You'll have to come more often."

Pendergast settled himself again into the cat-hairy chair, throwing one leg over the other.

"Emma Grolier," the old nurse said. "I recall her well." The watery eyes looked at him, narrowing with fresh suspicion. "I doubt she spoke highly of me or of anyone. What do you want to know?"

Pendergast paused. "I'm assembling information for personal family reasons and I'd like to know all about her. What was she like?"

"I see. Well, I'm sorry to say she was difficult. A thorny, fractious woman. Peevish. I'm sorry to be blunt. She was not one of my favorite patients. Always complaining, crying, throwing food, violent even. She had severe cognitive impairment."

"Violent, you say?"

"And she was strong. She hit people, broke things in anger. Bit me once. A few times she had to be restrained."

"Did any family visit?"

"Nobody ever visited her. Although she must've had family, since she had all the best care, a special doctor, paid-for outings, nice clothes, presents shipped in at Christmastime—that sort of thing."

"A special doctor?"

"Yes."

"His name?"

A long silence. "I'm afraid his name has slipped my mind. Foreign. He came twice a year, a grand fellow strutting in like he was Sigmund Freud himself. Very exacting! Nothing was ever right. It was always a chore when he arrived. It was such a relief when that other doctor finally took her away."

"And when did that happen?"

Another long pause. "I just can't remember, so many came and went. A long time ago. I do remember the day, however. He came without warning, signed her out and that was it. Didn't take any of her personal belongings. Very strange. We never saw her again. The Bay Manor at the time was in financial trouble, and it closed some years later."

"What did he look like, exactly?"

"I don't much recall. Tall, handsome, well dressed. At least that's my vague recollection."

"Is there anyone else from the nursing home I could speak to?"

"Not that I know of. They didn't stick around. The winters, you see."

"Where are the medical records now?"

"Of Bay Manor?" The old nurse frowned. "Such things are usually sent to the state archives in Augusta."

Pendergast rose. "You said she was mentally impaired. In what way, exactly?"

"Mental retardation."

"Not age-related dementia?"

The old nurse stared at him. "Of course not! Emma Grolier was a young girl. Why, she couldn't have been older than twenty-seven or -eight." Her look of suspicion deepened. "You say she was a relative?"

Pendergast paused only momentarily. This was stunning information, the significance of which was not immediately clear. He covered up his reaction with an easy smile and bowed. "Thank you for your time."

As he emerged once again into the bitter air, annoyed at having been smoked out by a half-deaf octogenarian, he consoled himself with the thought that the medical files in Augusta would fill in any missing details.

CHAPTER 58

Augusta, Maine

ALOYSIUS PENDERGAST SAT IN THE BASEMENT of the Maine State Archives building, surrounded by the defunct files of the Bay Manor Nursing Home. He was frowning at the whitewashed cinder-block wall, and one manicured fingernail was tapping the top of a deal table with evident irritation.

A diligent search for the medical records of Emma Grolier had turned up only a single file card. It indicated the complete records had been transferred by medical order to the care of one Dr. Judson Esterhazy, at his clinic in Savannah, Georgia. The date of the transfer was six months after Helen's alleged death in Africa. The card was signed by Esterhazy, and the signature was genuine.

What had Esterhazy done with those papers? They hadn't been in the safe of his Savannah house. It seemed almost certain he had destroyed them—that is, if Pendergast's theory, still taking shape in his mind, was correct. Chances were the existence of the nursing home bills was an oversight. *Emma Grolier. Was it possible...?* He stood up slowly, thoughtfully, pushing the chair back with great deliberation.

As he ascended from the basement and once again emerged into the subzero afternoon cold, his cell phone rang. It was D'Agosta.

"Constance has escaped," he said without preamble.

Pendergast stopped dead. For a moment, he did not speak. Then he quickly opened the door of his rental car and slid in. "Impossible. She has no motive to escape."

"Nevertheless, she escaped. And let me tell you, I hope you've got a raincoat handy, because the shit is about to hit the fan."

"When did it happen? How?"

"Lunchtime. It's bizarre. She was on a field trip."

"Outside the hospital?"

"Central Park Zoo. Seems one of the doctors helped her escape."

"Dr. Ostrom? Dr. Felder? Impossible."

"No. Apparently his name was Poole. Ernest Poole."

"Who the devil is Poole?" Pendergast started the engine. "And what in the name of heaven was a self-confessed baby-killer doing outside the walls of Mount Mercy?"

"That's the million-dollar question. You can bet the press will have a field day if they find out—which they probably will."

"Keep this from the press at all costs."

"I'm doing my best. Naturally, homicide is all over it."

"Call them off. I can't have a lot of detectives blundering about."

"No dice. An investigation's obligatory. SOP."

For perhaps ten seconds, Pendergast stood motionless,

thinking. Then he spoke again. "Have you looked into the background of this Dr. Poole?"

"Not yet."

"If homicide must occupy themselves with something, have them do that. They'll discover he's a fraud."

"You know who he is?"

"I'd rather not speculate at the moment." Pendergast paused again. "I was a fool not to anticipate something like this. I believed Constance to be perfectly safe at Mount Mercy. A dreadful oversight—*another* dreadful oversight."

"Well, she's probably not in any real danger. Maybe she got infatuated with the doctor, escaped for some sort of dalliance..." D'Agosta's voice trailed off awkwardly.

"Vincent, I've already told you she didn't escape. She was kidnapped."

"Kidnapped?"

"Yes. No doubt by this ersatz Dr. Poole. Keep it from the press and stop homicide from muddying the waters."

"I'll do everything I can."

"Thank you." And Pendergast accelerated onto the icy street, the rented car fishtailing and spraying snow, heading for the airport and New York City.

CHAPTER 59

New York City

Ned Betterton stood by the entrance to the Seventy-Ninth Street Boat Basin, staring out at the confusion of yachts, sailboats, and assorted pleasure craft, all rocking gently back and forth in the calm waters of the Hudson. He was wearing the only suit jacket he'd brought along—a blue blazer—and he'd purchased a gaudy ascot that he'd tucked into his collar, along with a white cap placed rakishly on his head. It was not quite six PM, and the sun was rapidly sinking behind the ramparts of New Jersey.

Hands in his pockets, he glanced out at the vessel he'd seen the German motor out to the day before, moored some distance from the docks. It was quite a yacht, gleaming white with three tiers of smoked windows—well over a hundred feet in length. There did not appear to be any activity on board.

Betterton's leave was up, and the calls from Kranston at the *Bee* had turned threatening. The man was furious that he himself had to cover the church meetings and other crap. Good—the hell with him. This was a hot lead, this yacht. It just might be his ticket out.

You call yourself a reporter? You couldn't report your way out of a douche bag! Betterton flushed at the dressing-down Corinne Swanson had given him. That was another reason he was back at the Boat Basin. He knew, somehow or other, Pendergast was involved... and *not* as an investigator.

It had been the blue blazer, actually, that gave him the idea. He knew it was a common courtesy for yachtsmen anchored in proximity of one another to exchange visits, share drinks, or otherwise pay a courtesy call. He'd pose as a yachtsman, go on board, and see what there was to see. But these were bad guys, drug smugglers—he'd have to play it very, very carefully.

He soon discovered it wouldn't be as simple as just strolling into the marina. The place was surrounded by a chain-link fence and sported a staffed guardhouse by a closed gate. A big sign read GUESTS BY INVITATION ONLY. The place reeked of money, sealed off from the hoi polloi.

He studied the chain-link fence, which ran along the shore, back from the water, and disappeared into some brush. Making sure no one was watching, he followed the fence into the brush, pushing his way into the growth along the riverbank. And there he found what he was looking for: a low gap.

He squeezed through, rose, brushed himself off, replaced the cap on his head, tugged his jacket smooth, and went walking along the shore, keeping to the brush. After fifty yards he could make out a boathouse ahead, and the beginning of the piers and docks. With another quick adjustment to his attire, he stepped out into the open and quickly scrambled down to the walkway above the pier, then began ambling along it as if he were just another yachtsman taking the air. A marina employee was working on the dock past the boathouse, where several dozen tenders were tied up at numbered spots.

"Good evening," Betterton said.

The man looked up, greeted him, went back to work.

"I wonder," Betterton said, "if you'd be willing to take me out to the yacht over there." He pulled a twenty from his pocket and nodded at the white vessel moored about five hundred yards off.

The man rose. He peered at the twenty, then at Betterton. "The *Vergeltung*?"

"Right. And please wait there to take me back. I won't be on board more than five minutes, maybe ten, tops."

"What's your business?"

"A courtesy call. One yachtsman to another. I've been admiring the boat and thinking of upgrading to something similar, myself. My yacht is over there." He waved vaguely at the anchorage.

"Well..."

There was a movement within the darkness of the boathouse and another man appeared, maybe thirty-five years old, with faded brown hair and a dark tan despite it being November. "I'll take him over, Brad," the new arrival said, scrutinizing Betterton.

"Right, Vic. He's all yours."

"And you'll wait for me while I'm on board?" Betterton asked.

The man nodded, then pointed to one of the marina's tenders. "Hop in."

CHAPTER 60

DR. FELDER PACED BACK AND FORTH BEFORE the leaded-glass windows of Dr. Ostrom's office at Mount Mercy Hospital. He took a long, deep, shuddering breath, stared at the brown marshes beyond, a chevron of geese flying south.

What an afternoon it had been—what a terrible afternoon. The NYPD had come and gone, having turned the place upside down, asked questions, disturbed the inmates, and ransacked Constance's room. One detective still remained on the premises for follow-up: he was now standing just outside the office, conferring with Dr. Ostrom in low tones. Ostrom glanced over, saw Felder was looking at him, frowned with disapproval, and turned back to the detective.

So far they'd managed to keep the story out of the papers, but that wasn't going to help him much. And it likely wouldn't last long. Already he'd received a call from the mayor, who had told him in no uncertain terms that—unless Constance Greene was returned to Mount Mercy with minimal fuss and zero collateral damage—Felder could start dusting off his résumé.

That it now appeared Dr. Poole had participated in the escape—perhaps engineered it—didn't really do him any good. The fact was, it was Felder's name on the outing request.

What could this Dr. Poole possibly want with Constance? Why would he take such great risks to spirit her away from Mount Mercy? Was he working at the behest of an unknown relation? Could Pendergast have been involved?

At the thought of Pendergast, Felder shuddered.

There was a commotion down the hall, near the guard station by the hospital entrance. A white-clad orderly walked toward Ostrom and the detective. Felder stopped pacing and watched while the orderly conferred briefly with Ostrom.

The director of Mount Mercy turned toward Felder. "There's a woman here to see you."

Felder frowned. "A woman?" Who knew he was here right now, save for Dr. Ostrom and the staff? Nevertheless he followed the orderly down the corridor and back to the guard station.

A woman was indeed waiting by the entrance: fifty-ish, short, thin as a twig, with fiery red hair and bright red lipstick. A faux Burberry bag was draped over one shoulder. She walked with a cane.

"I'm Dr. Felder," he said, letting himself past the guard station. "You wanted to see me?"

"No," she said in a high, querulous voice.

"No?" Felder repeated, surprised.

"I don't know you from Adam. And tracking you down wasn't exactly my idea of a pleasant afternoon. I don't have a car, and do you know how difficult it is to get out here without one? It was hard enough even learning *where* Mount Mercy is. Little Governor's Island—bah. I tell you, I nearly gave up twice." She leaned forward, tapping her cane on the marble floor for emphasis. "But I was promised *money*."

Felder looked at her in confusion. "Money? Who promised you money? What does this have to do with me?"

"The girl."

"Which girl?"

"The girl that gave me the note. Told me to bring it to Dr. Felder at Mount Mercy. Said I'd be *paid*." Another tap of the cane.

"Girl?" Felder echoed. *My Lord, it has to be Constance.* "Where did you see this girl?"

"From my back garden. But that's not important. What I want to know is this: are you going to pay me or not?"

"Do you have the note?" Felder asked. He felt himself flushing in his eagerness to see it.

The woman nodded, but suspiciously, as if she might be subjected to a search for admitting this fact.

With shaking hands, Felder dug into his suit pocket, pulled out his wallet, peeled off a fifty, and held it out to her.

"I had to take *two* taxis," the woman said, placing it inside her bag.

Felder plucked out a twenty, handed it over.

"And I'll need to take a taxi back. It's waiting outside."

Another twenty was produced—the last bill in Felder's wallet—and it vanished as quickly as the oth-

ers. Then the woman reached into her bag and produced a single piece of paper, folded in half. One edge
was ragged, as if it had been ripped from a book. She
handed it to him. Written on it, in Constance's precise
copper-plate hand, was the following:

> Please take this note immediately
> to Dr. Felder, care of Mount Mercy
> Hospital, Little Governor's Island.
> Please—IT'S A MATTER OF LIFE
> OR DEATH.
> Felder will give you a monetary reward.

His hands shaking even more, he unfolded the piece of
paper. To his surprise, the message inside was written
to somebody else—Pendergast:

> Aloysius—I have been kidnapped by a
> man who claims he is your brother-in-law,
> Judson Esterhazy. He was going by
> the name of Poole. I am being kept in a
> house somewhere on the Upper East Side
> but I'm to be moved shortly, I don't
> know where. I fear he means to harm me.
> There is something he's told me with
> peculiar emphasis more than once:
> Vengeance is where it will end.
> Please forgive my foolishness and
> gullibility. Whatever happens, remember

that I'm entrusting my child's ultimate
well-being to your care.
Constance

Felder looked up, suddenly brimming with questions, but the woman was nowhere to be seen.

He ducked outside, but she had disappeared. He went back inside and returned to where Dr. Ostrom and the homicide detective were waiting.

"Well?" Dr. Ostrom asked. "What did she want?"

Wordlessly, Felder handed him the document. He watched Ostrom start visibly as he read first the outside, then the interior message.

"Where is the woman?" Ostrom asked sharply.

"She disappeared."

"Good Lord." Ostrom walked over to a wall telephone, picked it up. "This is Dr. Ostrom," he said. "Get me the gatehouse."

It took only a brief exchange to discover that the woman's taxi had already left the grounds. Ostrom made a photocopy of the document, then gave the original to the detective. "We've got to stop that woman. Call your people. Catch up to her. Understand?"

The detective hustled off, unhitching his radio and speaking into it.

Felder turned to Ostrom as the director hung up the phone. "She's claiming her child is alive. What could this mean?"

Ostrom merely shook his head.

CHAPTER 61

ESTERHAZY WATCHED THE SUDDEN FLURRY of activity on the deck of the *Vergeltung* as the motorized dinghy approached unexpectedly from the marina complex. Using a pair of binoculars, he peered intently at it through the smoked windows of the main salon. At first—unlikely as such a direct approach would be—he wondered if it could possibly be Pendergast. But no: it was somebody he'd never seen before, perched somewhat precariously in the bow of the little vessel.

Falkoner came up. "Is that him?"

Esterhazy shook his head. "No. I don't know who this person is."

"We shall find out." Falkoner stepped out onto the rear deck.

"Ahoy, the yacht!" said the man perched in the bow. He was dressed, overdressed even, in nautical fashion: navy blazer, cap, ascot.

"Hello," Falkoner called out in a friendly voice.

"I'm a neighbor," the man said. "I was admiring your yacht. Am I disturbing you?"

"Not at all. Care to come aboard?"

"Delighted." The man turned back to the Boat Basin employee manning the outboard. "Be sure to wait."

The man nodded.

The yachtsman stepped onto the boarding platform at the rear of the yacht while Falkoner opened the stern transom to let him come aboard. Gaining the deck, the man smoothed down his blazer and extended his hand. "Name's Betterton," he said. "Ned Betterton."

"I'm Falkoner."

Esterhazy shook Betterton's hand in turn, smiling but not offering his name. As he smiled, the scratches on his face stung. There wouldn't be a repeat of that: Constance was locked in the hold, handcuffed, her mouth gagged and taped. And yet a chill ran through him as he recalled the expression on her face in the Upper East Side safe house. He'd noticed two things in that expression, as clear as he was alive: hatred—and mental clarity. This woman wasn't the basket case he'd assumed. And her hatred of him was unsettling in its intensity and murderousness. He found himself not a little unnerved.

"I'm moored over there—" Betterton jerked a thumb vaguely over his shoulder—"and I thought I'd just stop over to wish you a pleasant evening. And—to be honest—I'm captivated by your yacht."

"Very glad that you did," replied Falkoner, with a brief glance at Esterhazy. "Would you care for a tour?"

Betterton nodded eagerly. "Thank you, yes."

Esterhazy noticed his eyes were darting everywhere, taking everything in. He was surprised Falkoner had offered the man a tour—there was something vaguely phony about him. He didn't look like a yachtsman, the blue blazer was of a cheap cut, and the man was wearing ersatz deck shoes of the landlubber kind.

They stepped into the beautifully appointed saloon, Falkoner launching into a description of the *Vergeltung*'s characteristics and notable features. Betterton listened with an almost child-like eagerness, still looking around as if committing everything to memory.

"How many people on board?" Betterton asked.

"We have a crew of eight. Then there's me and my friend, here, who's just visiting for a few days." Falkoner smiled. "How about on your vessel?"

Betterton waved a hand. "A staff of three. Have you taken her out on any trips recently?"

"No. We've been moored here for several weeks."

"And you've been on board the whole time? Seems a shame, even on such a beautiful vessel, with all of New York spread out before you!"

"Unfortunately, I've had no time for trips."

They passed through the dining room and into the galley, where Falkoner brought out a copy of the evening's dinner menu, praising the yacht's chef as he did. Esterhazy followed silently, wondering where this was leading.

"Dover sole with truffle butter and a mousse of root vegetables," Betterton said, looking at the menu. "You eat well."

"Perhaps you'd care to share our dinner?" Falkoner asked.

"Thank you, but I've got another engagement."

They continued down a corridor paneled in tamo ash. "Care to see the bridge?"

"Absolutely."

They climbed a stairway to the upper deck and into the wheelhouse.

"This is Captain Joachim," Falkoner said.

"Pleased to meet you," Betterton said, peering around. "Very impressive."

"I'm happy enough with it," Falkoner replied. "You can't beat the feeling of independence a yacht like this provides—as you must know yourself. The loran system on board is second to none."

"I would imagine."

"You have loran on your boat?"

"Naturally."

"Marvelous invention."

Esterhazy glanced at Falkoner. Loran? That old technology had long ago been superseded by GPS. All at once, Esterhazy understood what Falkoner was up to.

"And what kind of vessel do you have?" Falkoner asked.

"It's, ah, it's a Chris-Craft. Eighty feet."

"An eighty-foot Chris-Craft. Does it have decent range?"

"Oh, sure."

"Such as?"

"Eight hundred nautical miles."

Falkoner seemed to consider this. Then he took Betterton by the arm. "Come on. We'll show you one of the staterooms."

They left the bridge and descended two levels to the living quarters on the lower deck. But Falkoner did not stop here, instead descending another staircase to the mechanical region of the vessel. He led the way down a hallway to an unmarked door. "I'm curious," he said as he opened the door. "What kind of engine does your yacht have? And what's your hailing port?"

They stepped into, not a stateroom, but a spartan-looking storage area. "Oh, I'm not really all that nautical," Betterton said, with a chuckle and a wave of his hand. "I leave all that to my captain and staff."

"Funny," Falkoner replied as he raised the cover of a sail locker. "I myself prefer to leave nothing to others." He pulled a large sailcloth tarp from the locker and unrolled it over the floor.

"This is a stateroom?" Betterton asked.

"No," Falkoner replied, closing the door. He glanced at Esterhazy, and there was something chilling in his look.

Betterton glanced at his watch. "Well, thanks for the tour. I think I'd better be getting back—"

He paused when he saw the double-edged combat knife in Falkoner's hand.

"Who are you?" Falkoner said in a low voice. "And what do you want?"

Betterton swallowed. He looked from Falkoner to the knife and back again. "I told you. My yacht is moored just down from—"

As quickly as a striking snake, Falkoner grabbed one of Betterton's hands and jabbed the point of his knife into the webbing between the index and middle fingers.

Betterton cried out in pain, tried to jerk his hand free. But Falkoner just took a tighter hold, pulling the man forward so that he stood on the sailcloth.

"We're wasting time," he said. "Don't make me repeat myself. Judson, cover me."

Esterhazy removed his pistol and stepped back. He felt sick. This seemed unnecessary. And Falkoner's obvious eagerness made it worse.

"You're making a serious mistake," Betterton began, his voice suddenly low, threatening. But before he could continue Falkoner took a fresh grip on the knife and then pushed it even deeper, this time into the flesh between the middle and ring fingers.

"I'll kill you," Betterton gasped.

As Esterhazy looked on with growing horror, Falkoner held the stranger's wrist in a grip of iron while he dug with the knife, twisting and probing.

Betterton staggered over the tarp, grunting but not saying anything.

"Tell me why you're here." And Falkoner twisted the knife deeper.

"I'm a thief," Betterton gasped.

"Interesting story," said Falkoner. "But I don't believe it."

"I—" Betterton began, but with a sudden explosion of violence Falkoner kneed him in the groin, then head-butted the man as he doubled over. Betterton toppled back onto the tarp, groaning, blood streaming from a broken nose.

Falkoner pulled one corner of the tarp over Betterton, like a sheet, then knelt on it, pinning Betterton's chest. He took the knife and let it trace a line up the soft underside of the man's chin. Betterton, unable to rise and half stunned, rocked his head from side to side, moaning incoherently.

Falkoner sighed, whether with regret or impatience Esterhazy couldn't guess, and then stuck the knife into the soft flesh just above the neck, below the chin, sinking it an inch into the man's palate.

Now Betterton finally screamed and struggled wildly. After a moment, Falkoner removed the blade.

Betterton coughed, spat blood. "Reporter," he said after a moment. The voice was a wet gargle, hard to understand.

"A reporter? Investigating what?"

"Death...June and Carlton Brodie."

"How did you find me?" Falkoner asked.

"Locals...Car rental...Airline."

"That sounds more credible," Falkoner said. "Have you told anyone about me?"

"No."

"Good."

"You have to let me go...Man waiting for me...in the boat—"

With a brutal slashing motion, Falkoner drew the knife hard across the reporter's throat, simultaneously leaping backward to avoid the jet of blood.

"Oh, my God!" Esterhazy cried, stepping back in shock and dismay.

Betterton raised his hands toward the wound, but it was an involuntary movement. As dark crimson flooded between the man's fingers, Falkoner drew the tarp around limbs that were already jerking spastically.

Esterhazy stared, transfixed with shock. Falkoner stood, wiped the knife on the tarp, straightened his clothes, wiped off his hands, looking down at the dying reporter with something very much like satisfaction. He turned to Esterhazy. "Little strong for you, Judson?"

Esterhazy did not respond.

They climbed back up two flights, Esterhazy feeling unnerved by the brutality and Falkoner's evident enjoyment. He followed Falkoner through the saloon and out onto the rear deck. In the shadow of the yacht, the motor launch was still waiting.

Falkoner leaned over the railing, speaking to the blond man in the launch, the one who had brought Betterton out to the yacht. "Vic, the body's downstairs in the forward cargo hold. Come back after dark and dispose of it. Discreetly."

"Yes, sir," said the man in the launch.

"You'll need an adequate story as for why your passenger isn't returning to the dock. He's a capital fellow, we've invited him on a short cruise."

"Very good, sir."

"I might suggest leaving the body in Riverside Park. Up in the low hundreds—that's still a sketchy area. Make it look like a mugging. I'd drop it out to sea but that would eventually be harder to explain."

"Yes, Mr. Falkoner." The man fired up the motor and turned back toward the Boat Basin.

Falkoner watched for a minute as the dinghy moved away. Then he glanced at Esterhazy. His face was tense. "A bloody clueless reporter and he found me. Found the *Vergeltung*." His eyes narrowed. "I can only think of one way: he followed *you*."

"Not possible. I've been exceedingly careful. Besides, I've been nowhere near Malfourche."

A long, slitted look followed this, and then Falkoner seemed to relax. He breathed out. "I suppose we can call that a successful dry run, *ja*?"

Esterhazy didn't answer.

"We're ready for this man Pendergast. As long as you baited the hook properly and are sure he will come."

"Nothing about Pendergast is sure," Esterhazy said at last.

CHAPTER 62

FELDER STOOD IN A FAR CORNER OF CONSTANCE GREENE'S room at Mount Mercy Hospital. Dr. Ostrom was there, along with Agent Pendergast and an NYPD lieutenant named D'Agosta. The previous afternoon, the police had taken away all of Constance's books, her private writings, various personal possessions, and even the paintings on the walls. That morning they had learned conclusively that Poole was a fake, a fraud, and Felder had had to endure a dressing-down by the real Poole, who savaged him for not checking the man's credentials.

Pendergast did not bother to hide his steely contempt for the way in which they had allowed Constance to leave Mount Mercy. Some of his displeasure had been directed against Ostrom, but Felder had endured the brunt of the man's icy wrath.

"Well, Doctors," Pendergast was saying, "allow me to congratulate you on the first escape from Mount Mercy in a hundred and twenty years. Where shall we mount the plaque?"

Silence.

Pendergast plucked a photograph from his suit pocket and showed it first to Ostrom, then to Felder. "Do you recognize this man?"

Felder looked at it closely. It was a slightly blurry shot of a handsome, middle-aged man.

"He looks rather like Poole," said Felder, "but I'm pretty sure it's not the same man. Brother, perhaps?"

"And you, Dr. Ostrom?"

"Hard to say."

Pendergast slipped a thin, felt-tipped pen from his pocket, bent over the photograph, and briefly worked on it. He followed with a touch of a white pen. At last he turned back to the two doctors and showed them the photograph without comment.

Felder stared at the photograph again—this time with a shock of recognition. Pendergast had added a salt-and-pepper Van Dyke beard.

"My God, that's him. Poole."

Ostrom nodded his miserable agreement.

"The man's real name is Esterhazy," said Pendergast, tossing the photograph on the empty table with disgust. He sat down beside the table, tenting his fingers, his gaze turned inward. "I was a damned fool, Vincent. I thought I'd run him deep into the bush. I didn't anticipate he'd double back on the trail and come up behind me, like a Cape buffalo."

The lieutenant did not reply. An uncomfortable silence began to grow in the room.

"In the note," Felder said, "she claims her child is still alive. How is that possible? The whole reason she's in here is because she admitted killing it."

Pendergast shot him a withering glance. "Before we

348 DOUGLAS PRESTON & LINCOLN CHILD

bring an infant back from the dead, Doctor, shall we
first recover the mother?"

A pause. Then Pendergast turned to Ostrom. "Did
this so-called Poole discuss, in specific psychological
terms, Constance's condition?"

"He did."

"And was his analysis consistent? Believable?"

"It seemed surprising, given what I knew of Ms.
Greene. However, its internal logic was sound and so
I assumed it was correct. He claimed she'd been his
patient. There seemed no reason to doubt him."

Pendergast's spidery fingers drummed on the wooden
arm of the chair. "And you say that, at his first visit with
Constance, Dr. Poole asked for a moment alone with
her?"

"Yes."

Pendergast glanced at D'Agosta. "I think the situation is clear enough. Crystal clear, in fact."

It wasn't at all clear to Felder, but he said nothing.

Pendergast turned back to Ostrom. "And it was this
same Poole, naturally, who first suggested Constance
be given an outing—off the grounds?"

"That's correct," said Ostrom.

"Who took care of the paperwork?"

"Dr. Felder."

Pendergast shot Felder a hooded glance. He cringed.
The FBI agent took a long, searching look around
the room. Then he turned once again to Lieutenant
D'Agosta. "Vincent, this room—and this place—hold
no further interest. We must focus on the note. Can
you bring it out again, please?"

D'Agosta reached into his suit pocket and took out

the photocopy Ostrom had made. Pendergast seized it and read it over, once, twice.

"The woman who delivered this," he said. "There was no luck tracking her taxi?"

"Nope." D'Agosta nodded at the note. "Not much to go on there."

"Not much," Pendergast said. "But perhaps, just enough."

"I don't understand," the lieutenant said.

"There are two voices speaking in this note. One of them knows Constance's ultimate destination—the other does not."

"You're saying that first voice is Poole's. I mean Esterhazy's."

"Exactly. And you will note that, perhaps inadvertently, he allowed a certain phrase to escape, which Constance quotes. 'Vengeance is where it will end.'"

"And?"

"Esterhazy was always overly pleased with his own wit. '*Vengeance* is where it will end.' Isn't that rather an odd construction, Vincent?"

"I'm not so sure, really. That's the whole point of it: vengeance."

Pendergast waved his hand impatiently. "What if he's speaking not of an *act*, but an *object*?"

This was followed by a long silence.

"Esterhazy is taking Constance to some *place* named Vengeance. Maybe it's an old family mansion. An estate. A business of some kind. That's precisely the kind of pun Esterhazy would employ—especially in a moment of triumph, as no doubt he viewed this to be."

D'Agosta shook his head. "That's pretty thin. Who would name something Vengeance?"

Pendergast turned his silvery eyes on the skeptical policeman. "Do we have anything else to go on?"

D'Agosta paused. "No, I guess we don't."

"And would a hundred NYPD officers, beating bushes and knocking down doors, have any greater chance of success than I, following up this possible lead?"

"It's a needle in a haystack. How can you possibly track such a thing down?"

"I know somebody who is exceptionally skilled in just this sort of thing. Let us go—time is short."

He turned toward Felder and Ostrom. "We are ready to leave, gentlemen."

As they departed, Pendergast walking so fast that Felder and Ostrom almost had to jog to keep up, the agent removed his cell phone and dialed.

"Mime?" he spoke into the phone. "It's Pendergast. I have another job for you—another very difficult one, I'm afraid . . ." He spoke rapidly and softly all the way to the entrance hall, before shutting the phone with a slap. He turned toward Felder and Ostrom, and in a voice laced with irony said, "Thank you very much, *Doctors*, but we shall find our own way out."

CHAPTER 63

Slowly, Constance regained consciousness. It was very dark. She was aware of both nausea and a splitting headache. She stood still a moment, slumped forward, confused, as her head cleared. And then, quite suddenly, she recalled what had happened.

She tried to move, but found that her hands were handcuffed to a chain around her waist and her legs were bound to something behind her—this time, very firmly. Her mouth was covered by duct tape. The pitch-black air was damp and smelled of diesel fuel, oil, and mold. She could feel the gentle rocking and the sound of water slapping against a hull—she was on a boat.

She listened intently. There were people on board—she could hear muffled voices above. She stood quite still, trying to collect her thoughts, her heartbeat slow and steady. Her limbs were stiff and sore: she must have been unconscious for hours, perhaps many hours.

Time passed. And then she heard footsteps coming closer. A sudden crack of light appeared, and a moment later a bulb went on. She stared. Standing in the doorway was the man who called himself both Esterhazy and Dr. Poole. He stared back at her, his handsome face scored both by nervousness and the scratches she herself had inflicted. Behind him, in a tight hallway, she could see a second, shadowy figure.

He moved toward her. "We're going to move you. For your own sake, please don't try anything."

She merely stared. She couldn't move, couldn't speak.

Taking a knife from his pocket, he cut the layers of duct tape that affixed her legs to a vertical structural post in what was now clearly a hold. In another moment she was free.

"Come on." He reached over and hooked his hand in one of her cuffed arms. She stumbled forward, feet numb, legs cramped, little sparks of pain shooting through them with each movement. He helped her get in front of him and eased her toward the tiny door. She stooped to go through it, Esterhazy following.

The shadowy figure stood outside—a woman. Constance recognized her: the red-haired woman from the adjoining garden. The woman returned her stare, coolly, a faint smile on her lips.

So Pendergast had not gotten the note. It had been futile. Indeed, it had apparently been some sort of ruse.

"Take the other arm," Esterhazy told the woman. "She's extremely unpredictable."

The woman took her other arm, and together they escorted her down a passageway toward another, even smaller hatch. Constance did not resist, allowing herself to be pulled along, her head hanging down. As Esterhazy leaned forward to undog the hatch, Constance braced herself; then she turned quickly, ramming the woman violently in the stomach with her head. With a loud *oof* the woman fell back, crashing into a bulkhead. Esterhazy swung around and she tried to butt him as well, but he seized her in a powerful embrace and pinned her arms. The woman scrambled to her feet, leaned over Constance, pulled her head back by the hair, and slapped her hard across the face, once, twice.

"No need for that," Esterhazy said sharply. He hauled Constance around. "You do what we say or these people will really hurt you. Understand?"

She stared back, unable to speak, still fighting to catch her breath.

He pushed her into the dark space beyond the hatch, then followed behind with the red-haired woman. They were in another hold, and in the floor was another hatch. Esterhazy loosened the hatch and opened it, revealing a dark, stagnant space. In the dim light, she could see that it was the lowest part of the bilge, where the hull came together in a V—no doubt in the bow area of the vessel.

Esterhazy merely pointed toward the dark, yawning mouth of the hatch.

Constance balked.

She felt a smack across the side of her head as the woman struck her hard with the flat of her palm. "Get down there," the woman said.

"Let me handle this," said Esterhazy angrily.

Constance sat down, placed her feet in the hole, and lowered herself slowly in. It was a bigger space than it looked. She glanced up to see the woman preparing to strike her again, this time with her fist. Esterhazy placed a less-than-gentle restraining hand on the woman's arm. "That isn't necessary," he said. "I'm not going to say it again."

A single tear welled up into Constance's eye and she shook it away. She had not wept in more years than she could remember, and she would not let these people see her weep now. It must have been the shock of seeing the woman—she realized just how much she'd been clinging to the slender thread of hope her note had offered.

She sat down and leaned against the bulkhead. The hatch shut behind her, followed by a squeak of metal as it was dogged down.

It was pitch black in the space—even darker than the hold had been. The sound of waves lapping the hull filled the bilge, making her feel like she was underwater.

She felt ill, as if she might be sick. But if she was, the duct tape over her mouth would cause her to aspirate, to drown. She could not allow that to happen.

She shifted, trying to get comfortable and focus her thoughts on something else. She was, after all, used to dark, small spaces. This was nothing new, she told herself. Nothing new at all.

CHAPTER 64

At two thirty in the afternoon—that is, just after rising—Corrie Swanson left her dorm room, hit the street, and headed for her cubby in the Sealy Library on Tenth Avenue. Along the way, she stopped at the local Greek coffee shop. It felt like winter all of a sudden, a cold wind blowing trash down the sidewalk. But the coffee shop was a warm oasis of dish clatter and shouted activity. She put down her money and slid out a copy of the *Times* from the middle of the pile on the counter, then bought a cup of coffee, black. She was turning to leave when her eye caught the headline in the *Post*:

Grisly Beheading in Riverside Park

With a sense of embarrassment she also took a *Post*. She had always looked on the *Post* as a paper for cretins, but it often covered the really gruesome crimes the *Times* primly shied away from, and it was her secret vice.

When she got to her cubby at the library, she sat down, looked around to make sure nobody was watching, and with a vague feeling of shame opened the *Post* first.

Almost immediately she straightened up, horrified. The victim was one Edward Betterton, on vacation in the city from Mississippi, whose body had been found in an isolated section of Riverside Park, behind a statue of Joan of Arc. His throat had been slashed so savagely, the head had almost been separated from the body. There was other, unspecified mutilation that might be signs of a gangland slaying, the *Post* said, although there were also indications it could have been a vicious mugging, with the pockets of the victim turned inside out and his watch, money, and valuables missing.

Corrie read the article a second time, more slowly. Betterton. This was awful. He didn't seem like a bad guy—just off base. In retrospect she'd felt sorry about the way she had reamed him out.

But this brutal killing couldn't be a coincidence. He'd been on to something—a drug operation, he'd said—even if he'd gotten the Pendergast angle all screwed up. What was the address of the house he'd told her about? She concentrated, feeling a sudden panic she wouldn't remember—and then it came: 428 East End Avenue.

She put down the tabloid thoughtfully. Pendergast. How was he involved, exactly? Did he know about Betterton? Was he really working on his own, with no backup? Had he actually blown up a bar?

She had made a promise not to interfere. But checking something out—just checking it out—even Pendergast couldn't call that "interference."

CHAPTER 65

SPECIAL AGENT PENDERGAST WAITED IN A RENTED CAR on the circular drive above the Seventy-Ninth Street marina on Manhattan's Upper West Side, examining through binoculars the yacht moored a few hundred feet offshore. It was the largest in the marina, close to one hundred and thirty feet, sleek and well appointed. As the afternoon wind shifted, the yacht swung on its mooring, revealing the name and hailing port painted on the stern.

Vergeltung
Orchid Island, Florida

A cold wind blew from the water, buffeting the car and raising whitecaps on the broad Hudson.

A cell phone, sitting on the passenger seat, began to ring. Pendergast lowered the binoculars to answer it. "Yes?"

"Is this my main Secret Agent Man?" came the whispery voice on the other end of the line.

"Mime," Pendergast replied. "How are you faring?"

"Did you find the yacht okay?"

"I'm staring at it now."

A pleased, raspy giggle sounded over the phone. "Ideal. *Ideal.* And do you think we, um, have a ringer?"

"Indeed I do, Mime—thanks to you."

"*Vergeltung.* German for 'vengeance.' It was rather a challenge. But then again, that ghostnet of zombified PCs I've appropriated all over Cleveland has been rather idle of late. It was high time I put them to work on something useful."

"I'd prefer not to know the details. But you have my thanks."

"Glad I was able to be of more help this time around. Hang loose, homeboy." There was a click as the line went dead.

Pendergast put the phone in his pocket and eased the car forward, heading down toward the entrance of the marina and up to the gate that led to the main pier. A man in a crisp uniform—an ex-cop, without doubt—leaned out of the adjoining guardhouse. "Help you?"

"I'm here to see Mr. Lowe, the general manager."

"And you are?"

Pendergast removed his shield and let it dangle for a moment. "Special Agent Pendergast."

"You got an appointment?"

"No."

"And this is in reference to...?"

Pendergast simply stared at him. Then he suddenly smiled. "Is there going to be a problem? Because if there is, I'd like to know it now."

The man blinked. "Just a moment." He retreated and spoke into a phone. Then he opened the gate. "You can pull through and park. Mr. Lowe will be out in a moment."

It took more than a moment. Finally, a tall, fit, nautical-looking man wearing a Greek fisherman's cap emerged from the main marina building and came striding over, his breath condensing behind him in puffs. Pendergast stepped out of the car and stood waiting for him.

"Well, well. FBI?" said the man, extending his hand with a friendly smile, his blue eyes flashing. "What can I do for you?"

Pendergast nodded toward the moored yacht. "I'd like to know about that yacht."

The man paused. "What's the basis for your interest?" He continued to smile genially.

"Official," said Pendergast, smiling in return.

"Official. Well now, that's funny," said the man. "Because I just called the New York field office of the FBI and asked them if a certain Special Agent Pendergrast was working on a case that involved the marina—"

"Pendergast."

"Excuse me. *Pendergast.* They said you'd taken a temporary leave of absence and assured me you were not on any active case right now. So one must assume you're moonlighting, flashing your badge under false pretenses. Which has got to be against FBI regulations. Am I right?"

Pendergast's smile did not waver. "You're right on all counts."

"So I'm just going to go back to my office, and you're going to go away, and if I hear any more about this I'm going to call the FBI back and report that one of their special agents is roaming around town, using his badge to intimidate law-abiding citizens."

"Intimidate? When I begin to intimidate you, you'll know it."

"Is that a threat?"

"That's a prediction." Pendergast nodded toward the water. "I presume you can see that yacht out there? I have reason to believe a serious crime is about to be committed on it. If that crime occurs, then I *will* be on the case—in the most official of all possible capacities—and you, quite naturally, will be investigated as an accessory."

"A hollow threat. I'm no accessory and you know it. If a crime is about to be committed, I suggest you call the police, Mr. Prendergast."

"*Pender*gast." His voice remained reasonable. "All I want from you, Mr. Lowe, is some information about that yacht, the crew, their comings and goings. To be kept specifically between ourselves. Because I can see you're a friendly man who likes to assist law enforcement."

"If this is what you call intimidation, it isn't working. My job is to protect the privacy of the clients who patronize this marina, and that's what I intend to do. If you want to come back with a warrant, fine. If the NYPD comes, fine. Then I'll cooperate. But not with an FBI agent waving some tin on his off hours. Now get lost."

"When we do investigate this crime, my colleagues—and NYPD homicide—will want to know why you took money from the people on that yacht."

A flicker passed across the man's face. "A gratuity is a

normal part of this business. I'm like a cabbie—tips are standard here. Nothing wrong with that."

"Naturally—until the 'tip' reaches a certain size. Then it becomes a payment. Perhaps even a bribe. And when said bribe is made for the purposes of buying pushback should law enforcement come by asking questions, well, Mr. Lowe, that *does* in fact make you an accessory. Especially when it becomes known that you not only threatened to kill me if I did not leave the premises, but also insulted New York's finest with vulgar language."

"What the hell? I never threatened you or the cops."

"Your exact words were: *I've got friends who'll put a bullet in your brain if you don't get the hell out of here. And that goes for the NYPD pigs, too.*"

"I said nothing of the sort, you lying bastard!"

"That is correct. But only you and I know that. Everyone else will think I'm telling the truth."

"You'd never get away with that! You're bluffing!"

"I am a desperate man, Mr. Lowe, and I am operating beyond the rules. I will do anything—lie, coerce, and deceive—to force you to cooperate." He removed his cell. "Now: I'm about to dial an emergency FBI number to report your threats and request backup. When I do that, your life will change—forever. Or...?" He raised one eyebrow along with the phone.

Lowe stared at him, quivering with rage. "You son of a bitch."

"I'll take that as a yes. Shall we retire to your office? There's rather a nasty wind coming off the Hudson."

CHAPTER 66

THE BUILDING ON EAST END AVENUE could not be dignified by the name *brownstone.* It was brick, not stone;
it was narrow; and it rose only three stories. A more
dismal and down-at-the-heels structure could not be
found on the Upper East Side, Corrie decided as she
lounged against a ginkgo tree on the opposite side of
the street, drinking coffee and pretending once again
to read a book.

The windows had firmly drawn shades that looked
like they had been yellowing for decades. The windows
themselves were filthy, covered with bars, and sporting
lead alarm tape. The stoop was cracked, and trash had
collected in the basement entrance. Despite the shabby
appearance, however, the building seemed buttoned
up pretty tight, with gleaming new locks on the front
door. And the bars on the windows didn't look old,
either.

She finished her coffee, put away her book, and
strolled down the street. The neighborhood, once
German, had become facetiously known as the "girl
ghetto," the preferred neighborhood for recent college

graduates, mostly women, newly arrived in Manhattan and looking for a safe place to live. The neighborhood was quiet, orderly, and undeniably safe. The streets thronged with attractive, preppy young women, most of whom looked like they worked on Wall Street or in one of the Park Avenue law firms.

Corrie wrinkled her nose and continued to the end of the block. Betterton had said he'd seen someone leave the building, but it didn't look like anyone had been there in ages.

She turned around and strolled back down the block, feeling dissatisfied. The building was part of a long row of real brownstones, and no doubt each one had a small garden or patio in the rear. If she could get a look at the back of the building, she'd be able to check things out a little better. Of course, it might just be part of the overheated imagination of Betterton. Then again, there was something almost believable about his story of Pendergast blowing up a bar, burning down a drug lab, and sinking a bunch of boats. And although Betterton had been wrong, she had to admit he looked both smart and tough. He didn't strike her as being someone who would be easy to kill. But kill him they had.

As she neared the center of the block, she eyed the two brownstones adjoining number 428. They were both typical, bustling Upper East Side buildings, with several apartments per floor. Even as she watched, a young woman exited one of the buildings, dressed in a spiffy suit and carrying a briefcase. The woman passed by her with nary a sideways glance, leaving a trail of expensive perfume. Other young women of the neighborhood were coming and going, and they all seemed to be of the same type: young professionals in business suits or jogging outfits. Corrie realized that her own Goth look—the streaked spiky hair, dangling metal, multiple earrings, and tattoos—made her stick out like a sore thumb.

What to do? She went into a bagel shop, ordered a bialy with lox spread, and sat by the window where she had a view down the street. If she could manage to make friends with someone on a ground-floor apartment on either side of the building, she might just talk her way into seeing the backyard. But you just didn't walk up and say hello to people in New York City. She wasn't in Kansas anymore...

...And then, coming out of the brownstone to the right of 428, she saw a girl with long black hair, wearing a leather miniskirt and tall leather boots.

Dropping a few dollar bills on the table, she bolted from the bagel shop and went walking down the street, swinging her bag and looking up at the sky, on a collision course with the fellow Goth coming the other way.

It had been so easy. Now the sun was setting and Corrie was relaxing in the tiny kitchen of the ground-floor apartment, drinking green tea and listening to her newfound friend complaining about all the yuppies in the neighborhood. Her name was Maggie and she worked as a waitress at a jazz club while trying to break into theater. She was bright, funny, and clearly starved for company.

"I'd love to move out to Long Island City or Brooklyn," she said, cupping her tea, "but my dad thinks any place in New York outside of the Upper East Side is populated by rapists and murderers."

Corrie laughed. "Maybe he's right. That building next door looks pretty creepy." She felt horribly guilty manipulating a girl she would actually like to have as a friend.

"I think it's abandoned. I don't think I've ever seen anyone go in or out. Weird—it's probably worth five million bucks. Prime real estate just going to waste."

Corrie nursed her tea and wondered, now that she was here, how she was going to get outside into the patio behind the brownstone, get over the eight-foot wall into the backyard of the creepy house next door— and then break in.

Break in. Was that really what she was going to do? For the first time, she stopped to think about why, exactly, she was here and what she was planning. She had told herself she was just going to check things out. Casually. Was it really the most intelligent thing to do: contemplate a B&E even as she was studying at John Jay for a career in law enforcement?

And that was only the half of it. Sure, she'd broken into more than her share of places before, back in Medicine Creek—just for the hell of it—but if Betterton was right, these people were dangerous drug dealers. And Betterton was *dead.* Then, of course, there was her promise to Pendergast...

Of course she wouldn't break in. But she'd check it out. She'd play it safe, peer through the windows, keep her distance. At the first sign of trouble, or danger, or anything, she'd back off.

She turned to Maggie and sighed. "I like it here. I

wish I had a place like this. I'm getting kicked out of my apartment the day after tomorrow and my new lease doesn't start until the first. Guess I'll go stay at a hostel or something."

Maggie brightened. "You need a place to crash for a few days?"

"Do I!" Corrie smiled.

"Hey, it will be great having somebody here. Living alone can kind of creep you out sometimes. Do you know, when I got home yesterday evening I had the strangest feeling that somebody had been in the apartment while I was gone..."

CHAPTER 67

By TEN PM, THE WIND HAD PICKED UP, raising faint white-caps on the dark surface of the Hudson River, and the temperature hovered a few degrees above freezing. The tide was ebbing, and the river flowed smoothly southward toward New York Harbor. The lights of New Jersey glowed coldly across the dark mass of moving water.

Ten blocks north of the Seventy-Ninth Street marina, on the ripprapped shore below the West Side Highway, a dark figure moved down by the water. It was dragging a broken piece of flotsam over the rocks—a battered remnant of a floating dock, some planks of wood adhering to an abraded chunk of marine Styrofoam. The figure eased the piece into the water and got aboard, covering himself with a rotten section of a discarded tarp. As the raft hung next to shore, the figure produced a stick, whittled flat at one end, which when dipped in the water became almost invisible and which subtly controlled the progress of what looked like a mass of floating detritus.

With a small push of the stick, the man shoved the

improvised barque away from shore, where it drifted into the current, joining other random pieces of flotsam and jetsam.

It moved out until it was a few hundred feet offshore. There it floated, turning slowly, as it drifted sluggishly toward a group of silent yachts in a mooring field, their anchor lights piercing the darkness. Slowly, the flotsam floated past the boats, bumping against one hull, then another, on its seemingly random journey. Gradually, it approached the largest yacht in the anchorage, knocking lightly against its hull and drifting past. As it neared the stern there was the very slightest of movements, a rustle and a faint splash, and then silence as the now-tenantless piece of garbage continued past the yacht and vanished in the darkness.

Pendergast, in a sleek neoprene suit, crouched on the swim platform behind the stern transom of the *Vergeltung*, listening intently. All was silent. After a moment, he raised his head and peered over the edge of the stern. He could see two men in the darkness, one relaxing on a sitting area on the aft deck, smoking a cigarette. The other was walking around on the foredeck, barely visible from this angle.

As Pendergast watched, the man on the aft deck raised a pint bottle and took a long pull. After a few minutes, he rose—unsteadily—and took a turn around the deck, pausing at the stern not five feet from Pendergast, looking across the water, before reinstalling himself in his nook and taking another long drink from the bottle. He stubbed out the cigarette, lit another.

From the small dive bag he carried, Pendergast removed his Les Baer .45 and gave it a quick check. He shoved it back into the bag and removed a short length of rubber hose.

Again he waited, watching. The man continued drinking and smoking, then finally rose and walked forward, disappearing through a door into the interior of the yacht, where dim lights glowed from various windows.

In a flash Pendergast was over the stern and onto the aft deck, crouching behind a pair of tenders.

Thanks to his new friend Lowe, Pendergast had learned there were probably only a few crew members on board. Most had gone ashore that afternoon, leaving, the general manager believed, only four on the vessel. How accurate this information was remained to be seen.

According to Lowe's description, one of the men was undoubtedly Esterhazy. And then there were the supplies Lowe had observed being loaded recently, including a long stainless-steel dry-goods box large enough to hide an unconscious person—or, for that matter, a corpse.

Pendergast briefly considered what he would do to Esterhazy if the man had already killed Constance.

Esterhazy sat on an engine room bulkhead next to Falkoner, the redheaded woman whose name he did not know, and four men carrying identical Beretta 93R machine pistols configured for automatic three-round burst action. Falkoner had insisted they retreat to the engine room—the most secure place on the boat—for the operation. Nobody spoke.

Soft footfalls approached outside the door, and then a triple knock sounded lightly, followed by a double knock. Falkoner rose and unlocked the door. A man with a cigarette in his mouth stepped inside.

"Put that out," said Falkoner sharply.

The man quickly stubbed it out. "He's on board," he said.

Falkoner looked at him. "When?"

"A few minutes back. He was good—arrived on a floating piece of trash. I almost didn't catch it. He climbed onto the swim platform and now he's in the aft deck area. Vic up on the flybridge is keeping track of him with the infrared night-vision setup."

"Does he suspect anything?"

"No. I pretended to be drunk, like you said."

"Very good."

Esterhazy rose. "Damn it, if you had an opportunity to kill him you should have taken it! Don't get cocky—this man is worth half a dozen of you. Shoot him at your first chance."

Falkoner turned. "No."

Esterhazy stared at him. "What do you mean, *no*? We already discussed—"

"Take him alive. I have a few questions before we kill him."

Esterhazy stared. "You're making a huge mistake. Even if you manage to take him alive, he won't answer any questions."

Falkoner gave Esterhazy a brutal smile, which stretched the already repulsive mole. "I never have problems getting people to answer questions. But I wonder, Judson, why *you* would have a problem with that? Afraid we might find out something you'd rather keep hidden?"

"You've no idea who you're dealing with," Esterhazy

said quickly, a stab of familiar fear suddenly freighting his anxiety. "You're a fool if you don't kill him right away, on sight, before he figures out what's going on."

Falkoner narrowed his eyes. "There are a dozen of us. Heavily armed, well trained. What's the matter, Judson? We've taken care of you well enough all these years—and now you suddenly don't trust us? I'm surprised—and hurt."

The voice was laden with sarcasm. Esterhazy felt the old fear grow in the pit of his stomach.

"We'll be in open water on our own boat. We've got the advantage of surprise—he has no idea he's walking into a trap. And we've got his woman tied up below. He's at our mercy."

Esterhazy swallowed. *As am I*, he thought.

Falkoner spoke into his headset. "Take her out to sea." He looked around the group gathered in the engine room. "We'll let the others take care of him. If things go awry, then we'll make our move."

Pendergast, still crouching behind the tenders, felt a rumble shudder through the yacht. The engines had been turned on. He heard some voices forward, heard the faint splash of a mooring pennant tossed overboard; and then he felt the prow of the boat swing westward, toward the navigational channel of the river, as the engines accelerated to full throttle.

Pendergast pondered the coincidence of his arrival and the boat's departure, and decided it was not a coincidence after all.

CHAPTER 68

Aboard the Vergeltung

ESTERHAZY WAITED IN THE ENGINE ROOM with Falkoner. The twin diesels, now running at cruising speed, were loud in the confined space.

He checked his watch. Ten minutes had passed since Pendergast came on board. The air of tension was gradually increasing. He didn't like this—didn't like it at all. Falkoner had lied to him.

He'd taken exquisite care in reeling Pendergast in. Constance had done precisely what he'd expected, escaping her loose bonds, writing a note and tossing it out the window of the safe house to his plant in the next garden. And since Pendergast was now on board, he had clearly swallowed the bait so carefully dangled—"vengeance," which of course in German translated to *Vergeltung*. It had been a balancing act, giving Pendergast just enough information to locate the boat but not enough to suspect a trap.

But now Falkoner was insisting on taking Pendergast alive. Esterhazy felt a twinge of nausea: he knew that one reason Falkoner wanted this was because he enjoyed torture. The man was sick—and his arrogance and sadism could still mess everything up.

Esterhazy felt the old sense of fear and of paranoia increase. He checked his handgun, racked the slide. If Falkoner didn't follow through at the first opportunity, he'd have to do it himself. Finish what he'd started on the Scottish moors. And do it before Pendergast—intentionally or otherwise—did in fact reveal the secret Esterhazy had kept from the Covenant for the past decade. Christ, if only Pendergast hadn't examined that old gun; if only he had let sleeping dogs lie. The man had no idea, *no idea*, of the madness he'd unleashed. Maybe he should have let Pendergast into the awful secret years ago, when he first married his sister.

Too late now.

Falkoner's radio crackled. "It's Vic," came the voice. "I don't know how, but we seem to have lost him. He's not behind the tender anymore."

"*Verdammter Mist!*" Falkoner said angrily. "How the hell could you lose him?"

"I don't know. He was hiding where we couldn't see him. We waited awhile and nothing happened, so I left Berger on watch in the main cabin and went to the sky deck to look from a better angle—and he was gone. I don't know how—we would've seen him no matter which way he went."

"He must still be down there somewhere," said Falkoner. "All the doors are locked. Send Berger onto the aft deck; cover him from your position on the flybridge."

Esterhazy spoke into his own radio headset. "A locked door is no impediment to Pendergast."

"He couldn't have gotten past the main cabin door without us seeing him," said Viktor.

"Flush him out," Falkoner repeated. "Captain, what's our position?"

"We're just coming into New York Harbor."

"Maintain cruising speed. Head for open ocean."

Viktor crouched on the flybridge of the *Vergeltung*, three stories above the surface of the water. The boat had just passed the site of the fast-rising One World Trade Center and was rounding the southern tip of Manhattan, the Battery on their left, lit up by a cluster of spotlights. The buildings of the financial district rose like clusters of glowing spikes, casting an ambient light across the water, bathing the boat in an indirect radiance.

Below him, the aft deck of the *Vergeltung* was softly illuminated in the glow of the city. Two outboard tenders—small motorboats used for coming and going when the yacht was at anchor—lay side by side on the port stern deck, each in its launching cradle, covered with canvas. There was no way for Pendergast to have gone forward without crossing the open deck. And they had been watching that deck like a hawk. He must still be back in the stern area.

Through the night-vision goggles, he saw Berger emerge from the main cabin, gun at the ready. Viktor lowered the goggles and raised his own weapon to cover him.

Berger paused a moment in the shadows, readying himself, then skipped alongside in the cover of the first tender and crouched behind its bow.

Viktor waited, his Beretta pointed, ready to unload at the slightest movement, the briefest exposure. He was ex-military and didn't care much for Falkoner's order to take the man alive; if this fellow showed his head, he'd take him down anyway. He wasn't going to risk the others for a live catch.

Slowly, Berger worked his way alongside the boat toward the stern.

Viktor's radio crackled, Berger speaking to him through his headset. "No sign of him behind the tenders."

"Make double sure. And be careful: he might have slipped back behind the stern transom, waiting to jump anyone coming out."

Keeping his weapon trained on the scene, Viktor watched as Berger crept from the first tender to the second.

"Not here," came the whispered voice.

"Then he did slip back behind the stern," Viktor said.

Viktor watched as Berger advanced to the stern rail, keeping to a low crouch. Then the man tensed and sprang up to full height, training his weapon on the twin swim platforms behind.

A moment later he dropped back down. "Nothing."

Viktor thought hard. This was crazy. "Inside. He might be hiding inside one of the boats, under the tarp."

Viktor shifted his gunsights to the tenders as Berger grasped the stern ladder of the first, swung it down, stepped onto it, and raised himself up. He leaned against the propeller shaft in order to lift the edge of the tarp and peer underneath.

Over the radio, Viktor heard a faint click, then an electronic beep.

Oh, Jesus, he knew that sound! "Berger—!"

A sudden earsplitting roar erupted from the tender's outboard; Berger screamed and there was a shower of dark spray as his body was kicked sideways by the whirling propeller, his side ripped wide open.

After an instant of horrified shock, Viktor raked the tender with multiple bursts from his Beretta, sweeping back and forth until the magazine was empty, the rounds shredding the canvas and punching through the boat, riddling anyone who might have been hiding within. After a moment, flames erupted in the stern area of the tender. Berger's body lay where it had fallen, unmoving, a puddle of black spreading out from beneath it.

With trembling hands Viktor ejected the empty mag and rammed another home.

"What's going on!" came Falkoner's furious voice over his headset. "What are you doing?"

"He killed Berger!" shouted Viktor. "He—"

"Stop firing! We're on a boat, idiot! You'll start a fire!"

Viktor stared at the flames licking up the canvas from the tender. There was a muffled *thump* and a shudder as more flames burst upward from the ruptured gas tank. "Shit, we've already got a fire."

"Where?"

"On the tender."

"Launch it. Get it off the yacht. *Now!*"

"Right." Viktor scrambled down to the main deck and raced to the tender. The man Pendergast was nowhere in sight—no doubt he was lying dead in the belly of the tender. He unclipped the stays fore and aft, threw open the stern transom, and hit the windlass switch. As the gears on the windlass hummed, the twelve-foot tender lurched back, sliding on launching rails; Viktor seized the bow and gave it an additional shove to keep it moving. When the burning stern of the tender hit the fast-moving wake, the water grabbed it and yanked the little boat off the deck, the chains snapping; Viktor was thrown off balance but managed to grab the stern rail, recovering quickly. The burning tender fell astern, spinning in the water, already sinking. It had taken the fire with it and most likely the dead body of the target. Viktor was vastly relieved.

Until he felt a stiff shove from behind, his headset yanked off simultaneously, and he went tumbling into the water after the burning tender.

CHAPTER 69

CROUCHING AGAINST THE PORT SIDE of the remaining tender, Pendergast watched the burning boat disappear into the darkness as the waters of New York Harbor closed over it. The cries of the man he had pushed overboard grew fainter and fainter, soon lost amid the sounds of the yacht, wind, and water. He put on the headset, adjusted it, and began listening to the alarmed chatter. From it he created a mental image of the number of players, their relative locations, and their various states of mind.

Most revealing.

As he listened, he shrugged out of the movement-hampering wet suit and tossed it over the side. Pulling his clothes from the waterproof dive bag he'd brought along, he dressed quickly, then tossed the bag overboard as well. After a few minutes, he moved to the bow of the tender. The flybridge at the top of the boat seemed to be vacant. A single armed man was now patrolling the sky deck. From each end of his perambulation the man had a clear vantage point of the aft deck.

Pendergast watched as the figure on the sky deck

stared out in the direction of the sinking tender, speaking into his radio. After a minute, he entered the sky lounge and began pacing back and forth before the wheelhouse, guarding it. Pendergast counted out the seconds it took him for each turn, then timed his own move, sprinting across the open main deck to the aft entrance of the main saloon. He crouched in the doorwell, the overhang now protecting him from view from above. He tried the door: locked. The window was smoked and the saloon beyond was dark, making it impossible to see inside.

The simple lock yielded to a brief attack. There was enough ambient noise to cover his movements. Though the door was now unlocked, he did not yet open it. He knew from listening to the radio there were many more people on board than he had originally anticipated—Lowe had been deceived—and he realized he had fallen into a trap. The boat was heading for the Narrows and no doubt the Atlantic Ocean beyond. How unfortunate.

Unfortunate, that is, for the survival chances of those on board.

Again he listened to the chatter, building an ever-clearer picture of the situation on the vessel. No clue as to Constance's whereabouts was offered. One person, clearly the man in charge, spoke in a mixture of German and English from a location with loud background noise—perhaps the engine room. The others were scattered about the yacht, all in place, all awaiting orders. He did not hear Esterhazy's voice.

From what he could gather, however, there was no one in the main saloon. With exquisite care he cracked open the door and peered into the dim but elegant space, paneled in mahogany, with white leather banquettes, a granite-topped bar, and plush carpeting barely visible in the ambient light. He looked around quickly, making sure it was empty.

He heard running footsteps in the companionway and a burst of radio chatter. Several men were on their way aft and would reach the saloon momentarily.

Quickly, he backed out of the door again, easing it shut. He crouched again in the darkness of the doorwell, ear to the fiberglass panel. The footsteps entered the saloon from the front. From the whispered radio chatter, he learned there were two of them. They were on their way to check on Viktor, last seen on the aft deck, who hadn't responded to his radio since launching the burning tender.

Excellent.

He eased himself around the corner from the door and pressed himself against the aft wall, concealed from above by the overhang. All was once again quiet in the saloon. The two men were waiting and listening as well, evidently spooked.

Moving with exquisite care, Pendergast reached an access ladder that ran to the upper aft deck; grasped a rung and slid himself up; and then, reaching out with one leg, transferred himself from the ladder to a small roof area above the saloon, still hidden from view of the sky deck by a large cowl vent.

Stretching out on the polished fiberglass, Pendergast leaned down over the overhang and—with one arm extended—lightly brushed the barrel of his gun on the door. It made a faint noise, no doubt magnified inside the saloon.

No response. Now the two men inside would be even more agitated. They couldn't be sure if the sound was random or not; whether someone was outside the door. That uncertainty would, for the time being, keep them in place.

Sliding back up on the roof above the saloon, keeping hidden behind the vent, Pendergast pressed the barrel of his Les Baer against the fiberglass roof and pulled the trigger. A massive explosion sounded in the saloon below as the .45 ACP Black Talon expansion round ripped a hole in the roof, no doubt filling the saloon air with fiberglass and resin dust. Instantly he skipped off the roof and slid back to the door-well as the two panicked men opened fire through the roof with their machine pistols, riddling the area where he had just been and thereby revealing their location within the saloon. One of them did the expected and came charging out the door, firing as he went; Pendergast, positioned behind the door, kicked him hard across the shins as he emerged and then struck him a simultaneous blow to the neck; the man's momentum sent him sprawling facedown on deck, unconscious.

"Hammar!" came the shout from within the saloon.

Without slowing, the agent charged in through the now-open door. The second man turned and let loose a burst, but Pendergast had anticipated this, throwing himself to the carpeted floor, rolling, and firing a single round into the man's chest. The man slammed backward against a plasma television and collapsed in a shower of glass.

Leaping to his feet, Pendergast veered left and exited the port saloon door, then flattened himself against the wall next to the recessed entrance. Hidden beneath an overhang, he paused once again to listen in on the continuing radio chatter, rearranging in his mind his picture of the vessel and the shifting locations of the men on it.

"*Szell. Respond!*" came the voice of the man in charge. Other voices jammed the frequency, asking in a panic about the gunshots, until the German shut them up. "*Szell!*" the man called harshly over the radio. "*Do you read?*"

Pendergast thought with satisfaction that Szell was beyond all reading.

CHAPTER 70

E STERHAZY WATCHED WITH GROWING ALARM as Falkoner spoke into his radio, "Szell. Hammar. Respond."

Static sounded over the speakers.

"Damn it," Esterhazy burst out, "I keep telling you, you're underestimating him!" He slammed his hand on the bulkhead in frustration. "You've no idea who you're up against! He's going to kill them all! And then come for us!"

"We've got a dozen heavily armed men against one."

"You don't have a dozen anymore," Esterhazy shot back.

Falkoner spat on the floor, then spoke into his headset. "Captain? Report."

"Captain reporting, sir," came the captain's steady voice. "I heard some shooting in the saloon. There was a fire on one of the tenders—"

"I'm well aware of all that. What's the status on the bridge?"

"All's well up here. Gruber's with me and we're locked and barred and heavily armed. What the hell's going on below?"

"Pendergast took out Berger and Vic Klemper. I sent Szell and Hammar to the main saloon and now I can't raise them. Keep your eyes open."

"Yes, sir."

"Maintain course. Await further orders."

Esterhazy stared at him. Falkoner's chiseled features remained calm and collected. He turned to Esterhazy and said, "This man of yours, he seems to be anticipating our every move. How is that?"

"He's a devil," said Esterhazy.

Falkoner turned toward Esterhazy and his eyes narrowed. He almost looked like he was going to say something, but then turned away, speaking into his headset. "Baumann?"

"Here."

"Your position?"

"Upper VIP stateroom. With Eberstark."

"Klemper's gone. You're in charge. I want you and Eberstark to join Nast on the sky deck. You go up the aft ladder. Eberstark, you go up the main ladder. If the target is there, catch him in the crossfire. Move with extreme caution. If you don't see him, the three of you sweep the sky and upper decks, fore to aft. Forget what I said about taking him alive. Shoot to kill."

"Yes, sir. Shoot to kill."

"I want Zimmermann and Schultz on the main deck, in position to ambush anyone coming down either of the two stairways. If you don't kill him on the sky deck, the pincer movement above will drive him below and forward, where they'll be waiting."

"Yes, sir."

Esterhazy paced the narrow engine room, thinking furiously. Falkoner's plan seemed a good one. How could Pendergast—*even* Pendergast—escape five men armed with automatic weapons on a confined boat, firing at him from two sides?

He looked at Falkoner, still calmly speaking into his headset. He remembered, with horror, the eager look in the man's eyes as he tortured and killed the journalist. It was the first time he'd seen Falkoner actually enjoying something. And he recalled Falkoner's eyes when he'd spoken of capturing Pendergast: that same eager, anticipatory look. Like thirst. Despite the warmth of the engine room, he shivered. He was beginning to realize that, even if Pendergast was killed, his problems with the Covenant were far from over. In fact, they might just be beginning.

It had been a serious mistake to plan this op on the *Vergeltung*. Now he, too, had placed himself at their mercy.

CHAPTER 71

PENDERGAST ASCENDED THE SIDE OF THE YACHT, clinging like a limpet to the exterior of the upper deck, using the drip edges of the windows as toe- and handholds. He reached the lower edge of the bridge windows. While the windows of the staterooms were smoked, making it impossible to see inside, the bridge windows were clear. As he peered over the edge, in the dim light from the electronics he could make out the personnel on the bridge: a captain and an armed mate, who was doubling as navigator. Beyond, in the sky lounge behind the bridge, was the single guard with an automatic weapon, pacing back and forth. Occasionally he would come out onto the sky deck behind the lounge, make a circuit, and go back in. Outside the sky lounge, the sky deck was clear except for an empty, uncovered hot tub and some banquettes.

The bridge itself was locked and barred. A yacht like this would have high security as a matter of course. The windows would be shatterproof and, judging from their thickness, possibly even bulletproof. There was no way in for him—none.

Pendergast crept along the slanting wall until he was just below the level of the toe-rail, where sliding glass doors opened from the sky lounge to the sky deck.

He reached into his pocket, took out a coin, and tossed it so that it clanked against the glass doors.

The man inside the sky lounge froze, then fell into a crouch. "Nast here," came the guard's whispered voice over the radio. "I heard something."

"Where?"

"Here, on the sky deck."

"Check it out," was the response. "*Carefully.* Baumann, Eberstark, prepare to cover him."

Pendergast saw the dim outline of the man, crouching behind the glass doors, peer out. When the man was satisfied the deck was clear, he rose, slid open the door, and stepped out warily, weapon at the ready. Pendergast lowered his head below the edge of the deck and, speaking into his own stolen headset in a hoarse, indistinguishable whisper, said: "Nast. Port side, over the railing. Check it out."

He waited. After a moment, the dark silhouette of the man's head appeared over the railing, directly above him, looking down. Pendergast shot him in the face.

With a gargled cry the man's head snapped back, then the body slumped forward, Pendergast helping catapult it over the railing. It struck the main deck rail and became hung up on it, sprawled partially onto the walkway. Grasping a post, Pendergast vaulted up onto the sky deck as a burst of chatter sounded over the radio. Leaping into the empty hot tub, he crouched low. He knew two more men were on their way to the sky deck.

Excellent.

They came thundering out onto the deck almost immediately, one aft and one forward. Pendergast waited for the right alignment, then leapt out of the hot tub with a single shot to startle them; the two men, as expected, let loose with automatic weapons and one of them fell, killed by his partner's crossfire; the other threw himself to the ground, firing wildly and ineffectively.

Pendergast disabled the man with a single shot, then leapt over the sky deck rail, dropping down to the main deck walkway below. Nast's dead body afforded an agreeably soft landing. He then vaulted over the main deck rail, grasping hold of two uprights to prevent himself from dropping into the sea. For a moment his legs dangled over the water, the hull sloping gently away underneath him. With a quick effort he found a purchase with his feet on a lower porthole drip edge.

There he waited, clinging to the hull, below the level of the main deck, listening. Again, the radio told him what he needed to know.

CHAPTER 72

DOWN IN THE ENGINE ROOM, ESTERHAZY PACED, aware of a growing sense of confusion and panic, which mirrored his own internal turmoil.

How the hell was Pendergast doing it? It was as if he were reading their minds...

And then suddenly he knew. *Of course.* It was so simple. And it gave him an idea.

He spoke, for the first time, into his own radio headset. "Esterhazy here. Bring the girl to the foredeck. You hear me? Bring her there quickly. We need to get rid of her; she's only an impediment to us now."

He shut off the headset and signaled Falkoner with a shake of his head not to use his own.

"What the hell are you doing?" Falkoner whispered harshly. "Who are you talking to? You can't get rid of her, we'll lose all leverage—!"

Esterhazy interrupted him with another gesture. "He's got a radio. That's how he's doing it. The son of a bitch has a radio."

Immediately comprehension bloomed over Falkoner's face.

"You and I will go topside. We'll surprise him when he comes to the bow to rescue her. Hurry. We'll collect what men we can."

They left the engine room and, weapons drawn, bounded up the stairway, then through the galley and out the hatch at the far end. There Schultz was waiting, gun drawn.

"There's been gunfire on the sky deck—" Schultz began.

Falkoner silenced him with a curt movement. "Come with us," he whispered.

The three of them moved swiftly and silently to the foredeck, then crouched behind the lifesaving containers. Not a minute later, a black-suited figure scurried up and over the rail on the starboard side, moving swiftly as a bat, then flattened itself behind the forward cabin wall.

Schultz took aim.

"Let him get close," whispered Falkoner. "Wait for a sure thing."

But nothing happened. Pendergast remained behind the cabin wall.

"He's on to us," muttered Falkoner.

"No," said Esterhazy. "Wait."

Minutes passed. And suddenly the figure came out of hiding, flitting along the foredeck at high speed.

Schultz let loose with a burst of fire, raking the fore-cabin wall, and the figure dove behind a forward davit, using the low steel bracing as cover.

The game was up; Falkoner fired, the rounds ricocheting off the steel with a loud clanging, sending off showers of sparks.

"We've got him pinned!" Falkoner said, firing again. "He can't get out from behind there. Careful what you shoot!"

An answering shot came from behind the davits and they instinctively ducked. In that momentary distraction, the black figure sprang out from behind its cover and literally flew through the air, sailing over the railing in a headfirst dive, vanishing over the side. All three fired but it was already too late.

Falkoner and Schultz rose, raced to the side of the boat, firing down into the water, but the figure had vanished.

"He's finished," said Schultz. "At this water temperature, he'll be dead in fifteen minutes."

"Don't be so damn sure," said Esterhazy, coming up beside them and looking aft. The dark water spread out, heaving and cold, the dim wake receding into nothingness. "He's going to get back on the boat using the stern swim rail."

Falkoner stared back and for the first time a crack appeared in his preternatural cool, beads of sweat popping up on his brow despite the frigid temperature. "Then we'll charge the stern. Take him as he comes back aboard."

"Too late," said Esterhazy. "At our rate of speed, *he's already back aboard*—and no doubt waiting for us to make that very move."

Pendergast crouched behind the stern, waiting for his assailants to come. The brief immersion had shorted out the headset. A pity, but the recent events implied that it had become useless anyway. He tossed it overboard.

The vessel swept along, traversing the Narrows. The Verrazano Bridge glowed overhead and they passed beneath it, the graceful arches of light swinging back behind them as the boat forged ahead, headed for the outer bay and the open ocean beyond.

And still Pendergast waited.

CHAPTER 73

FALKONER STARED AT ESTERHAZY. "We can still beat him," he said. "We've still got half a dozen men, armed to the teeth. We're going to mass the men, make a full-frontal assault—"

"I doubt you have that many left," Esterhazy cried. "Don't you see? He's killing us, one by one. No brute-force attack is going to work. We need to out-think him."

Falkoner, breathing heavily, stared at him.

And in truth Esterhazy *had* been thinking, furiously, since leaving the engine room. But things were happening too fast, there just wasn't time, Pendergast and Constance were...

Constance. Yes—it could work. *It could.*

He turned toward Falkoner. "That business of the woman flushed him out. That's where he's vulnerable."

"It won't work again."

"Yes it will. We'll use the woman—for real this time."

Falkoner frowned. "For what purpose?"

"I know Pendergast. Believe me, *this will work.*"

Falkoner stared at him. He wiped his brow. "All right. Go get the woman. I'll wait here with Schultz."

• • •

A short corridor connected the engine room to the forward cargo hold. Reaching the bottom of the stairs, Esterhazy sprinted down the corridor, threw open the door, entered, then slammed it shut, dogging it. No lock-picker could get through that.

The floor was spotless after the killing of the journalist the day before, the sailcloth gone. He went to the hatch in the middle of the V-shaped hold, undogged it, and threw it open. In the dim bilge, the young woman's face stared up at him: hair matted, face smeared with engine oil. As the light gleamed in her irises, Esterhazy was once again taken aback by the naked, overpowering hatred he saw in them. It was a most unnerving expression: suggesting unfathomable violence, yet overlaid with a kind of detached, frozen calm. Her mouth was gagged and taped; Esterhazy found himself grateful she could say nothing.

"I'm taking you out. Please don't struggle."

Snugging his gun into the waistband of his pants, he reached down and seized her hair with one hand, grasping her around the shoulders with the other. Her mouth and hands were still securely taped, but that did not prevent a struggle. He managed to pull her out, the baleful stare still fixed on him. Esterhazy pushed her toward the door, then he paused a moment, listening. Holding her in front of him as a shield in case they ran into Pendergast, he undogged the door, opened it, and pushed her forward, keeping his gun trained on the base of her skull. The corridor was empty.

"Start walking." Esterhazy directed her down the corridor to the forward stairway. They climbed it, ultimately emerging onto the foredeck. The vessel was moving through a moderate sea, into a cold headwind. The lights of Manhattan were a distant glow, the graceful arc of the Verrazano Bridge receding into the darkness behind them. He could feel the roll of the ship; they were now in open ocean.

Falkoner's face was even paler than when he'd left. "Nobody can raise Eberstark or Baumann," he said. "And look what happened to Nast." He pointed at the main deck railing, where a body hung limply, dripping blood.

"We've got to work fast," Esterhazy replied. "Follow my lead."

Falkoner nodded.

"You and Schultz hold her tight. But be very careful. I'm cutting her free."

The two men grabbed Constance. She had stopped struggling. Esterhazy uncuffed her hands, freeing her. Then he removed the tape from around her mouth.

"I'll kill you for what you've done," she immediately told him.

Esterhazy glanced at Falkoner. "We're going to throw her overboard."

Falkoner stared. "You do that and we'll lose our only—"

"Just the opposite."

"But she's just a lunatic! He won't trade his life for hers. He'll let her drown."

"I was wrong," Esterhazy said. "She's not crazy at all. Pendergast cares for her—deeply. Tell the captain to mark a waypoint on the GPS when she goes over. Hurry!"

They manhandled her to the rail. Suddenly she gave a short, sharp cry and began to struggle ferociously.

"No," she said. "Don't do it. I can't . . ."

Esterhazy stopped. "Can't what?"

"I can't swim."

Esterhazy cursed. "Get a life preserver."

Falkoner extracted one from a lifesaving container on the deck. Esterhazy grabbed it and tossed it to her. "Put it on."

She began to put on the life preserver. Her icy composure had returned, but her hands were shaking now and she fumbled with the latch. "I can't seem to—"

Esterhazy went over and buckled the front, bending over to tighten the strap.

With a sudden movement she brought her fist up, smashing him in the chin. He staggered and saw her nails once again clawing for his eyes. With a grunt of pain he twisted free and shook her off. She fell on the deck. Falkoner kicked her in the side, then grabbed her hair, hauling her to her feet while Schultz seized her and wrenched her toward the rail, pinning her arms. She cried out, head flailing, trying to bite them.

"Easy!" said Esterhazy sharply. "Don't hurt her or our plan will fail."

"Lift!" cried Falkoner, grabbing her by the shoulder. "Now!"

She struggled with sudden, frantic, shocking strength.

"Over!" called Falkoner.

In one galvanic movement they heaved her over the rail into the ocean. She landed with a splash and after a moment resurfaced, flailing, her cries rising for a brief time over the rumble of wind and water, then fading away rapidly as she disappeared into the darkness.

CHAPTER 74

P ENDERGAST BEGAN RUNNING TOWARD THE BOW as soon as he heard her cries. As he sprinted along the walkway, he glimpsed a flash of white plummeting into the water and saw Constance sweep past, then disappear in the darkness behind the wake.

For a moment he was paralyzed with shock. Then he understood.

He heard a voice coming from the forward deck: Esterhazy. "Aloysius!" it called out. "You hear me? Come out with your hands up. Surrender. You do that and we'll turn the boat around. Otherwise we keep going. Hurry!"

Pendergast, his .45 drawn, didn't move.

"If you want us to turn around, come into the open with your hands up. It's November—you know better than anyone how cold the water is. I give her fifteen minutes, twenty at most."

Again, Pendergast did not move. Could not move.

"We've got a waypoint of her location on the GPS," Esterhazy called out. "We can find her in minutes."

Pendergast hesitated for a final, excruciating moment.

He could almost admire Esterhazy's brilliant ploy. Then he raised his hands over his head and walked slowly forward. He came around the forecabin to see Esterhazy and two other men standing on the forecastle, weapons drawn.

"Walk toward us, slowly, hands over your head."

Pendergast obeyed.

Esterhazy came forward, took the .45 out of his hands, and stuck it in his own waistband. Then he searched him. The search was thorough and professional. Esterhazy removed his blades, a .32 Walther, packets of chemicals, wire, and various tools. He groped through the jacket lining and found other tools and items loosely sewed up inside.

"Take your jacket off."

Pendergast removed his jacket and dropped it on the deck.

Esterhazy turned to one of the others. "Cuff, secure, and tape him. Completely. I want him immobile as a mummy."

One of the men came forward. Pendergast's hands were cuffed behind his back with plastic straps. His mouth was sealed with duct tape.

"Lie down," said the third man, speaking with a German accent.

Pendergast complied. They cuffed his ankles, then taped his wrists, arms, and legs, leaving him prone on the deck and unable to move.

"All right," Esterhazy said to the German. "Now tell the captain to turn the boat around and pick up the girl."

"Why?" said the man. "We achieved our objective— who cares?"

"You wanted him to talk, right? Isn't that why he's still alive?"

After a brief hesitation, the German spoke to the captain through his headset. A moment later, the boat slowed and began to turn.

Esterhazy checked his watch. Then he turned to Pendergast. "It's been twelve minutes," he said. "I hope you didn't hesitate too long."

CHAPTER 75

ESTERHAZY TOOK UP A DOCK LINE. "Help me tie him to these cleats," he told Schultz.

His mind was working a mile a minute. He'd been faking bravura and an aura of command, but right below the surface he was almost beside himself with fear. He had to figure out a way to save his own skin now. But nothing came to mind. *What's the matter, Judson?* Falkoner had said. *You suddenly don't trust us? I'm surprised—and hurt.*

Esterhazy realized that the chances were good he was as dead as Pendergast.

The boat had come around and was now slowing as they neared the waypoint. Esterhazy moved to the bow, searching for the young woman while two spotlights from the bridge scanned the heaving sea.

"There!" said Esterhazy as one spotlight picked up a flash of reflecting tape from the life preserver.

In a moment the yacht had reached her, slowing still further and turning. Esterhazy jogged aft and snagged the life preserver with a mooring hook, hauling Constance around to the stern. Falkoner came aft and together they pulled her onto the platform, then carried her through the transom and into the main saloon, where they laid her on the carpeted floor.

She was semi-conscious but still breathing. Esterhazy quickly felt her pulse: slow and thready.

"Hypothermia," he said to Falkoner. "We've got to bring her core temperature up. Where's the woman?"

"Gerta? She locked herself in the crew quarters."

"Have her run a lukewarm bath."

Falkoner disappeared while Esterhazy removed the life preserver, unbuttoned and slipped off her soggy dress and underclothing, then wrapped her in a dry afghan that was folded on a nearby chair. He put plastic cuffs on her wrists and a much looser set around her ankles, leaving just enough slack for her to walk.

A moment later, the woman arrived with Falkoner. Her face was pale but she was composed. "The bath is running."

They carried Constance through the saloon to the forward stateroom master bath, where they lowered her into the lukewarm water. She was already reviving, murmuring something as she went in.

"I'm going forward to watch Pendergast," Esterhazy said.

Falkoner looked at him for a moment—a searching, calculating look. Then he smiled crookedly. "When she's revived, I'll bring her—and we'll use her to make Pendergast talk."

Esterhazy felt himself shudder.

He found Pendergast where he had left him, Schultz watching over him. He pulled up a deck chair and sat down, cradling the gun and looking carefully at

Pendergast. This was the first time they had been face-to-face since he'd left the agent, critically wounded and sinking, in the quicksand of the Foulmire. The man's silvery eyes, barely visible in the dim light, were, as usual, unreadable.

Ten minutes passed as Esterhazy went through every scenario, every possible plan to get himself off the *Vergeltung*—to no avail. They were going to kill him—he'd seen it in the look Falkoner had given him. Thanks to Pendergast, he'd caused the Covenant too much trouble, too many men, to remain alive himself.

He heard raised voices and saw Constance being pushed along the port-side walkway by Gerta, the red-headed woman, the threatening murmurs of Falkoner following. In a moment they emerged on deck. Zimmermann had joined them. Constance was wearing a long white terry-cloth bathrobe, with a man's jacket over it. Falkoner gave her one last shove and she fell to the deck in front of Pendergast.

"Feisty bitch," said Falkoner, dabbing at a bloody nose. "No problem reviving *her*. Tie her to that post."

Schultz and the redheaded woman pushed her toward a lifeline stanchion, then tied her to it. She did not struggle, instead remaining strangely silent. When they had secured her, Falkoner straightened up, dabbed his brow, and cast a cool, triumphant expression at Esterhazy. "I'll handle this," he said in a clipped tone. "This is, after all, my area of expertise."

He ripped the tape from Pendergast's mouth. "We wouldn't want to miss a word the man says—would we?"

Esterhazy casually glanced up at the bridge, a row of faintly glowing windows on the upper deck above and aft of the forecastle. He could see the captain behind the wheel, Gruber the mate to one side. Both were absorbed in their work, paying no attention to the drama playing out on the foredeck below. The vessel was now heading northeast, paralleling Long Island's South Shore. Esterhazy wondered where they were going—Falkoner had been more than a little vague on that point.

"All right," said Falkoner, taking a swaggering turn in front of Pendergast. He holstered his weapon and slid the combat knife out of its scabbard. Standing in front of the agent, he fondled it in the dim light, tested the edges, knelt, then pierced Pendergast's flesh with the tip and drew a thin line down the cheek. Blood welled up.

"Now you have a Heidelberg dueling scar, just like my grandfather's. Lovely."

The red-haired woman watched, a look of cruel anticipation gathering on her face.

"See how sharp it is?" Falkoner continued. "But that sharpness isn't for you. It's for *her*."

He strolled over to Constance and stood over her, playing with the knife, speaking to her directly. "If he doesn't answer my questions promptly and fully, I'm going to cut you. Rather painfully."

"He won't say a word," Constance replied, her voice low and steady.

"He will when we start chumming the water with bits of your body."

She stared at him. Esterhazy was surprised at just how little fear he saw in her eyes. This was one scary human being.

Falkoner merely chuckled and turned back to

Pendergast. "Your little quest, which we've only recently become aware of, has been most instructive. For example, we had thought Helen was dead these long years."

Esterhazy felt his blood run cold.

"Right, Judson?"

"It's not true," Esterhazy said weakly.

Falkoner waved his hand as if it was a trifling matter. "At any rate, here's your first question: what do you know about our organization, and where did you learn it?"

But Pendergast did not answer. Instead, he turned to Esterhazy, a strangely sympathetic look in his eyes. "You're next, you realize."

Falkoner strode over to Constance and grabbed her hands, which were cuffed behind the stanchion. He took his knife and sliced slowly and deliberately into her thumb. She stifled a cry, turning her head sharply to one side.

"Next time, speak to me and answer my question."

"Don't speak!" Constance said, hoarsely, not looking back. "Don't say anything. They're going to kill us anyway."

"Not true," said Falkoner. "If he talks, we'll drop you off alive on shore. He can't save his own life, but he can save yours."

He turned back to Pendergast. "Answer the question."

The special agent began to talk. He told—briefly—of discovering that his wife's gun had been loaded with blanks, and realizing that meant she had been murdered in Africa twelve years before. He spoke slowly, clearly, and utterly without inflection.

"And so you went to Africa," said Falkoner, "and discovered our little conspiracy to get rid of her."

"Your conspiracy?" Pendergast seemed to consider this.

"Why are you talking?" asked Constance suddenly. "You think he's going to let me go? Of course not. Cease speaking, Aloysius—we're both dead anyway."

His face alight with arousal, Falkoner reached down, grasped her hand, and took the knife, slowly cutting into her thumb again, much more deeply this time. She grimaced and writhed in pain, but did not cry out.

From the corner of his eye, Esterhazy noted that Schultz and Zimmermann had holstered their weapons and were enjoying the show.

"Don't," Esterhazy said to Falkoner. "You keep doing that, he'll stop talking."

"Damn you, I know what I'm doing. I've been at this for years."

"You don't know *him*."

But Falkoner had stopped. He held up the bloody knife, waved it in front of Pendergast's face, wiped the blood off on the agent's lips. "The next time, her thumb comes off." He smiled crookedly. "Do you love her? I suppose you must. Young, beautiful, spirited: who wouldn't?" He straightened up, took a slow turn around the deck. "I'm waiting, Pendergast. Go on."

But Pendergast did not go on. Instead, he was looking at Esterhazy intently.

Falkoner paused in his circuit, cocked his head to one side. "All right. I always keep my promises. Schultz, hold her hand steady."

Schultz grasped Constance's hand as Falkoner brandished the knife. Esterhazy could see he was, indeed, going to cut off her thumb. And if he did there would be no going back—not for Pendergast, and not for him.

CHAPTER 76

J UST A MOMENT," ESTERHAZY SAID.

Falkoner paused. "What?"

Esterhazy quickly stepped over to Falkoner and leaned in to his ear. "There's something I neglected to tell you," he murmured. "Something you must know. It's very important."

"Damn it, I'm in the middle of this."

"Step over to the rail. They mustn't hear. I'm telling you, it's of the *utmost* importance."

"This is a hell of a time to be interrupting my work!" Falkoner muttered, the smile of sadistic pleasure giving way to a scowl of frustration.

Esterhazy led Falkoner over to the port rail and walked him slightly aft. He glanced up: the view from both the bridge and the foredeck was blocked.

"What's the problem?" Falkoner demanded.

Esterhazy leaned over to whisper in his ear, placing a hand on his shoulder. As they drew together, heads bowed, Esterhazy brought his pistol up and fired a bullet into the German's cranium. A cloud of blood, gore, and bits of bone jetted out the far side, the blowback spraying Esterhazy directly in the face.

Falkoner jerked forward, eyes wide and astonished, and he fell into Esterhazy's arms. Esterhazy grasped him by the shoulders and, with a brusque movement, heaved the body up onto the rail and tipped it over.

At the report of the gun, Zimmermann came tearing around the corner. Esterhazy shot him between the eyes.

"Schultz!" he cried out. "Help us!"

A moment later Schultz appeared, gun in hand, and Esterhazy shot him as well.

Then Esterhazy backed away, sputtering and spitting, wiping his face clean with a handkerchief and returning to the small group, pistol drawn. Gerta stood there, staring at him, paralyzed.

"Walk over here," he told her. "Slow and easy. Or you're dead, too."

She obeyed. As she reached the edge of the cabin he grabbed her and, with the same tape used to tie Pendergast, bound her ankles, wrists, and mouth. He left her on the walkway where she wasn't visible from the bridge, then strode back to the aft deck, where Hammar was slowly regaining consciousness, groaning and muttering. Esterhazy bound him securely. He made a quick tour of the upper decks, found the wounded Eberstark, and bound him as well. Then he walked forward again to where Pendergast and Constance were restrained.

He looked at the pair. Both had witnessed what he'd done. Constance was silent, but he could see blood dripping from her injured finger. He knelt, examined it. The second, deeper cut went to the bone but not through it. He fumbled in his pocket, brought out a clean handkerchief, and bound the finger. Then he stood up and faced Pendergast. The silvery eyes glittered back. Esterhazy thought he could detect—barely—lingering surprise.

"You once asked me how I could kill my own sister," Esterhazy said. "I told you the truth then. And I'll tell you the truth again now. I didn't kill her. Helen's alive."

CHAPTER 77

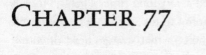

Esterhazy paused. A new look had come into Pendergast's eyes; a look he didn't fully understand. And yet the man said nothing.

"You think your fight's just with me," Esterhazy went on rapidly. "But you're wrong. It's not just me. It's not just this boat and this crew. The fact is you have no idea, *no idea*, of what you're dealing with."

No response from Pendergast.

"Listen. Falkoner was going to kill me, too. As soon as you were dead, he was going to do the same to me. I realized that just tonight, on this boat."

"So you killed him to save yourself," Constance said. "Is that supposed to solicit our trust?"

Esterhazy did his best to ignore this. "Damn it, Aloysius, listen to me: Helen is alive, and *you need me to bring her to you*. We don't have the time to stand around talking about it now. Later, I'll explain everything to you—not now. Are you going to cooperate with me or not?"

Constance laughed mirthlessly.

Esterhazy stared into Pendergast's frozen, unreadable

eyes for what seemed a very long time. Then he took a deep breath. "I'm going to take a chance," he said. "A chance that somewhere in that strange head of yours, you might just believe me—about this, if nothing else." Taking out a knife, he leaned over to cut Pendergast free, then hesitated.

"You know, Aloysius," he said quietly, "what I've become was what I was born to be. It's what I was born *into*—and it's something beyond my control. If you only knew the horror that Helen and I have been subjected to, you'd understand."

He sliced through the lines holding Pendergast to the stanchion, cut through the tape, and freed him.

Pendergast slowly stood up, massaging his arms, face still unreadable. Esterhazy hesitated a moment. Then he slipped Pendergast's .45 from his own waistband and handed it to the FBI agent, butt first. Pendergast took it, tucked it away, and without a word went over to Constance and cut her free.

"Let's go," said Esterhazy.

For a moment, nobody moved.

"Constance," said Pendergast, "wait for us at the tender in the stern."

"Just a minute," Constance said. "Surely you aren't going to believe—"

"Please go to the tender. We'll join you in a moment."

With a single, lingering stare at Esterhazy, she turned and walked aft, disappearing into the dark.

"There are two men on the bridge," Esterhazy said to Pendergast. "We have to neutralize them and get off this boat."

When Pendergast did not reply, Esterhazy took the lead, pushing open a cabin door and stepping over a motionless body. They passed through the main saloon and then ascended a stairway. Arriving at the sky deck, he opened the sliding glass doors and crossed the sky lounge. Pendergast took up a position next to the bridge door, drawing his weapon. Esterhazy knocked.

A moment later the captain's voice came over the intercom. "Who is it? What's happening? What was that shooting?"

Esterhazy put on his calmest voice. "It's Judson. It's all over. Falkoner and I have got them immobilized in the saloon."

"The rest of the crew?"

"Gone. Most of them killed or incapacitated—or overboard. But everything's under control now."

"Jesus!"

"Falkoner wants Gruber below for a few minutes."

"We've been trying to raise Falkoner on the radio."

"He ditched his radio. That man Pendergast got his hands on a headset and was listening in on our chatter. Look, we don't have a lot of time, Captain, Falkoner wants the mate below. Now."

"How long? I need him on the bridge."

"Five minutes, tops."

He heard the bridge door being unbolted, then unlocked. It opened. Immediately, Pendergast kicked it back, knocking the mate senseless with the butt of his handgun while Esterhazy rushed the captain, jamming his weapon into his ear. "Down!" he shouted. "On the floor!"

"What the—?"

Esterhazy fired the pistol to one side, then put the muzzle back against his head. "You heard me! Face down, arms spread!"

The captain dropped down to his knees, then lay prone, stretching out his arms. Esterhazy turned in time to see Pendergast tying up the mate.

He walked over to the helm, keeping his pistol trained on the captain, and throttled the twin diesels back into neutral. The boat slowed on its way to coming to rest in the water.

"What the hell do you think you're doing?" the captain cried. "Where's Falkoner?"

"Tie this one up, too," Esterhazy said.

Pendergast stepped over and immobilized the captain.

"You're a dead man," the captain told Esterhazy. "They'll kill you for sure—you of all people should know that."

Esterhazy watched as Pendergast went to the helm, scanned it, lifted a cage enclosing a red lever, and pulled the lever. An alarm began to sound. "What's that?" he asked, alarmed.

"I've activated the EPIRB, the emergency position-indicating radio beacon," Pendergast replied. "I want you to go below, launch the tender, and wait for me."

"Why?" Esterhazy was disconcerted at how suddenly Pendergast had taken control.

"We're abandoning ship. Do as I say."

The flat, cold tone of his voice unnerved Esterhazy. The agent disappeared off the bridge, heading to the lower decks. Esterhazy went down the stairs to the main saloon and to the stern. He found Constance there, waiting.

"We're abandoning ship," said Esterhazy. He pulled the canvas from the second tender. It was a 5.2-meter Valiant with a seventy-five-horsepower Honda four-stroke outboard. He opened the stern transom and threw the windlass into gear. The boat slid off its cradle into the water. He cleated it at the stern, climbed inside, started the engine.

"Get in," he said.

"Not until Aloysius returns," Constance replied.

Her violet eyes remained gazing at him, and after a moment she spoke again in that curious, archaic way. "You will recall, Dr. Esterhazy, what I told you earlier? Let me reiterate: at some point in the future, in the fullness of time, I will kill you."

Esterhazy snorted in derision. "Don't waste your breath on empty threats."

"Empty?" She smiled pleasantly. "It is a fact of nature as ineluctable as the very turning of the earth."

CHAPTER 78

ESTERHAZY TURNED HIS THOUGHTS TO PENDERGAST and what he was up to. He had his answer when he heard a muffled explosion below. A moment later Pendergast appeared. He helped Constance into the tender, then leapt in himself as another explosion shook the yacht. A smell of smoke suddenly filled the air.

"What did you do?" Esterhazy asked.

"Engine fire," said Pendergast. "The EPIRB will give those still alive on board a sporting chance. Take the helm and get us out of here."

Esterhazy backed the boat away from the yacht. A third explosion erupted, sending a ball of fire into the sky, streamers and burning bits of wood and fiberglass raining down around them. Esterhazy turned the boat and throttled up as much as he dared in the ocean swell. The boat pitched and yawed, the engine rumbling.

"Head northwest," said Pendergast.

"Where are we going?" Esterhazy said, still non-plussed at Pendergast's tone of command.

"The southern tip of Fire Island. It will be deserted this time of year—the ideal place to land unnoticed."

"And then?"

The boat ploughed through the medium sea, up and down, riding the swells. Pendergast didn't say anything, did not answer the question. The yacht disappeared in the darkness behind them, even the flame and black smoke that poured from it growing indistinct. It was dark all around, the faint lights of New York City a distant glow as a low-lying mist covered the waters.

"Throttle down to neutral," Pendergast said.

"Why?"

"Just do it."

Esterhazy did as ordered. And then, suddenly, just when a swell swayed him off balance, Pendergast seized him, slammed him to the floor of the tender, and pinned him. Esterhazy had a moment of déjà vu, when the agent had done the same to him at the Scottish churchyard. He felt a gun barrel press against his temple.

"What are you doing?" he cried. "I just saved your life!"

"Alas, I am not a sentimental man," said Pendergast, his voice low and menacing. "I need answers, and I need them now. First question: why did you do it? Why did you sacrifice her?"

"But I *didn't* sacrifice Helen! She's alive. I could never kill her—I love her!"

"I'm not talking about Helen. I'm talking about her twin. The one you called Emma Grolier."

Esterhazy felt sudden, massive surprise temporarily overpower his fear. "How . . . how did you know?"

"The logic is inescapable. I began to suspect it as soon as I learned the woman in the Bay Manor Nursing Home was young rather than old. It was the only explanation.

Identical twins share identical DNA—that's how you managed a deception that could persist even past death. Helen had beautiful teeth, and her twin obviously did as well. Giving her twin the one filling—matching it to Helen's—what a work of dental art."

"Yes," said Esterhazy after a moment. "It was."

"How could you do it?"

"It was either her or Helen. Emma was...very damaged, profoundly retarded. Death was almost a release. Aloysius, please believe me when I tell you I'm not the evil man you think I am. For God's sake, if you knew what Helen and I survived, you would see all this in a completely different light."

The gun pressed harder. "And what is it that you survived? *Why* did you arrange this mad deception?"

"Somebody had to die—don't you see? The Covenant wanted Helen dead. They thought I killed her in that lion attack. Now they know differently. And Helen is in extreme danger as a result. We've *got* to go to ground—all of us."

"What is the Covenant?"

Esterhazy felt his heart pounding. "How can I make you understand? Longitude Pharmaceuticals? Charlie Slade? That's just the beginning. What you saw at Spanish Island was a mere sideshow, a footnote."

Pendergast remained silent.

"The Covenant's rolling up their New York operation, erasing their U.S. footprint. The big boys are coming into town to supervise. They may be here already."

Still Pendergast did not reply.

"For the love of God, we have to get moving! It's the only way Helen will survive. Everything I've done has been to keep Helen alive, because she…" He paused. "I even sacrificed my other sister, damaged as she was. You have to understand. This is not just about you, or about Helen, anymore. It's bigger than that. I'll explain all, but right now we need to save Helen." His voice broke into a sob, quickly suppressed. He seized Pendergast's jacket. "*Can't you see this is the only way?*"

Pendergast rose, put the gun away.

But Constance, who had been silent, now spoke. "Aloysius, don't trust this man."

"The emotion is genuine. He's not lying." Pendergast took the wheel, throttled up, and directed the boat northeastward, toward Fire Island. He glanced toward Esterhazy. "When we land, you will take me directly to Helen."

Esterhazy hesitated. "It can't work like that."

"Why not?"

"I've taught her over the years to—take extreme precautions. The same precautions that saved her life in Africa. A phone call won't do, and surprising her with you would be too dangerous. I have to go to her myself—and *bring* her to you."

"Do you have a plan?"

"Not yet. We must find a way to expose and destroy the Covenant. It's either them or us. Helen and I know a great deal about them, and you're a master at strategy. Together we can do this."

Pendergast paused. "How long do you need to get her?"

"Sixteen, maybe eighteen hours. We should meet in a public place where the Covenant won't dare act, and from there go directly underground."

Another low murmur from Constance. "He's lying, Aloysius. Lying to save his own beggarly self."

Pendergast laid a hand on hers. "While you are right that his instincts for self-preservation are excessive, I believe he is telling the truth."

She fell silent. Pendergast went on, "My apartments at the Dakota contain a secure area, with a secret back door to get out when necessary. Across Central Park from the Dakota is a public area called Conservatory Water. It's a small pond where they sail model boats. Are you familiar with it?"

Esterhazy nodded.

"It isn't that far from the zoo," Constance observed acidly.

"I'll be waiting in front of the Kerbs Boathouse," Pendergast said, "at six o'clock tomorrow evening. Can you get Helen there by then?"

Esterhazy glanced at his watch: just past eleven. "Yes."

"The transfer to me will take five minutes. The Dakota is just across the park."

Ahead, Esterhazy could see the faint blinking of the Moriches Inlet light and the line of the Cupsogue Dunes, white as snow under a brilliant moon. Pendergast turned the tender toward it.

"Judson?" Pendergast said quietly.

Esterhazy turned to him. "Yes?"

"I believe you're telling the truth. But because the matter is so close to me, I might have misjudged you. Constance seems to think I have. You will bring Helen to me as planned—or, to paraphrase Thomas Hobbes, your remaining existence on this planet will prove nasty, brutish, and short."

CHAPTER 79

New York City

CORRIE HAD SPENT THE FIRST PART OF THE EVENING helping her new friend clean the place and cook a tray of lasagna—while keeping an eye on the building next door. Maggie had left at eight PM to work at the jazz club, and she wouldn't be home until two in the morning.

Now it was almost midnight and Corrie was finishing her third cup of coffee in the tiny Pullman kitchen while contemplating her kit. She had read, then re-read, her tattered copy of the underground classic *MIT Guide to Lock Picking*, but she feared that the new locks on the house might be of the kind that had serrated drivers, almost impossible to pick.

And then there was that lead alarm tape she'd noticed. It meant that even if she picked the lock, opening the door would generate an alarm. Opening or breaking a window would do the same. On top of that, despite the appearance of advanced decrepitude, there might be motion detectors and laser alarms scattered throughout the place. Or maybe not. No way to know until she was inside.

...Inside? Was she really going to do this? Before,

all she'd been considering was an external recon. Somehow, over the course of the evening, her plans had unconsciously changed. Why? She had made a promise to Pendergast to stay out of things—but at the same time, she had a deep, instinctual feeling that he was unaware of the full scope of the danger facing him. Did he know of what these drug dealers had done to Betterton and that Brodie couple? These were bad, bad guys.

And as for herself—she was no fool. She would do nothing whatsoever to endanger herself. The house at 428 East End Avenue gave every impression of being deserted—there were no lights on inside at all. She'd been watching the place all day: nobody had come or gone.

She was not going to step over the line of her promise to Pendergast. She wasn't going to tangle with drug smugglers. All she would do was get her ass in the house, look around for a couple of minutes, and go. At the first sign of trouble, no matter how small, she'd get the hell out. If she found anything of value, she'd take it to that pumped-up chauffeur Proctor and he could pass it on to Pendergast.

She glanced at her watch: midnight. No point waiting any longer. She folded up the lock picks and tucked them in her knapsack, along with the other gear: a small portable drill with bit-sets for glass, wood, and masonry, a glass cutter, suction cups, a set of wires, wire strippers and tools, dental mirrors and picks, a couple of small LED lights, a stocking for her face in case there were video cameras, gloves, Mace, lock oil, rags, duct tape, and spray paint—and two cell phones, one hidden in her boot.

She felt a certain mounting excitement. This was going to be fun. Back in Medicine Creek, she'd often performed break-ins like this—and it was probably a good idea to keep her hand in, not let herself grow stale. She wondered if she was really cut out for a career in law enforcement or if she shouldn't think about becoming a criminal instead... Then again, many people in law enforcement did have a sort of perverse attraction to criminality. Pendergast, for one.

She exited the kitchen onto the tiny back patio, which was surrounded on all sides by an eight-foot brick wall. The garden was overgrown, and several pieces of cast-iron lawn furniture were arranged around the patio. The lights of the surrounding rear windows cast enough illumination for her to see while sheltering her from prying eyes.

Selecting the darkest section of brick wall abutting 428, she placed a piece of lawn furniture against it, climbed onto it, then pulled herself over the wall and slipped into the backyard of the abandoned house. It was completely overgrown with ailanthus trees and sumac: even more perfect cover. She pulled a rickety old table over to the wall she'd just scaled, then moved ever so slowly through the overgrowth toward the back of the house. Absolutely no lights or signs of activity within.

The patio door was of metal and sported a relatively new lock. She crept forward, knelt, and opened her lock-pick set, selecting a tool. She inserted the pick and bounced it off the tumblers, rapidly establishing that this would be a very difficult lock to pick. Not for Pendergast, perhaps, but certainly for her.

Better look for an alternative.

Creeping along the back of the house, she spied some low basement windows in sunken wells along the rear wall. She knelt and shone a light into the closest one. It was filthy, almost opaque, and she reached down with a rag and began wiping it. Gradually she cleaned it well enough to see through, and saw that metal alarm tape had also been placed on this window.

Now, this was something she could work with. Taking out the cordless drill, she fitted a 0.5mm diamond tip to the end and fired it up, drilling two holes through the glass, one through the upper foil tape near the junction, and one through the lower foil tape, making sure not to sever the tape and therefore break the circuit. She stripped a copper wire and threaded it through both holes, using a fine dental pick to attach it to the foil on the inside, thus maintaining a complete circuit and, in essence, deactivating the alarm for the rest of the window.

Then, once again using the drill, she made a number of holes in the glass, outlining an opening large enough for her to slip through. Next, she scored a line on the glass with the glass cutter, connecting all the holes with one another. Affixing the suction cup, she rapped sharply on the glass; it broke neatly along the line. She removed the piece and set it aside. Although the lead foil was torn along the cut, it didn't matter: thanks to the copper wire, the circuit remained live.

She stepped back, glanced around at the surrounding buildings. Nobody had seen or heard her; nobody was taking any notice. She looked up at the structure before her. It remained dark and silent as the grave.

She returned her attention to the window. Wary of

a motion sensor, she aimed a flashlight through it, but could see very little save filing cabinets and stacks of books. The lead tape was a rudimentary alarm system, and she suspected that whatever existed in the interior—if anything—might be as lame. Using a dental mirror, she was able to direct the flashlight beam into all corners of the room, and spotted nothing resembling a motion detector, infrared or laser trip alarms.

She stuck her arm in and waved it around, ready to run at the first sign of a red light coming on somewhere in the darkness.

Nothing.

Okay, then. She turned around, stuck her feet through the hole, carefully worked her way in, dropped to the floor, then pulled her knapsack in behind her.

Again she waited in the dark, motionless, looking for any blinking lights, any indication of a security system. All was quiet.

She pulled a chair from one corner and placed it below the window, in case she needed to make a quick escape. Then she glanced around. There was just enough moonlight to make out the contents of the room: as she had noticed from outside, it seemed to be primarily a storage area, full of metal cabinets, yellowing paper files, and piles of books.

She moved toward the first pile of books and lifted the grimy plastic cover. It exposed a stack of old, identical, buckram-bound hardcovers, each one sporting a large black swastika in a white circle, surrounded by a field of red.

The book was *Mein Kampf,* and the author was Adolf Hitler.

CHAPTER 80

*N*AZIS. CORRIE LOWERED THE PLASTIC SHEET, taking care not to rustle it. A chill traveled down her spine. She couldn't seem to move. Everything Betterton had told her now began falling into place. The building had been around since World War II; the neighborhood had been a German enclave; that killer the reporter talked about had had a German accent. And now, this.

These weren't drug smugglers. These were Nazis—and they must have been operating in this house since World War II. Even after Germany surrendered, even after the Nuremberg Trials, even after the Soviet occupation of East Germany and the fall of the Berlin Wall, they'd been operating. It seemed incredible, unbelievable. All the original Nazis would be dead by now—wouldn't they? Who were these people? And what in God's name were they still doing after all these years?

If Pendergast didn't know about this, and she suspected he didn't, it was imperative for her to learn more.

She moved with great caution now, her heart beating hard. Although she had seen no sign of activity, no sign of anyone coming or going, there still might be people in the house. She couldn't be certain.

In the corner sat a table with some electronic equipment, also covered by grimy plastic. She raised one corner, slowly, silently, to find herself staring at a collection of vintage radio equipment. Next, she turned her attention to the filing cabinets, examining the labels. They were in German and she didn't know the language. She chose one at random, found it locked, and took out her tools. In a minute she had picked the simple lock and eased open the drawer. Nothing. The drawer was empty. But based on the lines of dust coating the upper edges of the drawer, it looked like it had until recently been full.

Several other drawers confirmed the same thing. Whatever papers that had been kept there were gone— although not long gone.

Taking out her flashlight and shining it briefly around, she spied doors in each of the far walls. One of them had to lead upstairs. She moved toward the closest, grasped its knob, and pulled it open with infinite care, keeping the squeak from the rusty hinges to an absolute minimum.

Her light revealed a room, tiled in white on the floor, ceiling, and all four walls. A naked steel chair was bolted in the middle, and under the chair was a drain. Steel cuffs dangled from the arms and legs of the chair. In the corner a hose was coiled up, detached from a rusty faucet.

She retreated, feeling faintly sick, and moved to the door on the other side of the basement room. This one led to a narrow staircase.

At the top of the landing was another closed door. Corrie listened for a long time, then grasped the doorknob and eased it open a quarter of an inch. A quick examination with the dental mirror showed a dusty, disused kitchen. She pushed the door wide and looked around the kitchen, then passed quietly through to a dining room, and then into an ornate sitting room beyond. It was decorated in a heavy, encrusted Bavarian hunting-lodge style: antlers mounted on paneled walls, massive carved furniture, landscapes in heavy frames, racks of antique rifles and carbines. A shaggy boar's head with gleaming yellow tusks and fierce glass eyes dominated the mantelpiece. She quickly scanned the bookcases and searched a few cabinets. The documents and books were all in German.

She moved into the hall. Here she stood, barely breathing, listening intently. All remained silent. At last she climbed the stairs, one at a time, pausing on each tread to listen. At the second-floor landing she waited again, examining the closed doors, and then opened one at random. It disclosed a room almost devoid of furniture beyond a skeletal bed frame, a table, a chair, and a bookshelf. A broken window looked onto the back garden, shards of glass still littering the sill. The window was barred.

She checked the other rooms on the second floor. All were similar—all bedrooms, all stripped—except for the last room. That one turned out to be a dust-choked photographic workshop and darkroom, and in addition contained several printing presses and primitive-looking photocopying machines. Racks of copper printing plates of all sizes lined one wall, many engraved with elaborate and official-looking patterns and seals. It appeared to have been an old document-counterfeiting operation.

Back in the hall, she climbed the stairs to the third floor. She found herself in a large attic that had been divided into two rooms. The first—the room in which she now stood—was very strange. The floor was covered by thick, Persian-looking rugs. Dozens of candles, large and fat, sat in ornate freestanding holders, pools of melted wax hanging stalactite-like from their bases. On the walls were black tapestries covered with bizarre yellow- and gold-colored symbols, some sewn on, others fashioned from thick felt: hexagrams, astronomical symbols, lidless eyes, interlocking triangles, five- and six-pointed stars. At the base of one such tapestry was emblazoned a single word: ARARITA. In one corner of the room, a series of three marble steps led up to what looked like an altar.

This was just too creepy, and she backed away. One last room, and then she'd get the hell out.

Shivering, she moved through a low doorway into the attic's second room. It was full of bookshelves and had once been a library, or perhaps a research room. But now all the bookshelves were empty, the walls barren save for a single, moth-eaten Nazi flag hanging limply against the far wall.

In the middle of the room stood a large industrial paper shredder of new manufacture, plugged into the wall and looking ludicrously out of place in what was otherwise a midcentury time capsule. On one side of it stood a dozen tottering stacks of paper, and on the other a series of black garbage bags full of the shredded result. A closet door stood open in the far wall.

She thought of the empty filing cabinets downstairs,

the vacant bedrooms. Whatever had gone down here was now quickly becoming history: the place showed every indication of being methodically stripped of its incriminating contents.

She realized—with a faint tickle of fear—that if this work was ongoing, it could pick up again at any time.

These were the only documents remaining in the house. Pendergast would no doubt want to see them. Quickly and quietly, she moved over to the stacks of paper, examining them. Most dated back to World War II and were on Nazi letterhead, complete with swastikas and old-style German lettering. She cursed her inability to read German as she ploughed through the documents, being careful to maintain them in their correct order and piles, trying to root out any that might prove to be of special interest.

As she worked her way down through the stacks, shifting papers and only examining one or two out of each huge batch, she realized that the documents on the bottom were more recent than those on top. She turned from the older documents and focused on these newer ones. They were all in German and it was impossible to ascertain their significance. Nevertheless, she collected those documents that looked most important: the ones with the most stamps and seals, along with others that were stamped in large red letters:

STRENG GEHEIM

Which to her eyes looked a whole lot like a Top Secret stamp.

Suddenly her eye caught a name on one of the documents: ESTERHAZY. She recognized it immediately as the maiden name of Pendergast's late wife, Helen. The name was sprinkled throughout the document, and as she sorted through the documents directly below, she found others with that name on it as well. She collected them all, stuffing them into her knapsack.

And then she came across a batch of documents that were not in German, but some in Spanish and—she guessed—the rest in Portuguese. She could muddle through Spanish, at least, but most of these papers seemed pretty dull: invoices, requisitions, lists of expenses and reimbursements, along with a lot of medical files in which the names of the patients were blacked out or recorded by initials only. Nevertheless she stuffed the most significant-looking ones into her knapsack, now full almost to bursting...

She heard the creak of a floorboard.

Immediately, she froze, adrenaline flooding her body. She paused, listening intently. Nothing.

Slowly, she closed her knapsack and stood up, careful to make no noise. The door was open only a crack, and a dim light filtered through. She continued listening and—after a moment—heard another creak. It was low, barely audible...like a cautious footfall.

She was trapped, in the attic, with only one narrow staircase leading down. There were no windows, no place to go. But it would be a mistake to panic; it might just be her overactive imagination. She waited in the dim light, every sense on high alert.

Another creak, this one higher and closer. No imagination: someone was definitely in the house—and they were coming up the stairs.

In her excitement over the papers, she'd forgotten to keep utterly silent. Had the person on the stairs heard her?

With exquisite care, she moved across the room to the closet standing open on the far side. She managed to get there without creaking any of the floorboards. Easing herself in, she pulled the door almost but not quite closed and then crouched down in the darkness. Her heart was beating so hard and so fast she feared the intruder might hear it.

Another stealthy creak, and then a faint groan. The door to the room was being opened. She peered out from the closet, hardly daring to breathe. After a long period of silence, a figure moved into the room.

Corrie held her breath. The man was dressed in black, wearing round smoked glasses, his face obscure. A burglar?

He walked to the center of the room, stood there, and finally removed a pistol. He turned toward the closet, raised the gun, and aimed at the closet door.

Corrie began to fumble desperately in her knapsack.

"You will come out, please," the strongly accented voice said.

After a long moment, Corrie stood up, swung the door open.

The man smiled. He thumbed off the safety and took careful aim.

"*Auf Wiedersehen*," he said.

CHAPTER 81

SPECIAL AGENT PENDERGAST SAT ON A LEATHER COUCH in the reception room of his Dakota apartment. The cut on his cheek had been cleaned and was now just a faint red line. Constance Greene, dressed in a white cashmere sweater and a pleated, knee-length skirt the color of coral, sat beside him. A soft light filled the room from behind scallop-shaped agate fixtures arrayed just below the ceiling molding. The room was windowless. Three of the walls were painted a deep rose. The fourth was entirely of black marble, over which fell a thin sheet of water, gurgling quietly into the pool at the base, in which floated clusters of lotus blossoms.

An iron pot of tea sat on a table of Brazilian purpleheart, along with two small cups filled with green liquid. The two conversed in low tones, barely audible above the hush of the waterfall fountain.

"I still don't understand why you let him go last night," Constance was saying. "Surely you don't trust him."

"I don't *trust* him," Pendergast replied. "But in this matter, I *believe* him. He was telling me the truth about Helen, there in the Foulmire—and he's telling the truth now. Besides—" he went on in an even lower tone—"he knows that, if he doesn't keep his promise, I'll track him down. No matter what."

"And if you don't," Constance said, "I will."

Pendergast glanced at his ward. A cold hatred flickered briefly in her eyes—a flicker he had seen once before. This, he realized immediately, was going to be a serious problem.

"It's half past five," she said, glancing at her watch. "In half an hour…" She paused. "How do you feel, Aloysius?"

Pendergast did not answer immediately. At last he shifted on the couch. "I must confess to a most disagreeable sensation of anxiety."

Constance looked at him, her face full of concern. "After twelve years…if it's true that your…your wife cheated death, why has she never contacted you? Why this—forgive me, Aloysius—but why this monstrous, overarching deception?"

"I don't know. I can only assume it has to do with this Covenant that Judson mentioned."

"And if she is still alive…Would you still be in love with her?" Her face flushed slightly and she looked down.

"I don't know that, either," Pendergast replied in a tone so low even Constance barely heard it.

A phone on the table rang and Pendergast reached for it. "Yes?" He listened a moment, replaced the phone in its cradle. He turned to her. "Lieutenant D'Agosta is on his way up." He paused a moment, then continued: "Constance, I must ask you: if at any time you have reservations, or can't bear being incarcerated any longer, let me know and I will fetch the child and clear all this up. We don't have to...follow the plan."

She silenced him with a gentle gesture, her face softening. "We *do* have to follow the plan. And anyway, I'm happy going back to Mount Mercy. In a queer way I find it comforting to be there. I don't care for the uncertainty and busyness of the outside world. But I will say one thing. I realize now that I was wrong—wrong to look at the child as your brother's son. I should have thought of the boy, from the very start, as the nephew of my...my dearest guardian." And she pressed his hand.

The doorbell rang. Pendergast rose and opened the door. D'Agosta stood in the entranceway, his face drawn.

"Thank you for coming, Vincent. Is everything prepared?"

D'Agosta nodded. "The car's waiting downstairs. I told Dr. Ostrom that Constance was on her way back. The poor bastard just about collapsed with relief."

Pendergast removed a vicuña overcoat from a closet, slipped it on, and helped Constance into her own coat. "Vincent, please make sure that Dr. Ostrom *fully understands* Constance is returning voluntarily—and that her departure from the hospital was a kidnapping, not an escape, entirely the fault of this phony Dr. Poole. Whom we are still looking for but are unlikely to find."

D'Agosta nodded. "I'll take care of it."

They left the apartment and entered the waiting elevator. "When you get back to Mount Mercy, make sure she's given her old room with all her books, furniture, and notebooks returned. If not, protest vigorously."

"I'll raise holy hell, believe me."

"Excellent, my dear Vincent."

"But...damn it, don't you think I should go with you to the boathouse? Just in case there's trouble?"

Pendergast shook his head. "Under any other circumstances, Vincent, I would accept your help. But Constance's safety is too important. You're armed, of course?"

"Of course."

The elevator arrived at the ground floor, the doors whispering open. They exited the southwest lobby and walked across the interior courtyard.

D'Agosta frowned. "Esterhazy might be organizing a trap."

"I doubt it, but I've taken precautions. In case anyone tries to interrupt us."

They passed beneath a portcullis-like structure and through the entrance tunnel to Seventy-Second Street. An unmarked car idled by the doorman's pillbox, a uniformed police officer behind the wheel. D'Agosta glanced around for a moment, then opened the rear door, holding it for Constance.

Constance turned to Pendergast, kissed him lingeringly on the cheek. "Take care, Aloysius," she whispered.

"I'll be with you as soon as I can," he told her.

She gave his hand a final press and slipped into the rear of the car.

D'Agosta closed the door after her, walked around to the other side. He gave Pendergast a last, intent look. "Watch your ass, partner."

"I will endeavor to follow your advice—metaphorically, of course."

D'Agosta got in and the car pulled out into traffic.

Pendergast watched the car disappear into the gathering dusk. Then he reached into his jacket, pulled out a tiny Bluetooth headset, and fitted it to his ear. Slipping his hands into the pockets of his coat, he crossed the broad avenue, entered Central Park, and vanished down a winding path, heading for Conservatory Water.

CHAPTER 82

AT FIVE MINUTES BEFORE SIX IN THE EVENING, Central Park lay under the drowsy enchantment of a Magritte painting: the sky above in vivid light, the trees and pathways below swathed in heavy dusk. The pulse of the city had slowed with the coming of evening; the cabs hushed by on Fifth Avenue, too lazy even to honk their horns.

The Kerbs Memorial Boathouse rose like a confection of brick and verdigrised copper beside the mirrored surface of Conservatory Water. Beyond it, past a fringe of trees dressed in autumn colors, rose the monolithic expanse of Fifth Avenue, the ramparts of stone blushing pink in the reflected glow of the dying sun.

Special Agent Pendergast made his way through the cherry trees of Pilgrim Hill and paused in the long shadows to scan the boathouse and its surroundings. It was an unusually warm fall evening. The oval pond was utterly calm, its mirror-like surface ablaze with the carmine and vermilion of the sky. The café adjoining the boathouse was closed for the day, and there were only a handful of would-be yachtsmen at the water's edge plying their model yachts. A few children sat or lay beside them, hands idly stirring the water, staring out at the little vessels.

Slowly, Pendergast circled the pond, passing the *Alice in Wonderland* statue as he approached the boathouse. A violinist stood on the stone parapet that rose before the lake, case open at his feet, playing "Tales from the Vienna Woods" with almost more rubato than the music could stand. A young couple sat on one of the benches before the boathouse, holding hands, whispering and nuzzling, identical backpacks beside them. On the next bench over sat Proctor, dressed in a suit of dark serge, apparently intent on reading *The Wall Street Journal*. A vendor of chestnuts and hot pretzels was closing up his cart for the day, and in the deep shadow behind the boathouse, in a cluster of rhododendrons, a homeless man was preparing his cardboard-box bed for the evening. A sprinkling of pedestrian commuters strode past on the various walkways leading to Fifth Avenue.

Pendergast touched his earpiece. "Proctor?"

"Yes, sir."

"Anything amiss?"

"No, sir. Everything's quiet. A couple of lovebirds who can't seem to get enough of each other. A vagrant who's just finished scrounging a meal from the trash. Now he's settling down for the night with what looks like a bottle of Night Train. An art class was painting the lake, but they left about fifteen minutes ago. The last model yachtsmen are packing up their boats. Looks like a go."

"Very well."

While they spoke, Pendergast's hands had clenched

unconsciously. Now he opened them quite deliberately, flexed his fingers. He made a successful effort to slow his heart to a normal level. Taking a long, deep breath, he emerged into the open, strolling to the short parapet surrounding Conservatory Water.

He checked his watch again: six o'clock exactly. He looked around—and then went quite still.

Two new figures were approaching from the direction of Bethesda Fountain, indistinct beneath the dark canopy of trees. As he stared, they crossed the East Drive and continued to draw closer, past Trefoil Arch, past the statue of Hans Christian Andersen. He waited, hands at his sides, keeping his movements slow and casual. Beside him, a young boy laughed joyously as two of the toy yachts collided while coming into port.

The figures, silhouetted by the evening sky, paused on the far side of Conservatory Water, looking in his direction. One was a man; the other, a woman. As they moved again, circling the lake toward him, he saw something about the woman—the poise of her bearing, the way her limbs moved as she walked—that momentarily stopped the beating of his heart. Everything around him—the yachtsmen, the lovers, the violinist, all the rest—vanished as he stared at her. As they rounded the edge of the lake they moved into a bar of evening light—and the woman's features came clearly into view.

Time itself seemed abruptly suspended. Pendergast could not move. She, after a moment's pause, separated from the man and came toward him with hesitant steps.

Was it really Helen? The thick auburn hair was the same—shorter, but just as lustrous as he remembered.

She was as slender as she'd been when he first met her, perhaps even more so, and she carried her long limbs with the easy grace he recalled so well. But as she drew close he noted changes: crow's-feet at the corners of her blue-and-violet eyes; those eyes that had stared sightlessly up at him on that terrible day among the fever trees. Her skin, always tawny and lightly freckled, had grown pale, even wan. Instead of the habitual self-confidence that had radiated from her like light from the sun, she had the diffident quality of someone who had been beaten down by the vicissitudes of life.

She stopped a few feet from him and they looked at each other.

"Is it really you?" he said, his voice little more than a croak.

The woman tried to smile, but it was a wistful smile, almost forlorn. "I'm sorry, Aloysius. So very sorry."

Upon hearing her speak—a voice he now heard only in dreams—another shock rippled through Pendergast. For the first time in his life, he felt his self-possession gone; he found himself utterly unable to think, completely at a loss for words.

She stepped up to him and, with the tip of one finger, touched the cut on his cheek. Then she looked beyond him, to the east, and pointed.

He followed her gesture, gazing through the trees of the park and toward Fifth Avenue. There, framed by the stately buildings, rose a swollen, buttery moon.

"Look," she whispered. "After all these years, we still have the moonrise."

It had always been their secret: they had first met under the full moon, and in the brief years that

followed they had made it an almost religious duty to
be together and alone once a month, to watch the rise
of the full moon.

This convinced Pendergast of what he already felt in
his heart: this was indeed Helen.

CHAPTER 83

JUDSON ESTERHAZY HAD KEPT A DISCREET DISTANCE from the couple and now took up a position in the eaves of the boathouse. He waited, hands in the pockets of his jacket, observing the peaceful scene. The violinist finished the waltz and segued smoothly into a sentimental rendition of "Moon River."

His fears of the Covenant receded somewhat. They knew Helen was alive now, and they were very powerful, but in Pendergast he had found his own powerful ally. Now all would be well.

A dozen yards off, the last yachtsman had removed his model boat from the water and was taking it apart and putting the pieces into an aluminum case lined with foam cutouts. Esterhazy watched as Pendergast and Helen strolled along the verge of the pond. He felt, for the first time in his entire life, an immeasurable sense of relief—that finally he was finding his way out of the maze of evil in which he had been entangled since his earliest childhood memories. It had all happened so suddenly he could barely believe it. He almost felt reborn.

And yet, despite the bucolic scene, Esterhazy still couldn't rid himself of that old, eternal sense of apprehension. He couldn't say why—there was absolutely no cause for concern. There was no way the Covenant could have learned of their meeting spot. No doubt his unease was merely habit.

Now he began strolling behind the two, hanging back, allowing them a few moments of privacy. The Dakota was a short walk across the park, along well-frequented paths. But for now...Their murmured voices drifted back to him as they slowly made a circuit around the small pond.

As they approached the boathouse again, Pendergast reached into the pocket of his jacket. He drew a ring from his pocket: a gold ring, set with a large star sapphire. "Do you recognize this?" he asked.

A flush came over her features. "I never thought I'd see it again."

"And I never thought I'd get the chance to replace it on your finger. Until Judson told me you were still alive. I knew, I *knew*, he was telling the truth—even when nobody else believed me." He reached for her left hand, his limbs still trembling slightly, preparing to place it on her ring finger.

But as he lifted her arm, he paused. The hand was gone. Only a stump remained, a jagged scar running across its end.

"But why *your* hand? I thought your sister..."

"The whole thing went awry. It was a horrific disaster, too complicated to explain now."

He looked back up at her. "Helen," he said. "Why

did you go along with this murderous scheme? Why did you conceal things from me—the Black Frame, Audubon, the Doane family, everything else? Why haven't you—"

She lowered her arm. "Let's please not talk about that. Not now. Later—we'll have plenty of time later."

"But Emma, your twin sister—did you know she'd be sacrificed?"

Her face turned very pale. "I only learned... afterward."

"But you never contacted me, ever. How can I—"

She stayed him with her good hand. "Aloysius, *stop*. There were reasons for everything. It's a terrible story, a *terrible story*. I will tell it to you, all of it. But this is not the time or place. Now, please—let's leave." She tried to smile, but her face was white.

She raised her other hand and wordlessly he slipped the ring onto the ring finger. As he did so, he glanced past her at the sylvan scene. Nothing had changed. Two distant joggers were approaching from the direction of the reservoir. A small child was crying, having gotten entangled in the leash of an excited Yorkshire terrier. The violinist was still sawing away industriously.

His glance fell on the last remaining yachtsman, packing up his boat, still clumsily trying to fit the pieces into his case. His hands were shaking, and despite the chill air Pendergast noticed a sheen of perspiration on his forehead.

A split second elapsed in which a dozen thoughts passed through Pendergast's brain—speculation, real-ization, decision.

Keeping his movements unhurried and calm, he

turned toward Esterhazy and made a casual gesture for him to join them.

"Judson," he murmured. "Take Helen and get her away from here. Do it calmly but quickly."

Helen looked at him in confusion. "Aloysius, what—"

Pendergast silenced her with a little shake of his head. "Take her to the Dakota—I'll meet up with you there. Please go. *Now*."

As they began to move away, Pendergast glanced toward Proctor, sitting on the bench a hundred yards off. "We've got a problem," he murmured into the headset. Then he continued strolling along the edge of the pond, toward the yachtsman, still struggling with his case. As he passed, he paused, keeping one eye on Esterhazy and Helen, moving along the path ahead of him.

"Lovely boat," he said, pausing. "Sloop or ketch?"

"Well," said the man with a sheepish look, "I'm rather new to this, couldn't tell you the difference."

With a fast, easy movement Pendergast pulled his .45 and drew down on the man. "Stand up," he said, "slowly. Keep your hands where I can see them."

The man looked up at him with a curiously blank expression. "Are you crazy?"

"Do it."

The yachtsman started to rise. Then, with a lightning movement, he yanked a gun from beneath his jacket. Pendergast dropped him with a single shot, the roar of the .45 ripping across the silence of the evening.

"*Run!*" he cried to Esterhazy and Helen.

Instantly, all hell broke loose. The two lovers on the

bench leapt to their feet, pulling TEC-9s from their backpacks and firing at Esterhazy, who had taken off at a run, pulling Helen along by the hand. The automatic fire cut him down, Esterhazy clawing the air with a scream as he fell.

Helen stopped and turned. *"Judson!"* she cried over the commotion.

"Keep running!" Esterhazy half choked, half coughed, writhing in the grass. "Keep—"

Another clatter of gunfire raked Esterhazy, flipping him over onto his back.

People were running everywhere, crying and screaming. Pendergast dropped one of the lovers with a shot from his .45 as he raced toward Helen; Proctor had leapt to his feet and, with a Beretta 93R that suddenly appeared in his hand, fired at the other lover, who had dropped down behind the bench, using her fallen companion as cover. As Pendergast tried to get a bead on her as well, out of the corner of his eye he saw the bum rise from his cardboard bed, extracting a shotgun from the bushes as he did so.

"Proctor!" Pendergast cried, "the homeless man—!"

But even as he spoke, the shotgun roared. Proctor, in the act of pivoting, was physically lifted off his feet by the impact and slammed backward, his Beretta clattering to the ground; he fell heavily, twitched, then went still.

As the homeless man turned to fire at Pendergast, the agent brought him down with a round to the chest, punching the man backward into the bushes.

Pendergast turned to see Helen, a hundred yards off, a low figure surrounded by fleeing people. She was still bending over her fallen brother, crying out in despair, cradling his head in her good hand.

"Helen!" he shouted, sprinting toward her once again. "Fifth Avenue! Head for Fifth Avenue—!"

The sound of a gunshot came from behind the bench and Pendergast felt a terrible blow to his back. The heavy-caliber round punched him to the ground, stunning him with its impact; his bulletproof vest stopped it but the wind had been knocked from him. He rolled over, coughing, and from a prone position returned fire at the shooter behind the bench. Helen had finally risen and was running toward the avenue. If he could cover her, suppress fire, she might just make it.

The bench shooter fired and a bullet kicked up a clout of dirt inches from Pendergast's face. He returned fire, heard the shot ricochet off the metal frame of the bench. Another shot came from between the slats; he felt a puff of air on his cheek as the bullet whined past his head and buried itself in his calf. Ignoring the fiery pain, Pendergast collected himself, emptied his lungs of air, and squeezed off another round; it passed between the slats this time, striking the shooter full in the face; she jerked backward, arms flinging out in surprise, and fell.

The shooting stopped.

Pendergast swept the scene of carnage with his eyes. Six bodies lay motionless around him: the two lovers, the would-be yachtsman, the homeless man, Proctor, Esterhazy. Everyone else had fled the vicinity, shrieking and crying. In the distance, he could make out Helen, still running, heading for a stone entrance leading to the Fifth Avenue sidewalk. Already he could hear distant sirens. He rose to follow, limping on his injured leg.

Then he saw something else: the two joggers—who had paused, then altered course away when the gunfire erupted—were now making directly for Helen. And they were no longer jogging. They were sprinting.

"Helen!" he cried, hobbling past the boathouse as quickly as he could, blood streaming from his leg. "Look out! To your left!"

In the darkness beneath the trees, still at a run, Helen turned, seeing immediately that the joggers were going to cut her off at the gate. She swerved away, heading for a grove of trees off the path.

The joggers veered in pursuit. Pendergast, realizing he could not catch up, dropped on his good leg and aimed the .45, squeezing off a round. But the target was more than two hundred feet away and moving fast, an almost impossible shot. He fired again, and then in desperation fired the final round from his magazine, missing again. Helen was sprinting toward a grove of sycamores alongside the Central Park boundary wall. In a furious movement, Pendergast ejected the empty magazine, slammed a fresh one home.

A scream resounded as the two joggers caught Helen, one tackling her, the two of them wrestling her back to her feet.

"Aloysius!" he heard her cry floating back toward him. "Help! I know these people! *Der Bund*—the Covenant! They'll kill me! Help me, *please*—!"

They dragged her back toward the gate to Fifth Avenue. With a groan of fury Pendergast staggered to his feet, stumbling forward, summoning the last of his ebbing strength, willing himself to stay on his feet. His wound was bleeding profusely but he ignored it, moving forward at a shambling lope.

He saw where the joggers were headed: a taxi, waiting at the Fifth Avenue curb. He would never make it—but the car at least was a good target. Sinking back down, head spinning, he fired at it, the round striking the side window with a dull thud, ricocheting off. Armored. He aimed lower, at the tires, squeezed off two more rounds, but the bullets ricocheted harmlessly off armored hubcaps.

"Aloysius!" Helen screamed as the joggers reached the taxi and flung open the rear door. They threw her inside and climbed in after her.

"*Los, verschwinden wir hier!*" he heard one of the joggers shout. "*Gib Gas!*"

The passenger door slammed shut. Pendergast stopped, took careful aim, preparing to shoot at the tires again—but the car screeched from the curb and the final round zinged harmlessly off the lower body.

"Helen!" he cried. "*No!*"

The last thing he saw, as a black mist rose before his eyes, was the taxi disappearing into a sea of identical cabs moving south on Fifth Avenue. As darkness rushed in, amid the sounds of rising sirens, he whispered once again: *Helen.*

He had found Helen Esterhazy Pendergast—only to lose her again.

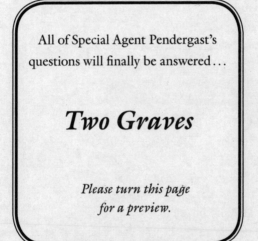

All of Special Agent Pendergast's
questions will finally be answered...

Two Graves

*Please turn this page
for a preview.*

+ FORTY HOURS

For the past forty hours she had been handcuffed and blindfolded and kept constantly on the move. She had been bundled into the trunk of a car, the back of a truck, and—she guessed—the hold of a boat. In all the furtive shuttling from place to place, she had grown disoriented and lost track of time. She felt cold, hungry, and thirsty, and her head ached from the savage blow she'd received in the taxi. She had been given no food, and the only liquid offered her had been a plastic bottle of water, thrust into her hand, some time back.

Now she was once again in the trunk of a car. For several hours they had been driving at high speed, apparently on a freeway. But now the car slowed; the vehicle made several turns; and the sudden roughness of the ride led her to believe they were on a dirt road or track.

Whenever she had been transferred from one makeshift prison to another, her captors had been silent. But now, with the road noise reduced, she could hear the faint murmur of their voices through the vehicle. They were speaking a mixture of Portuguese and German, both of which she understood perfectly, having learned them before English or her father's native Hungarian. The talk was faint, however, and she could only make out nothing beyond the tone, which seemed angry, urgent.

After several minutes of rough travel the car eased to a halt. She heard doors opening and closing, feet crunching on gravel. Then the trunk was opened and she felt chill air on her face. A hand grabbed her by the elbow, raised her to a sitting position, then pulled her out. She staggered, knees buckling; the pressure of the hand increased, raising her and steadying her. Then— without a word—she was shoved forward.

Strange how she felt nothing, no emotion, not even grief or fear. After so many years of hiding, of fear and uncertainty, her brother had come with the news she had long dreamed of hearing but had resigned herself would never happen. For one brief day she had been afire with that hope of seeing Aloysius again, of restarting their lives, of her finally living once more like a normal human being. And then in a moment it was snatched away, her brother murdered, her husband shot and perhaps dead.

And now she felt like an empty vessel. Better to have never hoped at all.

She heard the creak of an opening door, and she was guided over a sill and into a room. The air smelled musty and dead. The hand led her across the room, apparently through a second door and into an even mustier space. A deserted old house in the country, perhaps. The hand released its grip on her arm and she felt the pressure of a chair seat against the back of her knees. She sat down, placing her handcuffed hands in her lap.

"Remove it," said a voice in German, a voice she instantly recognized. There was a fumbling at her head and the blindfold was pulled away.

She blinked once, twice. The room was dark, but her long-blindfolded eyes needed no period of adjustment. She heard footsteps recede behind her, heard the door close. Then, licking dry lips, she raised her eyes and met the gaze of Wulf Konrad Fischer. He was older, of course, but still as powerful looking and as heavily muscled as ever. He was seated in a chair facing her, his legs apart and his hands clasped between them. He shifted slightly, and the chair groaned under his massive build. With his penetrating pale eyes, his dark tan, and his closely trimmed thatch of thick, snow-white hair, he exuded Teutonic perfection. He looked at her, a cold smile distorting his lips. It was a smile Helen remembered all too well. Seeing it, the apathy and emptiness was replaced by a thrust of fear.

"I never expected to receive a visit from the dead," Fischer said in his clipped, precise German, "and yet here you are. Fraulein Esterhazy—forgive me, *Frau* Pendergast—who departed this earth over twelve years ago." He looked at her, hard eyes glinting with some combination of amusement, anger, and curiosity.

Helen said nothing.

"*Natürlich*, in retrospect I can see how it was done. Your twin sister—*der Schwächling*—was the sacrificial pawn. After all your protests, your sanctimonious outrage, I see how well you have learned from us, after all! I almost feel honored."

Helen remained silent. The apathy was returning. She would be better off dead than to live with this pain.

Fischer peered at her intently, as if to gauge the effect of his words. He took a pack of Dunhills from his pocket, plucked one from the box, lit it with a gold lighter. "You wouldn't care to tell us where you've been all this time, would you? Or whether you've had any other accomplices in this little deception—beyond your brother, I mean? Or whether you've spoken to anyone about our organization?"

When there was no response, Fischer took a deep drag on the cigarette. His smile broadened. "No matter. There will be plenty of time for that—once we get you back home. I'm sure you'll be happy to tell the doctors everything...that is, before the experiments begin."

Helen went still. Fischer had used the word *Versuchsreihe*—but the word meant more to her than simply 'experiments.' At the thought of what it meant—at the memory—she felt a sudden panic. Instantly, she leapt to her feet and ran headlong toward the door. It was a mindless, instinctive act, done without thinking, borne out of the atavistic need for self-preservation. But even as she charged the door, it was opened, her captors standing just beyond. Helen did not slow and the force of the impact knocked two of them back, but the others seized her and gripped her hard. It took all four to restrain her and drag her back into the room.

Fischer stood up. Taking another deep drag on the cigarette, he regarded Helen as she struggled silently, fiercely. Then he looked at his watch.

"It's time to go," he said. He glanced again at Helen. "I think we had better prepare the hypodermic."

+ FORTY-THREE HOURS

The knock came at half past two in the afternoon. Kurt Webern put down the bottle of sweet tea he'd been drinking, dabbed at the corners of his mouth with a silk handkerchief, turned off his computer monitor, and walked across the tiled floor to answer it. A quick look through the eyehole indicated a respectable-looking gentleman.

"Who is it?"

"I'm looking for the Freiheit Importing Company."

Webern replaced the handkerchief in his breast pocket and opened the door. "Yes?"

The man stood in the hallway: slender, with piercing silver eyes and blond hair so pale it was almost white.

"May I have a minute of your time?" the gentleman asked.

"Certainly." Webern opened the door further and motioned the man to a seat. Although the man's suit was plain—simple black—it was of beautiful material, exquisitely tailored. Webern had always been something of a clotheshorse and, as he moved back behind his desk, found himself unconsciously adjusting his own cuffs.

"Interesting," the man said, glancing around, "that you conduct your business in a hotel."

"It was not always a hotel," Webern replied. "When it was built in 1929, it was called the Rhodes-Haverty Building. When it became a hotel I saw no reason to bother relocating my business. The view of Atlanta's historic district from here is second to none."

He took a seat behind the desk. "How may I be of service?" The visit, of course, was almost certainly a mistake—the 'importing' he did was for private clients only—but this wasn't the first time people had called on him. He had always made a point of being polite with such callers, to give the impression his was a legitimate business.

The man sat down, threw one leg over the other. "I have just one question. Answer it, and I'll be on my way."

Something in the man's tone made Webern hesitate before replying. "And what question is that?"

"Where is Helen Pendergast?"

This is not possible, Webern thought. Aloud, he said: "I have no idea what you're talking about."

"You are the owner of a warehouse in downstate New York. It was from this warehouse that the operation to abduct Helen Pendergast was put into motion."

"You aren't making any sense. And since it appears you have no business to conduct, I'm afraid I shall have to ask you to leave, Mister...?" As he spoke, Webern very casually opened the center drawer of his desk and placed his hand inside.

"Pendergast," the stranger said. "Aloysius Pendergast."

Webern drew out his Beretta from the desk. But

before he could aim it, the man, seemingly reading his mind, lashed out, quick as a striking snake, and slammed the pistol from Webern's grasp. It went tumbling across the floor. Covering Webern with his own weapon, which had appeared out of nowhere, the man retrieved the Beretta, put it in his own pocket, and returned to his chair.

"Shall we try again?" he asked in a reasonable voice.

"I have nothing to say to you," Webern replied.

The man calling himself Pendergast hefted the weapon in his hand. "Are you truly not attached to your own life?"

Webern had been very carefully trained in interrogation techniques—both in how to administer, and how to resist. He had also been schooled in how one of superior blood and breeding should conduct himself before others. "I'm not afraid to die for what I believe in."

"That makes two of us." The man paused, considering. "And what is it, exactly, that you believe in?"

Webern merely smiled.

Pendergast glanced around the office again, his gaze finally returning to Webern. "That's a rather nice suit you're wearing."

Despite the big Colt trained on him, Webern felt perfectly calm, perfectly in control. "Thank you."

"Is that by chance a Hardy Amies, my own tailor?"

"Sadly, no. Taylor & Merton, just a few doors down Savile Row from Amies."

"I see we share a fondness for fine clothes. I would imagine our mutual interest extends beyond just suits. Take ties, for instance." Pendergast caressed his own.

"While in the past I've usually favored handmade Parisian ties, like Charvet, these days I prefer Jay Kos. Such as the one I'm wearing at present. At two hundred dollars, not cheap, but in my opinion worth every penny." He smiled at Webern. "And who makes your ties?"

If this was some novel interrogation technique, Webern thought, it was not going to work. "Sienia," he replied.

"Sienia," Pendergast repeated. "That's good. Well made."

Suddenly—again with speed that more resembled an explosion than movement—Pendergast shot up from his chair, leapt over the desk, and grabbed Webern by the throat. Dragging him backwards with shocking strength, he threw up the sash of the nearest window and propelled the struggling Webern backwards into it. In terror Webern grasped the windowframe on both sides. He could hear the traffic on Peachtree Street twenty stories below, feel the updraft.

"I love the windows in these old skyscrapers," Pendergast said. "They actually open. And you were right about the view."

Webern clung desperately to the sides of the window, gasping with terror.

Reaching around with the butt of his gun, Pendergast smashed the fingers of Webern's left hand, breaking bones, then pounded on his right. With a cry, Webern felt himself shoved backwards into open space, his arms flailing uselessly, his legs still hooked over the window sill. Pendergast prevented his fall by grabbing his tie, holding him out at arm's length from the window.

Frantically, Webern pressed his calves against the window sill, choking and fighting to maintain grip.

"A man should always know his wardrobe—and his wardrobe's limitations," Pendergast went on, his voice still light and conversational. "My Jay Kos ties, for example, are made of Italian seven-fold silk. As strong as they are beautiful."

He gave Webern's tie a rough jerk. Webern gasped as one leg began to slip from the sill. He scrabbled to regain his footing. He tried to speak but the tie was choking him.

"Other manufacturers sometimes cut corners," Pendergast went on. "You know, like single stitching, two folds." He gave the tie another tug.

"So I want you to *be sure of* the quality of your tie before I ask you my question again."

Jerk.

With a harsh sound, Webern's tie began to rip. He stared at it, crying out involuntarily.

"Oh dear," Pendergast said, disappointed. "Sienia? I don't think so. Perhaps you've been deceived. Or you've been cutting corners, lying to me about your haberdashers."

Jerk.

The tie was now torn halfway across its fat end. From the corner of his eye, Webern could see a crowd gathering below, pointing upward, distant shouts. He couldn't breathe and he felt his head start to swim. Panic overwhelmed him.

Jerk. Rip.

"All right!" Webern screamed, scrabbling at Pendergast's hand with his own broken and twisted fingers. "I'll talk!"

"Make it quick. This cheap tie isn't going to last much longer."

"She's, she's leaving the country tonight."

"Where? How?"

"Private plane. Fort Lauderdale. Pettermars airport. Nine o'clock."

With a final, brutal tug, Pendergast pulled Webern back into his office.

"Schiesse!" Webern cried as he sprawled across the floor, in a fetal position, cradling his ruined hands. "What if my tie had torn completely?"

The man's smile simply widened. And suddenly, Webern understood—this was a man as far on the edge as a person could be while remaining sane.

Pendergast took a step back. "If you're telling the truth, and I recover her without incident, you don't have to worry about seeing me again. But if you have deceived me, I'll pay you another visit."

In the act of turning toward the door, Pendergast stopped. He loosened his own necktie, untied it, threw it towards Webern. "Here's the real thing. Remember what I said about cutting corners." And with a final, cold smile, he slipped out of the office.

Dear Reader,

We recently launched a new series of thrillers featuring an uncommon investigator by the name of Gideon Crew. The first book in this series, *Gideon's Sword*, was published in February 2011, and the second book in the series, *Gideon's Corpse*, was published in January 2012.

We are happy to report that the Gideon books were picked up by Paramount Pictures for a major series of feature films.

We hasten to assure you that our devotion to Agent Pendergast remains undimmed and that we will continue to write novels featuring the world's most enigmatic FBI agent with the same frequency as before—starting with the continuation of the story begun in *Fever Dream* and *Cold Vengeance*.

Thank you again for your interest and support. Please turn the page to read a sample from *Gideon's Sword*.

Warm regards,
Douglas & Lincoln

CHAPTER 1

August 1988

Nothing in his twelve years of life had prepared Gideon Crew for that day. Every insignificant detail, every trivial gesture, every sound and smell, became frozen as if in a block of glass, unchanging and permanent, ready to be examined at will.

His mother was driving him home from his tennis lesson in their Plymouth station wagon. It was a hot day, well up in the nineties, the kind where clothes stick to one's skin and sunlight has the texture of flypaper. Gideon had turned the dashboard vents onto his face, enjoying the rush of cold air. They were driving on Route 27, passing the long cement wall enclosing Arlington National Cemetery, when two motorcycle cops intercepted their car, one pulling ahead, the other staying behind, sirens wailing, red lights turning. The one in front motioned with a black-gloved hand toward the Columbia Pike exit ramp; once on the ramp, he signaled for Gideon's mother to pull over. There was none of the slow deliberation of a routine traffic stop— instead, both officers hopped off their motorcycles and came running up.

"Follow us," said one, leaning in the window. "Now."

"What's this all about?" Gideon's mother asked.

"National security emergency. Keep up—we'll be driving fast and clearing traffic."

"I don't understand—"

But they were already running back to their motorcycles.

Sirens blaring, the officers escorted them down Columbia Pike to George Mason Drive, forcing cars aside as they went. They were joined by more motorcycles, squad cars, and finally an ambulance: a motorcade that screamed through the traffic-laden streets. Gideon didn't know whether to be thrilled or scared. Once they turned onto Arlington Boulevard, he could guess where they were going: Arlington Hall Station, where his father worked for INSCOM, the United States Army Intelligence and Security Command.

Police barricades were up over the entrance to the complex, but they were flung aside as the motorcade pulled through. They went shrieking down Ceremonial Drive and came to a halt at a second set of barricades, beside a welter of fire trucks, police cars, and SWAT vans. Gideon could see his father's building through the trees, the stately white pillars and brick façade set among emerald lawns and manicured oaks. It had once been a girls' finishing school and still looked it. A large area in front had been cleared. He could see two sharpshooters lying on the lawn, behind a low hummock, rifles deployed on bipods.

His mother turned to him and said, fiercely, "Stay in the car. Don't get out, no matter what." Her face was gray and strained, and it scared him.

She stepped out. The phalanx of cops bulled through the crowd ahead of her and they disappeared.

She'd forgotten to turn off the engine. The air-conditioning was still going. Gideon cranked down a window, the car filling with the sounds of sirens, walkie-talkie chatter, shouts. Two men in blue suits came running past. A cop hollered into a radio. More sirens drifted in from afar, coming from every direction.

He heard the sound of a voice over an electronic megaphone, acidic, distorted. *"Come out with your hands in view."*

The crowd immediately hushed.

"You are surrounded. There is nothing you can do. Release your hostage and come out now."

Another silence. Gideon looked around. The attention of the crowd was riveted on the front door of the station. That, it seemed, was where things would play out.

"Your wife is here. She would like to speak to you."

A buzz of fumbled static came through the sound system and then the electronically magnified sound of a partial sob, grotesque and strange. *"Melvin?"* Another choking sound. *"MELVIN?"*

Gideon froze. *That's my mother's voice,* he thought.

It was like a dream where nothing made sense. It wasn't real. Gideon put his hand on the door handle and opened it, stepping into the stifling heat.

"Melvin..." A choking sound. *"Please come out. Nobody's going to hurt you, I promise. Please let the man go."* The voice over the megaphone was harsh and alien—and yet unmistakably his mother's.

Gideon advanced through the clusters of police officers and army officers. No one paid him any attention.

He made his way to the outer barricade, placed a hand on the rough, blue-painted wood. He stared in the direction of Arlington Hall but could see nothing stirring in the placid façade or on the immediate grounds cleared of people. The building, shimmering in the heat, looked dead. Outside, the leaves hung limply on the oak branches, the sky flat and cloudless, so pale it was almost white.

"Melvin, if you let the man go, they'll listen to you."

More waiting silence. Then there was a sudden motion at the front door. A plump man in a suit Gideon didn't recognize came stumbling out. He looked around a moment, disoriented, then broke into a run toward the barricades, his thick legs churning. Four helmeted officers rushed out, guns drawn; they seized the man and hustled him back behind one of the vans.

Gideon ducked under the barricade and moved forward through the groups of cops, the men with walkie-talkies, the men in uniform. Nobody noticed him, nobody cared: all eyes were fixed on the front entrance to the building.

And then a faint voice rang out from inside the doorway. "There must be an investigation!"

It was his father's voice. Gideon paused, his heart in his throat.

"I demand an investigation! Twenty-six people died!"

A muffled, amplified fumbling, then a male voice boomed from the sound system. *"Dr. Crew, your concerns will be addressed. But you must come out now with your hands up. Do you understand? You must surrender now."*

"You haven't listened," came the trembling voice. His father sounded frightened, almost like a child. "People died and nothing was done! I want a promise."

"That is a promise."

Gideon had reached the innermost barricade. The front of the building remained still, but he was now close enough to see the door standing half open. It was a dream; at any moment he would wake up. He felt dizzy from the heat, felt a taste in his mouth like copper. It was a nightmare—and yet it was real.

And then Gideon saw the door swing inward and the figure of his father appear in the black rectangle of the doorway. He seemed terribly small against the elegant façade of the building. He took a step forward, his hands held up, palms facing forward. His straight hair hung down over his forehead, his tie askew, his blue suit rumpled.

"That's far enough," came the voice. *"Stop."*

Melvin Crew stopped, blinking in the bright sunlight.

The shots rang out, so close together they sounded like firecrackers, and his father was abruptly punched back into the darkness of the doorway.

"Dad!" screamed Gideon, leaping over the barrier and running across the hot asphalt of the parking lot. *"Dad!"*

Shouts erupted behind him, cries of "Who's that kid?" and "Hold fire!"

He leapt the curb and cut across the lawn toward the entrance. Figures raced forward to intercept him.

"Jesus Christ, stop him!"

He slipped on the grass, fell to his hands and knees,

rose again. He could see only his father's two feet, sticking out of the dark doorway into the sunlight, shoes pointed skyward, scuffed soles turned up for all to see, one with a hole in it. It was a dream, a dream— and then the last thing he saw before he was tackled to the ground was the feet move, jerking twice.

"Dad!" he screamed into the grass, trying to claw back to his feet as the weight of the world piled up on his shoulders; but he'd seen those feet move, his father was alive, he would wake up and all would be well.

Dear Friend and Reader,

About a dozen times a year we send a short, entertaining note to a select group of our readers. It brings you information available nowhere else. We call it *The Pendergast File* Each missive includes a surprise or shock: an outlandish bit of Pendergast history, a marvelous giveaway, a contest, hidden clues to buried treasure, a sampling of horrible reviews, upcoming book signings, snide and nasty comments about reviewers we dislike, and other amusing tidbits.

In short, *The Pendergast File* is not your ordinary "newsletter."

If you would like to sign up for *The Pendergast File*, please go to our website, **www.preston child.com**, and click on the sign-up button. You can opt out at any time.

With warm regards,
Doug & Linc

P.S.: We will never, ever, under any circumstances, share your e-mail address or information.